THE OATH

KLAUS-PETER

WOLF

ZAFFRE

First published in Germany as 'Ostfriesenschwur' in 2016
by S. Fischer Verlag GmbH, Frankfurt am Main,

This paperback edition published in Great Britain in 2019 by
ZAFFRE
80–81 Wimpole St, London W1G 9RE

English translation by Bradley Schmidt
In grateful memory of Steven T. Murray

A CIP catalogue record for this book is
available from the British Library.

ISBN: 978-1-78658-034-4

Also available as an ebook

1 3 5 7 9 10 8 6 4 2

Typeset by IDSUK (Data Connection) Ltd
Printed and bound in Great Britain by Clays Ltd, Elcograf S.p.A.

Zaffre is an imprint of Bonnier Books UK
www.bonnierbooks.co.uk

'Gazing at the sea makes everything relative.'

Ubbo Heide, former chief of police in East Frisia

'What from the inside looks like a fantastic career ladder is sometimes viewed from the outside as nothing but a sorry hamster wheel.'

Chief Inspector Ann Kathrin Klaasen, Aurich Kripo

'Until "Beam me up" is invented, we're all a disadvantaged generation.'

Chief Inspector Rupert, Aurich Kripo

Ubbo Heide had spent the night enjoying his favourite pastime: simply sitting and gazing at the sea.

For him this was the most beautiful place on earth. Here, with this view of the natural might of the North Sea, even the wheelchair lost its hold over him.

Ubbo's thoughts took wing. He felt free and content. Suddenly everything seemed all right. Eventually, as the candle in the tea warmer flickered and burned out, he dozed off.

The early morning ferry brought the mail from the mainland to the island, along with the tourists.

Across from the Pudding Café the wind speed was measured at seven to eight on the Beaufort scale, which was officially called a moderate breeze and regarded by most coastal inhabitants as invigorating.

His wife Carola returned from the island's bakery with *Seelchen*, set the table and brewed a fresh pot of tea the way Ubbo liked it: black with peppermint leaves.

He was snoring quietly. She liked the familiar sound. When he fell asleep in his chair he snored like a seal with asthma. Lying down, especially on his back, he was as loud as a rusty buzz saw.

Carola Heide had brought along the *East Frisia* magazine and was reading an article by Holger Bloem as she stood by the table.

The postman rang the doorbell. Ubbo gave a start and pretended that he had been awake all along.

As Carola pushed open the door she said: 'They say the new chief of Kripo is one Martin Büscher from Bremerhaven. Do you know him?'

Ubbo smiled. 'Oh yeah, I know him.'

He rolled his chair over to the breakfast table and grabbed the magazine. Each new issue was more important to him than food.

Carola took cold cuts from the fridge and draped them carefully on a chopping board.

Holger had written about Ubbo Heide and his book of unsolved criminal cases. Thanks to him the book was now in its third edition. As a result Ubbo was occasionally invited to give readings and lead discussions. He, the former chief of the East Frisian Criminal Police, called the Kripo, was still plagued by his failure to solve a number of cold cases. And murderers and child abusers really belonged behind bars. In a self-tormenting way he enjoyed talking about these cases and the ineptitudes of the justice system, as well as his own failure to find the perpetrators.

These events made him feel like he was doing something meaningful by passing on his experiences. He always opened with the words: 'If it's true, ladies and gentlemen, that a person becomes wise from his mistakes, then a wise man sits before you. If not, then I'm simply an idiot.'

Holger Bloem had quoted this and called Ubbo Heide 'the genial father figure of the East Frisian Criminal Police.'

In the meantime, the postman came to the door. Carola opened the door for him and accepted a large package. It was addressed to Ubbo Heide.

'So who's it from?' Carola asked.

The return address was written with a fountain pen, and the ink was smeared.

She tried to decipher it.

'Do you know a Mr Ruwsch? Or Rumsch?'

Ubbo shook his head. 'Never heard of him.'

The package was at least as big as a two-layer cake or six bottles of wine.

Carola sawed away at the packing tape.

'Did you order something?' she asked.

'No, and it's not my birthday either.'

There were lots of polystyrene peanuts inside, surrounding a blue rubbish bag that was secured between a pair of freezer packs with a bungee cord.

Carola lifted the bag out of the box and placed it on the breakfast table. A few of the peanuts rolled onto the chopping board. One fell into Ubbo's cup of tea.

Carola cautiously stuck a bread knife into the trash bag. Air hissed out. She still couldn't see what was inside.

Ubbo sliced open a *Seelchen.* Since moving to the island of Wangerooge he'd learned to love this special type of roll, and his favourite toppings were honey or beer sausage.

Looking from this angle, Ubbo caught sight of hair and a nose and instinctively he reached to take away the knife from Carola. At the same moment his wife let out a shriek. There was a severed head poking out of the rubbish bag in the middle of their breakfast table, its tangled hair oily and plastered with dried blood.

Carola dropped the knife, which clattered onto the floor. She didn't faint but, reaching behind her into empty space, backed away from the table as far as she could go, holding her hands away from her body

'Is that a real head?' she asked breathlessly.

'I'm afraid so,' said Ubbo. He not only saw it, he smelled it too.

*

The matter couldn't be sugar-coated. For Büscher the transfer from Bremerhaven to East Frisia was a disciplinary action, regardless of the salary increase. He was supposed to take charge of this suicide mission and serve as boss to the legendary Ann Kathrin Klaasen.

One of the men wore a red tie, the other a blue. But they were both in agreement. The first would be only too happy to get rid of Büscher, and the other wanted to hire him.

They had agreed on what to do, and Büscher looked like a donkey brought to market and being sold to the highest bidder.

'There is a form of authority,' said the man with the blue tie, 'that is conferred by rank. As of now it's yours, Mr Büscher. But there is also another type of authority that emanates from the person himself. It's based on recognition of that person's actions. Naturally that's something you must earn. At the moment Ann Kathrin Klaasen possesses that authority. That's the reason for the failure of your unfortunate predecessor, Ms. Diekmann.'

He leafed through his papers and swallowed hard. To Büscher he looked like someone in urgent need of a beer. Dry-mouthed, he went on.

'Since Ubbo Heide retired, Ann Kathrin Klaasen has pretty much been running the station – although without any official commission. But she enjoys the loyalty of her colleagues. And that cannot be underestimated.'

He loosened his blue tie.

'She has apprehended four serial killers, and Bloem, the journalist, has turned her into a legend. Not to mention that we in-house have seriously considered appointing Ms. Klaasen as the chief of the Aurich-Wittmund Police Department. There were actually votes in favour of such a move. But in the end it wouldn't work. Her personality is just too abrasive and she's not a good team player. She's constantly at odds with the higher authorities, and extremely eccentric.'

His voice became hoarse and he cleared his throat, but no one offered him anything to drink. He tried to make the best of things.

'All the same, Ms. Klaasen cost an interior minister his job, and two state secretaries were fired. No one who takes political responsibility feels good in her presence, but that doesn't mean they don't like having their picture taken with her. She's very popular with the public.'

He could no longer suppress the urge to cough, and fished a throat lozenge from his trouser pocket.

'We have two graduates who have completed their studies at the German Police Academy in Hiltrup and have applied for the position.'

He waved away this remark, making a face. The lozenge was now stuck to his palate.

'Excellent people, without a doubt, but in this case it would be like handing a sheep over to the wolves.'

Büscher later recalled that at this moment he had looked down at his shoes. He noticed that the leather on the toes was worn, and they could use some polish.

The chap with the red tie, his superior from Bremerhaven, said: 'Now, don't look so dejected. The head of Central Criminal Investigation — that's really something! And you will be promoted from Chief Detective Inspector to *First* Chief Detective Inspector.'

The man with the blue tie glanced at the clock and mentioned an important appointment at the Interior Ministry. He concluded: 'We've even received an application from the police management in Osnabrück. But what we want here is an outsider who is not entangled or involved with anything or anyone. An assertive colleague with a lot of experience. In short – we want you, Mr Büscher.'

Both men had wished him much success but the chap with the red tie had given him such an odd look, as though he wanted to offer condolences.

Büscher viewed the Aurich station on Fischteichweg as something like Dracula's castle. Ann Kathrin Klaasen and her husband Frank Weller were still on holiday on Langeoog, so Büscher had three days to prepare for the first meeting. Maybe he could manage to win over a few people or at least understand the group dynamics before the actual witches' dance got going.

The weather was clear and sunny with a brisk wind from the northwest. He found a note on his desk, possibly left behind by mistake, or even as some sort of threat: *Whoever doesn't move with the times will perish with the times.*

An issue of the *East Frisia* magazine also lay on his desk. A framed article about Ann Kathrin Klaasen written by Holger Bloem hung on the wall in the hallway. In other places something like that might end up on the bulletin board or in a mailbox, and later in the wastepaper bin. Here it was treated like a holy relic.

Büscher genuflected in front of his new desk. His knees creaked unpleasantly.

I need allies here, he thought. I have to build up a network. Find a friend or at least a couple of people I can trust to some extent.

There is something that can tempt every fish; he'd learned that by going fishing. There were predatory fish that would snap at flashing, shimmering tin as long as it moved temptingly enough in the water. Others would swallow rotten fish scraps or a piece of meat. He knew that the bait had to be tasty for the fish, not the fisherman.

He heard footsteps in the hall, opened the door a crack, and peered out. It was Rupert.

Büscher sauntered the few steps over to the coffee machine. Rupert hadn't reckoned on meeting the new chief like this in the hallway. He had imagined a ceremonious official introduction with some big shot from the Ministry of the Interior, with speeches and definitely a modest toast. Perhaps not with champagne and caviar hors d'oeuvres, but beer and knackwurst at least.

At that moment Rupert was completely occupied with trying to come up with some advertising copy for the rifle club's new membership campaign.

Rupert mistook Büscher for the long-awaited 'technician' who was going to repair the coffee machine. It tended to spew out vegetable soup when you pressed the button for a *latte macchiato*, and hot chocolate if you wanted a *caffè crema*. Under no circumstances would it produce a plain black coffee. The machine had already been replaced three times. It was big, noisy, and basically just took up space.

'It's about time you people got this thing working properly!' Rupert yelled, kicking the machine where the metal was already dented.

Büscher gave Rupert a quizzical look.

'Hey, don't look at me like that! This is the third machine that doesn't work. How stupid can you be? Doesn't anybody work here who can fix this piece of shit? If not, send it back for a replacement. We've got enough idiots here.'

'I don't know a thing about coffee machines.'

Rupert grimaced. 'Yeah, I thought as much. But this time you picked the wrong man. All you boys should be jailed!'

Büscher cleared his throat. 'My name is Büscher.' He pointed to his name on the door. 'And this is my new office.'

Rupert had no idea how foolish he looked with his mouth hanging open. As if he were playing charades and trying to look like a human vacuum cleaner.

'You are— I mean, you're going to be—'

Büscher held out his hand. 'Head of Central Criminal Investigation.'

Rupert shook the hand. 'Chief Detective Inspector Rupert. Please excuse me. I thought you were—'

'An idiot. I got that.'

Trying to backtrack, Rupert said: 'I'm sorry. I was lost in thought. We're supposed to be thinking up an ad campaign to entice new members to join the rifle club and I'm working on a catchy slogan.'

'Very interesting,' Büscher said, feigning interest. Rupert swallowed the bait gratefully, and Büscher could feel him twitching on the hook.

'What do you think of this? *Join up! Learn to shoot! Make new friends!*'

Büscher nodded. 'Learn to shoot! Make new friends. Not bad. It puts sociability and camaraderie in the foreground.'

Sylvia Hoppe came racing up the stairs. She looked as if she'd hardly slept a wink and had overeaten at dinner. She was completely out of breath.

'Either everyone on Wangerooge has lost their minds,' she panted, 'or some nut has just sent Ubbo Heide a severed head in the post.'

Rupert smiled with relief. This disastrous news was just what he needed to get out of the embarrassing situation with the new chief. A severed head was just right.

Rupert blustered, 'OK, so what we're going to need is everybody on deck. Evidence response! Forensics! A helicopter and—' He glanced at Büscher. 'Sorry. Nice to meet you. I'd like to chat, but right now, as you've just heard, we've got a case to handle.'

Rupert was about to take off with Sylvia Hoppe when Büscher shouted: 'Hang on a minute! I'm in charge here. Is Wangerooge even in our jurisdiction? Isn't it in the Jever administrative district?'

Sylvia Hoppe pursed her lips and made a gesture as if right now she really didn't have time for such nit picking. 'It's in Friesland County!'

'Exactly. That's a job for our colleagues there.'

Rupert enunciated very slowly and carefully, as if Büscher were a bit thick: 'This is about Ubbo Heide! Our boss!'

Sylvia Hoppe grabbed Rupert. They had no time to waste.

'But I'm your boss now,' Büscher countered meekly. He wasn't sure whether those two even heard him. They were already heading downstairs.

Ubbo Heide, he thought. It would have to be Ubbo Heide. And then he realised that as chief he wasn't second in command behind Ann Kathrin Klaasen as he'd feared, but actually third. They were still calling Ubbo Heide their boss. There was a hierarchy here that had nothing to do with the official chain of command.

Most of all, he would have liked to return home and go fishing for pike in the Geeste River using a spinner, rather than hunting down criminals here in East Frisia.

It was the end of June. The pike season was open again. And apparently it was open season on him, too.

*

The package had been posted from a branch of the Deutsche Post in Norden at the shopping centre at 13 Gewerbestrasse.

Carrying a high-resolution mobile phone picture of the mailing label that he'd taken himself, Rupert flew directly from Wangerooge to Norden on the mainland. He didn't really enjoy the flight and when he saw seals lolling on a sandbank below him in the sun, he couldn't help feeling jealous.

They ought to be doing something with that landscape, he thought. Seals are on holiday pretty much all the time, while we cops have to settle for a few days per year.

A few minutes later he was standing outside the airport, looking for the police car that was supposed to pick him up. However, since it was high season, and two of the patrol cars were out of action, he ended up having to borrow a bike.

'Don't make such a fuss,' said Marion Wolters from the operations centre. Her voice sounded even worse than usual on Rupert's mobile phone. He had to hold the phone away from his ear.

'You could practically spit that far, it's so close. It would take a taxi longer to reach you than for you to ride a bike to your SUV. Besides—'

'Besides what?' Now he pressed his mobile phone tight against his right ear so he could drown out the noise of a twin-engined propellor plane with four tourists on board.

As if she had noticed, Marion Wolters raised her voice almost to a shout: 'Besides, it'll do you good.'

Her voice irritated the hell out of him. He hated being chided and decided to contradict her.

'What the hell are you trying to say?'

'I've read that men who take public transport to work have a much higher life expectancy than commuters who drive.'

'What bullshit.'

'It's true. It's practically been confirmed by scientists.'

'Did you get that out of the retirees' magazine or what?'

'No, I don't read the *Pharmacist's Weekly* like you do. It was in an ordinary illustrated magazine.'

'*Knitting Styles for the Frustrated*, or whatever it's called?'

'You don't have a clue, Rupert. The daily sprint on the platform to catch a connecting train keeps them fit. Running up and down the steps with a briefcase is just like going to the gym. Other people pay money to exercise. And if you ride your bike, that's priceless!'

'Oh, kiss my arse!' Rupert retorted, ending the call, so that she couldn't hear the rest of his reply. Let her guess what he'd said. It wouldn't take much imagination.

Rupert felt a tailwind, which made riding the bike much more fun. On Ostermarscher Strasse he overtook a line of cars, and when he rode across the car park to the shopping centre, the big glass doors opened to the atrium. He simply couldn't resist this invitation, so he rode into the building.

To the right was a bakery, and to the left of that a kiosk selling paperbacks and tobacco products. It also sold Lotto tickets and served as a post office branch and a florist's shop.

Rupert rode the bike past the racks of paperbacks and headed straight for the post office window.

Daniela Stöhr-Mongelli didn't like it when people parked their bikes or shopping trolleys inside her space. She politely but firmly informed him that this was a post office and not a cycle path. But that was where everything went wrong.

The petite dark-haired woman was precisely the type who triggered a complete vacuum inside Rupert's head. He began to act like a computer with a hard drive that's been erased. Only a few functions still ran flawlessly. He was able to maintain his equilibrium and breathe normally, and he could tell colours apart. But although he still knew his name and address, he both felt and looked like some kind of idiot.

He stammered out the words: 'Aurich Kripo. Homicide division. The name is Rupert.'

He attempted to smile, but his facial muscles seemed to have forgotten how.

'You're from the homicide division?' Daniela Stöhr-Mongelli said with an incredulous laugh. 'I would have thought you'd show up with flashing blue lights, not on a Dutch touring bike.'

At first Rupert wanted to explain his problems getting hold of an official car, but that made him feel even smaller. He didn't want to stand there and reveal that he didn't even have an official car to drive.

'I just arrived. I didn't want to be obvious.'

'From Wangerooge? On your bike?'

'No, I flew in and then . . . it doesn't really matter.' He leaned forward. 'No one can know that we're talking to each other. You might be in danger – mortal danger!'

She smiled, pointing to the queue that had formed behind Rupert, and asked: 'Do you want to let these customers go first?'

Rupert looked around. Four people were standing behind him. One waved his Lotto ticket and gave Rupert a friendly greeting. They knew each other from the Mittelhaus. Occasionally they diced for a round at the bar.

'Hello, Rupert.'

'Hello, Manni.'

With a generous gesture Manni indicated that he had all the time in the world. The others also nodded and crowded in closer so they could hear better.

Rupert held out the mobile phone photo to the young woman and asked: 'Can you remember who sent this? It's very important.'

She gave him a disarming smile. 'If you want to know who sent it, the return address is written right there.'

Rupert groaned. 'Yeah, but we can't really read it. What we can decipher is impossible to check. It says Ruwsch or Rumsch, from . . . it might be Hude. Then 277. The rest we can't read at all. Hude is in the Oldenburg administrative district, and there's nobody named Rumsch or Ruwsch living there.'

'Let me take a look,' said Manni, Rupert's pal, taking Rupert's mobile. He passed it around, and in the general hubbub Ms. Stöhr-Mongelli said: 'It was an Express Easy National package, weight limit up to 20 kilos, insured for 500 euros, which cost 29.90 euros. I think I remember now.'

Rupert was excited. 'And do you remember the man who sent it?'

'It wasn't a man. It was an old lady with a frame. She could hardly carry the package on her own. I think she was wearing those orthopaedic shoes, as if one leg was shorter than the other. She was standing right where you are now. I came out from behind the counter to help her put it on the scales. She also bought a small pouch of tobacco and rolling papers. Plus a copy of *The Courier*, if I recall. A lot of people post parcels here, and I don't remember all of them.'

'But you remember this one?'

'Yes, because she didn't look like she'd be rolling her own cigarettes. She bought an aromatic fine cut, almost more suited to a pipe than rolling papers. I think it had a vanilla or mango flavouring, but I'm not sure.'

Rupert scratched his chin. 'So if she didn't look like someone who rolls her own cigarettes, what exactly did she look like?'

Without pausing to think, Daniela Stöhr-Mongelli replied: 'more like someone who smokes filter cigarettes, or more likely a non-smoker. You see, when you work here you learn to read people. She didn't seem like somebody who would play the numbers. Just a simple Lotto game.'

'She bought a Lotto ticket?' Manni asked, and Rupert waved his hand as if he wanted to take over this line of questioning.

'No, she didn't. I don't really remember. But she looked like the type who would play the same numbers every time.'

'You certainly have excellent powers of observation,' said a woman who had come in to buy a TV guide. 'And you seem to have a good psychological sense too!'

Rupert appreciated her input. Playing the big boss, he now said: 'If you're ever looking for a new job, Ms. Stöhr-Mongelli, we can always use good people like you.'

Rupert's old drinking buddy Manni misinterpreted his remark. 'Oh, are you the new Kripo chief? It's about time.'

Flattered, Rupert puffed up his chest. 'Well, not exactly, but—'

Manni gave him a conspiratorial nod. 'So you pull the strings in the background as the real expert and leave the grandstanding to the others?'

Rupert smiled, hoping he was impressing the young woman.

'Why, is my life in danger?' asked Daniela Stöhr-Mongelli.

Rupert turned to her as he said to the others: 'Please keep back. This is a police investigation. I have to speak with the lady in private.' Then he whispered to her, 'You're the only person who saw the perpetrator. If you give me your address, I'll send a patrol car by occasionally to make sure nothing happens.'

Daniela Stöhr-Mongelli swallowed hard, gazing at Rupert with her big brown eyes.

*

The samurai sword had proved to be a bitter disappointment. He didn't want a repetition of such a disaster. It was a fine weapon, a *katana* from Gifu, forged of 420 stainless steel, the blade 70 centimetres in length. It felt good in the hand and looked wonderful, but he hadn't been able to sever the head with one blow. The blade got stuck and he'd had to pull it out and strike again, which had completely interrupted the flow.

*

Ann Kathrin couldn't stand the noise of the aeroplane engines and had to cover her ears. But she liked looking out of the plane window. The crows on Wangerooge were strutting across the runway as if they owned it. They didn't fly off until the plane was almost upon them. Clearly they had practised this a thousand times before, with nonchalance and composure.

Ann Kathrin smiled when she saw the crows hopping along the runway again as soon as they had landed. They kept an appropriate distance from the planes parked on the grass but had been disturbed by the noise of the plane landing and angrily cawed after it. A lone seagull was perched on the wing of an island-hopper, as if waiting for the pilot.

Ann Kathrin climbed out. The wind ruffled her hair, and she took a deep breath.

Ravens and crows, she thought, symbolise wisdom and knowledge in Nordic mythology. The god Odin always had two ravens that, like spies, informed him of everything that was going on around him. Apparently witches and sorcerers could morph into crows . She abandoned herself to that idea.

Weller glanced at his mobile phone, which he hadn't turned off during the brief flight. He didn't doubt that even during visual flying there were technical instruments that could be disturbed by a mobile phone. He'd simply forgotten.

Weller read the text from Rupert on his iPhone:

> We're looking for a frail old woman with a walker. The type who always plays the same Lotto numbers, and either doesn't roll her own cigarettes or is a non-smoker.

'Well then,' Weller grumbled, 'we might as well put out an APB on her, with all this information.'

Ann Kathrin looked at him as though she'd just woken up from a deep sleep. 'What did you say?'

Weller waved her away. 'Nothing.'

*

Ubbo Heide sat in his wheelchair and held out his arms to Ann Kathrin like a drowning man reaching for a life belt. She bent down to him, and he hugged her hard, as if he'd never let her go. And she felt a bit the same way. A strange symbiosis. Since her father's death, her mentor had become a sort of surrogate father, although they never discussed the matter. She could turn to Ubbo with all her cares and worries. He had always watched over her and patiently steered her along the right path.

Now the situation was reversed. She felt she had to protect him. He needed her advice. He had clearly suffered a huge shock.

Wangerooge was his retreat. The island that in some incomprehensible way had managed to defy the hectic pace of the world and preserve its innocence. Now, this perpetrator had desecrated that innocence.

And Ubbo felt responsible. Ann Kathrin could see it in his face. He believed that he had brought evil to the island. He felt guilty. Something inside him was refuting his right to keep living here because he had mysteriously introduced evil.

His wife Carola lay on the bed, dazed from a sedative and staring at a woodcut by Horst-Dieter Gölzenleuchter that Ubbo had given to her on her sixty-fifth birthday. It was from her father's estate, one of the woodcuts from his collection. Depending on how you looked at it, it depicted either a tree with branches stretching towards heaven, or a nude woman raising her arms in lamentation.

Today Carola saw the woman. In fact, she thought she could hear her sobbing.

She had spent all these years with this man, who, surrounded by the world's filth, had remained a good father and a kind man. She knew that images of victims often tormented him at night and kept him from sleeping. Sometimes she too had sensed the horror he'd witnessed. Here on Wangerooge, after his retirement, he had hoped to leave all that behind. But now, lying motionless on the bed, Carola realised that the images never ever cease.

Just as the Devil and God needed each other, her husband and crime belonged together. He was the antidote.

A tear spilled from her right eye and ran across her temple to her ear like an insect leaving a moist trail.

She heard Ann Kathrin and Ubbo talking in the next room. The wall was little more than a screen made of thin fabric.

'Do you have a hunch about this, Ubbo? Do you know this man?'

'No, I have no idea who the head belongs to.'

'Somebody is trying to get you involved in something,' said Ann Kathrin. 'Why would they do that?'

'You're wrong, Ann. I *am* involved. Maybe someone can't accept that I'm no longer the police chief. Maybe he wants me to keep investigating.'

'Who even knows that you two have a summer house out here? Or that you're actually here at the moment?'

'I could make you a list. Most of them are part of the firm.' He liked to say 'firm' when he meant their police station. 'My daughter Insa, of course, and a couple of friends.' A little sourly he added: 'But I don't think Insa actually knows where we are right now. We last talked to her about six or seven weeks ago. And a few of my wife's friends know about this place.'

Carola couldn't suppress a loud sob. As Ann Kathrin went to her, Weller's mobile played 'Pirates Ahoy!' He had stayed in the background, not wanting to interfere with Ubbo and Ann's conversation. He gazed out of the window at the sea while he took the call.

A TV journalist wanted an interview. His name was Joachim Faust, and it sounded like he expected people to know who he was. He was a bit put out when Weller didn't instantly express his awe.

'I don't watch much TV,' Weller said in apology. 'I prefer to read books.'

'We'd like to invite you and your wife to the studio so we could hear more about the severed head. She's in charge of the investigation, isn't she?'

'You must have the wrong number,' said Weller. 'My wife's name is not Ann Kathrin Klaasen, and she's not in charge of any investigation. She's a former kindergarten teacher who now works in St Pauli as a stripper. But only temporarily.'

Ubbo gave Weller a flabbergasted look.

'But I'm sure she wouldn't mind doing an interview with you.'

Weller listened for a moment. The journalist said no thanks.

Weller shrugged and said to Ann Kathrin: 'Too bad. Not interested. Since you have an unlisted number, all the press freaks try to reach you through me.'

'That's why we have a press agent,' Ann Kathrin snapped. Then she turned to Ubbo Heide and asked: 'Is the head still on the island? I'd like to have a look.'

Ubbo hunched his shoulders, and then nodded.

Weller groaned. 'I can go check with our local colleagues—'

'No,' Ann Kathrin said firmly, 'you're going to come with me and have a look.'

'But we'll be getting a report, Ann.'

'We have to know what we're talking about. There's a difference, Frank, between reading a recipe and tasting the food.'

He found that comparison extremely inappropriate, but gave in.

*

Marilyn and her brother Justin, who was two years older, kept digging deeper. Standing in the hole, the sand came up to their chests, but it still wasn't quite wide enough.

Today was a super day, Marilyn thought. It was here in Cuxhaven-Duhnen that her parents had met ten years before on holiday. She must have heard the story a hundred times, but she still never tired of it.

Mama and Papa first saw each other in a fish restaurant. They still intoned its name like it was some kind of miracle. Mama was sitting alone at a table eating her dinner. She was sad because the friend who'd come on holiday with her had gone home after a quarrel. Papa always told the story the same way. He said the sight of Mama had struck him like a bolt of lightning, dazzling him with her beauty.

Then Mama would always interject that she hadn't looked very good. She was sad, her eyes puffy from crying, and she was much too fat. She'd weighed at least five kilos more than she did today.

But Papa denied all that. At any rate he sat down at her table and announced: 'You are the woman of my dreams. We're going to get married and bring children into the world together.'

At first this had given Mama the creeps, and she had asked Papa to leave her alone and find somewhere else to sit.

This evening they wanted to have dinner at that same restaurant. So romantic. And Marilyn and Justin had promised to stay in the cabin and watch TV.

Today they really ought to bury Papa all the way. Of course they had to leave his head sticking out so he could breathe.

They always did this at least once every holiday, and each time they took a picture of Papa's head jutting out of the sand, flanked by Marilyn and Justin. They were usually holding ice creams, and Papa had beads of sweat on his forehead.

Marilyn thought that the hole was deep enough, but Justin wanted to keep digging. He liked to pretend he was a mole. Sandcastles were his passion.

He was using a blue tin shovel with a wooden handle. Marilyn had a little red trowel, which meant that she dug much more slowly.

Marilyn hit something hard. It made a funny sound. Squeaky. The trowel bent.

'There's something here, Justin.'

'Yep,' he said with a laugh. 'A pirate ship sank somewhere around here. If we find it we'll be rich because it had plundered gold on board.'

Marilyn always knew when her big brother was telling the truth and when he was trying to fool or scare her. His voice would change. He tried to sound like a grown-up, and his eyebrows settled into stern lines.

But then she saw something, like a naked beast, but without a pelt. A fat, dead, white worm or – no – worms didn't wear rings. And that looked like a dirty fingernail.

Marilyn shrieked, 'I found a hand!'

'Oh, sure!' Justin said with a grin and then leaned down to examine the object more closely.

Then he yelled: 'Papa! Mama!'

Marilyn had a feeling this was going to ruin her parents' romantic dinner. Suddenly she had no desire to watch TV alone with her brother in the unfamiliar holiday cabin.

*

A fat fly buzzed above their heads like a mini-drone sent by a foreign power to listen, observe, and maybe even frighten the people in the room.

Büscher's first official meeting as head of the department took place under extreme pressure. There was no time for everyone to get to know him, or for him to slowly exert his authority. He had to start from zero and proceed immediately to one hundred. They didn't even pause to introduce themselves.

He sat at the table next to the highly strung Rieke Gersema, who kept fidgeting with her glasses. Büscher didn't think they suited her. She wanted to set a time for a press conference, because apparently there were a zillion reporters waiting for news. The first rumours about jihadis in East Frisia were making the rounds.

Rieke Gersema, Büscher and Sylvia Hoppe had taken out their smartphones. Sylvia's had a touch screen, while Büscher and Rieke still typed on Blackberries with a keyboard.

Rupert referred to Büscher's message: 'The boys from forensics managed a real quickie this time. The victim was a man of about sixty. Blood type A positive. He still had all his hair. Medium blond sprinkled with white. General conclusion, a central European. When Ubbo unpacked the head, the man had already been dead for at least sixty hours. He was decapitated by two sword blows, so the perpetrator must have been an amateur. A beginner, in other words.'

Ann Kathrin could barely stand to listen to Rupert. She leaned her head on her hand in such a way that the others couldn't see her eyes.

'We have his teeth,' Rupert went on, 'so we'll probably be able to identify him eventually. But it'll take a while, of course.'

Sylvia Hoppe swatted at the fly and interjected: 'We're going over the missing-persons list, but haven't found him yet. In this past year alone, 125 men who match the description have vanished from the face of the earth. These include tax evaders and guys who'd rather go underground than pay child support.'

Rupert plopped his documents on the desk: 'That's all we know about him at the moment.'

'In Ubbo Heide's day there was always tea and *krintstuut*' – East Frisian raisin bread – 'or at least some cookies at meetings like this,' Weller complained. His stomach was growling.

Ann Kathrin cleared her throat. 'We do know a bit more than that, Rupert.'

'Such as?' Looking piqued, Rupert crossed his arms.

Ann Kathrin said, 'He was presumably a cabbie or truck driver.'

Everyone looked at Ann Kathrin. Büscher shifted position. His body language indicated he was paying rapt attention.

Rupert felt Ann Kathrin was mocking him. How could she make such a statement? He tried to ridicule her remark. 'Sure. And he loves butter-cream cake and reads Jerry Cotton paperbacks.'

As the fly buzzed around Rupert's head, Ann Kathrin went on, undeterred: 'His face was clearly tanned more on the left side than the right. The left side of his nose had traces of sunburn. At his hairline the skin damage indicates possible basal cell carcinoma, maybe already treated. People who drive a lot get much more sun on the left side, as is evident on his face and left forearm.'

Ann Kathrin's explanation impressed almost everyone present. Rupert begrudged her the triumph and countered: 'Then he can't have been a cab driver in England, because they drive on the left, and the driver sits on the right.'

Büscher caught on quickly to which way the wind was blowing. The group dynamics were all too clear. The women united behind Ann Kathrin Klaasen to form the power centre. There was macho dictatorship here. Nothing could come between Sylvia Hoppe, Rieke Gersema and Ann Kathrin Klaasen, especially no man.

Weller acted almost as first officer to Klaasen, and was also accepted by the other two women. Rupert, on the other hand, found himself in an extremely awkward position, but he wasn't nearly as foolish as everyone thought.

Sylvia Hoppe, who couldn't stand Rupert because he reminded her of her first husband, rolled her eyes, as if to signal how exasperated she was by so much stupidity.

Ann Kathrin refused to take the bait. She said, 'The perpetrator chose a return address in Hude and drove his SUV all the way to Norden to mail the package from that post office branch. He knew where Ubbo lived. Funny, it's almost like he could be one of us.'

'One of us East Frisians or one of us cops?' Weller asked.

'Either way he's somewhere in our vicinity,' said Ann Kathrin. 'That's one thing we can't deny.'

Büscher's mobile vibrated in his trouser pocket. He didn't take the call. It vibrated a second time and he noted with irritation the message that appeared on the display.

Rupert was watching the fly that was buzzing near his face, as if it wanted to land on his nose. It was flying slowly, provocatively self-assured. Rupert's right hand shot forward, not as a fist but open like a claw. He made a grab for the fly and believed he had caught it and crushed it, but when he opened his hand there was nothing but air. The fly was crawling around in the curls of his perm.

'Damn,' said Rupert, truly impressed by Ann Kathrin's deductive reasoning. 'Why do you always know more than we do when you look at a crime scene or a victim?'

She looked him straight in the eye. 'Rupert, almost nobody is as good at ignoring the obvious as you are. You do it perfectly.'

Rupert wasn't sure if that was a compliment or not. She always told him he was 'so good at something' or he 'did something perfectly'.

Sylvia Hoppe gave Rupert a thumbs up and nodded, as if Ann Kathrin's words had genuinely impressed her and Rupert could be proud of that.

Büscher asserted himself in a loud voice. 'We have the body to go with the head. In Cuxhaven-Duhnen some kids dug up a male corpse. Everything is there but the head.'

Ann Kathrin stood up. Frank Weller and Sylvia Hoppe followed suit.

'So, uh . . . are you going to take off for Cuxhaven?' Büscher asked.

'We'd all prefer to go to the Christmas market in Leer,' Weller teased him, 'but there's not much going on there in June.'

Büscher wondered how fast Ann Kathrin Klaasen could requisition a helicopter. And whether she'd face any resistance. In Bremerhaven he would have had to wait so long to go through the proper channels that he could have made it to a crime scene faster by bus and train. Here in East Frisia the bureaucratic obstacles, at least for Ann Kathrin, didn't seem to be as insurmountable. People knew each other, and things could be settled with a phone call.

He heard her say something on her mobile that set him wondering: 'Thanks, Hauke. I owe you one.'

Büscher still hadn't decided whether he should consider this a good thing or not. Although he really had nothing to do with the actual investigation, he flew out to the scene with them.

The police in Cuxhaven weren't surprised when Ann Kathrin, Frank Weller, Sylvia Hoppe and Martin Büscher showed up. A few pleasantries were exchanged, and everyone agreed to cooperate. The two chiefs even winked complicitly to each other.

Ann Kathrin was insistent that they hurry. She wanted to see the headless corpse.

The corpse lay naked on the autopsy table and was already being examined by two pathologists. One of them looked like he'd interrupted his summer holiday. He was suntanned from sailing, while the other doctor looked far from healthy.

It was cold in the room, and Ann Kathrin was shivering.

There were clear marks of shackles on the wrists and ankles of the dead man. Sand filled his navel. An ant was crawling on his right knee.

'We've found very little blood,' said the elder pathologist with the potbelly, 'so we don't yet how he was killed. He's been dead for a good seventy-two hours, perhaps longer.'

Ann Kathrin looked at Weller and said, 'The man wasn't killed here, only buried. What is the perpetrator trying to tell us? He used Hude for the return address on the package. Posted in Norden. Sent to Wangerooge.'

Weller pointed out the locations on an imaginary map in the air and drew lines to connect them. 'Cuxhaven-Duhnen. Hude. Norden. Wangerooge.'

'Decapitations,' said Ann Kathrin, 'are nothing new. There are decapitations in the Bible.' She counted them off on her fingers. 'John the Baptist was beheaded. Paul of Tarsus and Holofernes too. Even earlier, the Celts celebrated beheadings as mystical rituals. For them the head was the centre of the whole spiritual psyche. Just as today many people regard the heart as the location of the soul. The heads of the enemy were often embalmed and stored in treasure chests. In this way their evil power would be retained even in the hereafter. In some cases it was also thought that the power of a severed head would be transferred to whoever possessed it.'

Weller looked at Büscher and suspected the man was thinking: how does Ann Kathrin know all this stuff?

Weller knew the answer, of course, but asked the question for Büscher's sake. When people got to know Ann Kathrin, her vast knowledge could have a disturbing effect on them.

'How do you know all this, Ann?' Weller asked.

'It's all part of our job,' she said. 'Anything that seems to be a manifestation of the modern era is usually quite old. The guillotine of the French Revolution, no matter how terrible it sounds, was actually a progressive mechanism for killing a person without subjecting him to lengthy torture and suffering.'

'Thanks for that,' Sylvia Hoppe grunted.

The officers from Cuxhaven listened to Ann Kathrin with interest. They considered it an honour to be in the presence of the famous detective. The shorter of the two looked as if he might throw up at any moment, and Weller would have bet a month's pay that he would take sick leave within the next few hours.

'Decapitations,' Ann Kathrin continued, 'were viewed as honourable deaths, as opposed to hanging. In the Middle Ages beheading was reserved for the nobility. Everyone else was strung up. I think the first beheading to be uploaded to the Internet for propaganda purposes was in 2004, in order to spread fear and terror.'

Büscher clutched at his head. 'You mean that a video of this disgusting murder might already be online?'

Ann Kathrin rejected that idea. 'This case is unfolding quite differently,' she said. 'The perpetrator isn't interested in scaring the general public. His specific target is Ubbo Heide, our chief.'

I'm the chief here, Büscher wanted to say, but decided against it because it seemed petty for him to insist on his authority at that moment.

'And that means,' Sylvia concluded, 'that Ubbo knows the perpetrator.'

Weller didn't agree. 'Possibly, but in any event it means that the perpetrator knows Ubbo Heide.'

Ann Kathrin gave a curt nod.

Weller, the crime fiction fan, now quoted Sherlock Holmes from memory: '*When you have eliminated the impossible, whatever remains, however improbable, must be the truth.*'

It sounded as though he had come up with the quote on the spot, just to make a good impression on Büscher.

Ann Kathrin was looking at the left forearm of the corpse. 'Hmm,' she said, and this 'Hmm' was a clear sign to Weller that something was wrong. At the top of the scale, 'Hmm' might mean that something tasted good to her, and at the bottom, that it was inedible. But sometimes this murmured response meant: *Not with me*, or: *I've long since figured this out.*

'He's evenly tanned on one side and white as a sack of flour on the other. The weather here has been excellent over the last few days. Yet he has no sign of being sunburned.'

'So, not a cab driver after all?' Büscher asked.

'Probably not,' Ann Kathrin replied. She was standing at the foot of the autopsy table, touching the toes of the corpse. But she wasn't examining them very closely.

Like most of those present, Büscher asked himself why.

Ann Kathrin took her time, which annoyed the younger pathologist. The older one remained calm. 'Is something wrong?' he wanted to know.

Ann Kathrin said pensively, 'His toenails look like they've had a pedicure. And the calluses on his heels and the balls of his feet seem to have been carefully abraded. Even this corn here looks like it was treated recently.'

The officers from Cuxhaven glanced at each other and then at the pathologists. The younger one looked like he'd just been slapped. Now he seemed like a schoolboy.

'If the man was on holiday in Cuxhaven, he may have had a pedicure appointment at a local hotel,' Ann Kathrin went on. With an oblique look at the officers from Cuxhaven she added: 'That should be possible to check out pretty quickly.'

They both nodded. The older one sucked in his stomach.

*

He was happy to be able to do everything differently now.

It was easier to decapitate people than to lock them up forever. Now he had the cell almost finished. After his parents died he had renovated one half of the duplex, then the other. That had been less work than building this prison.

Almost everything he needed he could buy at local DIY stores, but he couldn't hire any construction help. He couldn't afford to hire anyone even for the most difficult jobs. And he couldn't trust anyone. Any witnesses would be dangerous.

Finally he finished the work. He used to claim he had two left hands. But now he was virtually an expert at any task. A real Renaissance man.

Being able to repair everything himself without relying on outside help made him feel good. There was something godlike about it. Omnipotence.

Yes, he was proud of this prison with the soundproof walls and the terrifying bars, intended to quash any thoughts of escape. He had polished them smooth. Now they shone like the chrome plating on his first motorcycle.

He had constructed two adjoining cells. He could control everything in here remotely. Turn the lights off and on and select the TV channel. There were two fully automatic fire alarms that would trigger the sprinkler system at the first sign of smoke.

The comfortable bed had a new interior-sprung mattress. There was a washbasin and a toilet. Three cameras monitored every movement of the prisoners inside the cells. Two more cameras were mounted outside, beyond the reach of any juvenile delinquents outside the bars.

Through a loudspeaker he could make announcements no matter where he was. He could monitor and control everything easily with his iPhone, even adjust the room temperature.

In the kitchen he had water and food supplies for at least two weeks. Beer, pizza and sirloin steaks for himself. Kale, beans, lentils and pea soup for the prisoners.

He drove to Emden and parked by the vocational college. He intended to snatch her before the day was out. It would be a shame to lose any more time. She attended classes at the college three times a week.

Pilates – Make Your Back Happy and *Lose Ten Pounds in Five Weeks, Cooking for Sports with Nutrition Plans* and a new one called *Killer Ab Training*.

He was also taking the *Cooking for Sports* class. That was the simplest way to get close to Svenja Moers.

He had to watch out for that girl Agneta Meyerhoff. She was after him like an animal, wanting a relationship or at least an affair. She kept touching him during class, as if by accident. This had actually turned out to be beneficial. Not only because it massaged his ego, but also because it prevented anyone from thinking he was taking the class because he was interested in Svenja Moers. To her he was above suspicion, and she paid no attention to him.

As always she had left her bike locked carelessly over near the bike racks. The luminous bright colours were like a beacon to bike thieves, and he seized the opportunity. He wouldn't even need a lock pick to remove the lock from the spokes. The red spiral cable attached to the combination lock seemed almost like the ribbon on a gift for thieves.

It took him less than ten seconds. He'd learned how on YouTube, like so much else. But he did wonder why the government allowed lock-picking lessons to be posted on the Internet, along with all the other instructional videos for DIYers. We're living in a crazy world, he thought.

He rode the bike around the corner, crossed the street, and rolled it into the Emden town ditch next to the city auditorium. Then he went back to the vocational college.

When the class is over, he thought, and she's looking for her bike, I'll offer, quite casually, to give her a lift home.

*

'We've got a headless body in Cuxhaven and a decapitated head on Wangerooge,' said Ann Kathrin. 'But that doesn't necessarily mean that the two belong together.'

Büscher drew himself up. 'Now you're really going too far, Ms. Klaasen. Surely you're not implying that—'

She held up her hands as if to fend him off. The younger officer from Cuxhaven jotted something down. Ann Kathrin stepped back from the table on which the body lay. 'I'm not implying anything. I just want to point out the facts of the case. We need to view the whole thing objectively.' Then she moved closer to the autopsy table.

Büscher considered all this a waste of time, but he said nothing in order to avoid an argument.

A few seconds later the pathologist with the holiday tan announced that the dead man's blood type was O negative.

Büscher smiled. 'You must be mistaken. The blood type is A positive.'

The doctor didn't look like he was used to being contradicted. He jutted out his chin and pursed his lips in an arrogant expression. 'Most definitely not, Inspector. A positive is a very common blood type, but this poor individual is O negative.'

Sylvia Hoppe seemed shocked.

'Why would he drive the body so far away, or send the head?' Weller asked.

'He mailed the head from Norden. On the way he might have had an accident or run into a police checkpoint. No one would dare drive for very long with body parts in the boot.'

'That means,' said Ann Kathrin, 'that somewhere there's another head and another body, which—'

Electrified by his own musings, Weller shouted: 'I bet he buried the second body in Norddeich!'

Sylvia Hoppe flinched and said, 'How on earth did you come up with that? Why specifically in Norddeich?'

'Well, the beach is similar to the one here. And it's not far from the car park for an SUV.' Weller raised his index finger and launched into a lecture: 'Criminals are creatures of habit. We have to understand that.'

Ann Kathrin put her hand on his right arm. 'All right, Frank. That's enough.'

'We should be getting back,' Büscher suggested with a glance at the clock, then added quietly but firmly: 'All leave is cancelled. We need every man on this.'

Sylvia Hoppe asked pointedly, 'And the women are free to take a quick trip to the Caribbean? Is that how we're supposed to interpret what you've just said?'

'No, of course not,' Büscher said with a groan, realising he had to watch out for her.

'So, are we supposed to go dig up the beach in Norddeich or what?' Weller asked on his way out.

The younger detective from Cuxhaven followed them out, trying to get Ann Kathrin's attention. 'Does this mean that the body doesn't belong to your stiff, and that there must be another head around here somewhere?'

Ann Kathrin kept walking. Weller turned to the officer and smiled at him. 'That's exactly what she was trying to say.'

*

During class he kept his distance from Svenja Moers. He'd smiled at her in a friendly way only twice, once in greeting and another time when she lost control of her paring knife and it accidentally flew out of her hand straight at him like a throwing knife. It struck his upper arm, not with the point but the handle. He handed it back to her with a smile, and she apologised profusely.

He paid no attention to her for the rest of the evening. Instead he let Agneta Meyerhoff flirt with him. For the third time she told him that her husband was away installing equipment, and sometimes she got so bored at home. She'd always been such a lively girl and was always looking for fun things to do.

Agneta left the classroom twice to have a smoke. Each time she invited him to come along, and if he wasn't mistaken, she even gave him a wink. But maybe she just had something in her eye; although she deliberately left the door open for him.

I can't be seen with Svenja Moers if she goes outside, he thought. I'll have to be gone by then, and when she's looking for her bike I'll come back and offer my assistance. Later the cops will try to reconstruct her last steps. Naturally they'll ask all the people taking the class, because they were probably the last to see her.

He smiled to himself. They would describe him as a friendly hippy. He was already looking forward to it. With his long red hair.

Again he felt that buzz of anticipation. He was in the zone now. This feeling was better than anything else. Being completely immersed in the moment.

His sense of smell seemed more intense than normal. He could hear the faintest sound in the room. If he listened hard enough, here in the kitchen he could even hear the whispering in the women's bathroom clear as a bell, as if there were no walls at all.

When he was in this state of mind, everything was good. Even the most impossible things went smoothly. If there were such things as lucky hormones, that's what his body emitted when he was in the zone. It wasn't some form of intoxication, but a state of clarity in which he had absolute control of everything. His senses were so alert and sensitive that he made no mistakes. He moved completely in the here and now and was totally aware of himself at every second.

He was fortunate. When he was in the zone, everything turned out in his favour, as if a higher power were arranging things so that nothing could thwart his plans.

Svenja Moers and Agneta Meyerhoff were standing around chatting outside the door after class. He took his leave with a curt nod to the two women and did not react to Agneta's loud remark, 'Right now a cool white wine spritzer is just what I need.' She stretched as she said it and yawned, as if she were both tired and looking for adventure at the same time.

Svenja didn't pick up on the hint. Maybe because she knew that Agneta Meyerhoff was looking for men and had no interest in women, whom she regarded as competitors.

When Agneta realised that the last man had come out of the college, she lost interest in chatting with Svenja and set off to have a drink somewhere.

Svenja looked for her bike. At first she thought she had just forgotten where she'd left it and was being scatterbrained again. Only last week she'd considered reporting her bike stolen, but then found it in front of a bakery where she'd never left it before. She was so often wrapped up in her own thoughts.

Every time she left the house after breakfast she would ask herself: 'Did I turn off the coffee maker? Is the candle on the table still burning? Did I turn off the cooker after I fried my eggs?'

How often had she gone back to check? And everything was always in perfect order. She did these things unconsciously and then never remembered. Also she was sure she'd left her bike securely locked somewhere. But where?

He spoke to her. 'Is there something I can help with?'

'I'm looking for my bike.'

He gave her a friendly smile. 'That's a coincidence. I came back because I forgot my glasses.'

She pointed to his face. 'They're right there on your face.'

He reached up and laughed. 'Oh! My old maths teacher must have been right.'

'Why?'

'He called me a forgetful fool. He said I'd never amount to anything except an absentminded professor, who shows up in class in the morning in his dressing gown and puts on his suit jacket to take a shower.'

She liked that. Anyone who could tell jokes about himself had to be a nice, harmless person.

He helped her look for her bike. It wasn't as easy to find as his glasses, he joked, scratching his thick, shaggy beard, as if there might be an animal hiding inside it.

After a while, when she realised that her bike must have been stolen, Svenja wanted to call the police, but he suggested he give her a lift home and she could call them the next morning. These days you could even post a police report on the Internet and wait for someone to respond. Or so he claimed.

She knew that filing a report never worked. Dozens of bikes disappeared and were never found.

She had already lost three bikes and considered it a waste of time even to report the theft. The important thing was to have theft insurance but the last time her bike was stolen the insurance company had refused to pay, so she no longer had a policy.

She complained loudly about the situation as she got into his car.

As he drove out of the car park, the radio came on automatically. It was set to Radio East Frisia, a non-profit station that had a studio upstairs in the college building. They hadn't buckled their seat belts and the car beeped annoyingly while a red light flashed on the dashboard.

'Yeah, yeah, yeah, I'll be a good girl,' she said, as if the car could understand her, and clicked the seat belt.

Then she asked him whether he'd ever visited the radio station's studio. She knew one of the DJs.

He didn't answer and when she glanced at him she saw his expression had changed. Suddenly he looked very tense.

The next instant his fist struck her on the temple, knocking her out cold.

Using the same hand, he pushed her hair out of her face and shoved her back in the seat so that anyone seeing the car would think they were just an ordinary couple. She looked as if she'd dozed off next to him.

*

When Ann Kathrin arrived at her house on Distelkamp in Norden, she went out onto the terrace barefoot. She deliberately headed for an area of the back yard that was covered with pebbles. Slowly, she placed her feet on the pebbles feeling the smooth stones underfoot.

Frank Weller called it 'her parcours therapy'. She liked to walk on the stones in order to calm down after a stressful day.

The carpet in the living room. The flagstones. The floor of the terrace. The pebbled area. And then the soft, closely cropped lawn. At the end of her route were pine boards that led to the sauna building.

There was room for six people, but so far only the two of them had been inside together.

She grounded herself with every step. Behind the sauna leaves and branches lay on the ground. A pair of hedgehogs lived back there, and her tomcat Willy liked to eat the cat food she put out for them. Here the bare earth under her feet felt much different from the lawn. Damper, and yet it made a crunching sound.

No, she didn't feel like a sauna today. She just wanted to get out of her head somehow, back into her own body. Above her feet she felt pretty good, but she was too tired to go for a walk along the dyke.

In the moonlight she looked over at Weller, both needy and terribly lonely. What he actually wanted to do was read a new mystery. He had bought two, and still hadn't decided which one to start first. *Shadow Oath* by Nané Lénard. The dedication in the front of the book was to those who bear the sadness for crimes that were never solved. That appealed to Weller. And he also had a copy of *Murderous Monaco* by Julie Gölsdorf.

Now he decided to let both books wait a while. When Ann Kathrin came back to the house he said: 'You're tired. Lie down and I'll massage your feet, then you can fall asleep.'

She agreed at once, and they promised each other not to talk shop. Instead she put on a CD of Ulrich Maske's *Thrill & Chill*. The music helped them both to leave behind the stresses of the day.

Weller sat on a cushion at the foot of the bed. That way he could massage her feet in a relaxed position. She stretched out her feet and moaned blissfully.

After less than ten minutes the pressure of Weller's fingertips on her soles began to fade. His massaging movements slowed, and finally he nodded off.

For a while both of them slept like that. Ann Kathrin stretched out on the bed, Weller half sitting and half reclining on the floor. Then he began to snore softly. She called his name and he grunted.

Not wanting to wake him, she slipped a pillow under his head and put a blanket over him. He rolled onto his side and grunted again.

The music of Ulrich Maske had long since come to an end when Ann Kathrin woke up with a start from a bad dream. She had seen Ubbo Heide and his wife, both looking shocked. Before them stood an open carton with a severed head inside. Carola Heide was clutching at her heart and gasping for breath.

Ann Kathrin sat up in bed. She reached out to the side of the bed where Weller usually lay.

'Frank!' she called. 'Frank!'

Like a ghost he got up from the floor. In the dark he couldn't tell whether he'd been out cold or had dozed off for a brief nap. He shook himself and felt for the light switch.

The glow from the bedside lamp spotlighted the bed like a stage. In the middle sat Ann Kathrin, surrounded by pillows.

'Yes? What is it?'

Ann Kathrin burst out: 'He's going to send the second head to Ubbo too!'

'Damn it, you're right,' said Weller, his mouth dry. It seemed inappropriate, but right now he felt a strong desire for a *doppio espresso*.

Ann Kathrin urged him to hurry. 'We have to stop that from happening. We need to search through the mail going to Wangerooge. Ubbo won't be able to cope with another shock like that.'

'Nor will Carola,' said Weller. 'But we'll need a court order to search the post office.' He looked at his watch. 'It's 5.11 now. We'll never make it in time for the first ferry. See about getting hold of a form to fill out.'

Ann Kathrin agreed with him. 'Right.' She looked determined as she combed her fingers through her hair. 'But we can't do both, Frank. Let's just intercept the mail before they put it on the ferry. We'll find the package and—'

Feeling muddle-headed and still half asleep, he muttered: 'But we need a court order.'

'It's too late for that, Frank!'

'OK, screw it,' he said, finally awake.

She nodded. 'Sometimes you've just got to do what you've got to do.'

*

Büscher had lain awake half the night. When he'd more or less been forced to accept the transfer to East Frisia, he'd had no idea how hard it would be to find a place to rent. Although there were plenty of people along the coast who lived in their own houses, if they had extra space, such as in the attic, they liked to rent out rooms to holidaymakers.

A widow asked him, 'Why should I rent the room for a monthly pittance to a surly working person when I can get the same amount per week from a happy tourist who even gives me flowers when he leaves?'

Finally, he found a lovely furnished holiday let in Esens that he could move into temporarily. It belonged to the East Frisian writer Manfred C. Schmidt. The cabin was fully equipped of course, so Büscher didn't need to bring anything but his clothes from Bremerhaven.

For the first time he realised what an mess he had lived in since his divorce. It was easier than he had thought to leave everything behind. So East Frisia became a real new beginning for him.

Unable to sleep any longer and worrying feverishly about what the workday would bring, he drove around the neighbourhood a bit to orient himself. He then parked the car and went for a walk by the sea, witnessing a wonderful sunrise from the top of the dyke.

Actually, he thought, every day that I miss this performance by Nature is a sin of omission. Maybe I should live like this . . . get up at dawn to greet the sun, watch it set after work and then go to bed.

Did you have to be retired in order to do this he wondered. Briefly, he felt depressed as he calculated how many more years he would have to keep chasing criminals. Then he decided to shorten the time until retirement by observing as many sunrises and sunsets as humanly possible.

He didn't even know exactly where he was. In front of him he saw a gigantic field full of wind turbines sprouting up from the ground like huge stalks of white asparagus. From here on top of the dyke the view of the rising sun seemed like a welcome respite for the soul. A way of recharging his batteries.

And mine were almost empty, he thought.

*

Frank Weller and Ann Kathrin drove from their house on Distelkamp to the town of Harlesiel. It took less than fifty minutes on the C4.

It was much easier and less complicated than they'd imagined. The mail was already loaded onto the ferry, but since everyone knew about the gruesome package somebody on Wangerooge had received, they all understood why the police needed to examine the mail, especially since Weller and Ann Kathrin weren't interested in letters or postcards.

There was no package of a suspicious size, and none addressed to Ubbo Heide. Despite this, Weller and Ann Kathrin did not consider their morning action futile. Rather, they felt relieved. They had done the right thing in protecting Ubbo Heide.

They had a cup of coffee and watched the ferry until it left the dock, heading for Wangerooge.

'Now we have more questions to answer,' said Weller. 'Where is the missing head that belongs to the body found in Cuxhaven? And where, damn it all, is the body that belongs to the head sent to Wangerooge?'

*

Obviously some people considered it amusing to call the police and report they'd found body parts. Right now Rupert had the third joker of the morning on the line.

'I found a piece of the principal's head in front of Ulrich High School.'

When Rupert heard the young, joking voice and the giggling in the background, he was instantly on guard. 'A piece of his head? What part? Nose? Ears?'

'No, a block.'

'A block?'

'Yes, he always went around with a mental block.'

'Listen here, you little shit. Do you realise that you're obstructing an official investigation of the homicide division? And now I have your phone number, your name, and your address.'

'B-but I – I'm not even calling from my mobile!'

Rupert was pleased that he'd landed a punch, and his opponent was already staggering.

'Thanks to our modern technology, all calls are recorded, analysed graphically and sonically, and instantly tracked geographically. Don't move from your present location. Two officers will be there shortly to bring you to the station.'

'Uh? What? Can you see me?'

'This guy's making a fool of you, Christian. Just hang up!' an adolescent female voice said. Either she had a summer cold or she definitely smoked too much.

Rupert laughed. 'So, Christian, didn't you know? That's the newest spyware that's been developed for us. Don't you ever watch *CSI*? As soon as you dial 911 or the police, the camera on your mobile turns on. That's an enormous help to us, and it saves a lot of lives. Didn't Mr Ulrich at your school tell you about it?'

'No, I . . ., um. Hey, that's bullshit.'

Rupert's voice took on a stern tone: 'How stupid can you be? If you don't want to be the only one charged, then do exactly what I'm going to tell you. Take your goddamn mobile phone and hold it so I can see the stupid faces of your friends too. Stretch out your arm, film the others, and then turn around slowly so I can get a shot of all of them.'

'But I—'

'That's a police order! This is the last time I'm going to tell you!'

'OK, OK. Fine.'

'Hey, Christian, what are you doing? Are you nuts? Shit, now you're filming me!'

Rupert had propped his feet up on the edge of his desk and was wiping away tears of laughter when Sylvia Hoppe entered the room.

'What's so funny?' she asked, then answered her own question. 'Did your wife finally tell you that it's not the size that matters?'

Rupert's good mood vanished at once.

*

Ubbo Heide and his wife Carola had decided to leave Wangerooge. They had actually reserved the summer cabin for more than three weeks, but since it was high season, and with this wonderful weather, they were sure other renters could be found. Ubbo hoped that the gossip hadn't specified exactly where on Upper Strand promenade the severed head had been delivered. He was afraid the news might attract morbid curiosity from tourists, while his wife was more worried that the house with the fantastic sea view would no longer be rented at all.

Ubbo had two engagements lined up to give readings from his book. One in Gelsenkirchen at the city library, and another two weeks later, at the market hall in Delmenhorst. Both events had been sold out for weeks, but Ubbo was contemplating not going. Would anyone be interested in his book? Or would they only want to hear about the head? Could he leave Carola alone? She still seemed quite shaken.

Actually his daughter Insa had promised to meet him on Wangerooge and accompany him to the readings. She had planned to drive him back to the ferry as well and then stay with them for a couple of days. But she hadn't called back, and Ubbo assumed that her plans had changed. He didn't really mind. She'd recently fallen in love and was probably rolling around with her lover somewhere with no idea of the nightmare her parents were dealing with.

He could no longer manage to travel for readings alone. Since he'd been in a wheelchair, these trips had turned into burdensome adventures.

On a ship or ferry he felt fine but he didn't like to talk about the fact that he was afraid to fly.

The Heides took the first ferry back to the mainland. They left the island on a sunny day that promised to be glorious. Cloudless, with a northwest breeze just strong enough to clear out the humidity.

Their car was parked in Harle in the long-stay car park near the airport, in row 18 way in the back, where the sheep pasture began. The sun was reflecting off the roof of the car, and Carola imagined with trepidation how hot it must be inside. She didn't tolerate heat well, and she had always appreciated efficient air conditioning. For her that was more important than the car's appearance or horsepower.

Ubbo could have waited at the entrance and had the car brought up, but he didn't like that sort of service. It made him feel useless. He'd rather bump across the meadow in his wheelchair.

A strong smell reached them on the wind, as if an animal had died somewhere nearby. The stench intensified the closer they got to their car. Flies were buzzing around the boot lid.

Ubbo knew right away what was going on. He clutched his wife's arm. 'Don't get in,' he said. 'I'll call Ann Kathrin.'

Carola refused to believe what they were both thinking. 'It could be a dead rat under the car,' she said, but Ubbo said sternly: 'Don't move, Carola. You might destroy evidence. He must have crossed the meadow here.'

'Do you really think that someone has put something in our car?'

Ubbo punched in Ann Kathrin's number.

She saw his name on the display and answered immediately her seal ringtone howled. She greeted him effusively, as if to ward off a premonition.

Ubbo said matter-of-factly, 'I'm afraid, Ann, that our perpetrator has stashed a few body parts that wouldn't fit in the package in the boot of my car. Judging by the smell, it must have been a while ago.'

Carola noticed that he said *my car*. He usually said *our car*. That was probably his last feeble attempt to keep her out of it.

The hot air above the car shimmered before her eyes. She was having a hard time breathing and couldn't quite read the number plate. It was blurred like in a photograph of a moving car. She saw only streaks of the tail lights, as if the car were driving away fast, but her mind was telling her that this was impossible, because the vehicle was parked right here and couldn't be moving forward without a driver.

Suddenly her throat was dry and she needed water badly. There was always a bottle of mineral water behind the backrest of Ubbo's wheelchair but she couldn't manage to take it out.

She felt dizzy, as if her legs would no longer hold her up and she sat down in the grass next to her husband's wheelchair. Not far from them three white butterflies were fluttering around an ice cream tub that someone had dropped on the ground. There was still chocolate ice cream around the rim.

*

Svenja Moers had given up all hope that she was just having a nightmare. Any chance of waking up and finding herself at home, having fallen asleep in front of the TV, vanished when she touched the bars of the cell.

She beat on them, and the shiny bars rang derisively.

When she was still married, she'd sometimes had the feeling of being in a prison. She had talked to a girlfriend about the cage in which boredom had stolen the wind from beneath her wings, making her forget that she'd ever had them.

Now she knew what a real prison was. It wasn't about a suffocating atmosphere, but about naked panic. This was the exact opposite of her marriage. Back then she was able to predict exactly what would happen next Monday at six, because the days were all the same, unaffected even by the change of seasons.

Now she had no idea what would happen, even in the next second. Far from being bored, she was scared to death!

She touched everything around her as if to reassure herself that that it was real. The walls and floors were covered in white tiles like an old-fashioned public bath, or a slaughterhouse.

There was a set of bathroom scales on the floor, the same brand she had at home. She felt it was mocking her. Why was it here? To signal normality?

Next to her cell was another one, a bit smaller and divided from hers only by bars. It looked even less comfortable. It had no bed, just a toilet without a lid. A water pipe stuck out from the wall, with a length of hose attached. There was no washbasin.

She wondered whether the cell next door was for more severe punishment. Was he going to put her in there? Would she have to sleep on the floor? Was her current cell, with the bed and washbasin, a privilege that could be taken away at any time?

After her second husband died she'd spent 'a brief time' in custody. At least that's what the press had called that eternity. Her idiot lawyer had taken five days to spring her. She still hated him for that.

Right now she'd be happy to have a lawyer. She would even settle for that miserable, incompetent mouthpiece from Leer.

She tried to get her panic and rasping breathing under control. She grabbed the bars and rattled them. Her hands left greasy marks on the shiny polished metal.

She yelled: 'Fucking heel, where the hell am I? I want out!'

It felt good to swear. Swear words made her feel strong in this intolerable situation. She wanted to yell the worst, nastiest swear words she knew. Maybe that would intimidate the bastard who thought he could hold her prisoner. No way did she want to appear to him as a crying, wailing female. But no matter how hard she tried, her store of swearwords was gapingly empty.

The thought of running out of swear words was sobering. What had happened to her? Hadn't two husbands feared her outbursts of rage? Her vulgar way of shouting them down? What had happened to that talent of hers?

*

The editor-in-chief of the *East Frisia* magazine, Holger Bloem, wondered about the visit. He had spoken briefly with Joachim Faust ten, or was it fifteen, years ago. Since then he'd often seen his picture in magazines for which Faust wrote tabloid-type articles.

The photos of him had obviously been run through a pretty good image-processing programme, which made them look more flattering than realistic. The makeup artists had done a great job on various talk shows where Faust had first been a guest, then later the host. On the TV screen he'd always looked young, sporty and dynamic.

Now Holger Bloem thought he looked rather bloated, prematurely aged, and sickly. His skin had the unhealthy, dull colour of a heavy smoker who had spent his life in air-conditioned offices with canteens that offered pizza with a double helping of cheese every day.

Faust was wearing a summer suit of light-blue linen and an apple-blossom-white shirt open to the third button. There was a heavy gold chain around his wrinkled, over-tanned neck. His bare feet were encased in sandals of yellow leather.

Joachim Faust was undoubtedly a famous man, but he had the whiff of an ageing small-town pimp.

Holger Bloem and Joachim Faust had met in journalism school. Even back then Holger hadn't trusted him. He thought the man was a conceited old goat who seized every opportunity that came along and whose goal in life was to fuck as many women as possible and make a pile of money doing it.

He seemed to think that fame and various scandals were the best way to achieve his goal, and so far the plan had been an outstanding success.

He greeted Holger with a handshake, displaying a powerful grip. Holger Bloem assumed that Faust had not come to apply as a freelancer for the magazine. They exchanged a few pleasantries and then left the editorial office. They went over to Café Ten Cate to have coffee and talk.

The beautiful weather had lured lots of people downtown to Osterstrasse. All the tables and chairs outside were occupied. They wanted a quiet booth with no eavesdroppers and there weren't even any seats for them in the ice cream parlour.

Naturally Faust headed for the smoking room in the café and instantly lit up a long French cigarette. Through the flame of his golden lighter he observed Holger.

'Still into sports and a non-smoker?'

Holger nodded. Faust laughed. 'Smoked fish keeps longer!' he said, blowing thick smoke onto the round tabletop so that it was deflected directly into Holger's face.

They ordered water, coffee and tree-ring cake from a server who was quite excited because this was the first day she'd been allowed to take orders.

'Are you also on the town council?' she asked timidly.

Bloem shook his head apologetically and waved through the glass door to Monika Tapper, who was bringing a customer a schnitzel in the non-smoking area.

The server-in-training smiled. 'Guided crime tours are really popular in Norden, and today they're coming here.'

The rookie server vanished to the kitchen.

Faust got on with his business. 'Tell me something about Inspector Klaasen's latest case.'

'About the severed head?'

'Yes. Or is there another case she's working on?'

Holger suddenly felt sick. He was squirming in his chair. Where was all this leading?

'Apparently you know more than I do. So far there has been no official press conference.'

Faust smiled smugly. 'This is not about the case, Holger. It's about Ann Kathrin Klaasen. And no one knows more about the inspector than you.'

'How am I supposed to take that?'

'Don't give me that. You praised her to the skies, made her into an icon. No one in Germany better symbolises everything we love about working women than Ann Kathrin Klaasen. Every actress tries to emulate and imitate her. Young women apply to the Kripo so they can be like her. And you've had a great deal to do with that, my friend.'

'Where are you going with this?'

'In Germany there is a simple journalistic principle,' Faust intoned. 'You can only tear down someone that you've previously built up. The higher someone climbs, the further he can fall.'

'And?'

'People want to see them fall, Holger. Let's not fool ourselves. Who's really interested in the next case that Ann Kathrin Klaasen solves? Yawn. We know all that. What we need is an Ann Kathrin Klaasen we can get excited about, a woman who has at last disappointed us and, in that way, become one of us again. So speak, my friend.'

Bloem looked at Faust in disbelief. 'Are you serious?'

'I'm looking for the fallen angel. The statue has to be knocked off its pedestal.'

'Why?'

'Because that's the kind of story people love. Then they no longer feel that they're so pathetic and small. We can only admire stars, but fallen stars do us good. The cardinal who abuses young boys is important for humanity. He gives every one of us sinners the opportunity to forgive ourselves, because other people, no matter how holy, are much bigger sinners than we are.

'The pop star, rich and famous, who doesn't pay his child support and even refuses to acknowledge his paternity, takes some of the load off every father who goes to bed at night feeling that he isn't a good father and hasn't spent enough time with the kids.'

Monika Tapper brought their orders, greeting Holger Bloem by name. This prompted Faust to flinch, because he was used to being recognised instantly and also greeted by name.

Here in Norden, Bloem was the star, not Faust. That hurt his ego. He'd wanted to show Bloem how famous and popular he was. But he'd realised long ago that in East Frisia the clocks ran differently from in the rest of the world. Hardly anyone here read the big slick magazines that he wrote for. Here the *East Frisia* magazine was more important.

And if my talk show was on, they'd all be out in the back yard grilling sausages, he thought grimly. Otherwise they'd recognise me. They always did in Munich and Berlin.

That too made him irritated with everybody up here, no matter how good their coffee and tea tasted. And they could take their tree-ring cake and rub it in their hair, for all he cared. He certainly wasn't going to eat it.

Bloem looked happy when he took a bite of the cake. Monika Tapper, who was very sensitive to mood swings, had noticed immediately the tension hovering over the table. As she left she said, 'If you need anything else, I'll be right over there. This is our last day with a smoking room. As of tomorrow we're a non-smoking café.'

Faust also saw this remark as directed at him and he tried to keep calm.

Bloem brought the conversation back to where they'd left off. 'And you want me to deliver Ann Kathrin Klaasen to you, is that it?'

Faust beamed. 'Bingo. You're sure quick on the uptake! And I won't leave you in the lurch. I'll invite you onto my talk show, and then you can talk about how disappointed with her you are and blah, blah, blah.'

Bloem was having a hard time sitting still but didn't show it. Faust was used to people who were eager to sell out their mother-in-law just to get on his show. They offered him money, their friendship, and of course a whole bunch of information. He had noticed at once that with Holger Bloem it was going to be much more difficult.

Bloem was simply staring at him. Faust made a sweeping gesture. 'There's ten thousand in cash in it for you if you've got something interesting to offer. Do you have access to her personal documents? They must be full of strange stories.'

Bloem didn't react.

Faust continued. 'She'll founder in the current situation. One way or another. That's just how it is. There's always something. Maybe she's too lax or too sharp. Too slow, or she reacts too hastily and we'll be after her, you get it? Then the press is going to ramp up the campaign against her, instead of merely ruffling her hair. I want her without makeup. Confused and pressured. Best would be in the arms of a lover. Although when I take a closer look at her – isn't she a closet lesbo? Did she screw her way to the top? That kind of thing is always good. And who in East Frisia Kripo is sleeping with whom and why?

Faust raised his cup like a glass of champagne to offer a toast. That should serve as a challenge to Holger Bloem, he thought. If he's up for it.

Bloem rubbed his hand briefly over his well-shaven jaw. He recalled a situation back in journalism school in which he'd asked himself: Why don't I just punch this guy on the nose?

He had controlled himself and not done it, because he was a gentleman. A man of his word, not a man of violence. But he asked himself whether, after all these years, this could be the right time.

Instead of punching Faust he took another bite of the delicious tree-ring cake and then said, 'This really hits the spot.'

Faust relaxed and leaned back. He certainly hadn't counted on winning over Bloem immediately. He'd thought Bloem would stall him for a while in order to drive up the price.

Holger Bloem motioned him closer. They put their heads together across the table, and Holger whispered mysteriously: 'I've been looking for a big emotional story for a long time. Who doesn't dream of knocking down someone who's loved by the public, a darling of the media who has so far been spoiled by good fortune?'

Faust was glad to hear that. 'Exactly. It's so unfair.'

Bloem agreed. 'Right. And it would great if a real character-assassin could be involved – a son of a bitch like you for instance!'

Faust's jaw dropped.

Bloem got up and headed for the door.

'Is that all you have to say, Holger? Is that really your last word?'

Bloem stopped at the glass door. The tour group with the city guide who were making the rounds of the crime scenes came into the café.

'No, Joachim, I've got something more to say.'

Faust's eyes opened wide. He was all ears.

'Get lost!'

*

This cell seemed bigger to her, more modern, somehow friendlier than the holding cell back then. This one was so new, as if a designer had come up with a model cell for detainees. It wasn't shabby and scratched up like the one in Aurich. At the same time it felt final in an intimidating way, while the cell in Aurich had suggested it was more of a way station. Here every square centimetre seemed to say: you're not going to get out of here. Get used to it. You're going to spend the rest of your fucked-up life in this tiled room, Svenja Moers.

*

The red-and-white crime-scene tape fluttered in the wind. A dozen sheep had gathered and were watching the evidence response team. Jens Warfsmann was kneeling on the grass in his white protective suit and searching for clues. From a distance it looked as though he was part of the flock and had merely wandered over to the other side of the fence.

Underneath his white hood he was sweating profusely. He had a hangover from the housewarming last night at his new neighbour's place. He swore he'd never drink schnapps again.

Jens had found a used condom in the grass and slipped it into a plastic bag. He could hardly believe it was from the perpetrator, but it was his job to secure any evidence, and not – based on the parametres of the case – to spend time evaluating it. He'd also picked up three cigarette butts, filter tips of various brands, and one filterless, hand-rolled butt, which smelled suspiciously as if there was not only tobacco in it but also hashish.

In the past, Jens had also enjoyed smoking a joint, but he stopped after he'd fathered two sons and found a job with the criminal police force after taking classes in night school.

Behind him he heard Klaasen and Weller talking to Ubbo Heide. He'd tried to convince the man in the wheelchair to go home, but former chiefs could be damned demanding and resistant to advice.

'We have to stop this, Ann. Carola can't take it anymore. She's had it. This isn't the way we'd pictured our retirement.'

Weller handed out bottles of water and suggested that Ann Kathrin and Ubbo should drink some. Weller thought he had to take care of them because they were ignoring the needs of their bodies and focusing all their attention on the case.

'The boot is undamaged, Ubbo. Somebody opened it and then closed it, without leaving a single scratch on the lock. There's only one explanation for that,' said Ann Kathrin.

All three of them knew what she meant.

Ubbo took a swig of water from the plastic bottle and grumbled: 'We had two remotes. One click to open or close the doors.

And each time the keys would beep.' He took another drink from the bottle. The plastic crackled. He went on as if he had to explain things in detail: 'So, the side mirrors fold shut. That's exactly how we found the car. First, the perpetrator must have known that we park the car here, and second, he had to have a key.'

'They aren't that easy to copy,' Weller put in.

Ubbo nodded. 'We lost one once. Or we thought we'd lost it.'

'When? Where?' Ann Kathrin wanted to know.

Ubbo dismissed the notion. 'No idea. It was my key, and I don't even drive anymore. Carola still has hers.'

'How is she doing? And where is she?' Ann Kathrin asked.

Ubbo straightened up in his wheelchair, trying to find a more comfortable position. 'She got a lift home with the patrol. I wanted to wait for you here.'

'That's fine, Ubbo. But you're not leading the investigation. I am,' Ann Kathrin clarified.

'Actually the state prosecutor is leading it,' Ubbo reminded her. 'Where is that washout, anyway?'

Ann Kathrin turned stern. 'Try to remember, Ubbo. The key is important. Who could have stolen it, when and where? When did you see it last?'

Pondering, he said, 'I think it was at the Reichshof restaurant. We were having dinner there. I'd just come out of hospital and was starting to adjust to the fact that my life had been turned upside down. I slammed the key on the table and said, 'From now on you'll have to drive us home from parties, Carola. And not only when I want to have a drink!"

He looked up at Ann Kathrin, who had the sun behind her. She moved over a bit.

'It was supposed to be a joke,' he explained, 'but I was in no mood to laugh. Have you ever felt like that? You want to scream but you're still cracking jokes?'

Ann Kathrin could see from Ubbo's expression that in his mind he was going down the list of guests who were also at the Reichshof that evening. In the past he'd had an almost photographic memory for people, but that was a long time ago.

Now he was trying to remember who'd been sitting at the next table. Who was over by the cloakroom? Who had said hello or looked away in embarrassment?

She was hoping he'd suddenly come up with a name. But then Weller suggested moving out of the midday sun, which was beating down on them so mercilessly. There was nowhere shady to sit.

Ubbo went on as if Weller hadn't spoken, 'But I don't think my key was taken at the Reichshof. If I even thought the murderer could have been right there, two tables away, calmly eating a filet mignon.'

'Do you remember using the car key again after that?' Ann Kathrin asked.

Before Ubbo could reply, Weller repeated his suggestion. 'We really ought to get out of the sun, people.'

Jens Warfsmann moaned, 'If you knew how much I'd love to come with you. These damned overalls are going to kill me.'

Weller made a move to push the wheelchair, but Ubbo insisted on propelling it himself. Weller and Ann Kathrin had a hard time keeping up with him, he was zooming so fast across the bumpy field. He ploughed right over several big molehills instead of going round them. His wheelchair rocked alarmingly.

Weller mused, 'You seem to like to go to Wangerooge quite often, Ubbo.'

'Yes, I do. Recovery is an island. Mine is named Wangerooge.'

Weller asked, 'Do you ever park your car at the outer harbour?'

Ubbo braked his wheelchair, and Weller banged into it. 'Why do you ask?'

'Well, everybody has to leave their car key there so that in case of flooding the cars can be moved to higher ground.'

'And you think,' Ann Kathrin interjected, 'that someone took the opportunity to get the key copied? We could easily check to see if a break-in was ever reported. I can't recall anything happening out there.'

Ubbo quickly quashed the idea. 'I've never parked at the outer harbour. Always near the airport, even though I hate to fly.' Without pausing he continued, 'I know what you're thinking. The perpetrator knows me.'

Ann Kathrin agreed. 'Yes. He knows where and when you go on holiday and where you park your car.'

Ubbo qualified that statement. 'Everyone going to Wangerooge parks here.'

'But he has your car key,' Ann Kathrin insisted.

Ubbo stopped and yelled at her, 'Yes, damn it! And he's trying to scare me!'

'No, Ubbo, I don't think so. He admires you. He sent a package to your summer cabin, beautifully wrapped like a birthday present.'

Ubbo crossed his arms stubbornly. 'But it wasn't my birthday.'

Weller looked at his wife quizzically. He asked himself where she was going with this.

She went on, 'And he deposited a second head, neatly packed, in your boot, without damaging the car in any way. Then he locked it up. Admit it, Ubbo. He likes you.'

Ann Kathrin's provocative statement rang true.

Ubbo sat up straight in the wheelchair and said, 'You're saying this is all some kind of love letter? Well, thanks a lot! I can definitely do without it. My wife has had a nervous breakdown, and the car is full of maggots.' He pointed to his vehicle at the end of the last row of cars. 'You can forget about that old heap. Who'd want to drive it now?'

'First the perpetrator deposited one head in the boot and then posted the other one. Why? He could have put both heads in the car at the same time. That way he wouldn't have run any risk.'

Weller asked, 'How long were you planning to stay on the island?'

"Three weeks,' Ubbo said.

'Obviously that was too long for the perpetrator. He wanted you to come home early. But why?'

They continued on, past the rows of cars, towards the cashier and the exit. A group of tourists was discussing what had happened. One young woman wanted nothing more than to go back to Sauerland. The calves of her legs and the backs of her knees were terribly sunburned.

'I wasn't going to stay on the island the whole time. I've got readings coming up in Gelsenkirchen and Delmenhorst.'

'How were you going to get there? Was Carola going to drive you?' Ann Kathrin asked.

'No,' said Ubbo, 'Insa was going to pick me up and take me there. Carola was supposed to stay on Wangerooge.'

Ann Kathrin said, mainly to herself, 'So you weren't even going to use your car.'

'No.'

'The perpetrator must have known that too. He didn't want the first head to sit in the boot for three weeks. That's why he posted the second one to you at the cabin. Apparently he could hardly wait for the game to begin.'

Weller sought eye contact with Ann Kathrin before he spoke. They hadn't agreed on what he now proposed. 'You should definitely do these readings, Ubbo.'

'Why?'

'Because I think this man will cross paths with you.'

Ann Kathrin agreed. 'Frank is probably right about that.'

'So now you can take me over to forensic. I want to examine the heads in peace and quiet,' Ubbo ordered.

'Do you think you can identify them?' Weller asked. He wasn't sure he thought this was a good idea. Ubbo looked terrible.

Ubbo gave Frank a reproachful glare. 'This must have something to do with me. And if I can't do it, who can?'

'One of the heads is at Pathology in Oldenburg, and the other one is on the way here,' Ann Kathrin told him.

'Then we'll go to Oldenburg first,' Ubbo said, using the same tone of voice as when he was still the chief in East Frisia. Friendly but firm.

Ann Kathrin and Weller were both wary of the idea.

She said, 'Wouldn't it be better if you stop by the house to see Carola first? She must be worried, and she needs you. We can bring you photos later, then you can examine them at your leisure.'

Ubbo sighed. 'I'm sure I don't have to explain this to you. Photos of corpses usually provide only a poor representation of reality. No, I have to see the heads for myself.'

Later, in the car on the way to Taubenstrasse in Oldenburg, Ubbo said, 'I've been through this before. Sometimes it really tore me apart. Part of me felt that I should stay with Carola and my young daughter. But another, stronger part told me that postponing the forensic examination would mean having to wade through mountains of paperwork or even redoing the examination.'

Ann Kathrin was driving. The windscreen was covered with dead insects. The windows were closed, and the air conditioning was running full blast. Ann Kathrin understood what Ubbo was saying. She felt the same way. 'How many times did my son have to realise that some criminal or murderer was more important to his mother than he was. I still hate myself when I think about that time I missed his first big birthday party because I was chasing some damn—'

She broke off and fell silent. Weller reached over to stroke her neck. 'It was the same with my daughter and me. It goes with the territory.'

'Eventually you get used to it,' Ubbo said from the back seat.

Ann Kathrin countered, 'No, Ubbo, you never get used to it. At most you can learn to live with it, but that's a long and painful process.'

*

It was humid in the cell. Svenja Moers was finding it hard to breathe. A gleaming film of sweat covered her face. Drops ran down her neck like slimy vermin creeping out of her pores. Her clothes were sticking to her body. Had he turned the heat up? Or had a feverish fear seized hold of her? She felt like tearing off her clothes. Maybe that's what he wanted.

How many cameras were watching her? Was everything being recorded for the Internet by a couple of sick guys?

Outside the bars, beyond her reach, was a steel door that now opened slowly with a humming sound. Illuminated by spotlights like a pop singer at a gala evening, he strode in.

She almost didn't recognise him. The red locks were gone. The full beard too. His face had an angular look. The thought that maybe the long hair and beard had been a disguise scared her. That would mean he'd been planning all this for a long time.

Of course he had. It was obvious that this prison hadn't been built in a couple of hours. Before her stood a man who might be insane, but who planned meticulously.

He looked to be in a good mood and was carrying a white tray with a plate on it. Before she could see what it was, she smelled it: cabbage. The tip of a sausage stuck over the edge, and a piece of bacon. Next to the plate were plastic utensils. A spoon and a fork. He'd even remembered mustard.

There was a serving slot between the bars. Full of determination he went over to it and shoved the tray inside. He did it without comment, as if it were a daily routine.

The smell disgusted her, but she accepted the tray anyway. Then she heard herself yell: 'You bring me cabbage with bacon, you sick bastard? That's a winter dish! It's the middle of summer. Are you trying to fatten me up so you and your idiotic friends can watch me turn into a whale?'

She threw the entire tray against the bars.

He didn't even duck. He stood there almost at attention without even attempting to avoid the food. A serving of cabbage landed in his face and on his shirt, and a piece of bacon on his right shoe. The sausage bounced off the cage bars and fell next to the tray in her cell.

He didn't say a word. He simply stared at her, not moving. Bits of cabbage fell from his face and plopped onto the floor.

His stillness frightened her. There was something robotic about him. Didn't he mind the hot cabbage in his face? Didn't he feel it? Did he not feel pain?

He just stood there. Then he left the room without a word. The steel door closed behind him with a whirr. The piece of bacon lay glistening on the floor.

His shoes had left behind spots of cabbage. The mustard was sliding down a bar of the cage like a tiny yellow snake.

The triumphant feeling inside her quickly gave way to a deep-seated fear.

*

Rupert actually wanted to order diggers to plough up the beach at Norddeich to search for the missing body. However, Sylvia Hoppe had requested tracker dogs instead and Büscher had ordered that everything should take place calmly, sensibly and without attracting a lot of attention. In a popular tourist resort in high season, ice cream stands looked far more appropriate than 'search and rescue dogs', as he called them. However, Büscher still believed that he'd made a wise choice by putting Rupert in charge of operations. It was important to delegate responsibility to his subordinates.

Büscher had misinterpreted Sylvia Hoppe's spiteful smirk. He assumed that she felt passed over, so he intended to give her an important assignment next time.

The dogs had to come from Aurich, so Rupert, Hoppe and four uniformed officers got to Norddeich shortly before the actual search and rescue team. They strolled from the guest house to the Diekster Kitchen and back before the canine unit arrived .

The queue at the ATMs by the beach was longer than on any other day. Even a few of the locals from Norden, who had always steadfastly refused to pay to use the beach, hurried to buy tickets from the meter when they saw all the police arriving. Everyone wanted to find out what was happening.

For years Wolfgang Mix from Bottrop had spent every summer holiday in East Frisia with his family, even as a child. His parents had always dreamed of being able to buy a house so they could spend their golden years here. They never managed to do that, but Wolfgang was hoping that he'd be able to realise that dream. He had two savings accounts and was a frugal man.

He had to laugh at the beach fees. 'The East Frisians are the descendants of pirates and robbers. Nowadays they no longer attack or kill people. They simply put up meters and expect us to rob ourselves. That's the modern form of piracy. Parking fees and beach meters!'

As the canine unit started the search of Dragon Beach, a dachshund from Oberhausen caught the scent of the body they were looking for, just beyond the blocked-off dog area of the beach. He began barking and digging excitedly outside the dog area so his owner, the bakery clerk Irina Schanz, came and got him. She took the dachshund, named Bello, back to the area reserved for dogs.

Now Bello was sniffing Joachim Faust's shoes. The journalist looked a lot like the man who had caused trouble in Irina's life many times. Someone who was vain, selfish and superficially cultured. But Faust wasn't interested in her or her dog. He was watching the police.

Ann Kathrin Klaasen wasn't there, but he thought maybe he'd be able to find someone who was willing to criticise the legendary hunter of serial killers.

When the headless corpse was finally found not far from the dog area of the beach, Faust watched as it was excavated. Wolfgang Mix from Bottrop recognised him and asked for his autograph. Faust always carried a few photos in his breast pocket just for this purpose.

At the very moment that he was signing his name on the photo, an exciting idea came to him. Another serial killer had struck right here once again. He would confront Ann Kathrin Klaasen with the theory that she attracted such individuals like moths to a flame. Yes! That would be the basis for his new article. She was dangerous for East Frisia, because she was like a magnet for dangerous felons.

Sylvia Hoppe was talking to the forensics team on the phone. Although Rupert was in charge of the operation, it was not beneath him to keep the rubberneckers at a distance and secure the crime scene with police tape.

Joachim Faust was taking pictures, and Rupert tried to stop him.

'It's a free country,' Faust lectured Rupert. 'I can stand around on a public beach as long as I want, and I can take pictures too. I don't need a permit for that.'

'Precisely,' said Mix, 'and we shouldn't need to pay a beach-use fee. What a rip-off!'

Rupert ignored Mix, but Faust knew that he'd hit home. Even as a kid Rupert had never been able to tolerate being lectured. Faust glanced over at Sylvia Hoppe. She should watch how her colleague Rupert dealt with these types of situations.

'Now just listen to me! If you'd like to spend the night in the drunk tank, you don't necessarily need to have a drink first. We can make certain arrangements, understand?'

Faust had already turned on his recorder. 'That's very interesting,' he said. 'You work with Ann Kathrin Klaasen and you're threatening to throw me in the drunk tank even though I haven't had anything to drink? Is that common practice here in East Frisia?'

Sylvia Hoppe was now standing next to Rupert. She'd recognised Faust from his very distinctive voice.

'My colleague didn't mean it like that,' she said. 'Anyway, right now we're digging up a corpse. The beach is full of people and it's quite a stressful situation.'

Rupert didn't understand the world anymore. Why was Sylvia being so nice to this windbag?

She whispered to Rupert, 'Apologise to him, Rupi. He's an important journalist, goddamn it. I've seen him on TV.'

Rupert scrutinised Faust. 'Journalist, eh? One of these blood-sucking reporters like Bloem?'

He couldn't stand reporters. If he was ever appointed the press spokesman for the East Frisian police it would be the worst conceivable disciplinary transfer for him.

'Apologise, Rupi!' Sylvia admonished him.

Lately the female officers had taken to calling him 'Rupi,' and he had no idea why.

Faust stood there with his arms crossed. In one hand he held a camera, and in the other a digital sound recorder.

Sylvia gave Rupert a nudge. 'This'll stress you out, Rupi. I promise you. You're picking a fight with the wrong person.'

'OK,' Rupert said and turned to Faust. 'Well, I . . . I didn't really mean it like that. I'd like to apologise.'

Faust smiled. 'That's not much of an apology.'

He was making it hard for Rupert. 'I'm not usually like this. Maybe I was a bit too brusque.' Rupert held out his hand to Faust. 'Are we OK?'

Faust kept his arms crossed.

'Don't be so ridiculous,' Rupert now said. 'I offered a sincere apology. And that's not something I usually do. Only when I have to confront an arrogant idiot like you, then I occasionally behave out of character and—'

Faust glanced at the red button. His recorder was running.

Rupert waved his arms in the air. 'As my wife always says, this only happens when the arsehole in front of me reminds me of the arsehole inside me.'

Sylvia drew Rupert away. 'Are you nuts?'

Irina Schanz, the bakery clerk from Oberhausen, could no longer hold on to her dachshund Bello. He seemed to consider the body he'd discovered to be his private property. Now he slipped underneath Kripo's crime-scene tape and sank his teeth into the corpse's left forearm.

Two uniformed police jumped into the sand pit and tried to pull the dog away.

Irina shrieked, 'Don't hurt him! Don't hurt him! He just wants to play!'

Faust kept taking pictures.

*

Maybe, Svenja Moers thought, the second cell isn't intended as punishment for me. Maybe he's going to bring in someone else. Maybe someone from our cooking class.

She almost wished there was another prisoner. For some reason she thought a man in the other cell would be preferable to a woman. She didn't know why, but she wished he'd capture a man.

She imagined holding hands between the bars. No, not with her Ingo. She couldn't imagine him being in the next cell.

Who would Yves Stern get, and when?

It was getting hotter. Her mucous was beginning to dry out.

The whole place smelled like cabbage and bacon. The floor was still covered with green stains. The slab of bacon lay shining on the white-tiled floor.

The tap refused to produce any more water. It just made a gurgling noise. Somewhere outside her prison he must have turned off the water.

I need weapons, Svenja thought. The plastic fork in her hand seemed ridiculous. Still, she found it encouraging that she was even looking for weapons. She told herself that it meant she hadn't given up.

Again the steel door opened with a whirr, as if controlled by a motor. And there he was, standing in the spotlight.

From the crook of his right arm dangled a Kaufhof bag.

He had bathed and changed his clothes. He must have used an apple shampoo, and something that smelled of coconut. His hair was fluffy, as if newly blow-dried. She noticed how intense her sense of smell was in this prison.

He held a camera in his hand and now searched for the best position from which to take a picture. He came very close to the bars of the cell.

'Oh wow, you're looking so chic,' she said, belligerently. That's a sharp shirt. From Kaufhof? Although it's not quite your style. Pigs should wear piggy pink, don't you think?'

He took a picture of her without a flash.

'What's that for?'

She wondered what he had in the bag. Did it contain the knife he was going to use to kill her?

The photos made her nervous. She didn't want to be photographed like this. And whatever he was planning to do, she wanted to spoil his fun.

She stuck out her tongue, rolled her eyes, and made faces.

He clearly didn't like that, and his displeasure goaded her on even more.

She gave him the finger with both hands, holding them close to her face so that they'd show in the pictures.

He lowered the camera. She'd managed to ruin his fun.

Opening the shopping bag he pulled out a big sketch pad and a black marker pen.

Does this perverse madman want to draw me now? She thought.

'If this is supposed to be a drawing class, can't you afford a professional model? The female students are queuing up for that sort of job these days. You don't need to grab a woman off the street.'

She noticed the strength in her voice. It was the courage of despair, the absolute will not to give up.

He put the pad and pen in the slot between the bars, but she refused to touch them.

'Take them,' he ordered her, 'and write: My name is Svenja Moers and I'm doing my punishment here.'

'No, I won't,' she said.

'Oh yes you will,' he replied. 'If you don't, there will be nothing to drink and nothing to eat. I can turn the temperature up to over 120 degrees. How long do you think you'd be able to stand that?'

So he did turn up the heat on purpose, she thought.

She picked up the pen and pad. Then she sat down on the edge of the bed and wrote. He was surprised to see her crack so soon.

He started taking pictures again. 'I can't quite see it,' he said. 'Hold up the pad and lean your chin on it so I can get a good shot. Then I'll turn the heat back down.'

She sat up straight and turned the pad so he could read it.

He took a picture, and then he lowered the camera. On the pad it said: *My name is Svenja Moers. Yves Stern has kidnapped me.*

At first he could hardly breathe. Then he raised his hand to loosen his collar. He was sweating too.

'You goddamned whore!' he snarled. 'You're going to regret this!'

He strode over to the door, but slipped on the chunk of bacon and landed smack on the leftover cabbage that was stuck to the floor. The camera dangled from his neck like a leash as he crawled out of the prison on all fours like a dog, dragging pieces of cabbage across the tiles.

'Great performance, Yves!' she yelled after him. 'Hope you got good pictures!'

Then she applauded him scornfully.

*

Weller almost didn't recognise Professor Hildegard. She'd changed completely since their last meeting. Her body no longer looked fit and sporty. She had dyed her hair a deep red and let it grow longer. Her complexion had changed too, or maybe she was wearing different makeup. She had put on a few kilos and looked almost as old as she really was. Weller appreciated feminine curves.

It did Ann Kathrin good to have Frank and Ubbo nearby. She felt secure with them.

The rooms in Pathology were pleasantly cool, and the odour of disinfectant had a calming effect on her.

The heads had been cleaned and forensics had treated them with chemicals for analysis, which Ann Kathrin noticed at once. Thanks to the clinical mode of presentation the decapitated heads no longer looked horrific. They looked like they had been prepared for a medical lecture and might not even be real. They could have been made of plastic.

'I can tell you something about these men,' said Professor Hildegard.

Ubbo Heide stopped his wheelchair. 'So can I.'

His remark had the impact of a balloon bursting. Even before Professor Hildegard could start her remarks, Ann Kathrin had lost all interest in what she might say. Instead she turned to Ubbo. 'You know them?'

He pointed to the head that had been found in the boot of his car. 'That one. I know him.'

Ann Kathrin said to the professor, 'Please send me the results. We have no time to waste. I'm sure you understand.'

The professor nodded, looking a little piqued. Generally she enjoyed these performances, when she had the chance to explain everything to police officers. She liked being the scientist. She liked to pepper her remarks with medical terminology, so that some Kripo officer inevitably had to ask her to translate it into layman's German. She always waited for that moment, and then she would revert to language that was generally understandable.

That moment, she thought, was sometimes better than sex.

She now felt that her expertise had been subverted, but she knew that to protest was pointless. Then Ann Kathrin Klaasen would start lecturing her and she'd have to listen to that old adage: most perpetrators are apprehended shortly after the crime is committed. The longer it takes to arrest the first suspect, the more difficult the case will be, because emotions cool and the suspects have time to work out a story.

In Professor Hildegard's opinion that was about the only thing anyone learned at the police academy.

She watched as her three colleagues headed for the door. She was pleased when Weller suddenly turned around, because he had another question that he absolutely had to ask. 'Tell me, Professor, did either of these men have skin cancer?'

Astounded, she stared at Weller. 'Yes, but only on the left side of the nose.' Even though she loved to give lengthy answers, she had to ask: 'How did you know that?'

Weller back-pedalled. He whispered, 'I can't tell you that. It might jeopardise the investigation.'

Then he strode off after Ann Kathrin and Ubbo, leaving a frustrated pathologist behind.

*

Weller drove while Ubbo Heide sat in the back, talking nineteen to the dozen. Ann Kathrin twisted around in the passenger seat so she could look at Ubbo, as if she wanted to read his lips. She couldn't fasten the seat belt, so a red light kept blinking, accompanied by a shrill beeping that was driving Weller crazy. It was making his head ache, like biting down on a cherry stone with an infected tooth.

Ann Kathrin didn't seem to hear it. All her attention was focused on Ubbo, who was thinking out loud.

'It's an old case from fifteen or twenty years ago. Little Steffi Heymann, barely two years old, disappeared on Langeoog, where she was camping with her mother. The girl was never found. Her father, Bernhard Heymann, had been involved in a terrible divorce battle with his wife. She was in the stronger position, and the court had awarded her custody of the child. For a long time the father was my prime suspect. He had moved to Switzerland, I think it was Appenzell.'

'This is driving me crazy!' Weller shouted, banging his hand on the steering wheel.

'Me too. Somebody is decapitating people in East Frisia.'

'That's not what I meant,' Weller clarified. 'That beeping sound is too much. It reminds me of going to the dentist.'

Without a word Ann Kathrin took hold of the seat belt and let it zip back without fastening it. Now she was kneeling on the passenger seat with her arms around the headrest and her back to the windscreen.

'And why would anyone put Heymann's head in your boot fifteen or twenty years later? That makes no sense.'

'No,' said Ubbo, 'it definitely does not. But it's him. I recognised him. I interrogated him three times and made him sweat. Sometimes he got tangled up in contradictions. I saw him protest and then flip out with rage. I put him through the wringer, the whole programme. Believe me, I know this guy.'

'You thought he'd kidnapped his daughter in violation of the court order? So that she could live with him in Switzerland?' Ann Kathrin asked.

'Yes, that's how it looked to us back then. At least for a while. But we couldn't prove it. He had cast-iron alibis and besides, the girl was never seen with him. A few days after the kidnapping – or maybe it was a couple of weeks, I don't know exactly anymore, but we still have all the documents – anyway, he was involved in a serious accident in Switzerland. His car rolled over a couple of times and was written off.'

'Had he been drinking?'

'No, he was sober as a judge. He said the accident was due to the highly stressful and tense situation, which was understandable. But they found traces of little Steffi's blood in the car. He explained that by saying he used to drive around a lot with his daughter. The funny thing was, though, that the blood wasn't in the back of the car, near the child seat, but in the boot. He even had a reason for that. Apparently the little girl had hurt herself and the first aid kit was in the boot. He claimed he had put her down in the boot, opened the first aid kit, and bandaged her hand.

The mother dismissed the whole story as a lie. The two of them could not agree on anything.

Some of my colleagues theorised that Heymann had decided to take Steffi to a mountain cabin owned by his fiancée, and to keep her there until the fuss died down. Then he had the accident, and out of guilt he buried his daughter's body in the mountains.'

'What did you think of that idea, Ubbo?'

He shook his head, as if not sure what to think after so many years. 'It's possible. He had applied for Swiss citizenship. After marrying his new wife – I think she was from St Gallen – there was no real impediment. Maybe he hoped it wouldn't be considered a kidnapping case. Maybe he thought the Swiss courts would grant him custody of the child or in any event prevent her from returning to Germany. Then what started as a family drama turned into a criminal case with a missing child. Still, it's possible. But he steadfastly denied everything.'

Now that the beeping had stopped, Weller at last felt he could think clearly. He began speculating out loud. He knew Ann Kathrin didn't like him doing this, but the words just kept pouring out of him: 'Maybe in the meantime the mother takes a lover, and he decides on some kind of act of revenge, to show her what a great guy he is.'

Weller realised that he was babbling and refuted his own theory. 'But then he probably would have presented the head to his wife on a silver platter instead of stowing it in your boot.'

'And what did the second dead man have to do with the case?' asked Ann Kathrin.

Ubbo swallowed hard, as if not wanting to admit his bewilderment. 'No idea.'

*

Büscher was standing at his office window on Fischteichweg in Aurich, looking down at the street. He felt as if he'd fallen overboard on the high seas and now would have to try and survive among the big waves without a life jacket.

He didn't even know in which direction to swim to reach the mainland. He saw no rescue boats and his own ship was sailing around near Bremerhaven. Out of reach.

He liked to think of himself as a tough guy, a lone wolf. But right now he was depressed. He didn't want to admit it, but he'd clicked on his wife's Facebook page. She had changed her profile.

He felt old, stupid and sleazy doing it, but damn it, what was so bad about checking up on his ex?

She looked good, and that was especially painful. Unlike him, she hadn't aged at all. She'd lost a few kilos and had stopped dyeing her hair. She was sunning herself in a bikini on a chaise longue.

Not a wicker chair on the beach by the North Sea. A chaise longue. Apparently somewhere in the Caribbean.

She and her new guy obviously could afford trips like that. She had uploaded a whole photo gallery to the Web. The two of them smooching, or laughing at beachside cafés, with foamy *latte macchiatos* in front of them.

Büscher tried to persuade himself that he was glad to be rid of her at last. Her capricious nature had simply not suited him. But when he saw Frank Weller and Ann Kathrin Klaasen being lovey-dovey, his heart ached.

His friends, if he'd ever had any, all lived in Bremerhaven. Here he had to struggle through things alone.

It was warm, so he opened the window. The wind made his shirt flutter and he held out his arms to feel the gusts caress his skin.

He wasn't toying with the idea of jumping, but at this moment he understood people who ended their lives that way. Instead of continuing to bear the burden, they chose a brief and easy flight.

He shook off the thought and closed the window.

I have to talk to the real chief of Kripo, he thought. Ann Kathrin Klaasen. If I can win her over to my side, then everything will go well. Maybe we could work together on an equal footing.

He sat down in the black leather easy chair, trying to find the most comfortable position. This office still didn't feel like it belonged to him. Would he ever feel truly at home here? Was he the wrong man for the job? Or could this be the start of a new, perhaps even better life for him?

He'd remove a few pictures from the wall and hang up some new ones. Naturally he couldn't start by removing the framed article about Ann Kathrin Klaasen from the *East Frisia* magazine. His colleagues wouldn't appreciate that.

But what sort of personal photos could I hang up? he wondered. A picture of my biggest success as an angler? The 6.2-kilo perch? Or the picture of me standing proudly next to the blue marlin that I caught in the Hemingway Cup on Mauritius?

Would that impress Ann Kathrin or scare her off? Every step he took could be wrong. He was on unfamiliar territory.

I have to talk to her in private, he thought. Just the two of us.

He decided to invite her out to dinner. He balled his fist and rapped three times on the desk.

All right, all right, all right! I'll invite her out to eat.

But then new problems presented themselves. Any restaurant he considered would instantly reflect on him personally. If they went to Schickimicki's, that would put him in a snobby corner, from which it would be hard to extricate himself later. Yet the place couldn't be too simple or too cheap. Above all it had to show her how much he valued her.

Büscher wasn't familiar with this area. If she had a favourite restaurant he might be able to find out what it was. Through Rupert, perhaps. But wouldn't that undercut his position? Wouldn't it send a signal that from now on everything would run according to Ann Kathrin's dictates and at her discretion? Wouldn't it be better to impress her with something new? Perhaps a restaurant she had never tried?

In Bremerhaven he would have known where to go. To Natusch. But here in East Frisia? Did she even like fish? Would it be correct to select local cuisine, to show her how down-to-earth his taste was? Or should he present himself as a man of the world by choosing a Chinese, Thai or Greek restaurant?

He was stumped by which restaurant to choose. The situation made it clear to him how difficult it was to get a foothold here.

Maybe, he thought, it's best if I let her decide, and just invite her to a restaurant of her choice. Yes, that seemed to be the best solution. And if everything goes well, he thought, we'll end up on a first-name basis and drink a toast to that.

He dialled Ann Kathrin's number.

In Bremerhaven he'd always used an aftershave that smelled like incense, but he hadn't brought it with him. Now he asked himself whether it was time for a change. Or maybe he should simply try to smell like himself. But he could hardly believe anyone would find that pleasant.

Women discussed such things with each other. But men? Could he really picture himself asking one of his co-workers: 'Tell me, what kind of aftershave do you use? Do you use cologne or skin creams?'

No, that was impossible.

*

He turned the heat all the way up.

I'm going to turn you into a prune, he thought grimly. Don't think you're going to get through this with your monkey business.

The floor had to be washed. Not a pleasant task, but the dirt interrupted his flow. He needed a clean, even clinical atmosphere to know that what he was doing was right and good.

Order. Clarity. Bacteria and viruses had to be fought. He loved disinfectants.

And he could hardly hire a maid to clean the anteroom to the cell.

He pondered how he could force his prisoner to wash the floor. Humiliation might be the very thing to break her resistance.

But he expected her to throw the water at him. When he tried to imagine what would happen next, he pictured her attacking him with the cleaning products, lunging at him with the mop and trying to fight her way to the exit.

No, she wasn't that desperate yet. He had to leave her in the cage. The anteroom wasn't secure enough. Not yet. Soon he would make her clean it with a toothbrush, but they hadn't reached that point yet. Her pride, her stubborn will, her defiance, must first be broken down by humiliation, fear and pain.

No matter how much it annoyed him, he had no choice but to wash the floor himself. To get rid of dirt, he would have to come in contact with dirt.

He pulled on the blue rubber gloves.

*

Without thinking much about it, Ann Kathrin decided to eat at The Galley. Weller had overheard the phone conversation. The new chief was apparently inviting them to dinner.

Weller knew the entire restaurant menu almost by heart. He thought about ordering his favourite, dyke lamb, or perhaps the beef roulades, which reminded him of the best days of his childhood, when he stayed with his grandma. That was when he escaped from his strict father, and the kind old lady would cook for him.

But then the conversation took an odd turn. Weller thought he could detect that he wasn't invited to come along, and he found that odd.

Ann Kathrin said goodbye to Büscher and put down the phone. Then she told Weller, 'I'm going out to dinner with Büscher.'

'Just you? Not both of us?' Weller asked.

'No. He expressly said that he wanted to go out to dinner with me.'

'If someone invites me to dinner, I naturally assume that you're coming along,' Weller said, a bit peeved.

Ann Kathrin shrugged. 'Come on, don't make this hard for me. He's our new boss.'

Weller raised his hands. 'OK, OK. I have something planned for this evening anyway.'

She looked at him in surprise. 'You do?'

He sighed as if he'd told her about it long ago, and as usual, she had forgotten. Resignedly he said: 'Boys' night out. Holger Bloem, Peter Grendel, Jörg Tapper, a few others.' He shrugged. 'We're doing a pub crawl. The Mittelhaus. The Cage. And to finish off maybe we'll drop in at Wolberg's.'

None of that was true, but Weller thought it was an excellent idea. All he had to do was call the boys.

*

Svenja Moers was sitting on the bed, bathed in sweat. The bastard had installed under-floor heating in this room, and the floor was already so hot that there were only a few spots where she could touch it.

She had drawn her legs up to her chest, her arms wrapped around her knees. She made herself as small as possible. She was breathing shallowly.

Worse than the heat was the stench. Everything smelled like cabbage and bacon.

The door opened again with a hum. The spotlights switched on once more for his grand entrance. But this time he clearly wasn't enjoying it.

His getup resembled that of a surgeon in the operating theatre. He was wearing a blue lab apron, long rubber elbow-length gloves and boots.

He carried a bucket and a mop.

'Oh, here comes the cleaning brigade,' she mocked him. 'It's about time. This pigsty stinks.'

'Shut up,' he snapped. 'Just shut up. You're making it worse.'

Then he began to mop the floor.

*

Maybe Ann Kathrin had suggested The Galley so she could see her friend Melanie Weiss and so that when Melanie greeted Ann Kathrin with a hug at the door, Büscher would feel excluded. At the same time he couldn't exactly greet the owner with the same familiarity. It would be inappropriate, since they had never met.

Melanie picked up on his discomfort and held out her hand. 'So you're the new guy?' she asked. Guests sitting nearby grinned and waved to him, and Büscher worried that he might blush. The phrase 'the new guy' could mean many things. The new chief or the new lover. It was too ambiguous for him.

He wrestled with his embarrassment and then said loudly enough for everyone in the restaurant to hear: 'My name is Martin Büscher, and I'm first detective inspector, head of Central Criminal Investigation.' That sounded a little too pretentious. He felt awkward, as if he might trip over his own feet.

The Galley smelled good. Fried ocean fish, coriander, lamb, and hovering above it all the scent of vanilla. The vying aromas were a bit bewildering.

Melanie Weiss had reserved a table for them. It was Ann Kathrin's favourite place to sit, though normally without Büscher. Steps led up to a sort of stage where there was a performance area as well as several tables. The table was next to a mural that gave guests the feeling of sitting outside by the sea.

Ann Kathrin greeted her neighbour, Peter Grendel, with a grin. He and his wife Rita and their daughter were seated nearby. They were looking forward to their steaks.

Some boys' night out, Ann Kathrin thought, wondering why Weller had made up such a silly story.

Büscher was debating whether to select a good wine or maybe a bottle of German champagne. He wondered whether a glass of champagne would be too much. He didn't want people to think he was a playboy. But Melanie Weiss brought them two welcome drinks on the house and instantly made a mark on their bill . She called the cocktails 'East Frisian blood'. It seemed to be Prosecco with blueberries. Buscher had never felt comfortable with the deep mysteries of mixing cocktails. That was something his ex-wife knew more about, but he didn't want to think of her at the moment.

He leafed through the menu without deciding on anything and wondered how he was going to start the conversation.

When Ann Kathrin finally ordered for herself, he simply nodded and said with a big smile: 'Excellent idea. I'll have the same.'

He raised his glass to Ann Kathrin and said, 'To the German language.'

And she gladly drank that toast with him.

He had planned so much in advance. He had a definite plan, and he wanted to win her over to it. But now everything was going haywire. It was part of his strategy to initiate the conversation, but he'd hesitated too long, because now she asked, 'So, why this secret meeting? Is this dinner work-related? It's not a date, is it?'

'Man, you people in East Frisia sure get right to the point,' he said under his breath. Then out loud he explained, 'I feel strange about being your boss. It's not easy, you must see that. I mean, my God—' He tried for an all-encompassing gesture but failed. 'You're a legend. Your reputation precedes you.'

Ann Kathrin dismissed the idea as if he'd fired off some flattery that she didn't want to acknowledge. So he tried once again. 'No, no, I'm serious. Basically it would make more sense for you to be in charge of the station, not me.'

Ann Kathrin shook her head, picked up her glass by the stem, and turned it slowly so that the berries in the cocktail spun to the top.

'No,' she said, staring at her drink, 'the best thing would be if Ubbo Heide were chief. There's no one better than him.'

'OK. Sure. But he's still recovering from that sad accident.'

She interrupted him. 'It was no accident. It was a knife attack.'

'At any rate, he's stuck in a wheelchair and retired. Believe me, Ms. Klaasen, if I could change things I would. I didn't apply for this position, but all of us have to try to deal with the situation. And if the two of us work well together, then it will be to everyone's benefit. I invited you here to express my personal admiration and tell you how much I respect you. As a colleague and as a woman.'

Oh no. Had he gone too far?

She smiled and raised her glass again. He was relieved to hear what she now said. 'I don't want your job. And I'll try not to make your work more difficult than it already is. As far as I'm concerned, I think we might as well be on a first-name basis, like genuine colleagues.'

Büscher welcomed the offer but it nettled him at the same time. As her boss, shouldn't he have been the one to extend the offer?

'I've already noticed that clocks run differently here from in the rest of the country. I'm from the coast too, but even though Bremerhaven is only a hundred and fifty kilometres away, I feel like I'm on a different planet.'

She agreed. 'Here we have our own way of life,' she said with a smile and drained her glass. She leaned her head back to make all the berries roll into her mouth. Then she turned to Melanie Weiss and held up her thumb. Not very ladylike.

'Another round?' Melanie asked, and Ann Kathrin nodded.

Büscher made short work of the starters from the kitchen, dried beans on roasted blood sausage with grilled onions, served on a curved spoon. He ate as if he had to get rid of the food as fast as possible, while Ann Kathrin talked to Melanie about what else Frank was magically cooking up in the kitchen. Whatever it was, Melanie called the appetiser '*amuse-gueule*', and Büscher pretended he knew how to spell it.

Ann Kathrin said, 'Yes, it's a real culinary delight.'

Why am I so damned nervous? Büscher asked himself. *I'm behaving like I'm on my first date. What's she going to think of me?*

He had actually planned to win her over by telling her a little about himself. But before he could begin, she said, 'For me and for many of my colleagues, Ubbo Heide was not merely our chief, but also a father figure. And he still is. Something like that doesn't just evaporate. He's seen us in crisis situations and led us through tough cases. He has supported us through our defeats, and he has celebrated our successes. He means a lot to all of us, but especially to me. My father served in the criminal police.'

'I know,' said Büscher, 'I know.'

'Without my father I might never have chosen this career path. To honour him I've tried to be the best I can be.'

'And you *have* been the best,' said Büscher.

But she shook her head. 'It may look that way on the outside, because I had good luck with a couple of cases and was in the right place at the right time. But from my own point of view it looks quite different. I often feel like a failure. I would rather run away screaming than be the chief of the East Frisian Criminal Police. Just recently my husband and I discussed whether we should open a fish shop instead of chasing criminals.'

Büscher admitted frankly, 'I would never be able to take on that role. I mean I couldn't be a father figure for the whole team. At most I could try.'

She didn't let him finish. 'Yeah, you've got some pretty big shoes to fill.'

Silently she ate her North Sea crab soup with deep-fried rocket. Even before the main course arrived, Ann Kathrin tried to get back to the case. 'The perpetrator must have had access to Ubbo's car. Ubbo kept a spare key at the Reichshof restaurant, which is practically across the street.'

'Right. I know where the Reichshof is.'

'He lost it. Or rather, that's where he saw it last.' She rummaged through her purse. 'We've got a list of all the guests he remembers. I'll bet if we pay him a visit, he'll be able to remember even more, and then we'd have a complete picture.'

Ann Kathrin noticed that Büscher seemed to take hardly any interest in these details. She leaned forward, and it looked as though she was going to whisper something very important to him. 'If you really want to score points with the team,' she said, 'the best thing to do is to show them that you're a talented investigator.'

Her words almost shocked him. 'I didn't really want to get involved in the operational—'

'They're used to having a boss with an exceptional understanding of criminal cases. Somebody with good instincts. They can all think logically.'

Büscher was glad when the East Frisian *snirtjebraa* arrived. He poked at the red cabbage with apples and the green beans with bacon as Ann Kathrin ate her food with zest.

'I know,' he said. 'You and Ubbo Heide, you are the type of Kripo detectives who can quickly catch a scent. You're like bloodhounds. I've never been that way. I mean, we need people like that, but I'm not one of them.'

'That's probably why you were made our chief,' Ann Kathrin said with a grin. 'How do you like the *snirtjebraa*?' she asked, shoving a forkful of new potatoes and gravy into her mouth. He tried to channel a connoisseur but failed.

He was not at all the new chief she'd imagined. But he was growing on her. There was something about him she liked a lot.

He was honest. And he wasn't conceited about his position. He tried to be a team player, something she found very hard to do.

*

I have to get back into the zone, he thought. This bitch is taking me out of it. She's got some nerve. She has no right to do that.

He was so furious at Svenja Moers. What the hell was she thinking?

In the shower he turned the water to steaming hot and then back to ice cold. He liked it when his skin turned red and started to prickle and burn. It made him feel alert, almost as if he was back in the zone.

Naturally it wasn't the best zone, where he had a firm grip on everything and the whole world felt like a huge theatre under his direction. All the others were either onlookers or had to dance to his tune.

The cold water wasn't cold enough for him. The sultry air was even heating up the water pipes.

Everything was blurring together in the world. He could no longer distinguish men from women; good from evil; hot from cold; organic food from processed industrial shit. It was all the same.

He felt that he had the power to put things back in their proper order. Black would be black again, and white would be white. Hot would be hot and cold cold. Women would be women and men would again be men. Crooks would be crooks, the sick would be sick. And the healthy would all be healthy.

He stepped out of the shower and without towelling off walked through the house. Here everything was in its place.

He hated disorder.

He paused by the bookcase. Books were always a problem. Should he put them in alphabetical order? Sort them according to size? Or by colour?

There were probably lots of other ways to arrange them. Once he'd arranged them by publisher, but that looked stupid.

Then by author. Even that didn't please him. A fat book next to a skinny one, a hardback next to a paperback; no, that didn't work either.

Now he had a paperback section and a separate one for hardbacks. The numbers on the backs of the books drove him crazy. The ISBNs were a hypocritical ordering system, nothing but sheer chaos. A bookcase couldn't be arranged that way. It made no sense.

Twice he'd pulled out all the books and tossed them on the floor in a fit of rage. If there was no way to sort them logically, why not just leave them in a pile on the floor like rubbish?

He'd even thought about consigning them to the flames. Yes, damn it! Anything that couldn't be properly arranged or lined up should be burned.

But he loved some of these books. They reminded him of his childhood. His mother had read him stories from these volumes. Like *Krabat and the Sorcerer's Mill.* But the book didn't fit in anywhere. Why weren't there more books in that format and size?

He had bought a few sets of collected works, simply because the books, arranged in their boxes, looked so beautiful. He had Ernest Hemingway next to Jörg Fauser and Friedrich Dürrenmatt.

Why, he wondered, did everything have to be so complicated? Why was there no EU edict to make all books the same size? Instead they were working on creating a straight banana and a standardised cucumber.

He went over to the monitors. He liked how the drops of water on his skin felt as they slowly evaporated. Only pampered mummy's boys who rushed off to work in their air-conditioned offices dried off with their microfibre towels softened in the dryer.

He'd read about Tibetan monks who sat down outside and meditated in their wet clothes, even in wintertime, allowing their body heat to dry them. That's the kind of man he wanted to be! Self-reliant, independent and strong. Beholden to no one, especially not to this insane society.

Considering how Svenja Moers was huddled up on the bed, she was probably on the verge of surrendering. Maybe she'd act up once or twice more, but then in the end she would accept her fate. She would pose for a suitable photo and do everything else he demanded of her. He was sure of that.

He pondered giving her a chance. Maybe she could clean not only her own cell, but also the anteroom. And then if she behaved herself, other rooms in the house too.

He wanted to crush her pride. Anyone who didn't want to live in filth had to learn to clean up. And as he knew only too well, that began with the small things. Most toilets were just as filthy as the souls of their owners.

Suddenly, Svenja Moers began to be move about as if she had noticed that he was watching her. She threw her hands in the air and roared as if talking to God.

'I'm thirsty, damn it, thirsty! Do you want to see me die of thirst, you maniac? What's this fucking washbasin for if there's no water coming out of the tap?'

He liked her like this. Pretty soon her prayers would turn more desperate. Very soon now. She would stop complaining and start pleading. Stop demanding and start negotiating.

*

Weller was already in the bedroom when Ann Kathrin came home. He was next to the little bedside light with a glass of red wine and his crime novel. But when he heard her he quickly turned off the light and lay down as if he had been asleep for ages.

He had hoped that she would come in and then have to apologise because she seemed to have woken him. But she just didn't come. She was pottering about endlessly in the living room and in the kitchen.

He could hear every single one of her steps. Then the clatter of a keyboard. Was she really checking her emails now?

He lay there waiting for what felt like a half an hour. Now he was upset that he hadn't just kept on reading. He had been in the middle of such an exciting part. He'd just snapped the book shut in the middle of a dialogue.

Hopefully, he thought, she's not so considerate as to lie down in the living room so as not to wake me. She should at least give me the pleasure of that little performance.

Then finally she came and, although she didn't turn on the light, each of her movements was loud enough that he had the chance, after all, to act as if she'd woken him.

He stretched and yawned, 'Oh! You?'

'No,' she giggled, 'how did you get that idea? It's not me, it's Marilyn Monroe.'

She smelled of the restaurant and as she moved closer to give him a kiss, he could smell alcohol on her breath, even though he'd just been drinking red wine himself.

'Well, that work meeting took a while,' he said.

She didn't react. Instead, she simply undressed and got into bed next to Weller. She sighed and said, 'Martin is completely different from what you'd think at first glance.'

'So you're on first-name terms now.'

'Well, as colleagues.'

Weller turned on the light and turned towards her. In that moment, her beauty hit him like toothache, as if he'd bitten into a bar of chocolate that unexpectedly contained a slightly too hard nut.

There'd been something caustic on the tip of his tongue but was glad that he hadn't said it. He just looked at her and knew that he was not the only man that she had that effect on.

'Martin is a very sensitive person. He thinks about so much and—'

'Well, congratulations,' Weller said, 'then he must have quite a head start on all of us.'

Even while the words were floating in the air he already regretted having said them.

Ann Kathrin laughed out loud. 'You're jealous!'

'No I'm not,' he grumbled, 'I'm just tired,' and turned his back on her.

Ann Kathrin ran her fingers through his hair and scratched his scalp.

'I'm tired,' he lied, 'I don't feel like it,' and he buried his face deep in the pillow.

What an idiot I am, he thought.

*

Rupert had brewed himself a pot of the strong local-blend tea. The scent filled the office. The white rose-patterned pot sat on a silver tea warmer, heated by a small flickering candle. Rupert drank his tea in his mother's honour, without sugar and cream, just as it was, black. She had come to East Frisia from the Ruhr region for love. His father had needed sugar and cream in his tea, but his mother had claimed it was fattening, to which his father had always answered by saying, 'Cream in tea isn't fattening, after all, the sugar dissolves.'

Rupert had generally felt closer to his mother than his father.

When Rupert saw the list of guests whom Ubbo and Carola could remember being at the Reichshof restaurant, he knew two things: first, the place was booming, and second, that checking each guest would be a hell of a job and would take up to a couple of days.

'How are we supposed to manage?' he asked Rieke Gersema. 'We need some help. And what are they supposed to tell us anyway? You think anyone will raise their hand and say, sure, I saw who stole Ubbo Heide's car keys that evening, but back then I just didn't say anything because I didn't want to ruin the excellent atmosphere?' He tapped the list. 'This here,' he prophesied, 'is pointless. We could get a couple of schoolkids who want to do an internship in to question the guests or—'

Rieke had brought along homemade apple cake that Rupert liked. He didn't mind helping himself.

He offered Rieke a cup of tea but she declined. She stood next to his desk, oddly distracted. He didn't have the slightest clue what she was doing in his office in the first place. Normally she kept her distance from him and didn't bring him any cake. The tray was enough for the whole police station and she said there was more to come.

Rupert wondered if it was her birthday and if he was the idiot who had forgotten again. Maybe he should give her something.

He hated games like Secret Santa, where you have to draw lots and then get a present for some random person. He had the habit of forgetting to do things like that.

'Super Rupert,' Rieke said, 'guess who asked me out?'

Rupert spoke with his mouth full. 'Probably one of those incredible guys who's been doing bodybuilding, has a six-pack, and rides a Harley, right?'

She poked him. 'Good grief, no! Joachim Faust!'

'But isn't that—?' the priggish pansy, Rupert was about to say, but swallowed his words just in time because he saw from the glimmer in Rieke's eyes how much she admired the man. I must be doing something wrong, Rupert thought. Why do women go wild for such phonies?

Was it really enough to have been on TV a couple of times to be attractive? Didn't anything else count?

'And what does he want from you?' Rupert asked. 'Probably not your apple cake recipe. Although I think you can be proud of that.'

Rupert grabbed a second piece. His desk was covered with crumbs now, but it didn't bother him in the least.

She seemed to be getting her hopes up over being asked out, and he didn't mind helping her get that idea right out of her head.

'I think,' he said, 'he's not that interested in you personally, Rieke. He wants some information on the case. He's already grilled me. On the beach, when we were there with the search and rescue dogs.'

'I know,' she replied. 'Apparently you were very insulting to him.'

'Well, if the truth is an insult, then lies quickly become flattery.'

She took a step back, tilted her head and looked at him from that angle.

'Something wrong?' he asked.

'Well, if the truth is an insult, then lies quickly become flattery; that's not yours, Rupert. It's a quote, right?'

'Yeah,' Rupert said, 'from my mother.'

Rieke Gersema half laughed, almost as if she was surprised that someone like him could once have had a mother.

She took her remaining apple cake and walked to the door.

'Don't get taken in by him,' Rupert warned. 'He's too stupid to tell the difference between a teabag and loose leaf.'

She turned around and stared at Rupert. She really wanted to say, '*You're not my father. I don't need that kind of advice from you.*' Instead she just repeated what he'd said, 'Too stupid to tell the difference between a teabag and loose leaf?'

Rupert nodded, satisfied with himself, and took a sip from his rose cup.

'Sure,' Rieke Gersema said, as if that settled it. 'What kind of woman would get involved with someone like that? It's the minimum of what can be expected: that a chap can tell the difference between a teabag and loose leaf.'

'Exactly,' Rupert said.

Rieke closed the door.

*

Ubbo Heide was glad he'd listened to his Carola. Ten years earlier, while the two of them were still fit and he was famous for his swinging throw in road bowling, she'd pushed him to have her parents' old house in Aurich, full of nooks and crannies, renovated to make it senior-friendly.

Senior-friendly, how that'd sounded to him back them. He had only agreed so he wouldn't cause an argument. Now he was reaping the benefits. He could move around all the rooms on the ground floor. Renovating the bathroom had worked out particularly well.

Peter Grendel, the bricklayer, who was something of friend of the family, had carried out all the work quickly, professionally, and inexpensively, and had enhanced the project with his own ideas.

The first-floor rooms were basically of no interest to him, but Carola had insisted on having a lift installed so that he could reclaim his own space.

He thought that maybe she needed these activities and he went along this scheme; just as he had her 'senior-friendly' planning.

Something completely different was occupying his mind. He thought he knew who the other head belonged to, the one

Carola had unpacked at the breakfast table on Wangerooge. Everything fitted together and at the same time it didn't.

He was surprised at himself that he hadn't confided in Ann Kathrin and Weller. He thought he knew himself so well but something inside was challenging his usual professionalism. He was ashamed of having been so wrong back then and feared becoming a victim of his own imagination again. He didn't want to leave the realm of logic and once again put together a puzzle made up of ideas, possibilities and speculations that produced a distorted, incorrect picture in the end.

He decided to take matters into his own hands. At least the initial investigative steps. First of all, he needed a sense of certainty before raising his suspicions again, and he hoped very much he wouldn't be right. He was retired. He'd never been very interested in the higher-ups' opinions, even when he was still acting in an official capacity. Now he couldn't care less. They'd lost all power over him. They wouldn't be able to shame him into resigning.

But he couldn't stomach the idea of looking bad to Anna Kathrin and Carola. He knew that for them he was a kind of monument to candour and criminalist expertise and he wanted it to stay that way.

Presumably his daughter Insa no longer, or never had, thought of him like that. She was his shining star and it hurt him to hear so little from her and to be such a small part of her life. While he wished her all the luck in the world, oddly enough he wasn't afraid to make a fool of himself in front of her. It was more about Ann Kathrin and Carola.

He tried to set aside these thoughts, so he wouldn't be in his own way with the work that lay ahead of him.

His usual box of tools wasn't at his disposal, with no access either to the computer with the picture files, or to the current list of people with warrants out for them. He still got the *Detective* magazine published by the police union. He had even written for it. But that wasn't any help to him now.

So, he went back to the notebook, squared, without lines, no larger than a postcard, so he could quickly make it disappear into his pocket, and a pencil. He always broke the pencils in half because they were too long for him otherwise. Then he sharpened them and put both halves in his jacket pocket. The tools he had started off with, long ago.

There were still a couple in his desk drawer. I can't drive everywhere so I'll just have to try to take care of some of it by phone, he said to himself. A phone call would be hard enough but he was happy to be able to excuse himself from having to meet Sophie Stern in person, although he knew that it wouldn't make his work easier.

He did it. Just now, while Carola was out shopping.

He retrieved an image of how he remembered her. A feminine woman, whose ideal weight was forty pounds over the official guidelines. A warm type. A passionate elementary school teacher.

She had no children of her own, a cause of regret to both her and her husband. Everyone who ever had anything to do with her knew her mantra: 'I have many children. I need an entire classroom if I want to greet them in the morning.'

He liked this woman and had immediately sensed that she herself had no involvement in the case but he didn't trust her husband for a second.

Yves Stern, son of a French mother and a German father, had something inscrutable, something shifty about him. His jokes were false, his laugh humourless, his grin fake.

Ubbo Heide's mother had called people like that 'fake fifties'. As a child, he'd frequently heard her use this expression and hadn't really understood it. It must have something to do with forged money, and when he saw Yves Stern, he thought he knew what his mother had meant.

Maybe, he thought, that was wrong and I'd just fallen into the trap of suspecting him to please my mother, who had already died at that point. Sometimes things from your childhood catch up with you. They may lead to the right conclusions or can cause people to make devastating mistakes in their otherwise normal, everyday lives.

He'd always been moved by his mother's fundamentally correct Christian values even though much of it had felt too parochial and small-minded.

In the case of Yves Stern, it was as if he had fallen into a pit his mother had dug for him without meaning him any harm. She had hoped to plant a tree there, but for some reason had never got round to it and in the end he had tripped.

He shook himself and massaged his face. He had to get rid of the ghosts of the past now and proceed with clarity.

He picked up the pad of paper and the pencil.

Ubbo Heide found the defensive tone of her voice when she answered even more difficult.

He asked again, 'Am I speaking with Sophie Stern?' To reassure himself that it was really her.

'Yes, and who is this?'

He cleared his throat. *If someone clears their throat during an interrogation, pay attention to that point in their statement. Maybe they only want to gain time, to cobble together an excuse, maybe it's embarrassing, or they have something to hide. Clearing one's throat is infrequently just clearing one's throat.*

'Perhaps you remember me. My name is Ubbo Heide. We were in touch about the disappearance of Steffi Heymann.'

She cut him off, taking a deep breath and hissing, 'I know who you are! And you have the gall to call me now? What are you thinking?'

'Mrs Stern, please calm down. Believe me, I don't want to bother you. But events have occurred that cast a new light on the case.'

'Well, how nice for you,' she grumbled. 'So now you can make trouble and ruin someone else's life. There have already been enough victims!'

'Please, Mrs Stern, I just have a simple question: may I talk to your husband?'

She laughed bitterly. 'You want to talk to my husband? Well, thanks a lot. Do you need someone to blame again? You've already destroyed his life. I don't wish you any harm, but if there's any justice, then you'll be in the pillory one day, and I wonder how many friends you'll still have then!'

As mean as her words were, Ubbo Heide was relieved to read between the lines and realise that Yves Stern was still alive.

'Mrs Stern, I really don't mean you any ill will. I just—'

'Go to hell!' she hissed and hung up.

Ubbo Heide looked at his notepad. What should he write down?

He noted the name Yves Stern and put a question mark after that. As head of the Kripo, he could have found out if Yves Stern was still alive in a couple of minutes. It was fundamentally more complicated as a private individual. But he tried to use his old knowledge.

Like many others who had at some point been suspected of something terrible, Stern had anonymised his address, and his telephone number was ex-directory. Ubbo thought it was a miracle that his wife could still be reached at the old landline number.

After a little thought, he called Rieke Gersema. This young woman had been the spokesperson for the East Frisian Kripo and Ubbo was of the opinion that she was good at her job. He had supported her from the start.

She addressed him as 'boss' and asked pleasantly how she could help him.

'I need some information on Yves Stern. His current residence.'

'Of course,' Rieke answered, 'Straightaway. Completely confidential of course. No one will find out.'

'Rieke, what makes you think that's necessary.'

'Well boss, I could hear it in your voice. It was always like this before every press conference: you told me precisely what all the journalists were allowed to know and what only Holger Bloem should hear.'

Rieke felt honoured that he had called her and not confided in Ann Kathrin and didn't concern herself with why he needed the information. She just gave him what he wanted.

*

Things had gone downhill for Yves Stern since the investigation had been concluded. Although nothing could be proved against him, he had still become a liability for schools. After parents had protested against his continued employment at the elementary school, he had initially been put on leave and ultimately granted early retirement '*due to illness*'. Psychological problems prevented him from entering a school or leading a field trip.

His marriage to Sophie didn't survive the stress and he moved to the Früchteburg neighbourhood of Emden, first to a place on Schützenstrasse, then to Steinweg.

The report specifically mentioned that both of these main streets had cycle paths that were used daily by schoolchildren, while he himself frequently used the 502 bus.

Ubbo asked himself who could have gathered the information about Yves Stern. It surely wasn't him. Or had he simply forgotten it?

He felt very perturbed at the thought that his memory was slowly starting to go.

Or had there been further investigations against Yves Stern later on? If yes, why hadn't his colleagues in Emden kept him informed?

Yves Stern had survived a suicide attempt and Sophie apparently had stood by him for a very long time. The divorce had only been finalised five years ago, although they hadn't lived together for many years.

Yves Stern earned a living as a part-time taxi driver in Emden. He had appeared twice on the authorities' radar. Once when he was involved in an accident and an examination of the taxi company had revealed that he'd been working off the books there for a while. The second time he'd verbally abused and ultimately assaulted an officer in Emden who was carrying out a traffic check.

If the information from Rieke Gersema was correct, and Ubbo Heide didn't doubt it for a second, then Yves Stern was now renting a place on Steinweg in Emden. His landline and mobile phone were both ex-directory.

Ubbo Heide pictured a life completely destroyed, and he blamed himself. No surprise that Sophie Stern was so furious at him.

Ubbo Heide cursed his wheelchair. His hand cramped around the pencil, as if he planned to slam the tip into his thigh to reactivate the nerves through pain.

He thought about his Christian childhood, which was full of stories about the lame walking again, the blind being able to see, and all of it without the assistance of modern medicine, but he was tied to this damned wheelchair.

How was he supposed to investigate all by himself? How would he get up the stairs to Yves Stern in Emden?

No, he couldn't ask colleagues, that would cause them a conflict of loyalties. That's not how it worked. He was already regretting that he'd called Rieke and somehow he had to take care of the rest himself.

And he wouldn't get his daughter and his wife involved either. He needed someone who was sufficiently curious but could simultaneously hold his tongue. Someone he trusted implicitly.

He called up Holger Bloem and said, 'Holger, I have a problem.'

'I can get away in about half an hour and could come straight over.'

'Thanks, Holger. If my wife comes back you don't necessarily have to tell her that we—'

Holger immediately reassured him, 'Got it.'

*

Svenja Moers could no longer tell if the heat from outside was wearing her out or if a fire inside her was causing fits of fever. She turned the tap fully on, but not a drop came out, and the hope that he would have mercy and turn the water back on diminished with every minute.

Her thoughts slowed and her movements became laboured. She felt as if she were sitting on a mass of chewing gum and had to fight the sticky resistance with every movement.

There was a mirror mounted over the basin but she hardly dared to look in it. She barely recognised herself. The pitiful person in the mirror had split lips and deep, black circles under her eyes. This woman had hardly anything in common with the fun-loving Svenja Moers she once had been. Her hair was stringy and greasy. Her eyes glazed over.

She felt like spiders were crawling over her face. She could feel their little, twitching legs but there was nothing there when she wiped her hand over her face. Still the feeling remained: spiders were creeping over her face, her forearms and the backs of her hands!

She was disgusted by herself. Simultaneously, the pressure in her bladder became unbearable; and a logical remedy for both emergencies came to her .

She had once given a presentation at the vocational college on how urine was once used as an elixir. Sick people used to drink their own urine. The Book of Proverbs supposedly gave evidence for this.

She didn't plan on giving him a show so she ripped off the bed sheet, crouched in a corner between the bed and a wall, draped it over herself like a tent and peed into the tooth mug.

Greedily, coughing and gagging, she drank the warm liquid and felt relief.

She would have preferred to stay under the sheet. There at least she would be safe from his gaze and the cameras, but here it was even stuffier and the tiles on the floor were as hot as the stone she had once eaten crispy roasted duck from at Jade Garden, the Chinese restaurant in Emden. Only now, she was the duck.

When she couldn't take it under the sheet anymore and had fled from the tiled floor back onto the bed, the door opened with a whirr.

He stood there smiling like an extremely friendly waiter. In his left hand he carried a tray bearing a glass with ice cubes and beside it a little bottle of Coke Zero. He had even thought to include a slice of lemon.

He lifted the bottle with some ceremony and poured the fizzy drink into the glass. A bubbling and hissing sound filled the room.

She stared at him, tooth mug in hand.

Perhaps she would be able to throw the cup through the bars and hit his head. It wouldn't kill him, but it would show him that she still wasn't finished.

'Do say if you're thirsty,' he laughed. 'Am I correct in assuming that the lady is watching her figure and reducing sugar intake? Diet Coke? Coke Zero? Or is being slim no longer of importance?'

'What do you want from me, Yves?' she asked. 'I thought you had a crush on Agneta Meyerhoff.'

His mouth twisted as if the thought of Agneta Meyerhoff nauseated him, and he returned the empty Coke bottle to the tray, holding it as if he were an experienced waiter and didn't have the slightest problem balancing a loaded tray in a tight space. He raised the full glass, clinked the ice cubes close to his ear, then drained it in a single gulp.

Belching with pleasure he said, 'Well, that was tasty. But you apparently have something better.'

*

Carola Heide and Holger Bloem arrived at almost the same time. Carola had bought a large basket full of fruit and vegetables. Slowly, she needed to get back to normality. There should be fresh food and she wanted to bake her own bread. She had even bought a new cookbook from the display next to the checkout. She wanted to familiarise herself with vegan nutrition. The thought of meat made her nauseous and she would eat vegetarian for the forseeable future. This was from someone who had always loved eating chicken, for whom an evening barbeque in the garden with friends had a magical effect. And someone who preferred a hearty meat sandwich to a layered cream cake.

She knew that the head on her breakfast table had changed her life fundamentally and she attempted to view the shock as an opportunity, a chance for a new, perhaps better life.

She liked Holger Bloem because he was a loyal and reliable man who acted rationally, even in difficult situations, just like her husband.

'What are you two up to?' she asked.

Holger and Ubbo didn't even have to exchange glances to come to an agreement. Carola shouldn't know about it.

Ubbo laughed. 'Well, we're off to make a splash in the Aurich nightlife. Grab a couple of drinks, visit a couple of strip clubs, and who knows, maybe we'll invite a couple of cute girls to spend the weekend in Paris with us.'

Carola let the boys have their joke. She liked that Ubbo was trying to get back to the sunny side of things.

'That's what men always say when they go off to drink lattes and talk about their prostate problems. Right?' She smirked.

Ubbo and Holger winked at each other briefly, then Holger pushed the wheelchair to the door.

Ubbo protested, 'I can drive my Harley myself.'

'Let me push,' Holger said, 'then I can get used to working a walker.'

Carola called after them, 'In case you girls can't cook and would rather eat with Mother, I've bought enough!'

They'd barely made it to the street when Ubbo burst out, 'Thanks for coming so quickly, Holger. My colleagues can't know what we're doing here.'

'Do you know what you're asking of me?' Holger asked. 'I don't enjoy abusing Ann Kathrin's confidence.'

'Me neither,' Ubbo admitted. 'I just don't want to upset the apple cart and put all the machinery in motion too soon. It's possible that all this is just a figment of my imagination. Of course, I'll inform the authorities if my suspicions are correct.'

'And leave the investigative work to them?' Holger demanded.

Ubbo nodded. 'Yes, damn it. But now please take me to Yves Stern on Steinweg.'

The house on Steinweg didn't look good. No one was investing money here to keep the place in shape. It was a building where a group of people were just trying to make as much money as possible without spending anything.

Yves Stern lived on the fourth floor.

'There's no lift,' Holger said. 'I'd like to carry you all the way up, Ubbo, but I've had a slipped disc before.'

'I know.' Ubbo said with a smile, 'I only need to know if he's alive. Just go up, ring the bell, and snap a picture of him, so we can be sure.'

'Won't he think it odd that there's suddenly someone in front of his door taking a picture of him?'

Ubbo showed him his phone. 'Can't you do it on the sly with something like this? The kids all do it at the bus stop. You think they're texting but in reality they're filming the girls getting on and off the bus.'

'Really? I hadn't noticed that.'

'Yep, Holger, you see the world from a different angle if you're in a wheelchair.'

Holger tried to return to the subject at hand. 'So I'm just supposed to determine whether or not he's alive?'

'I need one hundred percent certainty.'

Holger Bloem rang the bell but no one opened the door. Half-broken, the intercom dangled against the wall from three wires. It was quite possible that the bell didn't work at all. However, the main door on the ground floor opened with ease, and he walked up the stairs to the fourth floor.

Holger Bloem immediately felt that something wasn't right. There were three apartments, one of which appeared to be empty. The door was open and there were boxes inside. It looked as if someone had tried to pull off the wallpaper and then had given up in the middle of the job.

There was a blue doormat diagonally in front of the door to Yves Stern's apartment with the tip stuck under the door. White lettering that spelling the greeting *Hello* had turned blackish grey and the '*o*' was no longer legible.

Holger Bloem knocked and the door opened a crack. Holger dialled Ubbo Heide's number and held the phone to his ear. 'So he clearly isn't rich. I don't think he's home but the door's ajar.'

'Go inside and take a couple of pictures,' Ubbo Heide said, and Holger replied, 'The head of the East Frisia Kripo is suggesting I break into an apartment?'

'The former head. And it's trespassing at most. A good lawyer would make self-defence out of it. Can't you smell fire? Don't you feel an urgent need to check that nothing bad has happened?'

'I'm proud to be your friend,' Holger said, 'but believe me, Ubbo, I wouldn't want to be your enemy.'

Holger Bloem felt a surge of adrenaline and his heart was racing as he pushed open the door.

The mat under the door only offered slight resistance and Holger stood in an apartment where it was very clear a struggle had recently taken place.

'Either this place is a real mess or two people were in a massive fight here, or probably both,' he said and took a couple of pictures.'

An armchair was overturned and the table was diagonal to the sofa. It looked as if someone had jumped up from the sofa, pushing aside the table and then fallen over the armchair in an attempt to flee.

He took some more pictures and sent them straight to Ubbo, because he could imagine how impatient he was getting sitting in the wheelchair downstairs.

'There are even spots of blood on the edge of the table,' Holger said. 'I don't think I want to look any further here. This is more of a case for your crime scene techs.'

'OK. Orderly retreat, Holger. Don't touch anything.'

'That instruction's a little bit late.'

Holger Bloem hadn't any idea how fast he could get down the stairs. He tried to read Ubbo Heide's reaction to the news from his expression.

Ubbo looked petrified.

'What do we do now?' Holger asked.

'Now we call Ann Kathrin and confess.'

*

Playgrounds were dangerous for him. Almost as bad as the children's section at the public swimming pool.

He loved the littlest ones. He had no interest as soon as they could speak in complete sentences. But the smaller they were, the more difficult it was to get close to them undetected. The preschoolers were practically always under supervision, very infrequently moving alone, hardly ever far from home and were watched over by parents, guardians, preschool teachers, or – most dangerously – critical grandparents. Grandmas and grandpas could become unpredictable monsters when someone approached their grandchildren. Some retirees even looked like they were armed.

First Basic Rule: forget the little girls who are out and about with grandpa!

Elder siblings were ideal. He had an easy job of it with pubescent teenagers, who were annoyed because they had to watch their spoiled brothers and sisters. He could talk to them about music. He was always downloading the newest hits to his iPhone.

Pimply kids could be bought off with cigarettes. They thought it was cool that he listened to them. He addressed them properly and acted as if he considered them grown up. It was good for them, strengthened their self-confidence. They felt included and were too self-obsessed and inexperienced to realise that the focus wasn't them, but rather their younger siblings.

He'd fallen for that angelic boy in Störtebeker Park in Wilhelmshaven.

Marco's fourteen-year-old sister Lissa had the little rascal on her hands for several hours each day, and that had led to her losing touch with her friends.

By then he'd heard the whole boring story twice. How the great guy from her class that all the girls were crazy about – Patrick was his name – wasn't going out with her anymore. Instead, he was with that bitch from Käthe Kollwitz School.

He'd helped Lissa get a little free time. They had gone to the miniature railway together and had crossed the pond on a raft. By then other regulars assumed he was Marco's father.

He didn't want to backslide. He was attracted to girls, not boys, and convinced himself that this wasn't the beginning of something new. This wasn't dangerous, just something to take his mind off the real game – the one he wasn't going to play anymore.

He often talked to himself, calling himself 'Odysseus' because he felt as if he were tied to the ship's mast while the Sirens' songs drove him crazy. That's how much he pined for them. But he couldn't allow his ship to get too close to the cliffs. Otherwise he would inevitably be smashed into pieces.

That's why he kept his distance from little girls and tried to ease his suffering by being close to the boy. Marco was balm for his burning. His angelic blond hair. The skin soft as peaches. If he were a girl . . . but luckily he wasn't. So harmless . . .

Anyone seeing them would be more likely to suspect he had something planned with the older sister than with the boy.

He had to be careful. He couldn't trust people. Not even himself.

*

Büscher was astonished to see how casually Ubbo was brought back into his old office and that he moved around as if it were still his.

For his part, Büscher stood next to the window, feeling out of place.

Ann Kathrin, Weller and Holger Bloem were completely focused on Ubbo Heide. Even Holger Bloem, who was actually a journalist and had no business being there, if you asked Büscher, seemed to belong there in his own way. Much more than he did himself, Büscher thought.

He was waiting for someone to try to send him away and had already visualised how he would react. Should he leave the room with apologetic gestures or make it into a show and clear up a couple of things?

'Where's the map that always used to hang here?' Ubbo Heide asked, pointing to the white spot on the wall.

Büscher gulped. 'I took it down.' Büscher was glad he hadn't chucked it away but instead had placed it, folded, in the desk drawer from where he now took it and hung it back on the wall. Its corners had holes from the drawing pins. It felt like a defeat, considering Ubbo Heide didn't make any mention of it. Instead, Ann Kathrin asked him, 'So you think that Yves Stern is the second corpse?'

'We should consider it,' said Ubbo Heide. 'Yves Stern and Bernhard Heymann were friends. They'd frequently given each other alibis. Maybe true, maybe not. We couldn't ever prove anything.'

Weller chimed in. 'Yves Stern was your main suspect for a while in the Steffi Heymann case.'

'Yeah. I'd found something in his life that—'

Ann Kathrin looked at Weller. 'How did you know that?'

'Well, I read Ubbo's book about his cold cases; reading is fundamental.'

'At first I'd thought that Yves Stern was covering for Bernhard Heymann, maybe even helped him a little. At any rate, he was on Langeoog when Steffi disappeared. And then there were suspicious things in his story. Another child close to him had also disappeared. He was an elementary school teacher in Hanover. That must be where he met his wife.

'A girl from the first grade had disappeared back then. Nicola Billing. The child was missing for a long time. There were no ransom notes, nothing. Our colleagues spent months stumbling in the dark.'

'And he had something to do with that?' Büscher asked the room brusquely, basically to demonstrate he was still there.

Ubbo Heide waved him away. 'No, no, people, that's not how it was. It's also possible that we wronged him greatly. But it certainly looked suspicious that a second child close to him had disappeared. Nicola Billing's corpse was found in Lake Maschsee six months later. At the time I may have been a little,' Ubbo Heide chose his words very carefully, 'insensitive in the way I led the investigation. At any rate, the parents caught wind of it.'

Ubbo Heide wiped his lips with the back of his hand. He was shaking, if Ann Kathrin wasn't mistaken.

'Of course people thought he was guilty and Stern found himself in a nightmare. He lost his job and—'

'Holy shit,' Weller said, 'and now someone has decapitated him and sent you the head?'

'That's the way it seems,' Ubbo Heide said, looking at his knees.

'Why would anyone do something like that?' Ann Kathrin asked.

'My parents,' Ubbo Heide said, 'raised me in the faith that there's a God and a Devil. By now I'm not so sure if God exists. But the Devil surely does.'

Ann Kathrin wasn't satisfied with Ubbo's statement. 'That doesn't answer my question of why?'

Büscher felt uneasy. Everything seemed to be drifting off into a kind of philosophical conversation. In his experience, this had little to do with the everyday reality of police work. Although he considered it wasted time, he was silent and listened.

'Evil basically doesn't really exist in its pure form. I've only come across it very infrequently, in total sociopaths who want to see other people suffer. Usually true evil is dressed up as something good, logical, consequential. Only very seldom does someone evil really want to be evil. Many do the work of the Devil while believing in goodness.'

'You define evil as a mistake?' Ann Kathrin asked.

Ubbo Heide raised his hands as if he had to form the words in the air. 'No, as faulty reasoning. Even I myself have caused evil. I was, if you will, the Devil's henchman.'

Weller let out a stilted laugh. 'Hah! You of all people! If everyone was like you the world would definitely be better.'

'I'm sure Sophie Stern is of a different opinion. She believes I destroyed her husband, ruined their reputation and their marriage, and she's probably right about that. When I wrapped up my investigation the smear campaign against them continued but I had led the way.'

Holger Bloem had been listening quietly the whole time, practically motionless. Then he asked, 'And now you think someone finished the job?'

Ubbo Heide spoke through pursed lips. 'Two people who are connected with unsolved cases are dead. I led the investigations back then. We shouldn't ignore that.'

*

Rupert was enjoying questioning this witness for two good reasons.

First of all, the young lady was exceptionally attractive. She was exactly his type, although during the entire conversation he was asking himself why he was so fascinated by her, and if he had a type at all.

Was it the big eyes that were reminiscent of a startled deer that already sensed danger just before the hunter fired the decisive shot from his hide? Or her narrow hips? Would she drive me less crazy if she was fifty pounds heavier?

At any rate, he preferred questioning a beautiful young lady to an ugly old man.

Besides, Merle Ailts could remember that evening at the Reichshof restaurant. She raved about the food and described exactly to Rupert how the items were distributed on the plate. She made it so real that he could practically smell it, even though she looked like she lived off salad without dressing, mineral water, air and presumably a whole lot of love.

She probably jogs, Rupert thought, and has a sexy arse. Unfortunately he couldn't see it right now because she was sitting on it.

She wasn't wearing a bra under her tight T-shirt. Rupert hoped this fashion trend would soon go viral, and he had difficulty looking elsewhere because her nipples under the thin fabric were like sweet, ripe cherries that he would have greatly enjoyed trying.

He had summoned her to Reichshof, hoping that the guests would remember the evening better when on location. He ate and drank at Reichshof, putting it on his expense account, and labelling the whole thing 'site visit.'

'So, I was sitting over there, with my grandpa.'

'Why does a beautiful, young woman like yourself go out in the evening with her grandpa?'

She smiled and Rupert just melted. 'My grandpa is eighty-five and lives in a retirement home up north on Schulstrasse. He's no longer able to cope alone and he is well taken care of and enjoys himself . But once a month he takes me out to eat.'

Rupert had a measure of respect for how she dealt with her grandpa.

'And then,' he said, 'you listen to all the old stories, which you probably know by heart.'

She shook her head, making her gloriously messy hair fall across her face. She kept on running her hand through it to tidy it or sweep it off her face. She looked tousled, as if she were sitting on top of the dyke, not in Reichshof.

'No, on the contrary. He doesn't say very much. After all, not much happens to him. But he's interested in me. He wants to know what's going on in my life. You know, when we're sitting here, I talk all night. Sometimes I can hardly find time to eat.'

'You can tell,' Rupert grinned.

She looked at him, irritated, and smiled coyly.

So you were sitting there, your grandpa over there – and where was Ubbo Heide?' Rupert asked.

Merle Ailts pointed to exactly the right spot. Just as it was drawn on the plan.

'So you could see him the whole time?'

'Yeah, sure. I even heard how he talked with his wife. That table over there was fairly loud, a birthday party or something. He and his wife were very quiet, but all at once he exploded. He slammed his car keys on the table. My grandpa and I were shocked into silence, we thought there was a fight. But that's not the way it was. Basically it was a very tense situation. He said something like that from now on he could always have a beer because she'd be driving in the future.

'Did you know the two of them?'

'No, but I liked the look of them. I get along with older people. Sometimes better than with younger ones,' she said and lowered her gaze.

Rupert realised that she carried scars. She'd probably had a couple of terrible experiences with young guys in the past. Rupert liked that because it improved his chances.

He pegged her at middle, maybe late thirties, but he knew that he wasn't good at guessing.

'So you saw the keys lying on the table?'

'Yes. Definitely.'

'You know, for us right now it's all about these keys.' He leaned forward and spoke quietly, 'They are very important for us. Did you see anyone take them?'

She folded her arms across her chest, much to Rupert's disappointment.

She rubbed her upper arms, as if she were trying to warm herself up. 'No. If I'd seen that, I would have intervened. I mean, no one just watches as someone else gets something stolen from them.'

'Right,' Rupert said. 'But maybe you didn't recognise the theft as such. Do you remember anyone walking past, close to the table, or maybe stopping at the table? Possibly to exchange words with Ubbo Heide.'

'Yes. My grandpa.'

'What?'

'They know each other. And because Mr Heide was sitting in a wheelchair, my grandpa went over to him. But I don't know what they talked about. While they were talking,' she was slightly embarrassed, 'I was checking my phone. I was in the middle of a crisis with my boyfriend. He was crazy jealous and kept texting me every couple of minutes.'

'Of course,' Rupert laughed, 'a silly young chap has to be jealous when a beautiful young woman like you goes out to eat with her grandpa.'

'The two of them drank a Klötenköm together.'

'A what?'

'Klötenköm. Egg liqueur. That's what my grandpa calls it. Until recently he made it himself. His mother's recipe.'

'OK, sure,' Rupert said. 'So the two of them had a couple of shots. And were the keys still on the table when your grandfather left?'

'I don't know. But I can tell you something for certain: my grandpa didn't steal the keys. First of all, he doesn't drive anymore, and second, if he wanted to drive a car, he'd just buy one. My grandpa isn't poor. He gave me a VW Golf for my eighteenth birthday and has taxed and insured it for years, even though it's not really necessary because I—'

As nice as this conversation was for Rupert, he sensed that he wouldn't get very much further here. He would have liked to ask her for a date, but Merle Ailts looked at her phone and asked if it would take much longer because she had a – yes, Rupert even thought that she blushed at the word – date.

'Is there actually a difference between a date and a rendezvous?' Rupert asked.

She looked at him with eyes wide.

Rupert explained his question. 'Does date mean that you hop into bed the first time, while with a rendezvous you just drink lattes together and chat about the beauty of the landscape?'

Her lower lip sagged involuntarily. 'Do you want dating tips from me now or what?' she asked.

Rupert passed her his card. 'You can call me any time – in case you think of anything.'

'Now do you mean about dating or if I remember anything related to that evening? You know what, there was something else.' She looked back at her phone, as if she had to check if there was even time to tell the story.

'Someone from that table back there, from that birthday party, stumbled. I mean, I think he was already pretty drunk. He walked past Mr Heide's table with a glass of red wine in his hand, like he wanted to go to the bathroom, or was looking for his seat. Then he stumbled, grabbed the tablecloth, and pretty much pulled everything off the table. Anyway, Mr Heide's food landed on the floor. Waiters arrived immediately, everything was cleaned up, people apologised, and there was a new tablecloth. Things go like clockwork here. And Mr Heide didn't make a scene either. His wife was briefly upset because a shrimp had landed on her top. Anyway, I thought it was more funny than awful.

A shiver ran down Rupert's spine. Was this one of those moments that Ann Kathrin Klassen sometimes talked about? The instant when everything happens – when a story flips, a case is just about to be solved, the accused about to confess?

Now it all came down to asking the one right question. And Rupert did that. 'Were the keys back on the table afterwards?'

Merle Ailts shrugged her shoulders. 'No idea.'

The young woman didn't shake his hand when bidding farewell. Instead, she hugged him briefly and pulled him close. It was an electric moment for him.

That's the way they do it these days, he thought. After all, that's how we used to do it as well. When did we stop doing that? The brief hug, embracing the other before you parted ways? Instead, we just shake each other's hands.

His thoughts made him pause briefly. And in doing so, he did what his wife Beate had suggested. 'Sometimes it's better if you just keep your mouth shut, Rupert.'

Maybe this was one of those moments.

Martina Haver-Franke, the manager at Reichshof, was very helpful and was able to give Rupert a couple of important pieces of information. 'I know exactly which birthday party you mean.'

She couldn't remember the names of the people, but found everything in her notes. 'The table had been reserved by a Mr Kaufmann. The entire bill was paid with a credit card.'

She was able to tell Rupert the amount of the bill, the credit card number, and the holder's name. It had been a party of six and one of them, the birthday boy, Wilhelm Kaufmann from Brake, had paid for a wellness weekend at Reichshof for all six people and even paid for the meal.

'There's nothing better,' Mrs Haver-Franke said, 'than orderly bookkeeping.'

Rupert agreed. He drank another Pilsner while standing at the bar, and then he drove away with the feeling of having taken a step forward.

*

Rieke Gersema stomped into the bathroom, grabbed the silver tissue box, pulled out two tissues and blew into them, before taking the fastest route to bed. On the way, she passed three mirrors. The one in the bathroom, the one in the hall, and the dressing mirror in the bedroom.

She went to great lengths not to look in any of them. She knew exactly what she had now: her therapist called it post-coital depression.

She felt dirty and useless. Maybe that's why she only used each tissue once, and when she'd blown into it or used it to wipe her eyes, she threw it far away, as if there could be deadly germs stuck to it.

She took the box with her under her arm when she got out of bed to get herself something from the refrigerator, and spread the white paper clouds all around herself, like overgrown snowflakes marking her path through the house.

Sometimes ice cream helped. Straight out of the carton, with whipped cream from a can, piled high, making big mountains on the ice cream.

She thought it tasted disgusting, and that's exactly what she needed right now.

She was alone and could scream her thoughts out loud. 'It's never about me! Never!'

Joachim Faust had hit on her the whole evening, but he just wanted her to tell him secrets about Ann Kathrin Klaasen.

He makes a date with me, and the whole evening it's actually just about Ann Kathrin.

'Fuck, fuck, fuck!' she screamed and threw tissues at her unbearable image in the mirror.

That's the way it always was, she thought. Even at home. It was never about me. Not even with my parents. It was always only about keeping my father's violent temper under control so that he wouldn't beat up my mother again. Everything was directed towards preventing him from drinking too much and becoming a brute again. Looking ahead, we planned every evening. The television programme was selected based on what we hoped he would like the best. The apartment was cleaned so that he wouldn't find anything that could turn my mother or me into slobs in his eyes.

But he always found something, and in our attempts to placate him, we basically only humiliated ourselves and in the end still felt like failures because once again we hadn't succeeded. And then when he'd given my mother a black eye or had broken her arm, I was supposed to feel guilty about that, damn it. Yes, I was, because I thought that my mother was taking the beating that was actually for me, and that my parents would have been much happier without me.

And then I go to bed with that famous scumbag, that B-list guy. Or should I say C-or D-list?

Enraged, she bit herself in her left forearm. It felt good to feel the pain. At least that way she knew that she still existed.

What a terrible evening she had had! Right from the start, she had felt that it wasn't about her. Faust was charming, attentive. The wine was at the correct temperature. The way he had set everything up; all of it was spot-on. And yet the whole time she sensed: it's not about me.

And then – she especially hated herself for this – she didn't send him packing. Instead, she did everything so that he would think of her as an independent person.

She gave him what he wanted to know about Ann Kathrin, so they could finally change the subject, and in the end she openly offered herself up to him. She was ashamed of that now.

No, she hadn't gone to be with him because she found him so attractive. No, she didn't want to have a relationship with him. She merely wanted to play a role for once, to be seen.

When he was with her in bed and not with Ann Kathrin, when he felt her skin and she felt his, she sensed for a moment that she was really alive. Just a short moment.

Even as he pushed inside her, and his face contorted, making him look like he was on drugs, she would have preferred to stop and run away, but she didn't manage that. Now she somehow had to bring it to an end and forget it as quickly as possible.

Why do I do it, she thought. Why do I fall for guys like that? He just used my body, to pleasure himself! Did I get anything from it?

Not even then had it been about her!

In bed she could have been any one of the hundred others he'd been with. And she shuddered at the thought that he was now comparing her to them.

She jumped out of bed and stomped across her apartment again, feeling clumsy and moving awkwardly, the box of tissues stuck under her arm. She pulled out the last one, then went into the bathroom. There were another twelve boxes there; she'd bought two six-packs.

Now she looked at that stockpile and began to cry.

'I bought all these because I knew precisely what would happen,' she sobbed. 'I bought them even before I knew Faust. It could have just as well been another guy.'

She took two boxes off the shelf at once, and glanced at her phone on her way back into the bedroom. Was there anyone she could call? Isn't that what you had girlfriends for?

She even toyed with the idea of calling Ann Kathrin and yelling into the phone: 'I was with him as a replacement – because you weren't there!

But she didn't do that. She became very sad as she realised that she didn't even have a girlfriend who she could call.

Maybe, she thought, other people just talk to their mothers in this situation. But she hadn't done that in a long time. Her mother already had enough to deal with: with her difficult husband and her own life. She didn't want to add more fuel to the fire.

She'd always had the feeling that her mother could collapse under the weight at any time. If anything, she was the one who took her mother's problems upon herself. And for her mum she played the role of an uncomplicated, cheerful daughter who put people in a good mood, had a steady job, and who no one had to worry about.

She fell back into bed, yelling, 'Fuck', and chucked the box of tissues against the wall. 'It's all a fucking lie! My whole life is one big lie!'

*

Büscher, who had resolved to watch what he ate while he was up north, was already nibbling away at his second banana. The peel from the first one lay on his desk.

He was part of a generation of police officers who hadn't just learned to set up files, he also read files. Inside the interrogation records he not only discovered the suspect's personality, but also the officer who sent the conversation in the right or wrong direction. He worked his way through the files not only to become better acquainted with the people around him, but also perhaps because he had to feel occupied.

He immediately sensed something strange: Ubbo Heide had ordered that everyone from his team give a personal assessment of their conversation at the end of each interrogation. This wasn't of any interest in court and could even support the prejudice of an officer under some circumstances. But it was very helpful to the ongoing investigation when another person continued a colleague's work.

He hadn't given up this East Frisian habit during the short phase when Chief of Police Diekmann had been in charge there.

For instance, Ann Kathrin Klaasen wrote under the interrogation records:

Although the suspect wasn't inconsistent, the whole time I had the feeling I was being lied to. – Chief Detective Inspector Ann Kathrin Klaasen.

Büscher had never seen file notes like these, and in Bremerhaven they would probably have disciplined him or at least suggested that he was crazy if he'd done this.

Ann Kathrin had added the following sparse sentences under another interrogation: *This all sounds so unbelievable and it simply can't have been that way. The witness contradicted herself again and again. Despite this, I think she's an honest person who is in no way trying to lie to us, but truly believes what she says.* – Chief Detective Inspector Ann Kathrin Klaasen

Martin Büscher kept on flipping through the pages.

This individual is very narcissistic and likes the sound of his own voice. Although his statements agree with those of other witnesses, I assume that he didn't see anything, was possibly not even at the crime scene, but just wants the attention and enjoys the interrogation

like a minor star enjoys being interviewed in the gutter press. – Chief Detective Inspector Ann Kathrin Klaasen.

The banana just didn't make Büscher feel full. He had the feeling that the mush in his mouth was expanding. One banana was fine, but another one on top? He needed a fried herring, pickle, or even better, a big spread of fish with sautéed potatoes. They could leave off the salad for all he cared.

Now he was leafing through Rupert's files and was flabbergasted. He'd recorded the conversation with Merle Ailts very precisely, even meticulously, and then added the following personal note:

Merle Ailts would like nothing better than to be a mountain.

Büscher called Rupert in to find out what was behind this sentence, pregnant with meaning.

Rupert came in carrying a burger. There was mayonnaise and ketchup in the corners of his mouth, and he looked as though he enjoyed nothing more than eating a Big Mac with double cheese. Shamelessly, he continued to eat while he stood in Büscher's office.

Büscher asked, 'What does this mean? In your personal assessment of Merle Ailts you wrote: *Merle Ailts would like nothing better than to be a mountain.* Is that some kind of code I don't understand?'

Rupert returned the Big Mac to its cardboard box and placed it on the desk next to Büscher's banana peel. Büscher caught himself wondering what would happen if Rupert left the office quickly and forgot the Big Mac. Büscher could easily picture himself scarfing it down in two bites.

Rupert wiped his lips with the back of his hand. He spread out his hands and laughed. 'Please, she'd like to be a mountain.

What's not to understand!' He used gestures to emphasise his words. She just wants to stand around, be admired, and mounted from time to time.'

Büscher cleared his throat. 'This kind of thing,' he said, 'doesn't belong in a police file. It isn't serious enough.'

'Really? Ubbo drilled it into us to write our reports like this. If I were you, I wouldn't criticise him.'

'Your former boss surely didn't tell you that you should liken a woman to a mountain.'

'No, that's just my assessment. Trust me, I know plenty of her type.'

Now Büscher was less sure if it had been such a good idea to have been on a first-name basis with everyone from the start. Maybe a little distance would have been better in some cases – with Rupert, for example.

He tried to explain his view of things to Rupert. 'You just can't do this. You might as well write down the lady's dress size, her—'

Rupert looked at Büscher with interest.

'I mean, bra size and things like that, sexual preferences.'

Rupert nodded. 'Sure, I suggested that too, but the feminist faction was against it. Ann Kathrin staged a real revolt, and then all of them joined in.' He counted on his fingers, 'Sylvia Hoppe, Rieke Gersema and most of all Fat Arse.'

'Who?'

Rupert gestured his defeat. 'Marion Wolters from the operations centre. I'm good at guessing bra size. But Merle Ailts wasn't even wearing a bra. I mean, it would be a B, guaranteed, maybe 34 or 36.'

Büscher slammed his fist on the table. He hit the banana peel, which first stuck to his hand and then flew across the desk and landed on Rupert's hamburger box like a yellow octopus. 'Just shut up, Rupert! What is going on here is far too important for—'

Rupert pointed his finger at Büscher and finished the sentence that he'd heard from Ubbo Heide. 'Ubbo said everything is important! Many thousands of little pieces make a big puzzle in the end.'

'New bosses,' he grumbled, 'don't often grow old here. You think I don't know that you went out for dinner with Ann Kathrin? Something like that gets around fairly quickly in East Frisia. Did she set you against me? Are you batting for her team now?'

Rupert slammed the door behind him.

Büscher looked at the banana skin. Then he snatched it up, threw it into the wastepaper bin and grabbed Rupert's leftover Big Mac, biting down.

In his mouth, the fatty meat was still more appealing than that banana mush.

For a brief moment he yearned to be back in Bremerhaven.

*

He had to leave Svenja alone for a while now. He could see the pictures from all the surveillance cameras on his iPhone's display and even move them around so she wouldn't be unobserved for a second.

Despite that, he didn't like leaving her alone. She had brought herself to the edge of death with her rebellious ways. How long could she survive without water?

He had no interest in returning to find a woman who'd died of thirst. But he also didn't want to provide her with unearned relief.

He had to find a logical reason for turning on the water but didn't want to tell her that he needed to disappear for a while. It was better to leave her in the dark so that she wouldn't get any stupid ideas and have her resistance reinforced. Under no circumstances could she notice the pressure he was under. He would have to improvise again, even though he hated it. Why wasn't life predictable like a play?

He had read something similar by Clausewitz. '*All strategies of war are true until the battle begins. Then chaos rules.*'

And only those who were quick and spontaneous could win in the chaos. Improvising didn't mean just quickly winging it, but rather adjusting to the new situation in a calm and concentrated way in order to master it.

He'd practised that over the past couple of days. Again and again.

The door opened with a whirr, and he was standing in front of her.

She looked terrible. She wouldn't last much longer.

'I'm going to ask you three questions now. You will receive water if you answer them honestly.'

She was kneeling upright on the bed. Her eyes lay deep in their sockets. Her fingers were digging into her thighs. 'Turn off the heat,' she said. 'I'm suffocating in here. I need some fresh air! Give me water and turn off the heat.'

He ran his fingers along his shirt collar and laughed. 'It'll be even hotter than this in hell. This is like a kind of training camp, believe me. It's not up to you to make demands.

OK. And now my questions: did your first husband have life insurance?'

She yelled the answer to him, happy she could pass the test: 'Yes!'

She rubbed her thighs and nervously wobbled up and down on the bed.

'How much was it?'

'Fifty thousand.'

'And your second husband? He had life insurance too?'

'Yes.'

'And how much was it?'

'One hundred thousand.'

'So twice as much. That's what I thought.'

'What's the point of these questions? I've answered all of them right. Do I get water now?'

'That was only two questions.'

'No, damn it, that was four! It was actually four!'

The way she looked at him, she knew that he had complete control. He didn't have to keep his word to her. He could simply walk away, laughing, and let her die.

'Did you kill the men to get their money?'

'No!' she yelled. 'No, damn it, I didn't do that!'

'Too bad,' he said. 'You didn't tell the truth so there won't be any water.'

While listening to his own words, he thought: fuck, fuck, how could I be so stupid? Of course she wouldn't just admit to the crimes. Now I have to find another reason for turning on the water or I'll risk her croaking before I get back.

He was already wondering if it would actually be that bad if she died of thirst.

'Is this some kind of witch trial?' She shrieked. 'Do I have any chance? You put the witch in a bag, tie it, and throw it in the water. If she drowns, she's innocent, if not, she's a witch and will be burned?'

Her lower lip split and a drop of blood emerged, making a red film on her teeth.

Somehow I have to find a way to be more generous, he thought.

'Did you cheat on your husbands?'

'Yes!' she yelled. 'Yes, damn it! Both of them!'

'Were you happy that they died?'

She jumped up from the bed and went to the bars. She grabbed them and shook them. 'What are these questions about? Is this Judgement Day? Are you God?'

He slowly stepped back. It was supposed to look deliberate. Not like someone trying to sneak off.

Standing in the doorway, he turned to her and said, 'I'll give you water.'

The steel door had hardly closed when Svenja Moers was at the tap to turn it on. But she hadn't ever turned it off. In her panic she no longer knew which way you had to turn it to make the water flow.

She had no idea how long that lunatic would let the water flow so she needed a container to collect as much as she could. There was a plug for the wash basin. She pushed it in carefully.

The empty pipes made noises in the wall. Then with a gurgle, water squirted into the basin.

She cupped her hands under the tap and drank from them. It was delicious! It was life!

Energy returned with every gulp, and the knowledge that she wouldn't give up. Never!

She had survived her capricious mother, two marriages and a bankruptcy. She would survive this too!

*

They met in Ubbo Heide's apartment, not far from the police station.

Although it was very warm, his wife Carola had draped a rug over his knees, as if to protect him.

They drank tea, the way he liked it. Not with sugar and cream, but black with fresh peppermint leaves. The hot tea was refreshing, despite the sticky air in Aurich.

Ann Kathrin and Weller sat on either side of Ubbo. Each had only one cheek on the cushion, barely making use of the comfortable furniture, both looking as if they wanted to jump up, completely fixated on Ubbo and what they had planned.

Weller felt the slight pain in his back that he sometimes got when something in his life was off kilter and he had relationship problems. Now he tried to ignore it.

'The key to everything lies on Langeoog,' Ubbo Heide said.

'It's about Steffi Heymann. Someone's clearing up here. Is taking revenge or—'

He fell silent.

Weller added, 'Or is eliminating accessories because he's afraid he'll get caught anyway?'

Ubbo nodded. 'Conceivable.'

'Basically, we have to reopen the case and look closely at the individuals involved.' Ann Kathrin pulled out her pencil and notebook. 'Who did you work with back then, Ubbo?'

He smiled because she used the same writing utensils as him.

'I was part of a task force. The best people were mustered especially for this case,' he gestured, apologising for having put himself in the category of 'best people'. 'Do you know what a stir this caused in the press? The deepest of fears are unleashed when children are involved.'

'Were you in charge of the investigations back then?' asked Ann Kathrin.

'No. That was Chief Detective Inspector Wilhelm Kaufmann. But then he was removed from the police force.'

'Wilhelm Kaufmann?' Ann Kathrin asked. 'But he was at that birthday party in Reichshof.'

'Yeah,' Weller chimed in, 'Rupert found out.'

Ubbo Heide laughed. 'What? Rupert found that out? Didn't I tell you guys?'

'No,' Ann Kathrin said, 'I don't think so.'

'But that would have been important,' Weller said in a strange tone, as if he was afraid that Ubbo Heide was losing his memory.

Ubbo laughed uncertainly. 'You don't really think that a former colleague stole my keys so he could decapitate two suspects who we couldn't catch years ago?'

Weller and Ann Kathrin were silent. The two of them sipped their tea to bridge the resulting embarrassment, and Weller also reached for the raisin bread, which Carola had covered with a thick layer of butter. Weller raised his piece and motioned to Carola. 'Delicious. So delicious!'

'Ubbo, was Kaufmann guilty of anything?'

'Well, back then I supported him. We were all really nervous, and there were certainly excessive measures taken. I don't know all the details of his personal file. Back then I was furious when he was sacked. I think he completely left the police service. He opened a hotel on the River Unterweser, or somewhere. At any rate, he moved to Brake. I think he'd inherited his parents' house in Emden. Maybe he sold it and then used the money to start something new. I don't know exactly. We weren't the best of friends, but I respected him. He was a good man. Sometimes the good ones are sacrificed when someone high up fucks up.'

Ann Kathrin took a sip and then put her teacup down. She liked the ringing sound of the porcelain, so she lifted the cup again and replaced it on the saucer. She felt strange, as if the little girl inside her was just discovering the sounds that objects make. She had an almost irresistible urge to break the pencil she was holding in her hand just to hear the wood snap.

'We'll need Wilhelm Kaufmann. Do you think he'll be cooperative, or does he still hold a grudge against our lot?'

'No, I don't think so, he'll help us with this. He was a cop, through and through. We'll have to pull out all the old files and go over everything with him. He may remember some important detail.'

'Tonight,' Ann Kathrin said, 'is the reading in Gelsenkirchen. Do you really want to go, Ubbo?'

'Yes, of course.'

'Why do you do it to yourself?' Weller asked, although it had been his idea for him to go. Now he was worried that Büscher and Ann Kathrin would both go to Gelsenkirchen with Ubbo. He didn't like that idea at all, and if anyone went, he wanted to go too. Under no circumstances did he want to leave Büscher and Ann Kathrin alone for too long. He didn't like the thought of them spending a night together in a hotel.

Weller sensed that Ubbo would go through with it, despite all the difficulties. It was simply too important for him. So he suggested: 'I'll drive you. It's the least I can do.'

Ann Kathrin nodded. 'Sure, you can go together.'

Weller seemed relieved. 'Of course the officers in Gelsenkirchen will support us, Ubbo.'

Ubbo waved that idea away. 'For heaven's sake! I don't want a squad car in front of the door at my reading! How would that look?'

Ann Kathrin tried to put it differently: 'Oh please, you're the chief of police. Everyone will think it's completely normal that colleagues come to pay their respects when you present your book. The whole thing is practically an infomercial for the security services.'

'First of all,' Ubbo Heide said, 'I'm your former chief, and second it certainly isn't an advertisement because I'm only talking about unsolved cases, about mistakes that we made and—'

'Exactly,' Ann Kathrin said. 'That's what I think is so great. Only someone truly commanding can do something like that. We have to admit our mistakes and talk about our difficulties. That makes us human and part of society.'

'We'll probably need a good three hours to get to Gelsenkirchen. When do you need to be there, Ubbo?' Weller asked.

Ubbo Heide looked at his watch. 'The reading starts at eight o'clock in the city library. But I have an interview beforehand. I told the journalist Silke Sobotta from the *Stadtspiegel* that we could talk at seven.'

'Well then,' Weller said, 'we should go soon. The library has booked a room for Ubbo in the Intercity Hotel. We'll need a room too. They have a lift, so no problem at all for Ubbo.'

Ubbo was astonished by such prescient planning from Weller. Clearly the shop was in good hands in his absence. After all, he'd trained his people well.

Carola Heide suddenly appeared by the table and, looking into the teapot, asked if she should top it up and if it would make sense for her to accompany Ubbo.

'Sure,' Weller said, 'yes to both.'

However, Ann Kathrin saw from Ubbo's face that that was exactly what he didn't want. She placed a hand on Carola's forearm and said, 'You haven't had it easy lately, Mrs Heide. Perhaps it would be better for you to relax a little. Your husband is in the best of hands with us.'

Carola Heide looked at Ann Kathrin fondly. 'Yes. But he finds it difficult to dress and undress by himself. Even getting washed in the morning, he needs—'

'No problem,' Weller called. 'We'll take care of that. Right, Ubbo?'

'Don't worry, Carola,' said Ubbo. 'We'll manage.'

'Actually,' Carola added, 'Insa wanted to come with you, but I haven't heard from her in days.'

'Our daughter has her own life, Carola. We shouldn't bother her with our affairs.'

'Yes,' said Carola Heide, 'maybe you're right.'

*

Peter Grendel, the bricklayer, turned his yellow van into the Distelkamp car park. Joachim Faust was already standing there, waiting for him.

Peter Grendel mistook Faust for a tourist out for a stroll, not someone who wanted his services. Faust was approaching so he greeted him pleasantly.

Faust pointed to the ad on Peter's van: *Get Your Bricks on Route 66*. 'Great slogan,' he said. 'There's nothing better than a convincing ad these days.'

Joachim Faust was a weakling compared with Peter Grendel. Faust wore a white linen suit, combined with a formal blue shirt the same colour as his fabric shoes. To Peter Grendel, he looked like a dandy who had intended to go on holiday to the Caribbean, but ended up in East Frisia.

'Can I speak with you, Mr Grendel?'

Peter nodded and leaned on his van, listening.

'Do you know me?' Joachim Faust asked hopefully.

Peter Grendel shrugged his shoulders. 'Should I?'

Faust extended his hand. 'Faust. Joachim Faust. *The* Joachim Faust.'

Peter took his hand, shook it, and imitated Faust. 'Grendel. Peter Grendel. *The* Peter Grendel!'

He must have squeezed a little hard because Faust made a face.

There was something about the man that Peter Grendel didn't like, and it wasn't so much his outfit, it was his smell. He didn't smell like honest work, but of a strong perfume that seemed to Peter Grendel as if it had been used to cover something up. Peter grinned on the inside. Reminded him of Pepé Le Pew. He just couldn't stand the guy.

'You're considered a friend of Ann Kathrin Klaasen. There are a couple of newspaper reports. You've worked for her in the past. Is that right?'

Peter didn't answer. He just looked at the man and waited. What was he getting at?

'Well, whatever. It's probably not always easy to be friends with a famous woman. After all, she lives around the corner from you. House number thirteen, I believe.'

'What do you want from me?' Peter Grendel asked, crossing his arms over his chest. For Faust, he now seemed like an impenetrable obstacle.

'Well, I want to be completely open with you, Mr Grendel. I'm working on a story about Ann Kathrin Klaasen, and right now I'm gathering opinions about her. Stories, anecdotes. It shouldn't harm her if you talk to me.'

'Does Ann Kathrin know that you're talking to me?'

Faust smiled. 'No. But we can keep it to ourselves, Mr Grendel. I'll treat you to a round and then we'll have a talk, man to man.'

'No thanks,' Peter said, removing himself from the side of the van and moving towards the front door.

'Hey, hey, wait a second!' Faust yelled. He was now two steps behind Peter Grendel. 'Are there such dark secrets surrounding Ms. Klassen that you'd rather not talk about them?'

'I said *no*,' Peter answered. 'What part of that didn't you understand?'

Peter Grendel just kept on walking and Faust grabbed him by the T-shirt. Immediately, Faust knew that he had made a mistake; Peter stood still and turned around.

'Have you completely lost your mind? Do you really think I'm going to come up with random stories about Ann Kathrin Klaasen so you can teach her a lesson?'

'Well, I—'

'You know how you can tell if someone is a friend or not?'

Faust watched and waited almost meekly for the answer. He was thoroughly intimidated by Peter Grendel's appearance.

'Well, OK,' Peter said, as if he'd suddenly come around, 'I'll let you in on something: Ann Kathrin and me, we're in the Praise Club.'

'Praise Club? What's that?'

'The club members share their pure and unvarnished opinions – if they're alone. But a member of the club would never say a bad word about another on the outside. On the outside we praise each other to the utmost. That's the East Frisia Praise Club. You shouldn't even try and send in an application. You'd be more likely to win the Nobel Prize than become one of our members.'

Then Peter left him standing there and went inside. He was looking forward to having a barbeque with the neighbours that evening.

*

Weller was furious and failed completely to conceal the fact. Büscher had tried to change their plans at the last minute and had suggested that he would accompany Ann Kathrin and Ubbo Heide to Gelsenkirchen.

Normally bosses in his position were more concerned with questions of personnel and the overall structure of the institution and stayed out of the day-to-day activities. This job was more of a task for a bodyguard, and Weller couldn't imagine that Büscher had any other reason for going than to use it as a chance to hit on Ann Kathrin.

Büscher suddenly thought of something else: Weller should talk to those people who had been on the task force for Steffi Heymann. Weller turned down that idea, reasoning that he was basically still on holiday – but he wanted to be with Ubbo. In reality, Weller was both annoyed and slightly ashamed, feeling small and stupid for needing to keep an eye on his wife rather than watch over Ubbo.

He pictured the scene. Clearly Büscher liked to discuss a case over a glass of wine, and after the reading the two of them would sit at the hotel bar for another drink and wonder whether or not it had been worth it.

Had this always been the plan? Suddenly Weller asked himself why there had actually been two rooms booked. He'd be sleeping in a double with Ann Kathrin. Had Büscher been planning the whole time to go along and take his place? These feelings of resentment and mistrust gnawed at him.

Weller was driving a twenty-year-old Chevy, one of three confiscated American cars that the East Frisian Kripo used for undercover operations to save money. Rupert thought this was fantastic, but all three cars had automatic transmission and Weller didn't like that at all. It was an insult to his left foot. Whenever the car changed gear, his foot instinctively stomped the air.

Ubbo Heide and Martin Büscher sat in the back while Ann Kathrin was in the passenger seat.

Ubbo was preparing for his reading, searching for the right passages in his book.

Büscher warned Ubbo. 'Remember, if you give an interview, think about the fact that you're not the press representative for the East Frisian Police. That's Rieke Gersema. No statements about the current case.'

'You can't ask that of me, Martin. I'm appearing as a writer, not as the head of the Kripo.'

'But you wrote about this case, and of course they'll ask you about it. It'll be jam packed, and the press will rush you. Actually I wanted Rieke to come along, but she called in sick. Maybe the whole thing's too dicey for her.'

Ann Kathrin immediately defended her colleague. 'Oh no, Rieke is very dependable. If she called in sick, then she is actually sick. She wouldn't skive. We've been through lots of different situations with her.'

Büscher lifted his hands in defence. 'All right, all right. I didn't want to say anything bad about your friend. But there are times when it's inappropriate to be ill.'

Weller's mood lifted slightly. Was Büscher filling in for Rieke Gersema because he was concerned that the situation in Gelsenkirchen could get out of hand? Or was he just emphasising that he was filling in for her to distract from the suspicion that he actually only wanted to come along because of Ann Kathrin?

Under normal circumstances, Weller thought, Ann Kathrin and I would be sitting on Langeoog right now, looking at the sea and drinking espresso. Holidays could wait, but this couldn't.

If Büscher had had his way, I wouldn't be sitting here in this car right now, Weller grumbled inside. He would be on his way to a witness hearing, but Rupert had taken that over.

On the autobahn they got caught in a traffic jam caused by a construction site.

'We're cutting it fine,' Büscher said, and Weller barked back at him, 'We can't really put flashing lights on the roof and clear the streets just so Ubbo will make it to his interview on time.'

Ubbo Heide received a phone call. It was the journalist Silke Sobotta from the *Stadtspiegel* newspaper. She sounded sad and regretted that she had to call off the interview. She'd caught a stomach flu and wanted to keep her distance, so she wouldn't infect others.

'That's very good of you,' Ubbo said.

'I'm so very sorry. I really would have enjoyed talking to you. I was fascinated by your book. I like East Frisia and I could come up your way sometime, or if you're in the area again . . . Postponed isn't cancelled, even though I would have liked to report on this evening.'

*

Rupert would rather have interviewed a couple of brazen bees on Langeoog than the sacked Kripo man from the former special task force, of all people.

Twice now he'd half-heartedly tried to get hold of Wilhelm Kaufmann. When no one picked up the third time he rang, Rupert wrote: *Unsuccessful attempt to establish contact.*

Rupert didn't want to go home. His wife Beate was meeting up with her reiki friends, and there was so much 'good energy' in the room that Rupert could hardly stand it.

Rupert had a feeling that one of the reiki women was someone he'd once tried to seduce, and he would prefer not to run into her. That could be unpleasant, as he'd been married to Beate at the time. But it was possible that it wasn't her. He didn't know exactly. He had only seen her once on the balcony with his wife and, my God, there were dozens of women like that in his life. Rupert had trouble telling them apart. The differences blurred even more in his memory.

He would have liked to go to Gelsenkirchen as well. Not so much because he loved overtime or didn't want to miss a reading by Ubbo Heide, but because he believed the whole thing could become quite exciting. It could culminate in the arrest of a double murderer, and he really would like to be there for that. Although the longer he thought about it, he realised the whole thing could become nothing but an expensive business trip.

Because he wasn't making progress with Wilhelm Kaufmann, he decided to talk with Roswitha Wischnewski next. He'd googled her. She ran a massage practice in Oldenburg. Perhaps, Rupert thought, I could get a massage out of the deal. Could that be classed as undercover research?

He phoned her and was immediately intrigued by her voice when she answered.

Yes, he would like an appointment! Definitely better than with that former Chief Inspector Wilhelm Kaufmann.

Roswitha Wischnewski had significantly incriminated Yves Stern with her deposition. She had claimed she had seen him on the ferry from Langeoog to Bensersiel on the day in question, that he had travelled to the mainland and had been carrying a child.

Yves Stern swore solemnly that it hadn't been the little Heymann girl, but a tourist's child. She had asked him to hold the child because she wanted to be photographed leaning against the railing and the child had been fussy.

Unfortunately he couldn't remember the woman's name and subsequent efforts to find out whether she really existed came to nothing.

In the file Stern's statement had been evaluated by Ubbo Heide in a personal, hand written note, to be a lie.

Rupert drove to the massage practice in Oldenburg.

*

Ann Kathrin was lost in her thoughts. Ever since she had been confronted by the body parts, she had frequently thought of her mother, even though she had died peacefully in her bed at the nursing home.

At first, Ann Kathrin had visited her mother's grave almost daily. It was as if she still had something to tell her. Something she hadn't been able to during her lifetime. But whenever she stood by the grave her head was empty and she couldn't find the words.

Suddenly, just as she needed to be in Gelsenkirchen and couldn't turn around, Ann Kathrin knew what she wanted to say. She wanted to ask her mother for forgiveness and, although she didn't know exactly what for, she felt the urgent need to drive to the grave immediately.

Her thoughts was interrupted by Ubbo Heide addressing Weller, whose face he was observing the whole time in the rear-view mirror. 'My God, you look like you've eaten a dead cat. Are you felling all right, Frank?'

Weller cleared his throat. 'Sure, everything's great.'

Ann Kathrin explained her plan one last time. Everyone already knew the details but she did this not for them, rather to bring herself back to the present.

'So, this is what I was thinking: our fellow officers in Gelsenkirchen have pledged their complete support. Everyone who parks in the city library's underground car park will be recorded. Beyond that, there are two or three cameras in the room, meaning we'll have an uninterrupted overview of the guests afterwards.

'Mrs Piechaczek, the bookseller, has promised to send me a list of the addresses of all the customers who have booked tickets. She said on the telephone that there were also a surprising number of people coming from outside the city, people who weren't regular customers of hers. She'd received calls from Essen, Duisburg and Wanne-Eickel, but of course she didn't know if the addresses were correct.

'Ubbo will be sitting on a stage with two entrances. Frank will be on his left and I'll be on the right. I want to have pictures of everyone who goes into or out of the room later on. Together with the video analysis from the underground car park we'll have a fairly good overview.'

'Are you really so sure that he'll come?' Büscher asked, doubt in his voice.

Ubbo answered for Ann Kathrin. 'Yes, she is. And I am too. He tried to tell me something, and now he wants to know if I understood the message.'

'Exactly,' Ann Kathrin said. She exchanged a brief look with Ubbo. The deep level of understanding touched her so much she had to fight the tears for a moment.

She looked out of the window.

Ubbo placed a hand on her shoulder from behind and said, 'I know.'

*

Weller parked the Chevy directly in front of the Intercity Hotel behind the old post office. Next to the entrance stood a tall man who looked like a long-distance runner training for his next marathon. But he was taking a drag on a thin filter cigarette that would have been more at home in a woman's hands than in his athletic fists, strengthened by weightlifting.

Weller helped Ubbo Heide out of the car and saw that the man was walking directly towards them. Ann Kathrin watched him react very cautiously. Weller was still standing behind the wheelchair and immediately positioned himself so that he stood between Ubbo Heide and the approaching man, like a human shield.

The man tried to get past Weller by sidestepping him, but Weller was faster, ready to stop him with a punch or a kick. Wordlessly, the man conceded that he now had to explain himself if he didn't want to end up flat on the pavement with his hands cuffed behind his back.

He showed his open hands. 'Kowalski. I'm here to interview Mr Heide.'

Ubbo called out, 'It's fine, Frank! He's from the *Stadtspiegel*. Mrs Sobotta fell ill.'

Weller looked the man over critically, not speaking, just nodding and allowing access. Kowalski and Ubbo Heide shook hands in greeting.

'If you'd have a little time for me before or after the reading, Mr Heide, my readers would surely be very grateful, and I would too, of course.'

Ubbo Heide answered cordially. 'Why of course. I don't believe it would be possible to get a proper East Frisian-style tea, but I'd be glad to treat you to a cup of coffee.'

Kowalski nodded and proceeded to push the wheelchair. Ubbo didn't want to be pushed so he turned on the motor. Weller had actually been planning to walk alongside the two of them, but Ann Kathrin held him back. She didn't think it was necessary to be too obvious as a bodyguard here.

Ubbo went ahead with the interview while Büscher, Ann Kathrin and Weller discussed the evening's strategy up in the hotel room with their colleagues from Gelsenkirchen.

It wasn't comfortable, but Ann Kathrin had insisted that the meeting take place in the hotel, not in the Gelsenkirchen police station next to city hall, because they didn't want to be far from Ubbo. They all sat together in Büscher's room, safe from unwanted listeners.

The hotel room wasn't exactly suitable for a team meeting. Büscher and Weller sat next to each other on the edge of the bed while Ann Kathrin took the only chair in the room. The two police officers from Gelsenkirchen stood around slightly awkwardly.

One storey below, in the breakfast room, Ubbo Heide felt flattered because Kowalski had read his book, was well informed and actually even interested. Over the previous six months, Ubbo had often encountered journalists who wanted to interview him, but hadn't even read his book, and weren't interested in crime novels, but had to write the article. By contrast, a conversation like this one with Kowalski did him a world of good.

They were sitting at a small table not far from the bar. A lone drinker sat at the bar, staring into his beer. A couple, in the furthest corner of the room so as not to be disturbed, were cuddling and whispering together.

The woman from reception brewed coffee for Ubbo Heide and Kowalski.

'I'm actually a sports journalist,' Kowalski said. 'To tell you the truth, I wanted to play basketball, but there was a back problem standing between me and the Dallas Mavericks.'

Ubbo Heide smiled. 'I used to play road bowling with a passion. Are you familiar with it? It's a northern German, well, an East Frisian game.'

'You throw a ball on the road?'

'Yep,' Ubbo Heide laughed, 'exactly. But you didn't come here to talk sport with me.'

'No, certainly not. I'm fascinated by your book, *My Unsolved Cases*. Mr Heide, I wonder what kind of person you are. At the end of your career, you don't publish a volume of your successes – of which there undoubtedly were many – but rather your failures. You experienced all of these as defeats, am I right?'

'Yes, you could say that. If I was convinced I knew who the culprit was and I wasn't able to prove it, then I did consider this a personal failure. Sometimes it kept me awake at night. In some ways, the book was a kind of release, finally being able to speak freely and openly about these cases.'

'Isn't the whole thing more a failure of the justice system? I mean, you provided all the proof, and then they acquitted the criminal?'

Ubbo Heide shook his head and emphasised his words with an index finger lifted high. 'You're confusing proof and evidence. In each case I had evidence that pointed towards someone being the wrongdoer. Sometimes I was able to string together a chain of circumstantial evidence. But evidence is not proof. It's more than a hunch, it's a possibility, perhaps even a likelihood. But not more.' He tried to explain further. 'If your car was parked on the street, then it could be evidence that you were at the scene of the crime. But it isn't proof. If a lighter is found at the crime scene, that's initially evidence. But it's not proof. The lighter could have been stolen from you, maybe you lost it.'

Kowalski listened closely, but didn't take any notes. Instead, he placed a silver, Olympus-brand Dictaphone on the table. It blinked and he asked, 'Would you allow me to—'

'Of course.'

The couple in the corner giggled. The solitary drinker at the bar emptied his glass and requested 'another Pilsner'.

Now that he had turned on the Dictaphone, Kowalski spoke a high German that was particularly accented, as if the interview wouldn't be printed in the newspaper, but broadcast on the radio instead. 'So Mr Heide, your story is about unsuccessful trials based on circumstantial evidence.'

'Yes, as a matter of principle, it's a good thing that there are high standards in trials based on circumstantial evidence. There has to be a chain of evidence that suggests causality. But in the end, it comes down to how a judge evaluates it. Naturally it's easier if you have five witnesses who say I saw how Karl killed Eva. And then you have the knife with his fingerprints on it, and scratches on his face. And Eva has skin particles from Karl under her fingernails. That's it for Karl, he's not getting out of it. But it's seldom so simple.'

*

Things weren't as harmonious up in Büscher's hotel room as in the breakfast room of the Intercity Hotel. Ann Kathrin was almost breathless with indignation, and Büscher shook his head in disbelief. 'So basically we can call everything off, then?'

'The reading will take place without all that,' Weller interjected. Ann Kathrin could see that he was growing more and more resentful and was about to lose his temper completely.

What Ann Kathrin did then was something she had learned from Ubbo Heide. She summarised the conversation they had had so far, so that the others could have the chance to correct or retract something. She wasn't able to remain seated, falling into her interrogation mode. Three steps, turn, three steps. Instead of glancing at the suspect during the last step, she stared at the two officers from the Gelsenkirchen Police Department every time, making them feel increasingly uncomfortable.

'So, my fellow officers, if I've understood you correctly, this means we will receive neither a video recording from the underground car park, nor will cameras be installed in the event space. Instead we'll only be able to count on two officers protecting Ubbo?'

The detective with the crew cut, who looked young enough to still be at school, rocked from one leg to the other. 'It's not our fault. We didn't get the warrant. On the contrary. The whole thing violates data protection regulations, and we have to take them seriously.'

Weller slapped his palm against his forehead. 'Data protection regulations? We're dealing with a double homicide here and anticipate that the murderer will show up tonight!'

'That's pure speculation on your part, and it's very shaky,' the older officer pointed out. He smelled as if he'd just left the dentist's. His lower lip hung limply, and he was using a paper towel to pat the spittle on his lip. 'According to the judge, we would be making Gelsenkirchen's audience of people with literary interests into potential criminals and suspecting them without cause. The video tape would have consequences. You would examine every individual. We're not in East Frisia here. So we also have to provide administrative assistance. Friends, we neither have the legal right nor the capacity to—'

'To catch a double murderer,' added Weller.

'No, damn it! Now stop putting words in our mouths!' The officer from Gelsenkirchen ranted because he truly felt they were being treated unfairly. He tried to keep things formal, even though Weller kept on using his first name. 'If I had my way, we'd have all options at our fingertips. But we don't.' He fell silent and punched the air, as if he wanted to knock out the judge.

His partner came to his assistance. 'That kind of surveillance isn't straightforward. Later on people might be considered suspects at a murder trial just for having gone to an author's reading. Besides, how is this supposed to work later on? Do you want to film everyone at all of Ubbo Heide's events in the future, and then start a large-scale operation to check their alibis?'

Weller groaned. 'If you can't record in the event space, can we at least get the surveillance footage from the garage? A couple of registration numbers could be really helpful. I hardly think the perpetrator will come on the tram.'

The detective with the crew cut hummed and hawed. 'If I understood the judge correctly, we can't just hand over the film. There's no justification. The tapes will be deleted automatically later. They're just there to solve crimes. If a woman was attacked in the garage or a car was stolen, then we could use the tape.'

Weller jumped up from the bed and grabbed Ann Kathrin by the sleeve. 'Come on. I'm not going to listen to this any longer! We have two dead people, and they're waiting for a crime?' Weller slapped his hand against his forehead, producing a splatting sound.

'We're really sorry. We would have liked to help you. But legally we can't.'

Weller yelled at the officer: 'Blah, blah, blah!'

Büscher motioned to Weller that he should shut up.

*

The couple in the corner were kissing passionately, and the young woman had positioned herself in such a way that Ubbo Heide didn't see how she led her lover's hand under her T-shirt. The solitary drinker at the bar got a much better view.

Kowalski didn't register any of this as he tried to keep the conversation going. 'You were stabbed by a criminal in the line of duty, and you've been wheelchair-bound since then.'

Ubbo Heide interrupted him. 'No, I wasn't on duty. I was walking out of a café, with my wife. I became a victim in my free time, if you will.'

'Did that cause you to quit the service?'

'I didn't quit the service, I was retired.'

'Do you write books because you would still like to be a policeman?'

Ubbo Heide drank his coffee, giving himself a pause to reflect. Then he answered. 'I always regarded my work as a fight of good against evil. It's a nice feeling to be on the good side. Although I haven't been so sure recently.'

'What made you so contemplative?'

'Some people claimed that my work had destroyed their lives.'

Kowalski noticed that Ubbo Heide no longer felt comfortable and changed tack, afraid that otherwise he might end the conversation. 'Of course, our readers are also interested in how you view life differently now. Being in a wheelchair gives a completely new perspective on the world.'

'Right,' said Ubbo Heide. 'But I just ask myself sometimes if I'm really disabled or if I only become disabled when I can't get somewhere – because stairs are in my way, for example.'

Kowalski tested the recorder to see if everything was working. He appeared satisfied and continued. 'Is that the case in your private life as well? I mean, are you a policeman there too? Are you also looking for the truth there? What's it like for your wife to live with someone who's always right . . .'

'I wasn't always right. But I never claimed to be. I was looking for the truth. Besides, I want you to keep my wife and daughter out of this – your questions are becoming too intrusive for me.'

The journalist laughed. 'All right, all right. I like you, Mr Heide. You stand for everything that won't be around for very much longer – and what I really care about.'

Ubbo Heide looked at him quizzically, so Kowalski ticked a list off on his fingers. 'Books. Libraries. Video stores. Mailboxes. Postcards. Private space. All of that will sink into a digital sea.'

Ubbo Heide was thoroughly impressed by these words. He leaned back, starting to like this thoughtful person. Kowalski continued. 'For example, I only read real books, no e-books. I need paper in my hands. I have to be able to smell the glue and the printer's ink.' He laughed. 'I don't vape either, I smoke real cigarettes.'

He placed his pack on the table, as if he wanted to demonstrate he was a real smoker.

'But those are women's cigs,' said Ubbo Heide.

'Sure,' Kowalski grinned. 'My mother smoked that brand, and they were my first too. That's what started my passion. I stole from my mother's pack.'

He put the cigarettes away and glanced over at the bar. 'Can I get a mineral water?'

The woman behind the bar called, 'One or two?'

'Two,' answered Ubbo Heide, who was planning to pay the bill for the coffee and the water. 'And I'll take the bill.'

'Mr Heide, I know you don't have much time. Your event is beginning soon. Of course I'll be there listening. But I still have one more question: what do you think, is there a connection between the murders in East Frisia and your book?'

'What do you mean by that?'

'Well, you talk about cases in your book, after all, and now you've been sent a head in the post. Two people you suspected have been killed.'

Ubbo Heide waved him away, leaned forward, and spoke very quietly. 'Please, for heaven's sake, do me a favour: don't connect my book with the killings! It could be misunderstood as a cheap PR trick, you know. I don't want high sales at the cost of a serious crime. Two people are dead. I don't want to profit from the situation and I could be accused of that.'

The waitress brought two small bottles of mineral water and two glasses with ice cubes. Ubbo Heide was silent as she filled the glasses and only resumed speaking once she had disappeared behind the bar.

'This is a very sensitive topic and it could be that one of these cases will be reinvestigated at some point and solved. I don't want to derive any profit from that either. Do you understand me? My book is my book and the reality is the reality.'

'But you wrote a book about real cases. Don't you have to expect that?'

'I'm asking you! The situation is already bad enough. Once the connection is made by a newspaper, then all of them will pile in.'

'That won't harm the size of your print run.'

'No, but it will harm me. And the seriousness of the case and the associated investigations.'

Ubbo Heide was surprised that Kowalski didn't protest, saying instead: 'I respect your position, Mr Heide. You don't have to worry. I won't make the connection, even though it will naturally suggest itself to readers.'

Kowalski drained his glass in a single gulp.

Just then, Ann Kathrin, Weller and Büscher stepped out of the lift. Ann Kathrin saw that Ubbo Heide was exhausted. It wasn't that overtime face that she'd known from earlier years, when he'd pulled all-nighters. No. This was different. It was a kind of psychological exhaustion.

It's too bad that he still has the event, she thought. *He's basically done for already.*

She would have liked nothing better than to put him to bed.

'Ubbo, would you like to freshen up and lie down for a minute? Maybe you'd like something to eat before the reading?' Turning to Kowalski, she said: 'I think he needs a little break now. Evening events like this in front of an audience are a strain, and should never be underestimated.'

Kowalski was almost effusive in his thanks and, while leaving, from six or seven metres away, gave a thumbs up, promising: 'Don't worry, Mr Heide, I'll stick to our deal.'

Ubbo Heide smiled tiredly at Ann Kathrin. Then he produced a seal made out of marzipan and said, 'Jörg Tapper brought over a whole batch after the shock on Wangerooge. You wouldn't believe how terrible the marzipan is that gets sold to the rest of the world.'

Then he bit off the seal's head.

The two police officers from Gelsenkirchen were standing next to the lift with Büscher and Weller. They looked crestfallen. The one with a schoolboy's face offered his help, saying they were ready to sacrifice their free time to accompany Ubbo Heide to the reading. Büscher thanked them for their offer, but declined.

Weller was breathing heavily, as if he'd been in a brawl, or had at least exerted himself physically. He was pale and tight-lipped. Quickly, he strode towards Ann Kathrin and Ubbo.

'Listen,' Weller said. 'If we don't get any official help, then I'll take the photos. I'll just set up next to the door and snap everyone who comes in. Or we can check everyone's ID after the event.

'No,' Ann Kathrin said, 'we're not going to do that, Frank. That would be provoking a scandal. But your idea isn't that bad. You're going to play Holger Bloem here.'

'Huh? What?'

'Well, if Holger were here, then he'd be taking pictures constantly. And no one thinks it's strange when a press photographer takes pictures.'

Ubbo Heide remembered many similar situations, raised his finger and said, 'Yes, Holger sometimes stood behind me on the stage and took a picture so you saw not only my book but also the whole room and the audience.'

'Great idea,' said Weller, 'but then I'll need a real camera. I can't play the role of a press photographer using my phone.'

'How are we supposed to get a camera now?' asked Büscher, who had only just joined them. 'Should I ask one of the local police officers to get us one?'

Weller raised his hands. 'Don't even start! They'd need a warrant from the judge, and who knows how long that'd take and if they'd get it in the end. Maybe the judge would decide that we should make pen and ink drawings instead.'

Ann Kathrin warned him, 'Frank!'

'But it's true,' he railed.

Then Ann Kathrin pointed out, 'We can't really call Holger Bloem, Ubbo. Your event will be long over by the time he gets here.'

Just then, Ubbo Heide's mobile rang. The bookseller, Sabine Piechaczek, was on the line. She asked if she should pick him up, if everything was in order, and if he needed anything.

This question was very well timed. Ubbo coughed and said. 'Yes, you could do me a huge favour. A journalist from East

Frisia has accompanied me here and he was planning to take a couple of pictures and report on the event. But the thing is,' Ubbo laughed 'he's a little embarrassed by the whole thing. He has left his camera in East Frisia, the whole bag of expensive kit. Might you be able to help us out?'

'I don't have any professional photographic equipment, but I can get a digital camera.'

'That would be a great help. Is there anything I could do in return?'

'Yes,' she laughed, 'You can sign a couple of books for my shop later on.'

'Sure, of course,' Ubbo Heide said. They agreed to meet in the foyer of the city library.

Ubbo Heide ended the conversation and beamed at the three others from his wheelchair. 'Well,' he said, 'we have a camera now.'

'Great,' Weller grinned, 'then I'll play Holger Bloem tonight.'

*

The reception here was good. He was able to watch Svenja Moers in her prison on his iPhone screen. He zoomed in.

She had filled the washbasin to the brim with water. She was stocking up. Wet tiles glistened underneath the basin.

He zoomed in close on her face. She no longer looked so apathetic. Her eyes had a feverish glaze. It was as if she were looking at him directly. Did she know that he was watching her? Did the camera make sounds or detectable movements? He was upset that he hadn't checked that beforehand. He had to know everything exactly, wanted to have the situation completely under control.

Did she want to tell him something? Or was she talking to herself?

He knew the feeling. He sometimes talked to himself too. Hearing his own voice, reassuring himself. It made him feel good.

He looked around at the car, as always ready to disappear unnoticed. He couldn't be careful enough.

Here in the car park he felt unnoticed. There were only a few other vehicles close to his.

He turned on the sound and heard her yell. 'Yves! Yves, damn it! Let's talk! You can't seriously want to keep me prisoner here! What the fuck! Talk to me, damn it! Come here now and talk to me!'

Then she coughed, was quiet, and fought back the tears. But she was still able to hold them back.

That's good, he thought. Very good. I'll soften you up.

He turned on the radio remotely. There was no reason. He just did it to prove that he had control at all times.

She flinched, as if someone invisible had entered the room. She looked for shelter in a corner behind the bed.

As she listened to Radio East Frisia, a couple of words of low German dialect were enough to make Svenja Moers confident again. She stood up.

He tuned to a different station to demonstrate his presence. The cheery voices and jokes of the morning were probably the starkest contrast to the horrifying situation Svenja Moers found herself in. Through this she was truly made aware of the horror of her situation.

She broke down in tears, burying her face in the pillows so he couldn't see.

He stretched out on the driver's seat and closed his eyes. He was completely back in the zone.

*

Rupert enjoyed freedom because Büscher had only given him a couple of definite orders. The whole Heymann case would have to be reopened, and there were many people on the list who would have to be interviewed. Rupert preferred young women to old men, and he chose his appointments accordingly.

Roswitha Wischnewski had a husky voice that sent a chill up Rupert's spine. With that voice she would fit better in a dimly lit bar than a bright massage practice. Rupert called her a 'masseuse' but she made a point of being a massage therapist and chiropractor.

Chiropractor, how nice that sounded! As if she could master the positions that Rupert had never tried out with Beate. Was she one of those Kama Sutra-tantra specialists?

First of all, he flashed his badge to make an impression, stated he was investigating a sensitive matter and that he had a couple of questions. He had come to talk about an old case. She waved dismissively; she'd already spoken to them countless times. Why was the case being reopened now? She couldn't say more today than she had in her deposition back then. But she'd say this: she absolutely wasn't mistaken and was one hundred percent sure she had recognised Yves Stern on the ferry. He'd been holding that baby. She hadn't seen a woman, that had only been reported subsequently.

'Why is it,' Rupert asked, 'that you are so certain that you recognised Mr Stern? Was he your type? I can't really see it. He must have been at least twenty, if not thirty years older than me. Right?'

'Right,' she laughed. 'No, he wasn't my type. He was my teacher in elementary school. That's why I recognised him. I waved to him, but he didn't notice. At least that's what I thought at the time. But maybe it was just awkward for him that I'd caught him with a kid.'

'But if he'd kidnapped little Steffi Heymann from the island, why did he carry her so openly? He wasn't an idiot, right? I would have hidden her in the car.'

Roswischneski whooped. 'Yeah, that would have been even more obvious. In a car? On the ferry from Langeoog to Bensersiel? You haven't been living in East Frisia very long, right? Langeoog is a car-free island!'

'Yes,' Rupert admitted, 'right. Sure. I just wanted to test if you knew that.'

'Well, aren't you the clever one! You thought I hadn't even been on the island? Back then I even showed your colleagues my ticket for the ferry. I happened to have collected everything and put it in an album – yep, I had time for things like that. These days I have the practice.'

'Speaking of which,' Rupert said, 'could I maybe hire your services?'

To his surprise, she said, 'I'm actually fully booked until the end of August, but I've already finished for today. So if you insist.'

Rupert felt the chill go up his spine again.

'Undress and stand over there,' she said.

Her dominating voice suggested an impending adventure for Rupert. He'd actually been looking forward to a relaxing massage, but he could get that from his wife. Now he was intrigued to find out what techniques a chiropractor had mastered.

Sweating, he slipped out of his clothes with astonishing speed.

She sat behind him and gave commands like: 'Lift your left foot. Now place your legs shoulder-width apart and lift your right foot. So, now lift your knee up to your stomach. Yes. Now bend your back forward as far as you can.'

Rupert got his head almost down to his knees, his hands barely reaching the floor. All this time he was standing with his back to her, but he didn't get slapped on the bottom. Instead, she said simply, 'Thanks. And now please stand up again.'

Roswitha Wischnewski worked her way up his spine with a probing touch. Rupert sighed with pleasure.

'You're standing crooked. Your left leg is shorter than your right. That leads to pelvic obliquity, and presumably is causing pain in your sacroiliac joint.'

She placed her hands over the joint and pressed in exactly the place that had so often tortured Rupert. He groaned.

The lovemaking he expected didn't happen. Instead, she bent him so that his spine cracked and he was afraid he'd never walk again. He alternated between wanting to defend himself and simply surrendering to her.

After she had finished, she asked for forty-five euros and warned that the treatment could initially lead to a worsening of his symptoms. He would probably feel tired over the next twenty-four hours, but then he'd feel better.

She suggested walking a lot and starting with back muscle training and spinal exercises. She wanted to show him a few more tricks.

'Forty-five euros,' Rupert thought, paying dutifully. And he hadn't seen her breasts. What's the world coming to? Isn't there wild, uninhibited sex anywhere anymore?

He would have preferred his Beate's reiki rituals. He lay down on the bed, she placed her hands on his head, and he frequently fell asleep without finding out how the session continued.

Rupert's spine was pulsing when got back into his car.

Surely all the tourists with kids who left the island that day have been checked, he thought to himself. That can't be such a big problem. After all, they all registered their arrivals and departures in the hotels and bed and breakfasts and with the local administration. But Yves Stern's story could still be true. Maybe the mother with the child had been a tourist on a day trip who had left Bensersiel for a trip to Langeoog and had taken the last ferry back in the evening. Then she wouldn't be registered anywhere.

Rupert thought about whether he should go home now or stop for a couple of beers at Mittelhaus to avoid Beate and the reiki gang.

An incoming call brought him back to himself. The speakerphone was on, and Rupert learned from his colleagues in Cuxhaven that their investigations had come to nothing. They had checked all the men who had received pedicures in Cuxhaven and the surrounding area during the last week. All of them were still alive.

Rupert didn't know what to do with this finding, but was happy that so many men survived pedicures in Cuxhaven. He sent the information directly to Ann Kathrin's inbox.

*

Odysseus feared that the spirits of the murdered children had returned. Last night he had woken up screaming again and had seen them before him. They had been standing next to his bed and had shaken it.

Steffi Heymann held the lollipop he'd given her, and was sucking on it. Nicola Billing was sipping on the Coke that they'd shared.

Children were so easy to get and so easy to dispose of.

He never, ever wanted to do it again. He fought against it.

How much he envied those hetero men who could get married and then cheat on their wives as they pleased, had the brothel at their disposal, striptease bars and millions of hours of legal porn on the Internet. They had nothing to fear if they wanted to act out their sexual desires.

It wasn't even a problem anymore to be gay. Everything was possible. Everything was accepted. Only his damn sexual orientation would never be recognised. He'd given up hope.

People would always hate him for what he was. He hated himself for it.

He'd even tried therapy until the therapist stopped treatment for moral reasons, recommending a different place and stopping just short of notifying the police.

And the therapist didn't know everything, by any means. He thought they were talking about fantasies, not about lived experiences. Still, he had had no other choice but to kill that pin-headed intellectual. He couldn't afford witnesses.

He had never become part of a scene. He didn't download any pictures from the Internet. He didn't make any recordings of his crimes. He didn't exchange anything. He tried to live an upright, inconspicuous life.

His fantasies had caught up with him about a year ago. He knew that everything was leading to a repetition of the deed.

He didn't want to kill the effeminate boy. He only wanted to be close to him.

But in the last couple of days this had become increasingly difficult, since all hell had broken loose. He hadn't paid attention to the newspaper reports about a severed head on Wangerooge initially. He was preoccupied with completely different things, consumed with his own abyss, tied up in the struggle with himself.

But then he'd heard those names. Heymann. Stern. That reporter, Joachim Faust, was back in the middle of things and reopening the case. Somehow everything was connected with that Ubbo Heide, the detective from back then.

All of this seemed like a nightmare from a former life.

Had someone killed those men to remind him of his crimes? What was this about in the first place? Was the murderer also after him?

He considered this unlikely, but he didn't want to ignore any possibility. He had to be careful. He was on very thin ice.

For him Joachim Faust was a rat who'd sunk his teeth into a juicy piece of roast meat. He wouldn't give up and the Kripo surely wouldn't either.

Would he end up in front of a judge after all?

Everything had been looking so good for him, back then.

The deck would be shuffled again, and he didn't want to draw a bad hand. He had to stop the murderer.

First he had to forget about the baby-faced little boy from Wilhelmshaven. There were more important things. His own disguise.

He'd get that executioner. It was all leading to a fight.

He grinned. That wannabe jihadi surely wasn't used to his way of fighting.

I'll get you before you know what I look like, he thought.

He was good at that. He didn't need anyone to give him good advice or support him. He was used to living like a lone wolf. Completely autonomous in his own universe.

He'd come to Gelsenkirchen to get a feel for Ubbo Heide. Somehow it all led back to him. If the murderer showed up here he'd recognise him. He had a sense for things like that. There were victims and there were perpetrators. There was the picture, and those who could see. Just like there were men and women and creatures like him. And he could tell all of them apart.

But he didn't have to talk to them for that. He had his antennae and could sense it. He knew exactly who was like he was. Sometimes it was sufficient to spend a short amount of time in the same room with someone to know, or even just to walk past them.

Others heard a sound and could exactly place it within the scale. That's a C, that is a high A.

He recognised offenders, victims and his own kind.

*

The bookseller Sabine Piechaczek patiently explained the camera to Frank Weller. She didn't let it show how irritated she was that a professional photographer seemed so clueless, uninterested in diaphragms, lighting and the sharpness of the lens, shifting directly to automatic instead.

She found him likeable and forgave him for his ignorance, blaming nervousness, and said, 'If you're writing a piece about Ubbo Heide, then don't forget to mention that he has an unbelievable number of fans in the Ruhr region. I have ordered more than 120 copies of his book for the reading. People really value its honesty. Finally someone doesn't just claim to know the truth, but rather is searching for the truth. It's just good to know.'

Weller agreed. 'Yeah, sure,' and fiddled with the camera, accidentally taking a picture.

Ubbo Heide was already on stage in his wheelchair and doing a microphone test. It still sounded slightly muffled. Then suddenly there was an echo. But the sound technician was a master of his trade and after a brief period Ubbo Heide's voice came out of the speakers just like the original, only much louder.

Many guests were already waiting in the foyer. There was no reserved seating, so many of the audience had come very early to get good seats. The library director, Friedhelm Overkämping, was still holding the door shut. He wanted to have a word with Ubbo Heide . He noticed that Ann Kathrin Klaasen and Frank Weller were taking turns staying close to him, almost acting like bodyguards, and getting between Ubbo Heide and anyone who wanted to greet him.

Even he had difficulties reaching Ubbo Heide. He could feel Ann Kathrin Klaasen's gaze checking him out; she would have preferred to pat him down. Then she let him through but stood so close to him that he briefly started when reaching into his pocket for a tissue because his movement seemed to frighten her and she reacted to it by taking a swift step towards him. When she saw the tissue, she stopped and smiled.

Then the audience streamed into the room and a man immediately tried to get onto the stage. Frank Weller accidentally knocked his legs out from under him, looking as if he had lurched forward very awkwardly and stumbled over the other man. Now the two of them were on the floor together and Friedhelm Overkämping saw that Weller was patting the other person down.

'Hey, Willy,' cried Ubbo Heide, 'you here?'

Wilhelm Kaufmann scrambled up, gave Weller a furious look and walked over to Ubbo Heide. He shook his hand. 'I read that you were reading here and I wanted to come. Old boy!' He almost kneeled in front of Ubbo Heide's wheelchair and the two men hugged.

Ubbo Heide knew only too well that Wilhelm hadn't just come to listen to his reading. That was what he officially said out loud to everyone. Then he murmured into Ubbo's ear, 'Hey, is it actually true that they sent you Bernhard Heymann's head?'

Ubbo nodded. 'Yeah. And Yves Stern's.'

'My God, it all comes back so vividly. I absolutely have to talk to you.'

'Yeah. After the reading. I'm staying at the Intercity Hotel,' said Ubbo Heide. 'I'm glad that you're here, Willy. Really!'

Now Weller was walking around Ubbo Heide on stage, acting as if he were taking pictures of him. In reality he was trying to take snapshots of the audience and capture as many faces as possible.

He also saw the two detectives from Gelsenkirchen who had been so unhelpful in Büscher's hotel room. They had obviously decided to come anyway. They stood by the door next to Büscher, looking as if they'd had an accident and were afraid that everyone would smell what had just happened to them.

Even the journalist Kowalski was present. The man was a head taller than most of the other guests. He worked his way through to Ubbo Heide and presented him with a tin of sweets as a thank you for a truly great interview.

'I know how much you enjoy your sweets. I hope you like mints from Bochum, not just marzipan.'

Ubbo Heide regarded the pretty tin. He opened it and found white peppermint lozenges. He tried one right away and winked at Kowalski. 'Fantastic, your mints.'

Ann Kathrin saw that Weller was uncomfortable. He wasn't very good in the role of Holger Bloem, completely missing the calm composure with which the professional searched for the best perspectives for his shots. His movements seemed frantic and his cheeks were flushed. He felt that he was not being taken seriously as a photographer, as if everyone else had caught on long ago that he was a cop taking pictures for a possible manhunt. People kept on turning away at the decisive moment or leaning over and disappearing from the field of vision and he felt unable to get important people in the shot.

Weller felt like he was under fire during the event. He was unbelievably furious that things had not gone according to plan. He would have preferred to lock down the room and record the particulars of all those present. He was irritated that it couldn't be that easy.

'Why,' he hissed in Ann Kathrin's direction, 'does something terrible always have to happen before we can take action?'

'Something terrible has already happened, Frank,' she answered. 'Two people are dead. But it's possible that none of the people present here had anything to do with it.'

Weller thought he recognised the man who had been sitting at the bar in the Intercity Hotel. He tried to zoom in closer, but the man — if it was him at all — had taken a seat directly behind Kowalski, and he was at least half covered by the tall man.

Friedhelm Overkämping welcomed the guests and told them they should know how happy he was to have brought Ubbo Heide, a man who was currently very much at the centre of public interest, to Gelsenkirchen.

Sabine Piechaczek stopped selling books so as not to disturb the event. They had already sold three stacks of books and were uncertain if they would have enough. She waved to an intern, asking them to go back to the shop and get the books from the window display.

Carefully, Ubbo Heide began to read. His voice was a little shaky at first, but then it became firm and, within a few sentences, Ubbo had the audience under his spell.

'Sometimes as a young detective I could picture the crime vividly. I could see it just like a movie in my head, but I couldn't prove it. All too often, the judge would call my mental cinema speculation. The chain of evidence wasn't convincing enough. Expert witnesses tore it to pieces, lawyers pulverised eyewitness statements. Sometimes I left a court building as a defeated man while the culprit – I'd probably have to say defendant to be legally correct – triumphed. I always felt guilty then and I would wake up from nightmares drenched in sweat because the criminal had struck again, in my nightmares.

'I counted the crime as my own, felt guilty because I hadn't been meticulous enough in the investigations and hadn't been convincing enough.'

Ubbo Heide was repeatedly interrupted by applause. After about an hour Ubbo closed his book and drained a glass of water in a single gulp. He asked the audience to refrain from asking questions. He said he was completely exhausted and needed to leave soon. Everyone understood, but even so, a long line of people who wanted to have their book signed formed.

Weller seized this fantastic opportunity and was literally fluttering around Ubbo Heide with his camera, taking snapshots of his signing and always getting two or three of the people standing in line into the picture.

The Gelsenkirchen officer with a crew cut, whose name Weller didn't know, gave Weller a clear sign that he should photograph a certain person. However, Weller had already taken a couple of pictures of him and didn't want to be distracted.

A small, plump woman patted Ubbo Heide's hand. She looked as though she would have liked to smother him with kisses and beamed at him. 'Don't give up, Mr Heide. We need men like you. Please write in my book: *For Erika*. It would be a great honour for me.'

Ubbo Heide did as he was asked and even added two hearts.

*

Odysseus had found himself in the middle of the room, listening to the reading, and stretching out his antennae. But it had been different this time and he hadn't been able to tell the hunters from the prey. It was as if he'd lost his knack for it.

He'd come to find the killer, but now he had the sneaking feeling that the murderer had found him.

Hadn't the first two corpses been enough of a message to flush him out, so he'd finally show his face again?

Who the hell are you, he thought. Who are you? And what do you want from me?

There were police officers in the room. He'd recognised them immediately. The blundering press photographer on stage was certainly from the Kripo. The woman who was always close to Ubbo Heide was surely someone from his talent pool. He couldn't say if the bookseller was real or also a cop. Unquestionably, the two guys right next to the entrance were police.

Not long ago, so many law enforcement officers in one space would have made him nervous. Now he almost felt safe in their presence, and that made him worry. Had he become the hunted in the meantime?

He'd always sworn that he would never turn himself in, that he'd kill himself before his cover was blown and he was captured. People like him couldn't expect forgiveness. Neither from the courts nor in prison later.

Ever since the murder of Nicola Billing he'd been carrying a capsule that he'd purchased in Thailand at great expense. Supposedly it contained a poison stronger than arsenic. One quick bite was enough and he'd slip away from any court on earth.

A couple of times, during crises, he'd considered using the capsule, and today was one of those days. He felt it'd be better than being decapitated.

He saw Willy Kaufmann. That was that cop! When he looked in Kaufmann's direction the air seemed to vibrate, and the intense feeling of old returned.

He took a deep breath and had the feeling he wasn't sitting in Gelsenkirchen in the library, but at Flinthörn on Langeoog, barefoot in the sand, enjoying the sea air.

*

Sabine Piechaczek helped Weller remove the SD card from the camera after all the paying guests had left the room. She admitted she herself had borrowed the camera, but of course Weller was allowed to keep the card.

He wanted to pay for it, but she waved him away. She claimed it had been her pleasure and she'd rather have the article he was going to write about Ubbo Heide, so she could present it in her window display along with the new book from Ubbo Heide that so many readers were waiting for.

Weller promised that and felt bad for pulling the wool over her eyes. Then he went over to the officers from Gelsenkirchen and asked, 'Who was that guy I was absolutely supposed to photograph?'

'A dangerous man. He's spent some time in prison for aggravated assault and attempted murder.'

'Well? Does he have anything to do with our case?' asked Weller.

The Gelsenkirchen detective shrugged his shoulders. 'Who knows? But he was the only one in the audience that I knew.'

Again Weller tried to persuade the officers to hand over the footage from the cameras in the underground car park, but he was banging his head against a brick wall.

Ubbo Heide, Ann Kathrin Klaasen and Martin Büscher stood in the glow of a street light in front of the library and were on the look out for someplace that was still open.

'Back there,' said Ann Kathrin, 'there used to be a restaurant and a bar. Tigges. I wonder if it's still in business. My father often went there for a beer.'

Weller went into the car park to get the Chevy. He was dancing, even cheerfully, like a child who had a prank planned. Later on he wouldn't remember making the decision but Ann Kathrin guessed that at this moment he was clear about what he needed to do.

Weller took off his shirt and wrapped it around his head like a turban, buttoning it in such a way that his mouth and nose were covered. Only his eyes were still exposed. A sleeve dangled next to his left ear.

Most of the other parking spots were already free. Weller looked around for a suitable weapon and found it immediately. There was a wheel brace leaning against a column.

Raising the cold, silver part up high, he slammed it against the passenger-side window. The window cracked but held up astonishingly well and the wheel brace ricocheted off in Weller's direction. He ducked, narrowly missing being hit on the head and the wheel brace clattered onto the floor.

Weller picked it up and hit the window a second time. This time, it shattered and the alarm went off.

Weller was pleased with himself. Tugging his shirt back into place, he walked back up to where the two Gelsenkirchen officers were still standing with Ann Kathrin, Büscher and Ubbo Heide, waiting to say goodbye. The one with the swollen cheek spat a mixture of blood and mucus onto the asphalt.

'Hey,' Weller said, 'someone must have tried to break into our car during the reading. Luckily there are surveillance cameras. Let's get him!'

The Gelsenkirchen policemen looked at each other. The one with the droopy lip, who smelled of the dentist's, thought he'd worked out what Weller had done. But in the end he didn't care.

'Would it be possible,' Weller asked, 'to look at the footage with you right away, or will you send us the tape and we'll do the work for you?'

'That's not our responsibility,' said the man with the crew cut.

Ann Kathrin was insistent. 'This could have been an attempted assassination. Who knows if the culprit has put something in the car or wanted to try—'

The one with the fat lower lip raised both hands. 'Yeah, OK, damn it, fine! For all I care!'

*

There was good coffee at the Gelsenkirchen police station, and Weller wrote down every single license number as they watched the footage on the monitor together. Much of the audience had come by car and not all of them were from Gelsenkirchen, just as Sabine Piechaczek had said.

The cameras were synchronised with the motion detectors and only recorded when a car drove in or out.

When the man strangely disguised with a shirt over his head appeared on the screen Büscher hoped that he was dreaming. He was certain that it was Weller.

Büscher felt as if he were coming down with something. His heart was racing, his throat was dry and he felt hot and cold in waves. He looked over to Ann Kathrin and Ubbo Heide.

People said of Ubbo Heide that he approached life with cheery serenity. Büscher didn't think that was the case at all. First Ubbo talked all evening long about existential questions, about law and justice, castigating miscarriages of justice, and then he grinned to himself when he saw how his protégé Frank Weller had smashed a car to insight a manhunt.

The officer with the fat lip blasted Weller. 'You can't be serious! You set that all up just so you could—'

'Wait a second,' Weller said. 'Am I being accused of something here? I didn't do that myself. Guys! Why would I? Am I crazy? Am I considered a brute? Have I ever damaged a car in all my life? That guy may have a similar build, and he's also wearing a shirt like mine, but that shirt is mass-produced, there are thousands like it. But – as you can see – I don't have my shirt on my head, I have it on my whole upper body. No, no, no, you can't pin that on me!'

Büscher was breathing so heavily that it sounded like a deep, painful sighing.

'Now I have to defend Weller as well,' said Ann Kathrin. 'The car once belonged to a well-known pimp and drug dealer from northern Germany. We confiscated it. There were four kilos of heroin under the back seat. It's a distinctive vehicle. It's possible that some former victim recognised the car and wanted to take revenge on the owner. After all, nobody can tell that we have converted this criminal's car into a police car in the meantime.'

'Well,' Weller said. 'That's what you get if our funding constantly gets cut and we have to improvise.'

The fellow officer, who smelled like a dentist 's office, groaned in Büscher's direction. 'This has truly been a shitty day. And your goddamn squad has topped it off. My dentist only wanted to drill or nail an implant into my jaw and something went wrong so now I'm up to my neck in painkillers. I should really be in bed. And then these clowns from East Frisia come over and do something like this!'

Before Ubbo Heide left the building with his people, the one with the crew cut asked him to sign his book and whispered in his ear, 'I revere you, Mr Heide. We all wish we had a boss like you.'

*

They had a nightcap at the bar in the Intercity Hotel. They all needed one after such an evening. They leaned back against the bar and looked at Ubbo Heide, who was sitting in his wheelchair facing them and drinking a Pilsner.

They were the only guests and now Büscher vented, 'You were all in that together! How could you pull a stunt like that?' He patted the sweat from his neck.

'You smashed up a police car to set off the alarm!'

'No,' said Weller, 'not to set off the alarm, just to get at the number plates.'

'Do tell,' said Ann Kathrin with a smile, 'that was really you, Frank? I wouldn't have thought it of you.'

He grinned. 'Yes, dear, sometimes I can be a damn bad boy.'

Ubbo Heide held his hand in front of his mouth to stop himself laughing.

'What is this all about?' Büscher ranted. 'Legal, illegal, who cares? People! We're the Kripo!'

'Precisely,' Ubbo Heide said. 'We're here to solve the case.'

Büscher made a helpless gesture. 'Yes, damn it, what does that mean?'

'If you want to make an omelette, you have to break a couple of eggs,' Ann Kathrin said, and Weller interjected: 'By the way, I'm really hungry now. Can't we get anything to eat around here?'

Weller remembered that Rupert once claimed one of the best currywurst stands in the world was located in Gelsenkirchen, and Rupert really knew his way around things like that. But Weller couldn't remember where. He seriously considered calling Rupert and asking him for the address.

Then Wilhelm Kaufmann hesitantly entered the hotel. He walked over to the group at the bar and asked, 'Can I join you?'

'Sure, Willy,' Ubbo called with delight.

*

Svenja Moers had lost all sense of time. She could no longer trust her internal clock. How long had it been since she'd last seen Yves Stern?

Had he been away for a couple of hours or a couple of days?

She had actually begun to miss him. Ridiculous though it seemed, the prison was more tolerable with him than without him.

She hoped that nothing had happened to him. Maybe he had gone shopping. Possibly taken the autobahn. He was probably excited and in an emotionally difficult situation. Perhaps he hadn't been paying attention to traffic and had an accident.

What would happen to her, damn it? She'd simply starve to death.

She, who had lost her faith in God long ago, began to pray that Yves Stern was OK.

Perhaps, she thought, he's travelling and getting a prisoner for the other cell. She caught herself wishing him all the best.

'Please, dear God,' she begged, 'let nothing happen to Yves.'

Without him she had no chance of getting free from this prison.

Once she had realised that, she began to make a plan. She had to win over Yves Stern. She'd be lost without him.

She drank a sip of water from the basin. It was hard for her to look into the mirror. She looked terrible.

She slapped her cheeks.

I have to clean myself up. I have to try to make something of myself. I have to capture him. I can't look like a pile of compost.

She licked her index finger and wiped her smeared mascara.

She looked at the empty cell next to hers. She truly did not want to be alone anymore. And at the same time she was ashamed because she was wishing her fate on someone else.

She just needed someone she could hold tight.

*

Büscher kneaded his face. He was dog tired. 'Let's meet down here for breakfast at seven thirty. I want us to get an early start. We have a whole lot of work ahead of us in East Frisia.'

Weller looked at his watch. 'It's fucking late. I think we should give Ubbo a little more sleep.'

Büscher made a face. 'Fine. Eight thirty.'

'But we,' Weller said sheepishly, 'still have to repair the window before that. Otherwise there'll be a draught all the way back.'

'You'll think of something,' Büscher claimed. 'It's not my problem.'

He stood up from the bar with difficulty, almost as if it weren't easy to let go of the stool, and shuffled sleepily towards the lift. He looked as if he might fall asleep on the way there.

Ann Kathrin watched him go before looking indecisively at Weller and Ubbo Heide. Ubbo was engrossed in a conversation with Wilhelm Kaufmann and appeared to be uninterested in going to bed.

Ann Kathrin considered whether there was any reason why she should not leave him with Kaufmann down here at the hotel bar. Basically no, she thought. To her mind, Ubbo wasn't in the least danger, and alone, he would be sure to get more out of Wilhelm Kaufmann than if she and Weller stayed.

Ubbo winked at her as she said goodnight. She had the feeling that the reading had been good for him. The audience's adulation had made him euphoric.

Weller would have liked to have another beer, but Ann Kathrin motioned that he should come with her, leaving Ubbo and Kaufmann alone at the bar.

'Will you be OK on your own?' Weller asked.

Wilhelm Kaufmann gave the answer. 'I'm not driving back tonight. I'm staying here too so don't worry, I'll get your boss back to his room.' He added with a grin, 'And I'll tuck him in tight.'

Ubbo Heide gave Weller a sign that it'd be safe to pull back.

They had hardly disappeared into the lift when Wilhelm Kaufmann pushed Ubbo and his wheelchair to a table off to the side, away from the bar, ordered two more beers and said conspiratorially, 'Finally we're alone and can talk, man to man.'

'It's good that you came.'

'I thought I had to see you now, after what happened, Ubbo. We were both thinking the same thing back then. Heymann and Stern were up to their necks in it.'

'Yep,' Ubbo said, 'and now one of them is cleaning up.'

Then he produced the tin he'd been given from his wheelchair bag and put it on the table.

'Mints from Bochum. Want one?'

Wilhelm Kaufmann nodded and took one. They chewed while they were waiting for their next round of beers.

'I thought,' Kaufmann said, almost a little disappointed, 'you would talk more about the case. You did a proper poet's reading instead. My goodness!'

'I left out the case deliberately. I didn't want people to accuse me of profiteering.'

Kaufman threw his head back, tossed a peppermint bonbon high in the air and caught it with his lips. He cracked it loudly with his teeth, looked at Ubbo Heide and asked, 'Are you relieved because someone has got those two scumbags now? We failed back then. Although, if I think about it, we were actually pretty good. It was the fucking judge who shut us down.'

Ubbo Heide patted his wheelchair. 'Anyway, it wasn't me. And I can't say that it sparks joy when people are decapitated.

Although I would have wished that on those two if anyone. The thought of someone abusing children is somehow so unbearable; all those years, I was living in fear that they'd do it again. Coordinated somehow. Maybe they were just the tip of an iceberg of child abusers. I prefer the thought that Heymann only kidnapped his own child — and then maybe something went wrong.'

Wilhelm Kaufmann got upset. 'Don't get started with that *"He had an accident and the child died"* theory. I never believed that bullshit! Yves Stern is the key. Heymann was maybe even his victim. Or he sacrificed his daughter to Stern to get out of some kind of shit. What do you think – did Yves Stern blackmail Heymann?'

Ubbo Heide waved dismissively. 'What do I know?'

The waiter brought the two beers and the men each drank a big gulp. Ubbo's throat was dry from talking and reading aloud. He groaned with pleasure and placed the beer glass loudly on the cardboard coaster.

Using the back of his hand, he wiped the foam from his mouth, and then he shot his question like a poison dart, 'Did you take my car keys last time we met, at the birthday party in Reichshof?'

Wilhelm Kaufmann raised his arms as if he wanted to surrender. Then he laughed. 'Sure. I stole your car keys and then placed a head in your car boot. Believe me, I've frequently played with the thought of taking those guys out. I thought if the criminal justice system can't handle them, then maybe we have to do it. But I never did.'

'You lost your job back then because you were too rough with him.'

Kaufmann didn't look as if he was exactly proud of this, but then he said with a shrug. 'I smacked Heymann in the face. He didn't make a big deal out of it. But Yves Stern's lawyer was a crafty devil. He threatened to make me into a torturer in open court, just because I—'

'Did you punch him too?'

'No. I threatened him, saying if he didn't tell the truth I'd take him for a little ride and—'

'Then you choked him.'

'No, I just roughed him up a bit.'

Ubbo snapped at him. 'We're not in court, it's just the two of us.'

'Yeah, damn it, you're right. I completely lost it.'

'If I remember correctly,' Ubbo Heide said, 'at the time you went to see his wife and told her that he had confessed to the murder of Steffi Heymann.'

'Yes, damn it, I rolled the dice. I thought it would make her tell the truth. I wanted to break through that wall of silence, and then they made a huge deal out of it afterwards. Well, it cost me my badge.'

Ubbo Heide spoke quietly. 'And now you've taken revenge on both of them?'

'You really believe that?' asked Kaufmann, staring at him. Ubbo Heide couldn't hold his gaze for very long. He looked first at the sweets and then the tin and closed it. He placed it in his lap. 'I believe,' he said, 'I'm tired. I have to get to bed.'

'I'll help you.' Kaufmann stood up and pushed Ubbo towards the lift. His voice was hoarse. 'It changed all of us, Ubbo. You wrote a book to deal with all that shit; and I always go to Langeoog. At least two weeks every year. Always to the same place. I convince myself I'm on holiday there but in reality I'm not making any progress.'

Ubbo stopped the wheelchair so that Wilhelm Kaufmann had to stop too. As if he'd had enough of the heavy topic, Ubbo said, 'Everyone needs his own island. My island is Wangerooge. I'm there whenever I can be, sitting in the window and looking at the sea.'

'And you also try to do more than just get rid of the old demons there, right?'

'Yeah,' said Ubbo Heide, 'perhaps.'

Wilhelm Kaufmann pressed the button and the lift door opened immediately.

Ubbo Heide saw his own face in the mirror. He was shocked. The man he saw there seemed old, fragile and tired.

*

When she was in the corner next to the basin the angle was such that she could peer into the hallway as soon as the steel door opened. That's exactly where she was headed now because she heard sounds. There was the clatter of metal on metal. Then wheels rattling over the uneven floor.

She even toyed with the thought of seducing him. Yes, she was able to play the role of slut, the cock-hungry maid. That's how she had wrapped each of her two husbands and the other temporary guys around her little finger.

It was a role that she played. Nothing more. Copied it from television, down to the last ridiculous detail. Licking her upper lip with her tongue, a coy look, it was so easy to drive men crazy.

Perhaps, she thought, she'd be able to lure him into her cell. And then fight him to the death.

She pictured him kneeling on the ground, howling in pain because she had kicked him between the legs. Then she would punch his Adam's apple.

In her mind's eye, she could already see him lying in front of her on the floor. Then she had to be able to land a couple of kicks. She had to be tough. She only had this one chance, if any, she said to herself. She was ready to earn her freedom.

The steel door opened with a whirr. The lights blinked on after flickering briefly, and illuminated the entrance like a stage.

She stuck out her chest and positioned herself as lasciviously as possible.

I look terrible, she thought. If only I could have a shower at least, shampoo, a hair drier. A bit of makeup!

But what was this? She held up a hand because she was blinded by the light. He pushed something into the space. No, it wasn't him. A woman entered.

She was stooped and had straggly hair tied in a bun. Her skin was wrinkly and she had thin lips. Her shoulders were bent.

Svenja Moerst immediately took up a different position. She felt as if she had hit the jackpot: his mother!

He was still living with his mother, and she had found her way down here. She'll free me. She won't let her son get away with this mess. Dear Lord, thank you!

The old woman stood there with her walker and looked at Svenja Moers as if she were viewing an expressionist painting.

She looked interested and astonished but did not speak. It was as if Svenja wasn't a person, but a piece of art, an object.

First humming to herself, she began to sing quietly:

'There was an old woman

Who lived in a shoe.'

A chill ran up Svenja Moers' spine. Was the old lady crazy?

'My name is Svenja Moers. I'm being held in captivity. Do you have a key? Can you help me?'

The old woman nodded and continued:

'She had so many children

She didn't know what to do.'

Then she rocked back and forth in rhythm, just humming, and tried to turn the walker while dancing.

Svenja went to the bars and reached out for the old woman. 'Please help me! Is there a telephone here? Do you have a key?'

The old woman moved backwards slightly with her walker, as if she were afraid that Svenja Moers would attack her, although there wasn't the slightest chance of that.

The old woman tapped out a dance on the floor with her thick, orthopaedic shoes.

'She gave them some broth

And a big slice of bread'

She giggled and pointed at Svenja Moers with her long, thin fingers.

She seemed so friendly.

'She whipped all their bums

And sent them to bed!'

'At the end of the fairy tale,' yelled Svenja Moers, 'it was the goddamn witch that was dead, not Hansel and Gretel!'

The old woman retreated with a cackling laugh that reminded Svenja Moers of a seagull's cries.

'No! Don't! Stay here! I didn't mean to insult you! Please don't go! I'm in a dire emergency! This is not all right! Call for help! Bring me a telephone! Nothing will happen to your son, I won't testify against him, but help me get out!'

The steel door closed behind the woman and Svenja Moers heard the clatter of the walker.

Then she began to cry bitterly.

A psychopath who lived with his crazy mother had converted his house into a prison and put her in it like a plaything.

One thought depressed her but simultaneously gave her hope.

Presumably she wasn't the first. Someone who was so crazy must have drawn attention to themselves. Perhaps there was a chance that the police would get wind of it.

Surely the second cell wouldn't be empty forever. Maybe he would get caught attempting to kidnap someone else.

I have to survive, she thought. Time is on my side.

But then she tried to think back to every time she had met Yves Stern. Cooking together at the vocational college. The jokes. His deft way of handling a knife while cutting onions.

No, that man was in no way conspicuous. On the contrary. He seemed to be a normal pleasant man who you would be happy to accept a lift home from. More a gentleman than a pervert. More of a rational intellectual than a psychopath. Possibly a vegetarian, probably voted for the Greens. Yes, that's how she thought of him. On the outside he was a nice guy who looked after his elderly mother. He certainly didn't have a wife and children.

*

When Ann Kathrin was pulled out of her dreams by her phone's alarm clock the next morning, she needed a moment to realise the sad reality. Here she was lying alone in a hotel bed. She wasn't sitting in her beach chair on her balcony and her cat Willy wasn't winding his way around her legs, purring. Muted light cast bright spots on the wall, moving up and down like something alive.

Unusually for him, Weller hadn't left a message, but was simply absent without notice. She assumed he was helping Ubbo to get dressed.

When she entered the breakfast room she saw a freshly shaved Ubbo Heide biting into a cheese sandwich. He looked clean and was bursting with energy. In comparison, Martin Büscher's movements were puppet-like. He cracked his soft-boiled egg with extreme precision, his lips pressed together as if he were afraid that something dramatic could go wrong.

Ann Kathrin took this behaviour as a sign of stress which he was struggling to control. He was plagued by a fear of failure and looked as if he'd barely slept.

Ann Kathrin sat down next to the two of them and had a cup of coffee. She wasn't hungry. She looked around for Weller. Could he have already eaten breakfast? There weren't any dirty dishes lying around.

Weller came into the breakfast room at about nine, obviously in a good mood. He was light-footed, and seemed energised, as if a burden had been taken from his shoulders.

Everyone assumed that Weller had organised a replacement vehicle and that the Chevy would have to be repaired in Gelsenkirchen, but it was parked outside the door in the sunlight.

'Are you expecting us to travel in that?' Büscher asked angrily.

Weller nodded. 'Sure.'

'Won't it be a bit draughty?' Büscher asked.

Weller shrugged his shoulders. 'Why? I can close the window.'

'It's already been fixed?'

'Yes of course,' laughed Weller.

'How did you get it done that fast?' Büscher asked.

'Sometimes I can do miracles,' Weller grinned, winking at Ann Kathrin, and she nodded. 'That's right. Sometimes he can.'

*

Carola Heide waited impatiently for her husband. It was going to be a beautiful, sunny day and she would have liked to take a stroll with him in the park. She thought that they were both in urgent need of fresh air.

She ran to the door as soon as the bell rang, but they couldn't be back from Gelsenkirchen so soon.

The postman handed her a telephone bill and a postcard. It was from Insa, who in her small, spidery handwriting claimed she had fallen in love and was in Venice with her new boyfriend.

There was also a letter for Ubbo. What looked like an obituary announcement, framed in black, with no return address. Because Carola was in charge of social contacts, wrote birthday greetings and answered all the invitations, she opened the letter without a second thought.

The letter smelled of roses.

She used a breakfast knife to open the envelope. They were at the age when their best friends were dying off. She shivered despite the morning warmth.

But there was no obituary inside the envelope.

At first rose petals fell out, like the ones she had dried between the pages of books as a child. Then a photograph. There was a woman behind bars. She looked like she was afraid for her life.

Carola Heide dropped the letter on the table. She needed a glass of water.

She decided not to call Ubbo at once to tell him what had happened. Stress wasn't good for his heart and she also feared the call would mean they'd drive back too fast. She wanted to see him first.

Carola drank two large glasses of tap water and then she went back to look at the picture again. No, she didn't think it was a stupid prank. This was another message to her husband, just like the decapitated head they had received on Wangerooge. And once again the message lay on the breakfast table.

She overcame her repugnance and, without picking it up, looked very carefully at the woman in the picture. She had learned that it was important not to disturb any trace evidence.

No, to her relief, she didn't know this woman.

She left everything on the table, clearing away neither the butter nor the honey, nor the jam. She pictured the crime scene technicians walking through her apartment and she didn't like the thought at all.

She started cleaning up. But it was as clean and as tidy here as her childhood doll's house, which she had moved around and cared for on a daily basis, had been.

'Ubbo, please,' she quietly said to the window, 'hurry. Don't leave me alone with this horror for very long.'

She felt so deeply connected with her husband that she actually believed he could feel it.

Whether by a strange coincidence or as a direct result of her thoughts, just at that moment Ubbo said to Frank Weller, 'Hit the gas, boy. I want to go home. I've had enough.'

They drove non-stop for two hours until Ann Kathrin asked Weller to head for a service area. She had tried to control herself for a long time, but it wasn't working anymore and her bladder was almost bursting. They had left the Ruhr region long ago and there weren't so many facilities up north. Weller took the exit for a truck stop. There was a little toilet building, but it was broken and shuttered.

Ann Kathrin walked a couple of metres into the first trees she saw, and then crouched in the bushes.

'We'll take Ubbo home first, and then go directly to a briefing,' Büscher said in a commanding voice.

Ubbo Heide shook his head, and Büscher was worried that he was planning to participate in the meeting, maybe even lead it. But he said, 'There's a café just around the corner from my place. Please take me there first. After something like this I prefer to get my bearings again rather than take too much of this business home with me.'

*

Svenja Moers was looking for some way of measuring time. Not knowing if she had been imprisoned for days, weeks or months was having a disastrous effect on her. She needed something to orient herself in time other than his sporadic visits. She decided to at least catch a glimpse of his watch. He wore a watch, if she remembered correctly.

He stood in front of her seemingly satisfied. He was surrounded by an irresistible scent, as if he'd just come from a snack bar. There was a smell of freshly roasted chicken.

He held up a bag, waving it so that it rustled, as if the half-chicken inside was crispy but still alive.

'Yum. I brought something to eat. Looks like you have enough to drink. Have you been a good girl? Do you have anything to tell me?'

Yes, he wore a watch. But she couldn't read the face. And now she hardly cared about the time; after all, she didn't know what day it was. Only that chicken was important. Oh, how she wanted it! Meat. Protein. Energy.

She played her card immediately. 'I had a conversation with your mother.'

He was astonished. 'Would you look at that! With my mother?'

'Yes. She was with me. We got on really well.'

She tried to read from his face how he felt about this. She hoped he would care. Did he, like most boys she knew, want to present himself positively towards his mother? Not to look foolish in front of her, not be despised or judged by her? Regardless of how crazy the old lady was, she could be Svenja's trump card. Her lifesaver.

'I told her that you're a good son, Yves, and that we are just playing a game. Prison guard and prisoner. I don't think your mother has much understanding of S & M crap. Open up now, and let me out. We can work this out. We'll keep it all to ourselves. I told her that I've always liked you and only signed up for the cooking class so I could see you.'

He didn't react. He just stood there motionless and held up the bag with the roast chicken. Her mouth filled with saliva and Svenja Moers swallowed.

'Your mother would surely be happy if we cooked for her together. What do you think of that? Let's be a proper little family. I think it would be good for the old lady.'

He didn't use the hatch in the bars but just dropped the bag. It burst and grease ran out.

'What kind of goddamn slut are you?' he said as he turned around and disappeared behind the steel door.

Svenja Moers knelt next to the bars and reached her arm though them, stretching out her fingers for the chicken bag.

*

Marion Wolters tidied her hair and redid her smudged lipstick in the ladies. She practised the Rupi song, which had recently been rehearsed with the East Frisia police choir. It started with the line:

'Super-duper, Rupert,
Rupert goes at it like Superman,
He's his own biggest fan.
Super-duper, Rupert'

There were several verses, and several female colleagues had contributed ideas of their own. Marion Wolters lilted,

'A specialist at livin' large
If you ask him, he's in charge.'

Then someone in a cubicle behind her flushed.

Marion was startled and imagined Rupert was in the ladies and had listened to her. Hadn't the gents been closed recently because of problems with the pipes?

But then she was relieved to hear Sylvia Hoppe's voice. She carried on:

'What'd they do without that cat
They'd have no one to laugh at.'

Both women laughed. They didn't yet know when and how they would present the song, if they ever did, but that didn't matter. First and foremost it came down to enjoying singing and creatively processing the everyday stress and frustration that working with macho men entailed, as the police psychologist Elke Sommer put it.

*

The meeting in the Aurich police station had only just begun. Scherer, the prosecutor, was taking part to get a sense of where things were, which is why Weller didn't dare let him in on the heroics. The way Scherer had sat down on his chair suggested there was a storm brewing.

Rupert had something stuck between his front teeth that was driving him crazy. It felt like dental floss or sauerkraut. He kept bumping against it with his tongue.

Weller carefully read aloud the number plates that Marion Wolters had already started checking.

Prosecutor Scherer cleared his throat. 'Um, so have I got this right? Everyone who attended some random author's reading in Gelsenkirchen should be identified?'

'No,' Weller said, 'this was Ubbo Heide's reading.'

Scherer looked like he was about to vomit.

Weller continued, 'We'll check their alibis and—'

'Oh no,' Scherer said and erupted, 'you won't do that.'

Büscher was looking for a way to move away from this dicey topic. He leafed through a file.

Ann Kathrin smiled at Weller. She thought he was putting up a good fight against the prosecutor, who she felt more frequently slowed things down than moved them forward.

Scherer spoke spitefully in Weller's direction, finger raised. 'We're short on everything. We have neither the personnel nor a rational, tenable reason. This bears no relation to an efficient investigation, Mr Weller. Would I be right in saying it's more like looking for a needle in a haystack?'

Rupert said nothing and hoped that the lightning bolts wouldn't hit him. Also, he was afraid that whatever was stuck between his front teeth would dangle out of his mouth while he was talking. He continued to play with it with his tongue.

Then Büscher did something that Ubbo Heide had never done. He tapped his water glass with his pen. The sound immediately gave him everyone's attention. Ubbo Heide would have relied on his voice.

'We should,' Büscher said, 'direct our attention towards Wilhelm Kaufmann. After all, he didn't get kicked out because of some trivial charge.'

'Yeah, sure, we know. He really wiped the floor with Yves Stern back then,' said Ann Kathrin.

Büscher leaned forward. 'But that's not the only reason he was sacked.'

'What?' asked Ann Kathrin, and Büscher was all too happy to avoid the row between Weller and Scherer escalating. He made an effort to have a good relationship with his colleagues, but it was also really important that he had a constructive relationship with the prosecutor.

'There were rumours that he manipulated files and made extenuating evidence disappear.'

Rieke Gersema groaned and clutched her forehead.

'Rumours?' Ann Kathrin pressed. 'No one gets suspended because of rumours.'

Büscher pocketed his pen and took a sip from his glass of water. He wanted some thinking time without offering too much of a target.

'There were very specific accusations. He was never legally convicted, but—'

Ann Kathrin formulated a question. 'Did he attack Yves Stern to get him to talk or not?'

Weller whistled. 'That's the ticket, Ann! I think Kaufmann's our man.'

Scherer bristled. 'It's not Christmas, Mr Weller, and you're already writing your wish list.'

Ann Kathrin went straight in to bat for Weller. She couldn't stand those cockfights. Counting with her fingers she said, 'This is not just a wish list! First of all, Wilhelm Kaufmann knew exactly where Ubbo Heide was at the time in question. Second, he was familiar with Heide's fondness for Wangerooge. Third, there's a direct connection between him, Ubbo and the two dead men. Fourth, Wilhelm Kaufmann was in Reichshof when the keys to Ubbo's car disappeared.'

Weller was pleased by Ann Kathrin's contribution. 'And he was at the reading in Gelsenkirchen.'

Büscher nodded, but Scherer exploded. 'Gelsenkirchen, Gelsenkirchen! What the hell? You're barking up the wrong tree! Ubbo Heide had a reading there. So what? No one cares!'

At that very moment the seal in Ann Kathrin's phone started barking. Scherer thought the ringtone was as stupid as Weller's 'Pirates Ahoy!' Annoyed, he looked up at the ceiling. Then he held up his phone and showed that it was on silent.

'Hadn't we,' he scolded, 'agreed to mute our phones during the meeting?'

Rupert emphatically agreed with Scherer and looked under the table to check that his phone was also on silent. At the same time, he tried to remove the damn sinew from between his front teeth. Now he didn't care if the others were looking or not. Ann Kathrin provoked everyone's displeasure with her telephone conversation.

She made a sweeping gesture across the table, indicating that everyone should be quiet. Then she said, 'Yes, Ubbo?'

'Is everyone there?' he asked.

'Yes. Frank, Martin, Rieke, Prosecutor Scherer and Rupert.'

'Put me on speakerphone,' Ubbo demanded.

She did so, and even though everyone was already leaning over the table, she held up the device.

'I received a letter, with dried rose petals and a picture inside. It shows a woman behind bars. I think that it's a clue, just like the two heads. He has imprisoned a woman.'

'You know her?' Ann Kathrin asked.

'Yes. Her name is Svenja Moers. I investigated her once. She was suspected of having killed her second husband.'

'I remember,' Ann Kathrin said, more loudly than necessary.

'Damn,' Weller said. He spoke upwards, as if Ubbo Heide were floating just below the ceiling. 'And you also wrote about it in your book.'

'Yes,' Ubbo admitted, abashed, 'in the course of the investigation, I even considered it very likely that she was responsible for her first husband's death as well. But I couldn't prove it.'

'I'm surrounded,' Scherer commented, 'by amateurs!' Then he pointed to Ann Kathrin's hand, which was holding the phone hovering over the table like a threat, and asked sharply in Büscher's direction, 'Is he leading the meeting via iPhone now?'

Büscher just shrugged his shoulders. He looked resigned, on the point of throwing in the towel.

'I need the crime scene technicians here immediately. I don't suppose the guy is so stupid as to leave any usable finger prints behind, but—'

Rupert couldn't get rid of the sinew. It kept slipping between his fingertips.

'The letter was posted over in Gelsenkirchen,' Ubbo Heide noted. 'Yesterday.'

'Oh really!' Weller called out, slightly too enthusiastically, as if the news was a triumph for him. 'He was at the reading in Gelsenkirchen. I knew it!'

Prosecutor Scherer made a fist with his right hand and gritted his teeth with fury.

Rupert spat something onto the table.

Ann Kathrin immediately gave clear orders. 'I want to know everything about this Svenja Moers: friends, acquaintances, enemies.'

'Yes,' Rupert said, running his tongue over his teeth once again, 'let's find her, before Ubbo has her head on the breakfast table.'

'I'll send a picture to your phone. I hope it works,' Ubbo said. 'My wife can do it better. Wait a second.'

Ann Kathrin lowered her hand and placed her mobile on the table, so that the illuminated display could be seen. The phone was still connected. They could hear him talking with Carola.

'I don't think that he wants to decapitate Svenja Moers,' said Ann Kathrin. 'If he did, he wouldn't have sent Ubbo a picture.'

'What's happening?' Rieke asked.

The photo appeared on the display. All of them leaned over the table. Their heads almost touched.

'He's only bluffing,' Weller suggested.

Rupert's stomach growled as he said, 'He'll make her starve.'

'What the hell is going on here?' Scherer yelled.

*

Agneta Meyerhoff had prepared shashlik with beef and pork, the pieces of fillet separated by onions and peppers. The skewers lay in the red sauce, simmering away and filling the room with appetising scents. She had invited Yves Stern over for a meal. Her husband was still away on business, and they had only been communicating via text message for the past ten days. To make matters worse, he had applied for a job managing a construction site in Dubai.

Oh sure, that would bring in a lot of money. But she wanted to live right now. She yearned for laughter, tenderness and compliments, and had come to the conclusion that she needed a steady lover rather than frustrating one-night stands. These short sexual adventures hadn't really been good for her. In the end, she was usually glad just to get it over with and to get rid of the guy quickly.

Now she was looking for something steady on the side. She still wasn't thinking of getting divorced, but she needed a man to tide her over during lonely times.

Yves Stern had flirted hard with her at the evening cooking class. She liked men who were bigger than her, and he had a fine sense of humour, calling the world crazy and signalling that although the situation was hopeless, it shouldn't be taken too seriously.

His look told her: we're surrounded by idiots. Let's run away, Agneta!

She wore the lingerie her husband had given her for Christmas, but still hadn't seen on her. She thought it was particularly risqué that Yves should enjoy it before her husband.

She'd slipped Yves a note with her phone number and invited him over for a meal. Once, during the cooking class, he had snidely said that he'd prefer spicy shashlik to the miso soup with wakame seaweed, tofu, enokitake and green onions. He also wasn't really convinced by the instructor's claims about the bioactive substances isoflavone and saponin, which supposedly alleviated menopausal symptoms and could also prevent breast cancer.

Today she wanted to pamper him with shashlik, the new lingerie, and if he liked that sort of thing, she was even prepared to perform a belly dance. She'd learned how to do that at an evening class last year. He'd always stared over her way during the 'Killer Tummy Training' class when she did her sit-ups. She was exactly his type, she knew it. It's just he wasn't a world champion when it came to flirting. Not really shy, but reserved in a pleasant way. Not at all a suburban Casanova.

She was annoyed that he'd neither accepted nor declined. He just left the invitation hanging in the air, as if it hadn't been verbalised, or as if he hadn't understood.

At the same time, she liked playing with the possibilities. Of course Yves Stern would come. She was certain. There was just one question remaining: would she have her way with him before the meal or afterwards?

*

Ann Kathrin Klaasen had delegated all the tasks. Svenja Moers' friends and work colleagues were taken on by Rupert, Sylvia Hoppe and Schrader. Weller checked all the phones and telecommunications.

Klaasen took on the house in Emden herself. Alone. She wanted to get an impression of the person before the crime scene technicians changed the scents with their sprays and tinctures, making the atmosphere in the apartment unreadable. Yes, for Ann Kathrin it was if an apartment had a soul, and too many people and too much equipment chased away that soul like the northwest wind chased away the banks of fog off Norderney.

The place turned out to be a house in Emden's canal district with an overgrown front garden. There were brimstone butterflies, large tortoiseshells and painted ladies in the rose bushes and summer lilacs. Everything was so full of life. Insects were buzzing. Ann Kathrin concluded that a woman lived here who cared little what the neighbourhood thought. Between the well-tended front gardens, her little house looked like the gate to a jungle. Ann Kathrin thought it was thoroughly pleasant.

A white butterfly fluttered into her hair and got caught. She stood still, breathing gently until it flew away.

Yellow, salmon-pink and red roses big as fists surrounded the house like a magical protective wall planted by hippies. An overgrown arch of roses led to the front door. Ann Kathrin felt dizzy when she went through the gate. She stood still for a second and took a deep breath. She already felt better by the time she reached the front door.

The locksmith skillfully opened the door in seconds and only needed a signature from Ann Kathrin Klaasen.

She looked in the postbox. Inside there was a telephone bill and an ad from the German Automobile Club. The local paper was in the pigeonhole.

Ann Kathrin went into the house alone. Sometimes the hair on the back of her neck had stood up when she entered homes where a crime had taken place. That wasn't the case here. The horror, the terror was not hanging in the air. No smell of blood and fear. The air smelled stale and musty and she would have liked nothing more than to open a window. But there was no rotting smell.

There were roses fighting for their lives in one presumably homemade vase. In another there were droopy gerberas. The petals had already fallen. There was a dried, half-peeled orange on the living-room table in a bowl next to the grapes, which still looked quite good. So Svenja Moers had quickly eaten half an orange, but abandoned the other half to go somewhere.

And it was there that she had been snatched by the culprit, Ann Kathrin thought. It's unlikely that Svenja Moers had been taken from her home. Unless he knew her well and she went along voluntarily. At any rate, there wasn't a struggle here.

Ann Kathrin found the orange peel in the compost bin in the kitchen. So Svenja Moers had had time to leave her home in good order.

The teapot wasn't completely empty, and someone – presumably Svenja herself – had blown out the tea candle before it had burned down completely. Ann Kathrin estimated that there was still enough wax to burn for ten, maybe even twenty minutes.

So she didn't seem to have been in a hurry.

And lipstick on the teacup.

Ann Kathrin opened the refrigerator. Three jars of organic yoghurt. A bowl of raspberries. Cheese, wrapped in aluminum foil. Brie. Gouda. Appenzeller.

Washed carrots in the vegetable drawer, ready to eat. One bitten.

Two bottles of Prosecco. One was open, and there was a silver spoon poking out of the top. Ann Kathrin smiled. Her father had also tried this method of keeping opened sparkling wine from going flat.

A chopping board in the sink, a knife and a coffee cup. 'Langeoog – Holiday Has a Name' was printed on its side.

For a moment Ann Kathrin's thoughts went back to the island, to their aborted holiday on Langeoog. She saw Weller sitting in front of her, how he had eaten his beef in the Seekrug restaurant with an almost remote expression on his face. He seemed like he was on drugs. He had told her about the cattle that lived on Langeoog all year long and were only taken away from the island to be slaughtered. The owner, who he even knew by name, supposedly even accompanied his cattle on the ferry and rode with them to the mainland so they wouldn't be so afraid.

Later she even had to view the herd of cattle with Weller, and he wanted to be photographed with them.

When this is over, she thought, we'll go back to the island and finish our holiday. Then she remembered that her suitcase was still in Strandeck, the hotel next to the dunes.

Ann Kathrin slowly moved towards the bedroom. Enviously, she estimated that the divan bed looked like a king size. She and Weller slept on a narrower mattress.

To the left of the bed there was a bottle of still mineral water. The bed was rumpled. Bright, soft bed sheets. A summer meadow. Cornflower blue wallpaper. On the bedside table there was an open book about a diet that promised dropping ten pounds per month without starving.

In the bed, next to the pillow, a novel about someone unlucky in love. Ann Kathrin didn't know the author.

Nearby, a small bookcase held romantic novels and erotic literature.

There were only designer labels in her wardrobe. No cheap items, but nothing excessively ostentatious. Cashmere sweaters. Silk tops. Lots of cream and maroon. More skirts and dresses than trousers. Svenja Moers wasn't the type to wear jeans.

As well as women's clothing, Ann Kathrin found a tapered man's shirt, size 16, with a red wine stain, and a pair of briefs.

So she had a lover. He didn't live with her, but he'd left a dirty shirt and his briefs behind. So he had to have spare clothing here.

She looked around again and found another tapered man's shirt between Svenja Moers' blouses. In the bathroom there were three soft toothbrushes, light-blue, yellow and pink. And then a dark blue one with hard bristles. Two kinds of toothpaste. Many creams and feminine scents, no aftershave. One lady shaver, but no man's razor.

Ann Kathrin felt sure he was married or at least seeing someone.

She went back into the living room and looked at the bookcase there. Many specialist books and popular science. Two dozen diet and fitness advice books, a couple of books about astrology. Svenja Moers' sign was clearly Cancer; there were three books about that sign.

Many legal reference books and self-help books about how you could save your money from the anticipated economic crash and the impending hyperinflation. No one who was truly poor was concerned with questions like that.

Then an entire bookshelf of poetry: Rose Ausländer, Hugo-Ernst Käufer, Ringelnatz.

Watercolours on the walls. Coastal landscapes. Animals in soft colours. Each picture was A4-sized and glazed. Every picture bore the initials S.M.

Ann Kathrin pictured a woman who paid attention to her body and liked to surround herself with nice things. She had been widowed twice and had possibly had a part to play in the deaths. At any rate, her losses hadn't harmed her financially. Instead, she had profited significantly. She practised painting and pottery. She was full of zest and had visitors. At night she read romantic novels and erotic literature in her big bed. She was possibly a little embarrassed by these books and had other, more presentable literature in the living room.

She had left the house or was lured out.

Ann Kathrin looked at the pile of newspapers. The local paper from Emden. The second to last issue.

She probably bought a daily every once in a while, maybe only on Saturdays. Or someone regularly emptied her letter box, Ann Kathrin thought.

A *Cosmo*. An *East Frisia* magazine. An underwear catalogue. A booklet summarising the courses offered at the vocational college.

Ann Kathrin leafed through it. Two classes were circled. An exclamation mark beside the 'Cook and Sport' class.

Bingo, Ann Kathrin thought. She sat down on the leather chair, which was turned away from the television, as if it wanted to demonstrate to its owner that she should be more interested in books than in TV programmes.

Ann Kathrin called Weller. 'She was taking evening classes. I want to know what and—'

Weller interrupted his wife. 'The last time her phone was registered was on Wednesday just after eight o'clock, and guess from where.' He answered his own question. 'At the old vocational school!'

'I need a list of all the people who were in classes with her.'

Weller said gleefully, 'I went through all the drivers of vehicles who were at Ubbo's reading in Gelsenkirchen.'

'Good.'

'Don't you want to know?'

'Later.'

'What is it, Ann?'

'I don't want to lose her, Frank. We can't make any mistakes. This woman is still alive. I can feel it.'

'There's only one connection between Svenja Moers, Stern and Heymann: Ubbo investigated all their cases and wrote about them!'

This wasn't new information for Ann Kathrin, but the way Weller said it, it sounded like a revelation.

'What do you want to tell me?'

Weller leafed through Ubbo's book, although he knew the sentences by heart. 'Listen to this: *I was really committed to putting her between bars, but I failed. I was convinced of her guilt, but I couldn't prove without a shadow of a doubt she committed the murders. I never forgave myself and hope that she hasn't found her next affluent husband by now.*'

'Fuck,' Ann Kathrin groaned. She felt sick, tired and ill.

'Yes, Ubbo wrote that. In the book he only called her the *rose princess*. Someone has found out her name. That wouldn't be too hard if you had access to newspaper archives or our police computers, for example.'

'*Rose princess*?'

'Because she supposedly loved roses and always gave her men roses.'

'I feel sick,' Ann Kathrin said and getting up she walked into the kitchen for a glass of water.

*

Ingo Sutter was on his way to Svenja Moers. As always, there was doubt mixed with anticipation when he was on the A28 approaching from Oldenburg. Should he really risk splitting up with his Heike? He knew she could be a hellcat. A merciless warrior was hidden underneath the disguise of a charming wife.

She knew about his secret accounts in Switzerland. She had accompanied him twice to Zurich. They had stayed at Hotel Scheuble in the Niederdorf neighbourhood. Alarmed by the state of Lower Saxony's purchase of a CD containing data on Swiss bank account holders who had supposedly been dodging taxes, he had withdrawn all his money and deposited the amount in Swiss francs in a safe. As he had explained to Heike, it came down to saving taxes, not getting interest.

The tax investigators got most of their tips from resentful and cheated spouses who wanted to take revenge. He could see his Heike doing something just like that. There would be meetings with lawyers and trials awaiting him instead of a new, free life with Svenja. Pretrial detention and maybe even a real prison instead of nights of love in good hotels with a view of the sea.

He thought of sports stars who had been caught for tax evasion. He surely didn't have to fear such a media circus, but in Oldenburg he was a well-known businessman, a member of his congregation's parish council and on three other boards. He had repeatedly been photographed as a member of the Lions Club when presenting generous cheques to organisations for people with disabilities.

He had his freedom and his good reputation to lose, not just money. Regardless, Svenja was worth it. He was a completely different person with her. He felt free, better, healthier. He told her the old stories, and for him it sounded as if he were telling them for the first time. He was rediscovering his own life with her.

There was a bouquet of roses on the passenger seat. Red and white long-stemmed roses that smelled fantastic, just what she loved.

Yes, damn it, he wanted to live with her, and just like every time he made that decision on his way to her, he hit the gas and drove twenty, if not thirty kilometres over the limit, depending on how strong his will for change was. In the end, not much was left except a ticket that reminded him of how powerful his resolve must have been.

Usually it cost twenty to thirty euros, as much as a good meal at his favourite Italian restaurant or the feeling of being full.

*

Ingo Sutter wasn't irritated by the fact that the door was ajar. After all, the date had been set for a long time.

He stepped through the arch of roses and sprinted the final few metres to the open front door. He pushed it open, shouting with glee, and hoping he would find her ready for love. He whinnied like a horse and called, 'Here's your stallion, you wild mare!'

There stood Ann Kathrin Klaasen. He was so shocked that he staggered and fell. The bouquet of roses burst out of its paper wrapping.

'Hello. My name is Ann Kathrin Klaasen. I'm a police detective. And who are you?'

She avoided the word 'homicide' because she didn't want to cause any unnecessary panic.

Completely in contrast to his effusive entrance, Ingo Sutter now seemed stiff, old and befuddled. It took some effort for him to pull himself together. He was wearing a light, silver-grey summer suit that was woven through with thin red and blue threads, giving the fabric a rainbow-like sheen with every movement.

'I'm . . . I just wanted . . . Well, why are you . . .? Where is . . .?'

He, the otherwise so articulate businessman, who was able to eloquently win over people and achieved nothing less than brilliance in motivating employees, was now stammering and looking for words.

Ann Kathrin helped him. 'You're married and now you're worried that your wife will find out. But don't worry: adultery isn't any of our business. We have reason to believe that Mrs. Moers was kidnapped, and we hope that you can be of assistance in our search for her, Mr—'

'Sutter. Ingo Sutter,' he said, acting as if he had only just remembered his name. 'What, kidnapped? When? By whom? What do the kidnappers want?'

Before he could bombard Ann Kathrin with additional questions, she wanted to know, 'When was the last time you saw Mrs Moers?'

He acted as if he had to think. 'She hasn't answered my texts for two or three days. But that isn't unusual. Sometimes she's texting me constantly and then again . . .' He showed his empty hands.

'When did you last get a message from her?'

He looked at his phone. 'On Wednesday at 4 p.m. That's when she confirmed our date for today.' He read aloud, 'I'm looking forward to you, my wild stallion.'

*

Joachim Faust actually would have preferred to have a prime-time show. He belonged in the evening slot, not in one of those dinky magazine programmes for an uneducated, low-brow audience that was already bored on the sofa, zapping through the channels. But he had to take what he could get. For now!

In the end, this case would catapult him into the really important talk shows and the primetime slot. He'd been obliged to use the Whaleseum up north as the set. He should have gone into the studio in Hamburg, but the producer had immediately agreed that conducting the interview in the skeleton of a whale gave an unbeatable backdrop. She asked herself why none of her colleagues had thought of it. It looked good, gigantic, and it belonged on the coast, just like this whole story. So everything was in the right place right away. It was about death, and it was about East Frisia. This way everyone got it from the start. She was sure that her segment would be broadcast multiple times.

Faust had once had a brief affair with this producer. More gymnastics than sex. More wellness than passion.

It had been an amicable split. In the meantime she had married a department head, probably exactly three years too late, Faust thought. At any rate, she signalled to him that she'd have some time after the shoot.

Unfortunately Faust had to talk to a presenter whom he considered a complete idiot, because he was younger, looked better, and spoke German coloured by Oxford English, which was meant to communicate to the ladies that they were dealing with a cosmopolitan stud. Even though he'd only temped at the BBC for six months. Ever since then he acted as if he couldn't speak proper German.

Faust would have preferred to have a blonde female to work with – preferably under thirty. But he had to grin and bear it. Faust felt old compared with the presenter, who was named

Hinnerk or Henrik or something like that. Clumsy and fat. In short, unattractive. But he didn't want to run for Mr Universe today, he wanted to demolish a monument: Ann Kathrin Klaasen. Her amateur investigations in two spectacular murder cases dealt him some trump cards.

Hinnerk or Henrik, or whatever the pompous twit was called, announced Joachim Faust as a 'legendary journalist' who had repeatedly gained attention with explosive reporting.

Sure, lay it on thick, Faust thought angrily. I'm essentially upgrading your show here. Later people will talk about how I was your guest, you cretin.

'Today we're proud to welcome the journalist Joachim Faust in this special setting up north. His bestselling interviews were in the top twenty several years ago. And yes, ladies and gentlemen, we are inside a whale skeleton.' He knocked against the bones with his fist. 'These are real bones from a fifteen-metre-long bull sperm whale. It was stranded off Norderney in 2003.'

Faust could hardly believe it. Now the pretty boy was going on about whale bulls! Perhaps he had made a mistake. Instead of making him look good and introducing him as something special, now the damn skeleton was stealing the show.

The producer was standing next to the second spotlight and was giving her presenter signals, motioning him to get to the point. Then she winked at Faust. He put on his famous cheesy grin and looked into the camera, so that the audience, and in particular the women in the audience, had the feeling he was looking them directly in the eye and talking to them personally.

Several tuned out, others felt spoken to. And that's exactly what Faust was looking for.

'In all modesty,' he said with a smile, 'it was the top ten, not the top twenty. And it wasn't a collection of interviews, it was reportage about the rich and the beautiful in our republic.'

The presenter tried to take the reprimand as a joke. He knew there was nothing more disarming than humour.

'The rich and beautiful? Well then, I'm sure not to be mentioned.'

'That's right,' Joachim Faust grinned and deployed his most potent weapon: his Mr Irresistible smile. This label had been following him since his schooldays. '*Now he has his Mr Irresistible smile on again.*'

His classmates had a cocktail that tasted disgustingly sweet, but the girls liked. It got you drunk really fast and sometimes made you horny too, and that's why it was called a 'Mr Irresistible'. Faust thought he didn't need such means. Instead, he poured on the charm and tried out his irresistible look, which had spread legs many a time.

The presenter, whose name appeared on the screen, and undoubtedly started with an 'H', knew he'd have lost if this conversation progressed from preliminary skirmish to duel, so he said, 'You're following a very hot case, Mr Faust. Tell us about it.'

Faust threw himself into a pose. 'A psychopath is killing in East Frisia. He's already decapitated two people and sent the heads to the police.'

You scumbag! Tell the truth! Not to the police, to Ubbo Heide. Psychopath? Do you want to make me into someone with an illness? Someone who can't keep it together?

'The juicy part is that both of the heads landed in the jurisdiction of the famous – or should I say infamous – detective Ann Kathrin Klaasen. Clearly someone wants to challenge her.'

'You've been getting really close in the past few days. You're a confidant of the police in East Frisia. How should we see people like that, Mr Faust?' the presenter asked.

'Well, I don't think Klaasen's been blinded by her success, but I fear it has narrowed her view, watered it down, if you will.'

'I mean the perpetrator, not Ms. Klaasen. Have you had the chance to talk with profilers?'

Don't confuse me, you jackass, Faust thought, and tried to communicate that to Hinnerk or Henning with a glance.

'The perpetrator is mentally disturbed. Craves recognition. He's not a typical sex offender. This isn't about the gratification of sexual lust. He's demanding attention, which explains the odd killing methods. For the perpetrator it's like a piece of theatre. We're all in the audience. At the moment we're in the first act. He's building the tension. Other exciting elements will follow soon.'

'You mean murders?'

Faust shrugged his shoulders expressively, showed his empty hands, and pointed the corners of his mouth down, like taxi drivers are fond of doing when they say, 'Sorry, I'm not free.'

'I don't know what this sick mind will come up with so we all need to keep a watch.'

Sick mind? Craving recognition? Demanding attention? Then you're talking about yourself, you shithead! What are you thinking? Mocking me in public? Distracting from Ubbo Heide, from the Steffi Heymann case? What are you doing, damn it?

'At any rate, Ms. Klaasen won't solve this case quickly. Sure, there may have been a couple of serial killers who got caught in her web. But now someone's killing innocent people and to me it seems like she doesn't have a plan, is tired and maybe even burned out.'

Innocent people? What shitty journalism! You bastards! You goddamn bastards . . .

*

Weller parked in front of the vocational college. He had an appointment with Mr Feier, its director. Generally it was possible to go through unofficial channels, which might not be recommended, but were all the more effective for that.

His phone rang, playing the opening melody from Bettina Göschl's song 'Pirates Ahoy!' Weller saw Ann Kathrin's portrait on the screen, accepted the call, and settled himself in the driver's seat as if he were in an easy chair.

'Frank, you've done your share of fishing.'

'Sure?' He had no idea where she was headed.

'When you catch an eel, how do you kill it?'

He'd trained himself not to ask why she wanted to know something. He simply assumed that she had a reason. 'Fishermen are supposed to stun a fish before killing it, usually with a swift blow to the head. But it's hard with eels, they're such primordial creatures. They are difficult to kill, let alone stun. A stab to the heart works best, but most fishermen can't find it. It's tiny and the eel is squirming.'

'So what do you do?'

'Most people cut the head off – not really in accordance with etiquette – at least that's what I always did as a boy, and so did the people I knew.'

'That's what I thought.'

He couldn't hold back after all. 'Why do you ask?'

'And you chop a chicken's head off as well. When I was a little girl and on holiday on a farm the farmer slaughtered a chicken by chopping off its head. I watched and never wanted to eat meat again.'

Frank Weller didn't remind her that she hadn't kept this resolution. Instead, he said, 'And Ubbo Heide called Heymann and Stern an eel and a rooster in his book!'

'Exactly. That's why I called.'

She ended the conversation and for a moment Weller sat there, lost in thought. Then, just as he was about to get out, he received a WhatsApp message from Sylvia Hoppe with a link to a TV segment. He clicked on it and immediately Faust appeared on the screen.

Weller was immediately seething with rage and informed Ann Kathrin, but she had also received it from Sylvia Hoppe that same moment.

'I even spoke to one of Ms. Klaasen's neighbours because the police in East Frisia seem to have established a moratorium on speaking to the press. The guy was a hulk. Hands the size of oven mitts. A bricklayer. He confirmed that in East Frisia there is a "Praise Club", as he called it. They stick together against outsiders and don't say anything that could harm anyone in their club. Compared with the situation in East Frisia, the famous Cologne

Clique seems like a birthday party for Christian Boy Scouts. Merely the fact that a married couple is investigating together is unbelievable.' He demonstrably twisted his mouth in disgust. 'When it comes down to it, they could even refuse to testify in court so as not to incriminate their spouse.'

Weller angrily made a fist. Then he sent a WhatsApp message to the group. 'What a dick!'

The first answer came from Sylvia Hoppe and was a question. 'What does that bastard want?'

'I'll take him to task,' Weller promised and decorated his message with two symbolic steam clouds.

Rieke joined in. 'This is bad news.' And as if everyone had forgotten, she added, 'I'm the press spokesperson.'

'No one's accusing you of anything,' Sylvia Hoppe said. She wanted to immediately put herself in Rieke's shoes and support her.

Then Ann Kathrin wrote. 'Isn't he basically right in everything he says?'

Weller exploded. 'Right? Are you kidding? I'll punch him in the face if I get my hands on him.'

Ann Kathrin reacted with an odd calmness, apparently unimpressed by Faust's accusations. 'His analysis of the perpetrator's personality makes sense. The murderer is staging a kind of play, but not for the general public, as Faust believes, but for a select audience, for us. He wants to impress us.'

'That means,' Weller spelled out the consequences, 'he's on the inside?'

'Yes,' Sylvia Hoppe and Rieke Gersema immediately agreed, 'he's part of the firm.'

'So Wilhelm Kaufmann after all?' Sylvia Hoppe conjectured.

Rupert chimed in. 'I only know one thing: it wasn't me.'

*

Prosecutor Scherer reached for the telephone and called Martin Büscher. He didn't waste time with an opening gambit or a polite greeting. He was direct in a way typical for East Frisia. He assumed that Büscher must have seen the segment already and that if he hadn't, he was an uninformed moron who had been let down by his employees.

'Mr Büscher, you have a problem. Take care of it, otherwise you won't last in East Frisia, I can promise you that. Once people start talking about someone, then—'

'Yes, damn it,' Büscher blustered, 'but what am I supposed to do? I can't serve the guy with a gagging order!'

'Didn't they teach you how to handle the press in Bremerhaven?'

'I wasn't hired to be a publicity manager!' Büscher defended himself. 'We're living in a free country so we have to have a free press too.'

'Exactly! Get them on your side. You'll have better cards then. Anyone who has the press against them is done for fast. Every word from that man is correct. It's just too bad that he had to draw the public's attention to those words. Remedy those shortcomings!'

Büscher knocked against the phone and said with a disguised voice, 'Mayday. Mayday. Spaceship to Earth. I didn't make the problems on this planet, they were here when I arrived.'

Scherer hung up. Then he looked at the phone as if Büscher were standing in front of him. 'You too,' he said grumpily.

When he had woken up, he had already sensed today wasn't his day. Why hadn't that stupid presenter invited him onto the show? I could have told him exactly the same thing as that Faust, just more objectively and knowledgably. But unfortunately prosecutors didn't have press agencies like rock stars, politicians or writers. It annoyed him that Ubbo Heide had written that book. He considered it an attack on the justice system, even an attack on himself.

Now he asked himself why Ubbo Heide hadn't been a guest on the show. Was this trouble on his horizon? Did he have to expect to be publicly humiliated by that Aurich fossil?

No, he didn't have to fear that because Ubbo Heide hadn't mentioned him at all. That's what upset Scherer the most. He didn't even make an appearance in that damn pathetic piece of work. And that cast a completely false light on the work of the Kripo. They were depicted like heroes and the blame was passed on to the judicial machinery. Not a word about the separation of powers in our country.

Scherer was worried by Ubbo Heide's new book, which was already being talked about, although it hadn't yet got a title. He didn't know what he was more afraid of: being mentioned in it or not being mentioned at all. Ubbo Heide hadn't used real names before anyway, presumably to avoid getting sued. Many were simply given letters, Mr A, Mrs B. Those were minor figures. Others received proper names, usually from the animal kingdom. Mrs Fox. Mr Dog.

Scherer asked himself whether if he was mentioned at all, it would be just a one-letter existence: Prosecutor X said; or if he would receive a real name. If so, what kind of animal would Ubbo Heide choose for him? A miniature pinscher? Cockatoo? Lion or Rhinoceros? Such names weren't neutral. They already said something about the person and were supposed to reflect their nature.

For example, his wife, with whom he'd been getting along better recently, called him 'my little golden hamster'. When she said that, it usually sounded very loving, although it was undoubtedly a reference to the fact that he liked to stuff too much in his mouth when he was eating. But he didn't want to appear in Ubbo Heide's book as Prosecutor Goldhamster.

*

Weller was greeted warmly by Mr Feier at the vocational college. Naturally, Feier noticed Weller's fury; he could practically hear his stomach acids bubbling.

Weller spoke with a very gentle diplomat's voice so he wouldn't let his rage show. Mr Feier offered tea and biscuits, and Weller bit into the biscuits like a poisonous snake bit into a rat it wanted to kill and eat.

Feier knew Svenja Moers. She was a regular at the college and was always attending classes. Mr Feier had quickly printed out a list for Weller. In such an important case – when the life of Mrs Moers was possibly at stake – Feier wanted to be helpful.

Weller only skimmed over the names, but one of them seemed to stand out, waiting to be discovered. Weller suddenly only saw those letters: YVES STERN.

All the trouble with Faust was immediately forgotten. Weller asked, 'Did this Stern chap attend any of your other classes?'

Feier looked on the computer. 'That'll be easy to check. But I believe . . . only one.'

Weller excused himself, saying he had to make a call.

Ann Kathrin immediately picked up. 'Yes, Frank?'

'Stern attended a cooking class with Svenja Moers.'

'Yves Stern?' Ann Kathrin asked, irritated.

'Yep, Yves Stern.' Weller turned to Feier. 'Can you determine the last time Yves Stern and Svenja Moers were at the class?'

'Sure, that's not a problem. There are attendance lists. But we can also ask the class teacher. According to my information, they have both attended every class so far. Most recently on Wednesday.'

'Did you hear that, Ann?' Weller asked.

'Yeah, Wednesday. But Yves Stern was long dead. Unless the man whose head was lying in Ubbo's boot wasn't Yves Stern.'

'I think that's out of the question. We have his DNA and—'

'Someone,' Ann Kathrin, 'is giving us the runaround.'

'You can say that again,' Weller ranted. 'What does that bastard have planned?'

'He wants to take us somewhere, but I have no idea where.'

The printer rattled and Mr Feier handed Weller a piece of paper.

Weller took a deep breath. He waved to Feier and went into the hallway so he could talk to Ann Kathrin without being disturbed. She had taught him not to hold his breath in moments of shock. He was supposed to do the exact opposite: exhale and then take a deep breath. 'That way you can best separate yourself from the bad vibes, instead of letting them inside your body,' she had said.

He fared well with that. Even bad cases didn't take away his breath anymore. He'd learned strange things from her in the past few years. Sometimes she seemed like a creature from another planet, one that had only taken on a human body so she could move freely among people.

'Guess where Yves Stern lives, according to the information he provided?'

'Frank, this isn't a quiz,' she warned him.

'In Hude, on Ruwschstrasse,' he crowed.

'The sender of the package,' said Ann Kathrin. 'That's him. The killer definitely attended that class and now he has Svenja Moers in his power.'

'And why does the scumbag call himself Yves Stern?'

'He wants to point out a connection. He wants us to connect the dots.'

'Yeah. Or he just wants to confuse us.'

'A street in Hude that doesn't even exist,' Ann Kathrin murmured, as if talking to herself. 'Why?'

Then she ended the conversation with Weller and he went back into the room with Mr Feier.

*

Ingo Sutter had taken the time to pack a few things he wanted to take. He looked at Ann Kathrin guiltily. He was clearly more afraid that his wife would find out about the affair than he was worried about Svenja Moers. Ann Katrin was sure that he was telling the truth and would have liked nothing better than to turn the clock back.

What kind of sissy are you, she thought, and hoped that Svenja Moers, should she survive this nightmare, would dump him. In her experience, life crises ultimately led to more clarity or at least to insights. This man loved himself and his affluent position much more than anything else in this world. Svenja Moers didn't stand a chance, regardless of how good the sex was with her.

'From countless crime shows you probably know that you can't change anything about a crime scene,' she said, and pointed to the bag with his things. 'It could be interpreted as you wanting to cover your tracks.'

He went pale, opened his mouth, but couldn't say anything.

'Yep, you're basically erasing all traces. Traces of adultery. Go back to your wife. Try to become what you now wish in the depths of your soul you'd stayed: a faithful husband and . . .' She handed him her card. 'Give me a call if you think of anything else. Most of all, whether Mrs Moers spoke about acquaintances, men or exes.'

Cringing, he took the card and said. 'Her ex-husbands are both deceased.'

'Yes, I know. Tell me something new.'

'Can I go now?'

'Yes and take your roses with you. They'll certainly make your wife happy.'

*

After so many years together, Carola Heide could see that her husband had changed. The smart decision-maker, who always tried to at least give the impression that he had everything under control, seemed unsure of himself, even in need of some muscle. The athlete who had got up before sunrise on holiday to do his stretches on the balcony, his push-ups and knee-bends to stay fit, was now in a wheelchair and had trouble dressing and undressing by himself.

On the one hand, he had become a popular writer, in demand for discussions and interviews, but on the other, his life was somehow going downhill and hers along with it.

That night she had dreamed that he'd been decapitated and his head was on her breakfast table.

Was that where this all was going?

Her daughter Insa, from whom she hadn't heard anything for far too long, was here and in need of support, advice and being mothered. But although Carola very much wanted to be there for her daughter, she couldn't do that just now. She herself needed help and someone who could give her the feeling of being held.

Still in the doorway, she hugged her daughter more fiercely. Insa quickly felt uncomfortable; there was something engulfing, even stifling, about the embrace. Her mother seemed so needy and Insa asked, 'Mum, what's the matter?'

Her only answer was to hug even harder, clutching her.

'Is something wrong with Dad?' Just for the moment, Insa's own concerns were wiped away. The thought that her father could die, perhaps even be buried without her finding out, flashed through her body like an electric shock. But there were telephones! Smartphones! Emails!

No, that couldn't be! Her father was alive or had only died a few minutes ago.

At the same time, Insa asked herself if she'd actually given her parents her new phone number. She'd switched providers, not just because the new one was cheaper and had better coverage, but mostly to get rid of a couple of frenemies who had become a nuisance and could trace her via an app on her phone:

'Hey, I noticed you're in Düsseldorf too right now. Then let's do something together, you crazy girl!'

She was using a pseudonym on Facebook instead of her real name and her profile picture was of a tree, not a face.

Had she got rid of her parents along with all those annoying people?

She felt guilty and terrible. Her mother was stuck to her like glue and she led her inside.

The place looked good. Clean as ever.

'Where's Dad?' Insa asked.

The two women sat down on the sofa. There was so much to say.

*

Joachim Faust hoped, even expected, that the show from the Whaleseum would also make him famous in the north and Norddeich. He went off – without taking along the producer – to show himself to the astonished public. But he wasn't recognised at Diekster Kitchen next to the dyke, where he ate a plate of fish, or on Dörper Lane, where he strolled with deliberate slowness, stopping in front of Grünhoff and looking into the display window as if he'd never seen a teapot before.

He'd parked his car in the car park. He'd paid a one-euro fee, which seemed laughably small, but then had printed out the receipt for tax purposes. After all, he was here to work.

He drove to Norden, parked behind the old school, and hoped to at least provoke some attention here in the shopping street.

Before he went into the credit union headquarters, he stopped briefly in front of the big lion and admired it with effusive, large gestures, as if he had to bow down before the creature. In reality, he only hoped he would be recognised by passing tourists. That didn't happen.

Inside the Credit Union he printed out his bank statement, looking left and right, but even here there weren't any screaming fans waiting for him.

At least there were tourists sitting in front of Mittelhaus, drinking dark beer with sugary strawberries. A woman watched Faust with the corners of her mouth turned down. She was here with four men, her husband and three sons, and had promised to drive. They had all already had a round, and were cheery and a little tipsy.

One son tried to cheer up his mother, poking her and calling, 'Look, isn't that the total moron from TV?'

'Not so loud!' She hissed.

Faust elected not to go into Mittelhaus.

Café Ten Cate was still busy. He took a seat. The buildings were already casting long shadows, and you couldn't sunbathe anymore. But he was here looking for compliments, not to get a tan.

He ordered coffee and a beer. He could tell that that people were talking about him. They huddled together looking in his direction, or they consciously looked away so as not to embarrass themselves.

He enjoyed it. He needed it, like others needed the medication prescribed by their doctor. He cheerfully ordered, 'another cup of that excellent coffee'.

Monika Tapper approached his table. She smiled. It strained. She swept a strand of hair out of her face. 'You don't need to pay.'

He felt flattered. Now that his status as a public figure had been recognised, every café or restaurant naturally wanted to count him as one of their guests. He was pleased and beamed at Monika Tapper.

'Thanks, that's nice but I wasn't actually planning to pay just now. Your coffee is good, and I'd like to have another.'

Her husband Jörg appeared behind Monika Tapper.

'You misunderstood my wife. We don't care for you as a guest.'

Faust thought he had misheard. Or was this a joke? One of those East Frisian jokes that were so hard to understand? But the way Jörg and Monika Tapper looked, the café owners weren't pleased about something.

Now Jörg Tapper spoke very slowly, as if he had to explain something to a child. 'My wife has tried to tell you nicely. You're not wanted here. Anyone who is unpleasant about our friends can drink their coffee elsewhere.'

There was a cheerful lady with windswept hair sitting at the neighbouring table, eating strawberry cake with whipped cream. She yelled, 'Yep, that's East Frisia! Love it or leave it!'

Someone clapped. 'Bravo, Brigit!'

Monika Tapper nodded in Brigit's direction.

Jörg Tapper clarified, 'Ann Kathrin Klaasen is one of our regulars,' and Monika emphasised, 'And she's my friend. A kind-hearted person. And we won't hear anything against her.'

Faust stood up awkwardly, as if he had difficulty getting up. He needed some time to formulate some kind of response to make a good exit. It was impossible for him to retreat so beaten. Too many people were watching and listening.

Brigit, sitting with her granddaughter, was so happy about his defeat that she gave a thumbs up in the direction of Monika and Jörg Tapper.

An old, bent woman was supporting herself on her walker and giggling like a witch in a fairy tale.

'Well, screw you all, you ignoramuses!' Faust cursed and stamped off in the direction of Neuer Weg. Just before he reached Weissig's fish shop, he was stopped by a young, extremely attractive woman. She was wearing white trousers that were very wide from the knee down, but were outrageously tight on her thighs and crotch. 'You're Klaus Faust, right, the TV man? Can I have an autograph?'

Although his name was Joachim, not Klaus, and he would have never called himself a television man, but rather a high-quality journalist, just now he didn't care. He accommodated her request, eyeing her impressive bosom. There was a slogan printed on her T-shirt in large type: *Shock Your Parents*, and smaller below: *Read a Book!*

She was pleased by his willingness and bounced up and down with excitement. 'Please write: *For Trudi*.'

'So your name is Trudi.' he deduced.

'No,' she laughed, 'my name is Danni. The autograph is for my granny, not for me. She always used to watch your talk show.'

The series of defeats seemed to not have ended for the day. He dutifully signed the card.

'Please write today's date too, but nice and big. My granny can't read very well anymore.'

Faust groaned.

In other cities when he gave autographs on the street, everyone wanted one and a crowd would form. It was different here. The people in East Frisia clearly had their heroes and stars. Ann Kathrin Klaasen was one of them and he'd insulted her. Unforgiveable.

If I'd bought a house here, now would be the time to sell it, he thought. But luckily he hadn't.

But then some other people came over and stopped and stared.

'Did you want an autograph?' Faust asked and put on his irresistible smile.

'No, thanks, we're just waiting for Danni.'

Well thanks, Faust thought, that's enough now. But then to add insult to injury, the bricklayer Peter Grendel came up behind him and jeered. 'Don't take it personally. They are like that round here. If the Pope lived here and went shopping, then they'd say: Look at that, the Pope is shopping. And you're not exactly the Pope, you're a show-off with extremely uncomfortable shoes.'

Faust looked at his five-hundred-euro shoes and asked himself what was wrong with them. He hurried to get to his car. In the car park, he saw the old lady with the walker close to his car. Although he couldn't care less about her, it occurred to him to wonder how she could have come over so quickly from Ten Cate.

She beckoned to him with her finger, reminding him even more of a witch. She was dressed completely in black, with a starched white collar.

'Mr Faust, can I have an autograph too?'

Finally, someone had got his name right.

He whipped out his autograph cards and approached her.

'Should I write your name on it? Is it for you?'

'Yes, please,' she coughed.

Then he saw the blade. It was a long knife. It reminded him of an undersized Samurai sword. He didn't protect himself, although he saw the blade and still would have had the opportunity to jump to the side or run away. Perhaps he was too vain to admit that an old, feeble lady could present a danger for him.

She rammed the blade in between his ribs from below.

He slumped to his knees. His mouth was open and gurgling noises emerged.

She grabbed his hair, pulled his head back and cut his throat. The blood spurted and although he wasn't dead, he knew that he would die. He was already lying on the ground. He saw his blood running down the car door in long rivulets.

Then she cut out his larynx. He was already in heaven when she placed his own larynx between his lips. Or in hell. Or wherever souls go when they leave the body.

*

Insa hadn't felt so close to her mother for a long time. It felt good to be useful, and that eased her piercing pain. Romantic partners came and went or were a long time coming. But she was a daughter and would be that for the rest of her life. This warmed her like soup on a frosty winter evening.

She held hands with her mother and listened to her. She had already brewed two cups of calming herbal tea and the apartment smelled of sage, cinnamon and coriander.

Ubbo Heide called it 'girly tea'. He was stubborn in only accepting real, East Frisian tea, or peppermint tea if he was feeling really bad. Best of all, he liked strong black tea with fresh peppermint leaves instead of sugar or cream. Carola mentioned that now so she could say something nice, something that didn't trigger any fear.

Insa was happy to be alone with her mother. There had always been frequent mother-daughter talks, without Dad. But not for a long time.

She knew that she'd have to tell the truth now, and it was unbelievably embarrassing. 'I think I know how the killer got the car keys, Mum.'

Carola looked at her daughter with her crystal-clear eyes, and wiped a tear from her face. 'What, you know?'

'You lent me the car when you went you went to Wangerooge for three months in March, because my old VW—'

Carola Heide remembered. 'Yeah, I remember!'

'I thought I had lost the car keys at a party. I probably just had one too many, and then . . . well, at any rate the keys were gone the next morning. I thought someone must have gone off with the car. But it was still exactly where I'd parked it, it was just that the keys were gone. I thought I might have lost them when I was dancing. It was so embarrassing. I didn't want to come across like the stupid, careless daughter who gets drunk and then loses track of the keys to Daddy's car. I had a copy made. Your authorised garage, where you buy all your cars, was very helpful; they also promised they wouldn't rat on me. I didn't know that—'

Carola didn't seem upset, but very decisive. 'We have to tell Ubbo. We can't keep that information from him.'

Insa understood, but as Carola dialled Ubbo's number and held out the phone for her daughter she felt as if she had drunk slurry rather than herbal tea.

*

Ubbo Heide sat at his old desk in his former office and, with Büscher, went through all the names of the car owners who had attended the reading in Gelsenkirchen. They also looked at all the pictures Weller had taken.

Rieke Gersema was with them. She had lost so much weight that her blue glasses constantly slipped down her nose.

'There is one strange thing. In keeping with Ann Kathrin's request, everyone was asked for an alibi.'

Büscher interrupted her. 'Alibi? We don't even know when the crimes occurred. What are we going to do with an alibi?'

Rieke grinned mischievously. 'No, that's right. They were asked where they were when Ubbo had his reading. And everyone said they were in the city library at the event.'

'Of course, where else?' Büscher nodded. 'Big surprise?'

'Exactly. Except for one. He claimed he hadn't been there.'

Büscher was flabbergasted.

Ubbo smiled. 'Nice one, a basic but simple trick.'

'Who and why?' Büscher asked.

Rieke found the picture. 'This one here, next to the woman with black – almost violet – hair.'

'Hmm,' Büscher grumbled.

'But unfortunately,' Rieke said, 'there's a simple answer. There's something going on between these two, and his wife isn't supposed to know . . . classic!'

'People used to take their lover out to eat,' said Büscher, 'even go dancing or to the cinema. Do people go to readings these days?'

Ubbo Heide felt flattered. 'Apparently!'

Just then his phone buzzed. Ubbo saw his own landline number on the screen and answered. He was expecting Carola and greeted her with a, 'We're in the middle of a meeting, dear.'

Insa's voice made him prick up his ears. He raised his hand, just like he'd frequently done when co-workers were with him and he had to take an important telephone call. His raised hand halted everything as if it had suspended the laws of nature and stopped the world for a short time. Everyone fell silent and waited, and only when his hand had sunk again did everything continue as normal.

Büscher wasn't familiar with this unwritten rule. He was crunching a biscuit and the sound was inappropriately loud in the silence. Rieke's look let him know he should stop, and he swallowed what was still in his mouth almost without chewing and thought: well great. The old boss calls the shots, and the press spokesperson forbids me from eating while he's talking on the phone. Where the hell have I landed?

Ubbo Heide concentrated, listening to his daughter. So as to not interrupt her flow, he said only 'yes' or 'no problem' or 'sure' at the most. After she had told him the embarrassing truth, he asked, 'Where was the party?'

'In Hude,' she answered.

For Ubbo it was another piece in the puzzle that needed to be put together. 'Everything's OK, Insa. It's good that you're with Mum.'

Ann Kathrin entered the room. She briefly nodded to Ubbo and took a seat. That also irritated Büscher. Ubbo didn't seem annoyed by her tardiness. He seemed proud that she considered the meeting so important that she came at all.

'I need a list of all the people who were at the party. I want the names of everyone who could have had access to the keys.'

He listened. Then he comforted his daughter. 'No, my child, you're not making anyone a suspect. You're simply telling the truth. Only who was where when. That's not betraying your friends. The culprit has a woman in his power. We have to do everything to help her. We'll see each other later. I might have to work a bit late today.'

'But Dad, you're retired!'

'I know, child, I know.'

Ubbo looked around the room, as if he had to reassure himself that Rieke and Büscher were still there; he lowered his hand.

'The keys were stolen in March. That means our man planned everything long in advance and had at least four months to prepare. We have to take a closer look at Hude and Langeoog.'

'That also means,' Ann Kathrin deduced, 'that the culprit knows Insa and knew that you had lent her your car.'

Ubbo Heide clenched his right fist and bit into the back of his hand. 'Crap,' he cursed, 'you're absolutely right!'

Ubbo Heide hadn't got any further when Büscher's phone rang. He was pleased because that way he could dispel the impression that he was completely unimportant here. He also raised his hand, as if he'd learned by watching Ubbo Heide. But then he immediately spat out the news like something disgusting he'd almost swallowed.

'A body has been found in Norden in the car park behind the old pirate school! That singer—'

'Bettina Göschl,' Rieke prompted.

'Yeah, exactly. That Göschl woman found the body and says it's Joachim Faust.'

'Oh no,' Rieke said, 'please no.'

She looked so shocked that Ubbo Heide suspected there had been a personal relationship between Rieke and the dead journalist. Büscher only thought that she was dreading the expected media circus.

*

He spread cinnamon, sugar and pieces of apple over the pancake. The whole kitchen was filled with the aroma. He'd eaten the first few hot straight from the pan; his favourite food as a child.

Sometimes, when he had so much grown-up stuff to take care of, he wanted to be a child again afterwards. He needed it then. Apple pancakes or rice pudding. All of it with lots of cinnamon. He like to watch kids' movies then or read comics. He had a whole box of them up in the attic. *Sigurd. Akim. Nick.* All of them illustrated by Hansrudi Wäscher. But also *Fix and Foxi.* He'd never liked *Mickey Mouse.*

He stacked the pancakes on top of each other. He'd liked the sight of such a pile as a child. But however much he regressed, a part of him always remained stuck in the world of adults.

His phone lay next to the stove. He'd eavesdropped on the Kripo meeting, as if he'd been in Ubbo Heide's old office himself. The reception was excellent. Better than he had expected. There were so many techological possibilities these days.

The death of that appalling journalist had caused shock rather than amusement or relief in the general public.

What kind of people are you guys? he asked himself. Someone publicly bashed you, mocked you and revealed your suspects, and instead of regarding his punishment as justice and celebrating his death as a victory, you hunt the person who did you a favour.

He held a pancake high in the air and snapped at it with his teeth. He tore a good piece out and chewed with delight.

You're the big babies, he thought, not me. You're just playing police, you're just acting like you're fighting evil. But while evil becomes stronger and stronger, you fill out forms and ask for time off for holidays and play by the rules that someone in a fancy office thought up for you, but never applied to real life.

Then he considered whether or not he should take Svenja Moers a pancake. She hadn't earned it, after all.

*

Odysseus was shocked. His head pounded and he pictured a furious goblin on a motorcycle who, stuck inside there, kept on driving against his skull in the hope that it would burst.

Some crazy, stupid idiot had cut little Marco's hair. Now the angelic image was gone.

At first Odysseus had thought Marco's sister was watching over another, strange child, to earn a couple of extra euros, but then he looked Marco in the eye, and immediately recognised him.

The blond hair wasn't just shorter, it was gone. A radical cut. They had turned an elfin being into a military head with a shaved neck. The illusion of a girl became the reality of a boy.

Odysseus immediately lost all interest in him. Little Marco recognised Odysseus and ran to him cheerfully, but he felt repelled by the child and didn't want to hold him or play with him. The monster in his head wouldn't stop raging until he had found a new toy, a real girl. And it was senseless to deny that. He was back to square one.

He had tricked and repressed himself and that urge for a long time. Now the pressure was back.

He didn't know who had cut Marco's hair, but he hated their guts.

Marco's sister Lissa also had a new haircut and had hoped she would get compliments and filter cigarettes from Odysseus. But at first he ignored her, looking right through her, as if she were made of air. And then, when she grabbed his elbow and spoke to him, his look hit her hard. There was so much hate! Withering rejection.

He registered her shock and needed a moment to switch back from the role of sadistic sex offender to the friendly, eternally youthful, ordinary guy.

'Were you both at the same hairdresser?' he asked and added, laughing, 'You should sue him for damages.'

Now he was no longer the murdering monster who was sometimes even afraid of himself, but the nice neighbour who had himself completely under control. But Lissa no longer believed him. She'd seen the dark side of his nature flare up, his crazy bloodlust. She didn't want any more compliments, or any cigarettes.

Odysseus almost fled Störtebeker Park. He no longer wanted to stay in Wilhelmshaven. He pedalled his heart out at times like these, on the run from himself, burning off energy until he was totally exhausted. Every time he lay somewhere next to a bicycle path in the grass, drenched in sweat, dehydrated, his calves hurting, he understood that it didn't matter how far he ran from the chosen child, that goblin had come along with him and was already looking around greedily for a new girl.

Preferably four or five, best of all only two or three years old. Still completely pure. Totally innocent, guileless and full of life yet to be lived.

Did anyone like eating sheep or mutton? No, it had to be lamb, young and legs still shaky just before death.

He started to cry. That tiny goblin inside him was stronger than he was. He was just its slave, its minion, its conscience-stricken servant. Perhaps, he thought grimly, it would be better to bite into the capsule that he had bought in Thailand. He imagined it would be better to die than once again become the goblin's tool.

He had ridden around aimlessly for almost fifty minutes and was next to the dyke. He could see Spiekeroog and Wangerooge from here. The wind ruffled his hair. He opened his mouth towards the sea, allowing the purifying power of the wind to push inside him.

Seagulls were suddenly there when he decided to die, greedily fluttering around him, as if he was already a piece of carrion, and they were planning to pick out a couple of juicy pieces from his body. He tried to shoo them away, waving his arms wildly and screaming.

Then he felt better. He continued to hold his face to the wind, but closed his mouth. His heart was racing.

There was something sublime about having one's own death in one's hands. The clarity of the possibility freed him from all constraints. He looked at the sea and felt a primal connnection with the seagulls, as if he could fly away with them and finally be free, through his own willpower. This power made him larger than everyone else, larger than the cultivated people who ate beef and pork, but would rather starve than eat a human, larger than all the civilised population with its diplomas, salary brackets and prenuptial agreements.

He spread his arms and laughed loudly into the wind.

Yes, he was truly free if he claimed the power of simply leaving the world. Like you walked out of a loud restaurant where the food didn't taste good: turning your back on the rude waiter, ignoring the bill, leaving nothing behind but a half-full plate.

Now he could even laugh about the goblin in his head, and it quickly became subdued. It was no longer driving a motorcycle, feeling afraid because it would die along with him. The goblin, unlike him, loved life. That made it vulnerable. Weak. Conquerable.

And now, in this cheerful lightness, in this limbo between life and death, he also sensed the identity of that Samurai warrior who had beheaded Stern and Heymann. Only one person had

had that expansive feeling of superiority during the reading in Gelsenkirchen, viewing everyone else as insects. He didn't know the name, but he knew the face.

How blind I must have been not to have sensed him, he thought. It was that policeman, who'd already caught his attention on Langeoog. A hothead. Aggressive, perhaps even intelligent – at least compared to his colleagues. Nowhere near as intelligent as him: Odysseus.

At some point the case had been taken out of his hands and he had been removed from the field. Maybe that's why he had pegged him as harmless. Although now he wanted to know more. He needed that power.

The mind, he thought, is a good servant, but a bad ruler. You can't give it too much latitude, or it will ignore everything that it can't understand, categorise and sort.

But he wasn't as stupid as others like him, who collect newspaper articles or even trophies. No. He had all his keepsakes in his head. That way no one could take them away, and they were safe from every house search.

But he hadn't remembered the name of that cop. At the time he had seemed irrelevant. Now he decided to look for him on the Internet. Surely there were the old newspaper reports from the archives online.

Before you come to me, I'll come to you. I won't take my life yet. First I'll get you, and then a cute little girl. Perhaps . . .

He asked himself if he only thought these things to calm his raging mind or if he really would do it. At any rate, that cop was his first target, as soon as he had found out his name.

*

Ann Kathrin Klaasen, Frank Weller, and Rupert were at the crime scene before forensics, but not before Holger Bloem. The whole city seemed to know already.

Bettina Göschl was in the back of a police car with the door open. The singer was pale and jittery. She had blood on her hands and face.

Melanie Weiss had come running out of The Galley bringing water, a coffee and a blanket for her. Then she handed her a tissue so she could at least clean herself a little. She'd touched her face with her bloody fingers.

The journalist Holger Bloem didn't want to photograph the body for ethical reasons, but had recorded some reactions from tourists and locals from Norden.

Dark rainclouds emerged over the Credit Union bank. The wind pushed them further, and an initial shadow on the car park was followed by the first raindrops.

Even the most hard-bitten were shocked by the sight of the body. Traces of tyre marks led to the other side of the car park towards The Galley.

'It looks like,' Rupert said, 'the culprit fled by bicycle.'

'No, those aren't bicycle tracks,' Ann Kathrin disagreed, 'more like a buggy or—'

'A walker!' Rupert crowed. 'Sure, the grandma from the estate car!' He was proud of his flash of inspiration.

'Can you take a couple of pictures?' Weller asked Holger Bloem. 'The damn rain will wash away all the traces before forensics—'

'What do you need?' Holger asked drily.

Weller pointed to the trail of blood. 'This first.'

'We need something in the picture so we can determine the proportions later!' Ann Kathrin called to them.

'Do you still smoke?' Holger asked Weller.

Weller shook his head. 'Not anymore, sadly.'

Holger Bloem turned to the cluster of bystanders. The people were in a state of shock, but didn't leave despite the rain.

'Does one of you have a packet of cigarettes?'

Lars Schafft knocked one out of his packet and held it out to Holger. But Holger took the whole packet and placed it next to the trail of blood. Then he took pictures. A couple of drops stuck to the packet, ironically exactly where 'smoking kills' was printed.

'You can keep it,' Lars Schafft offered, 'I want to give up anyway.'

The rain thinned the blood and dissolved the traces into small rivulets, just as forensics arrived.

Rupert questioned the bystanders. He was primarily interested in the old lady with the walker, who looked like a typical Lotto player.

'The culprit,' Ann Kathrin declared, 'didn't come by car. He didn't park here, and fled the scene with a stroller, walker or whatever, in the direction of the pedestrian zone.'

Weller poked Bloem. 'Samurai warrior escapes with walker instead of getaway car. How do you like that headline, Holger?'

Holger Bloem didn't answer. He felt sick. He preferred to take pictures of ships, gardens or island landscapes.

Peter Grendel pushed his way through the crowd to his neighbour Ann Kathrin. 'Is that the scumbag from TV?'

Ann Kathrin nodded.

'I just talked to him over there, and there really was a lady with a walker.' Peter pointed to Rupert. 'So it was exactly as the idiot suggested.'

Ann Kathrin looked seriously at her friend and neighbour. 'A lady with a walker?'

'Yes, a feeble old lady. If those tracks are hers, she probably didn't even see what happened. She looked nice, just an old granny who you'd hold the door open for or help to cross the road.' Peter pointed to the body that was being covered to protect it from the rain and the people staring. 'At any rate, not a granny who would kill like that.'

'Maybe she was a witness and doesn't even know it. Or is walking around the city, traumatised.'

'Did anyone see,' Rupert yelled into the crowd as loud as he could, 'who cut the larynx out of that windbag?'

Ann Kathrin was astonished by his insensitivity. Peter Grendel whispered in her ear. 'I'd stop your colleague before there's trouble.'

Ann Kathrin immediately accepted Peter's suggestion and reprimanded Rupert. 'We're at a crime scene, Rupert, not in a bar. And the deceased deserves to be treated with respect.'

Rupert gave her a clueless look. 'And you're telling me that! Did he insult me or you?'

'That's not at all important anymore. Either you tone it down or I'm going to send you away.'

Weller spoke with Bettina Göschl. She was still sitting in the back of the police car but had her feet outside, as if she might leave at any minute. She was taking alternate small sips of water and coffee and had wrapped the blanket from The Galley round her shoulders. Melanie Weiss stood next to her, leaning against the open door of the police car.

'I can't help you anymore,' she said to Weller. 'I parked over there. I wanted—'

Melanie answered for her. 'She wanted to come to us. We're having an event today with songs and crime novels. It's been sold out for weeks. But it won't happen now. I hardly think that Bettina can sing in this state.'

Bettina Göschl drank another sip of water and agreed. 'I'm afraid I have to go home. I want to have a bath and go to bed. This has really taken it out of me.'

Weller still pressed her, trying to bring a little bit of normality to the crazy situation. He'd learned that a chat about normal things that had nothing to do with a homicide often helped witnesses to remember more. He knew Bettina and called her by her first name. After all, they lived in the same street.

'I have your pirate song as a ringtone,' Weller said.

Bettina smiled at him. 'I know. But I still can't help you, Frank. I just saw the body and all that blood, and then I called you right away.'

'How did you get blood on your hands and clothes?' He regretted the question immediately. The answer was just as he had expected. 'I bent over the man, wanted to help him, but he was already dead.'

Straightaway, Weller turned around and walked over to Ann Kathrin.

'He must have changed clothes. With the mess the culprit made here, it would be impossible for him to have escaped through the pedestrian zone without being noticed. He must have been covered in blood.'

Ann Kathrin agreed. 'The old lady must have been a strong young man,' she said. 'Using a walker like that and wearing a disguise he could easily get close to any victim. He probably even stowed a change of clothes in the walker.'

'But wouldn't people notice a young man with a walker?' Frank Weller asked, more of himself than his wife.

The doctor came up to the two of them and snapped off his rubber gloves.

'Basically this man was killed twice. A deep stab to the upper torso shredded his internal organs, and then the culprit cut his vocal cords and extracted his larynx. Someone probably wanted to silence him, once and for all. More in the report.'

In the meantime Peter Grendel had worked his way through to Bettina Göschl. He suggested he drive her home and she accepted his offer with thanks.

*

Svenja Moers heard her stomach rumble, like an internal voice.

She had consumed the roast chicken long ago and would have liked to fashion a weapon out of the bones. Had she read about something like that or was she not remembering correctly? Didn't Stone Age people or the Aborigines make tools and weapons from bones?

But little chicken bones were hardly suitable as weapons for cutting or stabbing. Besides, she felt she was being watched the whole time.

When she was small, her mother had often told her. 'God above sees everything.' She had acted as if someone somewhere was keeping track of her every move. She wanted to look good and be without reproach at the Final Judgement. She imagined it to be like a doctor's waiting room. God sat behind his desk, wearing a white gown. He also had a doctor's face, just with a halo, and his assistant was an angel. She still thought her childhood fantasy cute.

This time presumably her judge would be less lenient. Without question, Yves Stern wasn't just inclined towards sadism, he was mad, a dangerous criminal. Capricious and mean. But she had to try to get him under control. Put him on a leash. Just as she had been able to do with her husbands. She knew men could be manipulated. Over the years she had learned this much. And now was her only chance.

Had Ingo realised that she'd been kidnapped? Was there anyone at all who missed her and would call the police? Her Ingo, the fine Mr Sutter from Oldenburg, didn't seem a likely candidate. The longer she was here, the more it became clear to her that he would never leave his wife. Perhaps he was scared that she could betray him to the tax authorities. Perhaps he still loved her and enjoyed having two women in his life: a wife with whom he could play the perfect family man, and another woman to satisfy his sexual fantasies. Locked up behind bars, she began to despise him. He wouldn't come and save her.

The slightest noise resonated like a motor in the sticky air and it was hard to breath. Every movement caused currents of air that she felt on the skin of her upper arms and neck.

She heard the tapping of a cane. The door opened with a hiss and a whirr. Air flowed into the room from outside. Svenja took a deep breath and felt oxygen flowing into her blood along with adrenaline. She shuddered with excitement. The old lady was back again!

She slowly came closer, leaning on a cane. She walked, bent forward as if she had a problem with her spine, as if she had a hunchback.

Her hair was white and tied into a knot. She wore a black dress, buttoned up, double breasted. Her buttons shone golden, as if they had been carefully polished. She had thrown a shawl, which looked handmade, over her shoulders.

'Please help me, Mrs Stern! I'm sure your son is a good boy! But he needs help. A doctor! A psychiatrist! He's having a crisis.'

The old lady stood very still, supporting herself with two hands on her cane. She tilted her head and looked critically at Svenja Moers, as if to decide whether Svenja was real or a hallucination.

Svenja Moers wondered if the elderly lady was suffering from dementia.

'Look, Mrs Stern, these are iron bars!' She banged against them. 'If you have a key, please let me out!'

'Key,' said the lady, sounding to Svenja like an echo, as if she'd yelled into a deep canyon from the top of a mountain.

'Yes, key! Where is the key?'

The old lady waved her cane in the air, and the shawl almost slipped from her shoulders. She repeated, 'Key?'

'If you don't know where the key is, then at least bring me a phone so I can call someone! People will be worried about me. As a mother you should understand that. Don't you always want to know where your son is and if he's safe? Please, please, bring me a phone or a computer – anything.'

The old woman leaned back on her cane again and then bent forward. Slowly, very slowly, she turned her head away. 'My son,' she said, 'Yes, yes, my son. You want to seduce him. You want to take him away from me.'

'No, damn it, I don't! If you let me out, I'll leave right away. I don't want anything from your son.'

She knew it was a mistake, but she couldn't stop herself. She would have liked nothing more than to pelt the woman with objects, just like she'd done to her first husband.

'Your son is crazy! He's pretending to be God! He's sick! Sick!'

'That's what that journalist said too, darling. That Faust, the dirty rat.'

'You mean Faust from the television?' Finally she's talking to me, Svenja thought. Maybe everything will work out after all.

'Do you know what happened to him?' the old lady asked stepping closer to the bars.

Just a little closer, Svenja Moers thought, just a tiny bit more, and I'll be able to grab you. She didn't know what she'd do then, but maybe he would let her go in exchange for the life of his mother. At the moment she held poor cards. She had to make sure the deck was shuffled again.

'What did Faust say? Does he know Yves?'

The old lady babbled something and spat. She retrieved pictures from under a cloth. They were colour prints on white A4-sized paper.

So she must have access to a printer and where there's a printer, a computer can't be far away, Svenja Moers thought. Then she started. The pictures showed a man in a pool of blood. His neck was cut open and he had something between his lips.

'He'll never say anything stupid again.' She cackled like a witch.

The old lady ran her right hand through her white hair and ripped the wig from her head. The giggle became a loud, chuckling laugh. Mean and vulgar.

Svenja Moers leaped back, even though there were bars between them. She bumped against the bed. Her shock was so great that she barely noticed the pain, even though there would be a big bruise later.

'Yep, you're surprised, you little bitch? It's me! And now you're thinking about that guy, aren't you? Norman Bates, who had his mother sitting in a chair as a mummy. *Psycho*!'

While he was speaking, he climbed out of the dress and stood up straight. The fragile old lady became an athletic man with no trace of a hunchback.

'But I'm not crazy! I'm not running through the house and yelling for my mother. I just chose the perfect disguise to move around without being recognised. No one who is chasing after a killer looks twice at a nice old lady. This way I get through every roadblock.'

He pointed to the photos on the ground. 'He fell for it. I think even as he was dying he thought he had been killed by a granny.'

Svenja's knees went wobbly and she had to make an effort to stay standing. She reached back into the air but there was nothing to support her. Just the bed below her.

He grabbed the bars, as if to test how solid they were. 'OK, and now back to you. It's obvious that you killed your first two husbands. And what about number three? Good old Ingo Sutter? The honourable member of Oldenburg society? Let me guess – at the moment he's easily worth half a million. The house isn't quite paid off and things haven't gone so well in the last few years, but after the divorce he'll still be worth at least half that. And then there's the maintenance for the wife and kids. She'll take you to the cleaner, believe me. She's copied the most important documents long ago and deposited them with her lawyer. A real piece of shit, if you ask me. Known for messy divorces. Oh, you don't need to act so clueless! Your Ingo will lose a lot. So if I were in your shoes, I'd think about killing her before the divorce rather than waiting to get him after you're married. Then you could comfort the mourning widower.'

She sat down on the edge of the bed, her body as stiff as a candle, and tried to push her feet down firmly against the floor. Her legs quaked.

Intoxicated by his own words, he continued, 'He's worth double – at least – if you send her into the great beyond early. And if you get married after waiting a bit – for the sake of decency – he can have an accident or die of . . .'

The shaking started from her knees and spread throughout her whole body. It was as if she could hear her own blood rushing through her body. Loud and unpleasant, like a warning signal.

He pushed his head through the bars up to his ears. His nose moved like an elephant's trunk. He could smell her fear.

'Oh, I can see it in you. I can smell it. You had the idea long ago – it's so obvious. Does he already know? Or maybe he even gave you the idea? Do you talk about these things, when you're lying in bed next to each other after sex? Most couples smoke afterwards. Some eat ice cream. I personally like a beer and a cigarette. I'm completely normal when it comes to that. And you? Come on, talk to me!'

She tried to get the shaking under control by pressing her palms to her knees. It didn't work. But her mind was crystal clear. She had to try to get him into the cell and then risk a struggle. If she stayed behind these bars she would only become weaker and eventually die.

You're only a man, she thought. I'll get you, or I'll kill you.

'Sometimes,' she said, trying to smile, 'the chocolate cake afterwards was better than the sex.'

He pulled back his head and opened his mouth in astonishment. The lipstick made him look strangely feminine. Powder from his face had stuck to the metal bars and two indentations next to his ears made his face look as if it had recently been stuck in a cake tin.

He made a face. 'Chocolate cake?'

She nodded. The shaking subsided. He had responded to her. He hadn't won the game yet, even if his hand was damn good. And she was encouraged by the thought that he was insane, while she was acting with a clear head.

'Yes, chocolate cake. Best with a scoop of vanilla ice cream.'

'And that was better than the sex?'

She looked thoughtful. 'Sometimes,' she said, hesitating, and then corrected herself, 'Often.'

He's really listening me, she thought. I'm starting to get through to him.

She acted as if she were taking him into her confidence. 'To be perfectly honest it was most of the time.'

He pushed off the bars with both hands, turned around once and snapped his fingers. 'I knew it! I could see it from a way off. You're frigid!'

'Oh no,' she laughed, and hoped that she didn't sound offended. 'No I'm not.'

Arms akimbo, he said, 'So you're telling me you have multiple orgasms, are you?'

The words sounded silly coming from his mouth, as if he was talking about things he had no knowledge of. '

'Of course!' she exclaimed. 'My second husband was a tantra master.'

She looked at him. He hadn't expected that and had trouble meeting her eyes.

'No, he wasn't,' he chided.

'Yes, he was!'

'You're lying!'

'I'm the one who'd know!'

He walked around nervously and clumsily stumbled over the dress lying on the floor. Now it seemed like he was the one behind bars, not her.

He waved his arms in the air. This created a slight breeze on her skin, as if someone had just turned on a fan. He stood still, pointed at her, and almost barked it out. 'If he was such a wonderful lover, why'd you kill your Tantra master, damn it?'

'I didn't.'

He waved her away tiredly. 'Let's not start with that again. I thought we were done pretending.'

He bent over, lifted the dress with the golden buttons off the floor, and went to the door.'

'No!' she called. 'Please stay! Don't leave me alone.' The steel door was already whirring shut behind him when she heard herself cry. 'But I love you! Stay!'

She stood still. Had she really just yelled that at him? Had he heard it? Or was the metallic sound of the door too loud when he was on his way out?

Then the door opened again. He danced up to her, wiping under his nose with the back of his hand and smearing the lipstick across his face.

'What did you say?' he hissed in a reptilian way. 'You love me?'

She stood up straight, like a soldier at roll call, and nodded silently.

If you ever come into my cell, she thought grimly, *it'll be a life and death struggle.*

She decided to attack his neck, his eyes and his genitals. A kick between his legs and a finger in his eye would take a lot out of him.

He came closer. She wasn't shaking anymore now that she had a plan.

Just come in here. I'll rip out your fucking Adam's apple. I don't even need a knife. My fingernails should be enough.

'Shall I open the door and come to you?'

She ran her tongue over her lips and nodded again. She didn't say anything. She was afraid her voice could betray her.

As if he sensed it, he demanded, 'Say it again.'

'I-I love you.'

She thought it sounded believable. Appropriate for the charged situation. Not exactly passionate, but a little aggressive.

He moved from one leg to the other, hopping around like a rapper on cocaine and gloating, 'You mean you want to sleep with me, here and now? We'll have wild, uninhibited sex on the bed there?'

'Yes, I'd love to! Come in. I can hardly wait.'

So, now I've got you. You're also nothing but an idiot controlled by his dick. Come on. Come.

She wondered if she should start taking off her top. Would that push him over the edge or make him wary?

She moved her hips to see if she could attract his attention.

Oh yes, she could!

Now she reached under her breasts and lifted them briefly, moving as if she had to put everything into the right place. All the time, she was only paying attention to his eyes. She could move his gaze wherever she wanted to.

Open the fucking door! Come on, do it!

She saw him on the floor in front of her, crying with pain and disappointment. But could you even cry with your eyes gouged out? Should she leave one of his eyes?

He played with the key.

Yes, you stupid motherfucker, enjoy your power one last time. It'll be over soon. Forever. I've put two husbands into the great beyond. It wasn't fun. Not for any of us. But I'll enjoy it with you.

She felt wolfish, cunning, positively superior.

As if he'd guessed her thoughts, he suddenly made a cutting gesture through the air, as if wielding an imaginary Samurai sword.

'So you did do it, right?'

'Did what?'

'With your husbands. Feigned love, lulling them into a false sense of security and then—' He made a throat-cutting gesture. 'You're one of those death spiders, or whatever they're called. Those creatures where the female eats the male while mating.'

'They're called wasp spiders and the males sacrifice themselves. It's the most they can do for their progeny.'

'You,' he laughed, 'won't ever get me. You're in here for life, my dear. Life in prison!'

He turned on his heel and walked through the shiny steel door, provocatively aping a feminine swing of hips. There he turned around one last time, pointed to her, promising: 'This is the final destination for you. You're done for, baby. You could get some relief if you write down your confession, but other than that . . . ' He ticked off the possibilities. 'One meal a day. Fresh clothes once a week. Maybe I'll even turn down the heat and turn on the radio. Maybe.'

He reached to the right, touching a switch, and the door closed by itself.

*

Everyone who had attended the cooking class with Svenja Moers and the supposed Yves Stern had to be questioned. Rupert saw Ms. Meyerhoff and was immediately enthused by the job. She was so much his type that it was almost as if she'd been made for him.

If there was a God, Rupert thought, he sent me to this woman to make up from the suffering of the last few days and weeks. Thank you, Lord! I want to be your loyal servant and your courageous warrior. Whatever you need.

Rupert had his own way of praying, but at that moment he thought he had a great connection with heaven.

Agneta Meyerhoff led him into her apartment, and the way she walked ahead of him, every step was a promise to Rupert.

Maybe she does yoga or dance, he thought. It's possible that she works out on the step machine every day. At any rate, she had firm calves and a tight arse. But not so much that she seemed manly. Rupert loved curves. Too much sport and fitness was not always a good thing.

She wore a maroon dress that stopped just above the knee and had a slit down the back. Her black nylons had a silk sheen and a seam up the back that sparked Rupert's interest.

She offered him either ice tea or an espresso. Because he hesitated, she asked, 'Or are you allowed to have a beer? I also have Prosecco.'

Rupert decided on a beer. She fetched it from the fridge, telling him that her husband was away on business, and they only saw each other once every few weeks. Usually at the weekend.

Rupert looked at the ceiling. Thank you, Lord.

Rupert thought beautiful women who were aware of their bodies were fantastic. Neglected beautiful women who were aware of their bodies were a godsend.

She held out an East Frisian brew.

'Well?' she asked, 'Glass?'

'Bottle is fine,' Rupert said opening the bottle and taking a long swig. He liked dark, traditional beer from Grossefehn.

She'd given him a small bottle. At home, Rupert always had a six-pack of the litre bottles in his garage.

He poured her a glass of Prosecco from the half-full bottle. The wine already seemed flat and stale to Rupert, and he was happy that he hadn't chosen Prosecco. Only women drank that kind of thing anyway.

Liqueurs, cocktails, Prosecco, lattes – none of that for real men, Rupert thought.

He decided to get to the point. He wanted to get the necessary questions over with and then he had nothing else to do for the evening that couldn't be postponed if the need arose.

He was imagining having another beer or two and then staying the night here. But they hadn't reached that point yet. They still had to circle around each other a couple of times for the sake of decorum, although everything was essentially settled between them, Rupert thought. The way she looked at him, he could look forward to a passionate night.

He asked about Svenja Moers and if she had noticed whether anything might be going on between Moers and Yves Stern.

Agneta repositioned herself, pushed out her chest and declared with slight annoyance that she had noticed nothing of the kind. On the contrary, Yves had constantly given Agneta compliments, and they'd also planned a date, but unfortunately it hadn't happened.

She looked thoroughly insulted. Rejected women were easy prey for guys like him, Rupert thought, but it was important to be cautious. The neglected ones were happy that anyone was interested in them, wanted to take revenge on their spouse by having an affair and boost their self-confidence. In contrast, the insulted, rejected ones could become dangerous. They could become angry if you only wanted a one-night stand.

Maybe he should write a book about women. He could hardly imagine that anyone knew more about the feminine soul than him.

'He hit on you – and then jilted you?' Rupert feigned shock. 'No way!'

The way she looked at him her eyes seemed to take up the whole of her face.

'What an idiot,' Rupert added, shaking his head.

Flattered, she licked her lips and toasted him.

Then he switched to attack mode. The castle was ready to be stormed.

'It feels like we're getting on well,' he said, and she agreed.

'Unfortunately we still have a couple of items to work through. So this Yves Stern is a very dangerous man. He has – and this is very confidential – in all likelihood kidnapped Svenja Moers. You could be the next victim on his list.'

She held a hand in front of her mouth in shock. 'Me?'

Rupert moved closer. 'Well, if you were supposed to meet with him, then I assume that he was planning to kidnap you.'

'But why?'

Rupert twisted his mouth and leaned over. 'I mean, of course none of this is official yet, but I think he's just a perverted sexually motivated murderer, and because you're a very attractive woman with significant erotic charisma . . .'

'Really? You think that about me?'

'Oh yes. I'm an expert – he probably wanted to kidnap you, but then something got in the way.'

'Oh my God, that means I'm in great danger; he knows where I live. I invited him over. He has my telephone number—' Cold with fear, she rubbed her arms.

'I'm here now,' Rupert said. 'I'll grab him if he comes.'

'Does that mean I'm acting as your decoy now?'

Rupert ran his hand over her hair. She accepted the gesture with appreciation.

'Don't worry. Nothing will happen to you. I've been trained in hand-to-hand fighting.'

Rupert pulled out his iPad and showed her pictures of the men Weller had photographed in Gelsenkirchen.

'Please look very closely at these pictures. Is one of them Yves Stern? Do you recognise any of them?'

She didn't touch the device, as if she had too much respect for it, or was afraid of the men on the screen. She just nodded and muttered when she had seen enough and Rupert swiped over the touchscreen with his finger to push new pictures into view.

'No, Yves Stern looks completely different. A little hippy-ish. But very tidy and clean. He seemed intellectual, slightly removed from reality. Certainly not a handyman, more of a philosophical type. Mop-headed.' She motioned a bushy, superb head of hair. 'Thick, wavy, red hair, such nice curls. I like that.'

Rupert grabbed his short curls. 'Like me?'

She smiled at him. 'No, much more volume, and longer too.'

Rupert was slightly disappointed.

She continued. 'And then a huge full beard.'

'Do women like that kind of thing?' Rupert asked.

She pulled back her head and raised her shoulders giving herself a bird-like look. 'Well, I've never kissed someone with a big, bushy beard. Does it tickle?

Rupert shook off the question. 'No idea. I've never kissed someone with a big, bushy beard either. What else can you tell me about him? Every detail is important.'

'Well, he wore round, metal-framed glasses, quite studenty.'

'John Lennon spectacles?'

'Yeah, exactly. He wore jeans and sweaters rather than a suit. Significantly taller than me. Lean.'

Rupert followed up. 'A jogger?'

'No, he didn't really seem like a jogger. More like a vegetarian – but I'm not completely sure, if I think about it – after all, we were in a cooking class together, I would have noticed that. No, he just looks like someone who's diet-conscious.'

Rupert gestured big biceps. 'Ripped? Would it make sense to look for him at a gym?'

'I don't really think so,' she said. 'The way he looked, he would be more likely to visit a library than a gym. And if he goes to the cinema, it would be arthouse stuff, not a Hollywood blockbuster.'

Rupert tapped at his iPad. 'Should we look at the pictures again? Maybe the full beard and hair weren't real. Criminals like to change their appearance so they won't be recognised.'

Carefully, she touched Rupert's hair and played with a curl. 'But this is real,' she said.

He gulped. She was almost too bold for his liking. He wanted to conquer her, but it felt like she was taking him.

'So you're sure your husband's not coming home?' he asked.

She pulled Rupert closer. 'Don't turn me off by talking about my husband. I'm not asking about your wife.'

She took his head in both hands and turned him to the right angle. Then their mouths came ever closer. But she didn't just kiss him; she started by nibbling at his lips. Then she gently licked his neck, as if tasting him.

Hopefully I won't go home with a hickey again, Rupert thought. He was afraid that Agneta would latch onto his neck at any minute. She was so unpredictable.

Rupert felt like a beginner when she began to kiss him for real. As if it were his first sexual experience. This woman confused him.

She opened his shirt, and her fingers crawled over his upper body like small animals looking for nourishment. On the one hand, he wanted her so much that he would have liked nothing more than to make love to her right there on the chair or on the carpet. On the other hand, he felt a strange urge to flee and escape into the fresh air.

She noticed his hesitation with irritation and, briefly separating, she drank a sip of Prosecco. She threw her hair back, looking fantastically tousled and full of passion.

'If you need to take any kind of medication, so we can have a little fun, now would be the right moment—'

'I – what? No. Where's that come from? I don't need anything like that!' He added proudly. 'And I never have!'

Then he began to worry. If she were accustomed to doped men, how would he compare if she made love to him unplugged, so to speak.

'Do you want another beer?' she asked.

He smiled. Yes please! These little bottles are more the thing for a kid's birthday party.'

She went to the fridge for him and Rupert understood what the word 'lascivious' meant.

On the way there, she slipped out of her skirt and stepped over it as if nothing had happened. Then, which pleased Rupert greatly, she bent over to grab the beer from the fridge. It was on the very bottom shelf.

*

It wasn't good for him to listen to Ubbo Heide. It took him out of the zone. He felt criticised and misunderstood, especially now that Ubbo was speaking with Ann Kathrin Klaasen. The confidence between these two excluded him.

He'd turned the sound up to maximum. When no one was speaking, the device hummed like an over-revved engine.

He was baking a chocolate cake for Svenja Moers. It was an ancient family recipe. The cake had already been in the oven for forty minutes. He knelt down and looked at it. He liked the rising dough in that light.

He wanted to serve it with vanilla ice cream. Just as she'd said she liked. That it was often better than the sex before.

He was excited to see what she'd think of his cake.

He wanted to shock her. He imagined the thoughts that would race through her head when he stood in front of her with this *post-coital dessert*. Would she look like that idiot Faust had, just before the blade glided between his ribs and into his flabby body – like into warm, mushy shit?

But even though that act of punishment had gone so smoothly, it hadn't taken him back to the zone. Everything felt terribly strained and he was fatigued. The feeling that everything would go his way was missing. He had to push through so much resistance; the universe wasn't on his side.

But this was only because of that unreasonable Ubbo Heide and Ann Kathrin Klaasen. She was a typical police officer. She viewed Stern and Heymann as victims just because they had been killed rather than perpetrators who had been punished. She was a bad influence on Ubbo, pushing him in the wrong direction.

That whole anti-death penalty faction, that army of gullible do-gooders, had contributed to the putrefaction and dulling of society. They handed the state over to serious criminals and organised crime.

This incompetent and ludicrous justice system was no longer able to deal with criminals and long ago had begun to protect rapists from libel. It financed therapy for murderers and organised courses to retrain organised criminals. These narrow-minded believers in justice were ultimately ruining the rule of law. This country needed sharp knives to win the fight of good against evil. A reaper. Him.

But he couldn't do it without allies. Had he completely misunderstood Ubbo Heide? Ann Kathrin Klaasen's voice alone got on his nerves.

'Many people call for paedophiles to be beheaded, Ubbo. Our culprit carried out the deed. In your book you expressed the hope that Svenja Moers would be put behind bars forever before she did it again—'

'Stop it, Ann, please stop! You're completely right. He's working through my book. It's been ages since I last felt this bad. I would like nothing more than to hide somewhere and bury my head in the sand. Do you think he'll keep on going? Should we give all former suspects from the book police protection? There are twenty-three of them. No one would approve that.'

That'd be even better, he thought grimly, pulling on the oven gloves and taking the cake out of the oven.

He sprinkled icing sugar on the hot chocolate cake. Then he tried a piece right away.

'We don't have any other choice,' Büscher said. 'The press will slaughter us if the next one dies or is kidnapped.'

'So protection for twenty-three people?' Weller asked.

The cake was too soft, too mushy. He couldn't even get this right! Not even a simple kids' cake.

'I have to do everything alone and this group of criminals will get protection from the government.' He cursed and slammed the warm chocolate cake against the wall.

Ubbo cracked something between his teeth and kept talking. 'Besides, Faust doesn't fit into the pattern. I think we can clearly assume we are dealing with the same perpetrator, but Faust doesn't appear in my book. And now he's lying next to Heymann and Stern in the forensics department.'

'I watched Faust's last show three times now. It's possible it was the trigger for his murder.' Ann Kathrin said, 'And there's a transcript of the conversation. I always like it when things are put into writing, it requires more precision.'

'Yes, I read that too. He basically insults all of us. Me, you, the entire East Frisian police.'

Ubbo Heide was chomping again.

'What are you eating?' Ann Kathrin asked.

'Those mints from Bochum. Would you like one? They are really addictive.'

'No, thanks, I have enough problems already.'

The device crackled. Either Ann Kathrin Klaasen wasn't talking loudly enough or she was too far away from the receiver.

'Ubbo, he called the perpetrator a psychopathic killer. And that's probably exactly what he is. Faust sketched a clear picture of his personality. But I don't think that's why he had to die.'

'Why then?'

'Because he attacked all of us. Think about it, Ubbo. The killer identifies with us. He's one of us.'

Ubbo Heide spoke loudly. 'Knock it off! You're not telling me our former colleague Willy Kaufmann—'

'You said it, Ubbo. At any rate, I think it's someone who's frustrated. Someone who was passed over for promotion, or left the service. He feels unfairly treated. He has a big score to settle with the rest of the world. He can handle weapons. He is strong enough to behead humans and to overcome strong men in their homes. He knows our rules. He knows you. Your car. Your daughter. He leaves clues where he knows we'd have to follow them up because that's just what we do. But he also knows that these traces won't lead to him. I've been asking myself if he doesn't even have an assistant among us.'

'Oh, just knock it off, Ann. Assistant? He probably has a few secret sympathisers since murdering Faust, but certainly no assistant!'

He rubbed his hands together. That was just what he needed. Helpers and sympathisers. And best of all, Ubbo Heide himself.

He hadn't played all his trump cards yet. He'd only just started the game, and everything would go his way in the next hand.

The pieces of cake that were stuck to the wall followed the laws of gravity and slid to the floor.

He'd get her to clean that up, he thought. Later.

He wanted to bake her a new chocolate cake. A better one. But he couldn't stand mess and rubbish lying around. That mushy cake on the wall and the floor caused him pain. Either he had to get her out of the cell immediately and force her to clean it up or he'd do it herself.

He couldn't bear to leave everything as it was. Not for a couple of hours, not even for a couple of minutes. He just couldn't. He fetched the dustpan and brush from underneath the sink and started to sweep up the crumbs and the fist-sized, sticky pieces of cake. He put a big chunk in a soup bowl. Then he opened the freezer and took out the vanilla ice cream. He deposited two large scoops of ice cream on the cake and garnished the whole thing with two gooseberries and a squirt of whipped cream from a can. Then he stuck a spoon in it.

He reassured himself that the fountain pen was in his breast pocket. It was the same kind that Ubbo Heide had loved using when he was still working.

Then he balanced the dish, carrying it through the hallway like a well-trained waiter. He straightened up before reaching the switch for the steel door. He had to regain control of everything. Master of the universe. King of fortune. Vanquisher of facts.

He wanted to get back in the zone. The door whirred open.

Svenja Moers was perched on the bed, staring at him.

'Chocolate cake with vanilla ice cream,' he said triumphantly.

She thought he was playing another game with her and wasn't planning to give her the cake. But it was different this time. He pushed the dish through the slot in the bars. The dessert was piled so high that the spoon collided with the bars and fell off.

She inhaled the scent of the food. She immediately realised that it would make her sick, but she didn't mind. The ice cream alone was a short trip to paradise. She could feel it in her mouth before the spoon reached her lips. Then she dug in greedily, as if the bowl could disappear at any second.

'A small preview of a better life to come,' he prophesied. 'After this you'll write your confession and . . . '

He didn't continue, waiting for her reaction. She looked up at him, swallowed, and nodded.

He removed the fountain pen from his pocket and placed it in the slot.

'You can write on the back of those prints. Faust's dead body in the pictures gives the confession enough weight. After all, we're talking about life and death. That's what it's been about the whole time.'

She was shovelling so greedily that she choked and had to cough. When the dish was empty, he started pacing in front of the bars and dictated to her:

'Your confession should be addressed directly to Ubbo Heide.'

'To who?'

'Ubbo Heide.'

'To the cop who made my life such a misery? Because of him, I almost—'

'Yes, that's exactly who.'

It doesn't matter at all what I write, she thought. I can retract everything later. Forced confessions from situations like these are worthless.

Besides, she'd heard you couldn't be charged for the same crime twice – double jeopardy – so she'd get out of it anyway. This confession was a letter to the outside world. With it she could draw attention to herself and her situation. Perhaps it could serve the police as a sign pointing the way to her.

She burped and clung to this shrea of hope.

'So write: Dear Mr Ubbo Heide – no, don't! This is better: Honourable Mr Heide. My name is Svenja Moers, and I'm right where I belong: behind bars.'

She wrote. Her breathing rattled, as if she were suffering from severe bronchitis. She had trouble writing the right words. She didn't want to make any mistakes. He wasn't exactly the kind of guy who generously overlooked mistakes.

Should she use contractions? Should she write 'I'm' or 'I am'?

She tried a compromise, giving the reader as much room for interpretation as possible. Maybe she used an apostrophe, maybe not. Her shaky hands didn't make it any easier.

'This is my confession.' He considered. Write that: Confession. And don't even dare try to smuggle in any words, signs or clues. I'm still treating you nicely, in keeping with Western law. If you prefer Sharia, then just try tricking me once more!'

'No, don't, please, I'll do everything. OK. Confession. And now I'm just supposed to write how I—'

He snarled at her. He had an enormous amount of adrenalin in his system. 'No,' he yelled, 'you only write what I say! No tricks! So write: It was all exactly as you, Mr Heide, described in your book. You were right on every single point. Unfortunately the judges and prosecutors didn't recognise you and your criminal work. Instead, it was torn to pieces in court by splitting hairs. The trial was a triumph of lies. Like a Nuremberg Rally of evil. I'm writing 'unfortunately' because—' He came very close to the bars. With his piercing gaze, he tried to read what she had written so far. His whole body seemed to vibrate. A sour smell came from his mouth. 'Because otherwise I would be sitting in one of your nice prisons, with a recreational programme, educational classes, televisions in cells, visiting hours and medical care. Here in this makeshift prison it's just me and,' he took a deep breath because he had difficulty saying the words, 'just me and the executioner.'

'Executioner?'

'Yes, damn it, write executioner.'

She looked at him. He was serious. A tear fell on the paper.

She wrote: 'The executioner.'

His words were like the hoarse barks of a vicious dog. 'And now sign with your own name.'

For a moment she feared he would demand that she sign with blood. But he didn't. He'd abandoned that idea as too dramatic. No one at the police station would doubt the authenticity of the letter. It was full of fingerprints, and one of Svenja Moers' tears had even fallen on it.

He'd actually wanted to force her to clean the kitchen, but he couldn't wait to post the letter. It was supposed to be waiting on Ubbo Heide's desk tomorrow morning.

He passed her an envelope and instead of sending it to Ubbo's private address, had it addressed to the police station in Aurich: Aurich Police Station, Mr Ubbo Heide, Fischteichweg 1–5, 26603 Aurich. He did not want to give Ubbo the chance to make it simply disappear.

*

It wasn't worth it anymore for Odysseus. Back then, Detective Wilhelm Kaufmann had investigated Heymann and Stern because he'd recognised himself in them. His unrealised yearnings. Hadn't closet homosexuals been particularly stringent haters and pursuers of gays under Fascism because they were always fighting against an isolated part of themselves? At least that's how history had explained the connection back then. He himself was gay and had come out after twenty years of marriage.

Odysseus had adored that man because he had stood up for himself and he knew that he could never publicly reveal his fantasies without being locked up forever.

Back then, before he had snatched little Steffi on Langeoog, he had been about to talk to his old history teacher. If he had been able to reveal himself to anyone to ask for help, then it was him.

But in the end he hadn't done it for fear of rejection, shame and because he wasn't sure that his teacher wouldn't have called the police. Instead, he'd taken Steffi and lived out his fantasies.

He shook himself. He had to get rid of those thoughts and focus on Wilhelm Kaufmann. He'd watched him back then, after the crime on Langeoog. He'd studied the papers in Café Leis, eaten delicious cake and drunk his tea. The police had been searching everywhere for little Steffi Heymann, every ferry to Bensersiel was trawled with a fine-toothed comb. By the second day after Steffi's disappearance, every passenger had been traced. He simply waited it out, read the newspaper and watched the police carry out their search.

He had noticed Wilhelm Kaufmann at the time because Kaufmann had stared at the children, rather than the women with their long, tanned legs in those short, swishing skirts.

He's like me, Odysseus had thought back then. It was amusing that someone like him would become a detective and not a teacher at a school or daycare centre so as to be close to the objects of his desire.

Did he recognise me too, back then on Langeoog, when I looked deep into his dark soul? Had he been carrying around that secret ever since?

They had let him go. He had lived in seclusion for a while. People like them could live inconspicuously. Our disguise it our greatest weapon: normality.

It felt like he were talking to Kaufmann now. Only in his head, of course, but that's the way it often was.

You tried to be like them. But you never succeeded. It doesn't make any difference if you put on a uniform or a tailored suit, Wilhelm. You can shed your skin as often as you want, you'll still remain a predator. People will never accept you because you lay hands on their spawn. There came a point where you couldn't take it anymore and started to kill people like you. At first only in your dreams. Sure. A brief fantasy during the day. Then later, when the desire got stronger and stronger, you started planning, and then when the first one died from your blade, you felt some relief. Was it as if you'd chopped off a part of yourself?

Perhaps I'll ask you all these questions myself. Before I kill you. I know that you'll come for me, too. Back then there were a couple of hundred male tourists on the island. How many minutes did you have to check each of us? And you didn't even have the child's body. Just the idea that the father could have kidnapped his own child with the help of his friend.

But you already sensed that something different had taken place. When you were looking for Steffi with your ridiculous Boy Scout methods, the two of us exchanged words. You gave me the flyer with Steffi's picture.

The police are requesting your assistance. Little Steffi Heymann is missing.

I took a flyer. As if I was too stupid to read, you asked me, 'Have you seen this child anywhere? She's been missing for two days.'

'I know,' I answered, 'I know.'

Your flyers did nothing. They were all show. As if there weren't any papers, no TV. I don't want to even get started on the Internet.

Then we met again, near the Melkhörn dunes – or was it between the Pirola dunes on the way to the dairy? At any rate, you were riding a bicycle and were surrounded by a flock of children. You looked happy and I bet you didn't even notice me.

And then that night by the sea, that was you too. Right? It couldn't be a coincidence. Did you follow me? Did you already know everything back then?

I was out for a stroll near Flinthörn. There wasn't a soul for miles around. I wanted to be close to the dead body. I sat on that wonderful spot in the sand and meditated. Carried out a dialogue with the dead child. Perhaps the sea had already claimed it, but the presence of a soul that hadn't had the chance to lose its innocence was easy to sense.

Are you sensitive enough to feel something like that, Kaufmann? You acted more like a tough guy in life generally, and in your career. For a moment I even suspected you had come to steal the body.

Are you like that? Do you trust yourself around the little ones who are alive?

I bet you used to sneak around mortuaries. Sure you did. You can't fool me. And now you want to get rid of me because it wasn't enough to kill Stern and Heymann. But even if you slaughter all of our kind – and believe me, there are lots of us – even then, Wilhelm, you'll still be what you are: one of us.

*

The young woman who stormed into the police station on Fischteichweg seemed upset and belligerent.

Marion Wolters stepped out of the way and was – perhaps for the first time in her life – happy that Rupert was standing close to her. She knew she was too fat for his taste, but he still roved her body with his eyes, as if he would like nothing more than to tear off her clothes. Perhaps she should get involved.

Rupert registered how Marion Wolters quickly retreated. As it happened, he did quite enjoy conversing with beautiful young women, but the narrow-hipped blonde was positively surrounded by a cloud. For the first time, Rupert understood to some extent what his wife Beate meant when she said that a person had a dark aura. Perhaps there really was such a thinig, and he had recognised it.

'Can I help?' he asked in a manner that was quite friendly for him.

She screamed at him. 'You criticised Joachim Faust unfairly! None of you gave him even the slightest chance! You bullied him, humiliated him and ultimately killed him!'

Rupert pointed to himself. 'Me?'

She waved her hands in the air. 'You! All of you! You pig-headed East Frisians!'

Rupert suggested with arm movements that she should calm down. 'I understand that you're upset. It's obviously been a difficult loss for you.'

'You have no idea!' she yelled.

Rupert had learned that in order to calm the torrent of emotions from an agitated, aggressive person, he first had to establish an objective relationship with them.

'My name is Rupert. Chief Inspector Rupert. And who are you?'

'Rupert?' Now she really got going. 'You called him a pussy and an arrogant twit!' She gasped for breath like someone who was drowning. 'Did you revel in his death? Did you protect the killer? Intentionally let them go?'

'Now listen up, young lady! Just because you had a thing with Faust, which I assume you did, it doesn't mean you can come in here making a fuss!'

Rupert's words hit hard. The air the woman had just inhaled with so much effort slipped away. It seemed like she was shrinking.

Rieke Gersema had wanted to walk past Rupert into the hallway. Now she stayed behind him, leaning against the wall and listening.

'I mean,' Rupert said, 'he probably promised you everything under the sun to get you into bed. But believe me, nothing would have come of it. That Faust guy was so . . . he talked everyone he wanted right into bed.'

Tears welled up in Rieke Gersema's eyes. She turned around and ran back into her office. Irritated, Rupert turned around.

The young woman in front of Rupert took advantage of the fact that he was temporarily distracted. Her right hand shot out without warning, fingers spread wide, and she hit him across the face. He took a second to process what had happened as she was digging frantically through her handbag.

Was she looking to pull out a weapon? Would she try to shoot him here, in the entrance to the police station? Maybe she was planning a mass shooting to avenge her murdered lover. As

Rupert jumped the woman and ripped her bag away from her he believed he was saving the lives of his clueless colleagues. He flung the thing across the hallway, twisting the young woman's right arm behind her back and then they fell to the floor together.

Marion Wolters hurried over.

'The purse!' Rupert called. 'She tried to pull out a weapon!'

Marion Wolters reached into the bag and checked. 'There's no weapon inside. Only this.' She held up a Dictaphone and some cosmetics.

Rupert released the woman. She kicked his shin and scratched his face.

'My daddy recorded everything and sent it to me! He said that you're all in on something and there are skeletons in your closet. That's why you destroyed him. He was on to you!'

Rupert straightened up with some effort. 'Your daddy?' he asked, dumbfounded.

'Yes, you fool! I'm his daughter. He was a better father than you'll ever be, you . . . you . . .'

She couldn't think of a swearword word bad enough.

Then she barked, 'You East Frisian idiot, you!' but looked disappointed at her own choice of words. She ripped the Dictaphone out of Marion Wolters' hands and held it up in the air. 'I'm going to offer this to the radio or the television – whoever wants it. I'm going to destroy you! My daddy had a lot of friends in the media. You have his life on your conscience! I'll destroy you, you filthy animals!'

Rupert wanted to take the Dictaphone away from her again, but as he moved forward far too quickly, his sacroiliac joint shot a bolt of pain through his body, as if someone had jammed a hot knife in his back.

He remained bent over, not even managing to reach out his arm, and said in a distorted voice, 'That . . . that is . . . possibly evidence. A piece of evidence in a homicide! You can't just—'

'Yes,' she crowed, 'and it's evidence against you, you jerks!'

She strode to the exit.

Rupert tried to get Marion Wolters moving to follow the young woman, but Wolters stayed put and looked stoically at Rupert.

'If that tape is what I think it is, Rupert,' Marion Wolters said, 'then you're not going to come across very well to the media, my dear.'

Accusingly, Rupert hissed. 'Yeah, thanks! And you're letting her get away with it, fat arse!'

Marion Wolters turned her back to Rupert. Walking away, she not only showed him her wide, child-bearing hips, she also gave him the finger.

Rupert held on to the wall. He urgently needed Ibuprofen, or at least a double vodka.

Rieke Gersema, the press spokeswoman, saw dark clouds approaching. She ran after Faust's daughter to try and prevent the worst. But when she got outside the young woman was nowhere to be found.

*

The morning couldn't have been busier. For Rieke Gersema it seemed as if her phone was ringing louder than usual. She had already dissolved and drunk two aspirin to ward off a headache, and was starting to develop stomach pains. Journalists had seldom posed such hard questions and been so persistent.

As press spokeswoman, she felt as though she were the one in the dock.

Büscher didn't have any time for her concerns. He dismissed her with a wave of his hand.

If he'd had his way, he would have simply opened the letter. But Ann Kathrin insisted on bringing in Ubbo Heide. She tried to reach him by phone. After all, the letter was addressed to him.

It was lying on the otherwise empty conference table, illuminated by an office lamp. Büscher had only touched it with tweezers.

'Postmarked Emden,' he said, 'I'd bet a month's pay it's from our perpetrator.'

'Well, that can't be very much,' Weller needled him. He didn't like the way Büscher looked at Ann Kathrin. Even the way the two talked was too intimate for Weller's taste.

Weller had slept poorly and had dreamed that he was still married to his ex, Renate, who had cheated on him multiple times while he was babysitting or working nights. He was still furious with her and wasn't planning to let anyone pull the wool over his eyes again.

Ann Kathrin stood, her back turned to the others, whispering on the phone with Ubbo Heide. Büscher considered this a real affront. He addressed the other members of the team loudly, looking into each of their eyes. 'The letter was sent to our police station but addressed to Ubbo Heide. What does the culprit mean by that?'

Sylvia Hoppe shrugged her shoulders, preferring not to say anything, but Weller couldn't keep his mouth shut. 'He wants to imply that he doesn't accept you as our boss, Martin.'

The way he said Martin implied that only an idiot could have that name.

Her phone pressed to her ear, Ann Kathrin looked at her husband, rebuking him.

Büscher looked rattled. 'Well, this case puts us all to the test. If the killer really is someone from our ranks, then—'

Rupert limped into the room, bent over. 'Apologies, colleagues, but . . . my sacroiliac joint—'

Sylvia Hoppe interrupted him. 'Yeah, sure, OK. Don't bore us with your medical history.'

Ann Kathrin spoke into her phone. 'Thanks, Ubbo,' and hung up. She nodded at Büscher. 'Ubbo is already on his way over here. But we're supposed to open the letter right away and not lose any time. He'll be here as soon as possible.'

'How kind,' Büscher scoffed and carefully went to work with the letter opener.

It was so still in the room that the cutting of the paper sounded like a viper's hiss.

They huddled round. Although everyone was reading the text for themselves, Büscher read aloud:

'This is my confession . . . It was all exactly as you, Mr Heide, described in your book. You were right on every single point.'

Weller murmured, 'Most of us know how read!'

But Büscher continued:

Unfortunately the judges and prosecutors didn't recognise you and your criminal work. Instead, it was torn to pieces in court by splitting hairs. The trial was a triumph of lies. Like a Nuremberg Rally of evil. I'm writing 'unfortunately' because otherwise I would be sitting in one of your nice prisons, with a recreational programme, educational classes, televisions in cells, visiting hours and medical care. Here in this makeshift prison it's just me and the executioner.

Rupert groaned, and it was unclear if this was triggered by the letter or by his sacroiliac joint.

Rieke Gersema put into words what was going through her head without thinking. 'So Ubbo was right. It really was her.'

Ann Kathrin reacted unusually stridently to Rieke. 'I don't want to hear anything like that again! This here,' she pointed to the letter, 'is a disgusting document. A confession possibly produced under torture. Luckily we're living in a country where no judge would ever recognise something like this.'

Weller placed a hand between his wife's shoulder blades. But as if his touch had been a starting signal, she now began to pace back and forth like a caged animal. Loudly, she questioned her colleagues. 'What does this letter tell us about the perpetrator?'

'He's read Ubbo Heide's book,' Weller said.

'He hasn't killed her yet,' Rupert chimed in.

Ann Kathrin looked at Büscher. He passed, as did Rieke and Sylvia.

Then Ann Kathrin ticked off what she thought she knew. 'He's clearly from our world. Perhaps he even works in this building. He feels as if he's been treated unfairly. He thinks that he's better than most of us and—'

'He's upset about the justice system. He considers the judges and laws too lax,' Weller said.

Ann Kathrin continued. 'Even worse. He thinks the justice system dances to the criminals' tune.'

Büscher cleared his throat. As the boss, he needed to say something. 'From his perspective, he's doing good—'

'Seen superficially, yes,' Ann Kathrin said. 'But he uses this to live out his sadistic impulses. All these justifications aim to legitimise what he does. He wants recognition, even praise from us, particularly from Ubbo Heide. He thinks he's doing our work, and even better than us. At any rate, we know him, and he knows us. He has been frustrated by us more than once. He's probably very intelligent and plans meticulously. So we're looking for a man who was passed over for promotion. Someone who thinks he belongs in the front row and was thrown on the scrapheap. Someone who doesn't feel like he's taken seriously.'

Rupert raised his arms as if he were turning himself in. 'OK, you guys, you got me, I give up!'

'Shut up, Rupert!' Weller hissed. 'This isn't a laughing matter!'

Something inside Weller rebelled against Ann Kathrin's analysis. She'd taught him that you should always take your feelings seriously, and that's exactly what he did now. 'That might all be the case, Ann. But why should he be from our ranks, even from this building? Can't it just be some kind of justice fanatic who's read Ubbo's book and is a little obsessed and considers himself the . . . What did he call himself?'

'Executioner,' Sylvia Hoppe whispered, looking like someone other than her had said it.

'Executioner!' Weller scolded. 'A person calling himself that must have a screw loose. We'd notice if one of us had lost his marbles, right?'

Sylvia Hoppe whispered in Rupert's direction. 'Which puts you back in the game!'

'Hopefully in prison they will cut the free time and the educational courses he hates so much,' Rupert railed.

Rage was causing a powerful energy to build in the room.

Ann Kathrin got serious. 'He simply knows too much internal information. For example, where Ubbo goes on holiday.'

It wasn't easy for Weller to humiliate his wife in front of everyone, but he still said it. 'I'm afraid you're mistaken, Ann. For example, there was a feature on Ubbo Heide in the Harlingerland paper. Almost a whole page. There he talks about his favourite island and that he loves sitting on Wangerooge looking at the sea and that he'd written the last pages in his book there and . . .'

Weller fished the folded newspaper article out of the inside pocket of his jacket and smoothed out the paper on the table. 'This picture here was taken in his holiday cottage. Here you can see the sculpture honouring the seafarer up on the esplanade. With a little spatial awareness, you can work out exactly which apartment the picture was taken in. Ubbo became a public figure by writing that book. Don't be mistaken, Ann. I googled him yesterday and within half an hour I'd found out more about him than in the ten years we worked together.'

Ann Kathrin acknowledged Weller's objection and said, 'The boys from the lab need to examine the letter and envelope for micro-traces. DNA on the adhesive surface and so on.'

'You're out of date,' Rupert ridiculed. 'These days no one licks stamps. They're self-adhesive.'

Ann Kathrin motioned at the letter. 'But not the envelope, Rupert.'

'You think he's so stupid that—' Rupert waved her away without finishing the sentence and made a face like he'd just licked an adhesive strip himself. He wiped his lips with the back of his hand.

'Everyone makes mistakes at some point. Even more so if he feels as superior as this scumbag clearly does,' she continued. 'The paper has to be tested for impressions. Sometimes things like this have been used as a pad beforehand.'

Büscher agreed with Ann Kathrin. 'In Bremerhaven we once had a kidnapper who'd written his Christmas cards before the note. With warm greetings to his mother and siblings. He was very surprised when his doorbell rang.'

The door opened, right on cue, and Ubbo buzzed in in his wheelchair. No one except Ann Kathrin had expected him so soon. Everyone made space for him as a walkway to the table with the letter formed.

No one said a word. Even 'hi' would have been too much in the circumstances.

*

As he listened to them, he could picture their faces exactly. If he closed his eyes, it was as if he were in the room, in Aurich police station on Fischteigweg, in the conference room on the second floor.

Ubbo Heide's voice was serious but clear. 'I rue the day that I got the idea to write this book. I have pulled the plug on the second volume of course. My publisher has twenty-six thousand pre-orders and they're going crazy. But I said that I didn't want the book to appear under any circumstances.

'You mean,' Rupert said, 'you don't want to give the culprit any more material?'

'Yes, I don't want to be responsible for there being any more victims.'

'But we'll get him, Ubbo, before he's murdered his way through your entire book,' Weller interjected.

He blew smoke rings and sent them to the ceiling like signals. He got back into the zone when he listened to them.

What amateurs you are, he thought.

Büscher tried to take the lead but his voice betrayed the fact that he had nothing, absolutely nothing under control.

'So should I assume that the perpetrator will simply work his way through the book? Isn't that a bit too obvious, people?'

Weller interrupted him. 'The Steffi Heymann case is the book's opening chapter.'

'Yes, but,' Büscher argued, 'Svenja Moers doesn't come until chapter three.'

'Right,' Ubbo Heide said, 'because the suspect from chapter two died three years ago.'

'Fuck!' Rupert cursed. 'What a fucking mess!'

'Yes, you can say that again. If I only I hadn't written that book!'

Rupert had always thought reading books was stupid and now felt validated.'

'But that means,' Weller said, 'we can set a trap for him with the fourth suspect. The culprit in chapter four is—'

'No,' Ann Kathrin said, 'that's too simple. He's expecting that. The whole time I've had the feeling that this man knows exactly what we're doing, as if he's listening to us here, sitting at this table, and laughing at us.'

That's exactly what I'm doing, he thought, and took a drag, deep into his lungs.

'He's not just working from the front to the back,' Ubbo Heide said. 'He's selecting his victims based on a different principle.'

'Which one?' Ann Kathrin asked.

'He's only taking the cases where Willy Kaufmann was involved.'

'But that was just in these early cases,' Ann Kathrin pointed out. 'Svenja Moers and Heymann. Kaufmann wasn't even on the force after that.'

'Right,' Ubbo Heide said, 'but in the last case in my book—'

'The homicide in Syke?'

'Yeah, exactly.'

'The woman was raped and then murdered. What does that have to do with Wilhelm Kaufmann?' Ann Kathrin asked.

Ubbo Heide coughed, and it seemed to the culprit as if the cough was caused by his cigarette smoke. He waved his hand and would have liked nothing more than to apologise to Ubbo Heide. Then he kept on listening.

'The victim was his niece. His sister's daughter. He really annoyed his colleagues at the time. He tried to get involved in the investigation and initiated private research. He was desperate to catch the killer, especially as that could also redeem him so he could return to the police force. For his colleagues on the case it was a complete nightmare. I was sent there at the time because we had had a similar case in Bensersiel, where the woman had survived. She was able to describe the attacker, but—'

'Yes. We all read your book, Ubbo,' Weller said.

There was a bang, as if someone had smacked the table. He imagined that Ubbo Heide was that person, but then Ann Kathrin's voice was so sharp, as if she were yelling directly into his ear. 'Why the hell didn't we know anything about that?'

'Well, he wasn't a suspect, just a relative of the victim.'

'Yes, how come?' Rupert asked, 'And why isn't that in the book?'

Weller groaned. 'There aren't any names at all in the book, you idiot! Maybe you should read it.'

'Is it required reading now? Rupert asked.

'Yes, damn it, it's practically part of the file.'

Büscher sounded almost whiny. 'And what was the name of the guy you suspected back then, Ubbo?'

'The victim from Bensersiel gave us a clear description and we could have caught him, but then two friends gave him a bulletproof alibi. His poker buddies.'

'And it wouldn't surprise me,' Ann Kathrin said, 'if we soon find all three with their throats cut.'

Weller nodded in agreement. 'Yes, and with cards in their mouths.'

He started to roll a new cigarette. It's not such a bad idea, he thought, and pictured the astonishment in the Aurich police station if he did exactly what they'd just suggested.

But then he smiled and said, 'You will all be surprised. I'll shock you all. I'm very good. I'm sure you won't be expecting my next move.'

'I want,' Ann Kathrin said, 'Wilhelm Kaufmann to be under surveillance round the clock. And everyone from that poker group as well.'

'Yes,' Büscher groaned. 'And I get to worry about how I'll get the personnel and the resources, and best of all, keep everything secret.'

'Right,' Ann Kathrin said, 'that's exactly what we thought.'

*

Ann Kathrin Klaasen and Ubbo Heide retreated to Café Philippe so they could talk without being disturbed. There wasn't much going on there. When Ann Kathrin walked through the door she had the feeling she was falling through time back into the seventies. Ubbo Heide really liked the place.

They sat down at a corner table and ordered plum cake and coffee. Ann Kathrin opened the conversation. 'You don't trust anyone in the force at the moment, do you?'

Ubbo nodded grumpily, and simultaneously shrugged his shoulders. 'He's always a step ahead of us, Ann. I pretty much could have told you that the number plates in Gelsenkirchen wouldn't be any help, as original as I thought Frank's move was. This man knows exactly what we're doing – he wouldn't park nearby. He knows where the surveillance cameras are, and he knows that we'll be checking. We won't get anything from the letter either. If there are clues, he will have planted them to confuse and mislead us.'

'So he's one of us after all?'

'Everything inside me resists the idea. But I'm certain that this is someone that we've trained ourselves.'

'We'll stick close to Willy Kaufmann from now on,' she said, and pressed her hands together, as if to demonstrate that.

Ubbo Heide placed his hands on the wheels of his chair. 'He's already in the know,' he boomed. 'He wants to play with us a little until he gets bored and our attention slips. And then he will—'

Ann Kathrin's seal started barking even before the waiter had brought the coffee. With a single, fluid motion, she lifted her phone to her ear and answered it. The connection was very good.

'The good news first. We have twelve people for the round-the-clock surveillance,' Frank Weller said. 'Four per shift.'

'And the bad news?' Ann Kathrin asked.

'I wanted to invite Kaufmann in for a conversation. I thought we'd bug his place during the talk. But he isn't answering his landline and his mobile tells me that he's unavailable at the moment. We can't even locate it, he's turned the thing off.'

'Keep trying,' Ann Kathrin said. She wanted to end the conversation, but then she sensed Weller wanted to say something else.

'Ann, I'd actually prefer to put out a warrant for him.'

'No, then he'll be warned. He'll be looking to get close to us, and if we get to his next victim soon, then we can grab him there,' Ann Kathrin said.

Ann Kathrin ended the call, placed the phone on the table and looked at Ubbo Heide.

Ubbo hadn't heard Weller, but deduced from Ann Kathrin's words. 'They've already lost him?'

Ann Kathrin nodded.

She'd ordered two pieces of plum cake without whipped cream, but they came with cream. Ubbo said Ann Kathrin could eat his portion too. She didn't want to, highlighting the fact that she'd put on weight, but at the same time, spooned a large proportion of the cream into her coffee. She watched as the floating island of cream slowly dissolved.

Ubbo Heide weighed his words carefully. 'The fact that you can't get hold of him doesn't mean anything. He's from a different generation, Ann. Just like you and me. But he's even more critical of the digital age. He wrote memos by hand, didn't even want to use a mobile phone while on duty because it drove him crazy that he could be tracked. Apparently he read George Orwell at school. He was always afraid of the surveillance state.'

'Like everyone who has evil intentions,' Ann Kathrin chimed in, but Ubbo didn't accept that.

'No, Ann, it's a real danger. There are cameras everywhere and everyone with a phone in their pocket has their own Stasi tracker. It's not just criminals who are worried. It could also be the beginning of the end of our freedom.'

'Maybe you're right, Ubbo,' she said, 'but at this moment I'd prefer it if we knew where he was.'

'The first thing he'll do is go after Volker Janssen.'

'The rapist?'

'The presumed rapist, the one our witness from Bensersiel identified. The justice system exonerated him back then, but he had some trouble from a women's group. They sprayed "rapist" on his car and his front door, and kept following him with their hate. He deserved it. Then he moved to Achim.'

'To Achim?'

'Yeah, to Achim. Similar behaviour to Heymann and Stern. Anyone who has been pilloried so publicly tries to start again somewhere new – looking for somewhere to hide.'

At first Ann Kathrin hesitated to say it, but then she burst out. 'Ubbo, you're acting as though you wouldn't mind if he snatched Janssen and brought him to justice.'

'Yes, damn it, I'd like that. But I know that it's not OK. Now don't pin me down like that, Ann. Don't be so hard on me. We have to stop this criminal and defend the rule of law, even if the system sometimes seems weak or unjust to us.'

Ann Kathrin sipped at her coffee, returning it carefully back to her saucer without making the slightest sound, and said, 'I don't think he'll go for Janssen first.'

'Why not?'

'He sent us that terrible confession from Svenja Moers. He'll try to put Volker Janssen under such pressure that he also confesses.'

'But how?'

'I assume first he'll get one of the poker players who covered for Janssen. That way he can give him the biggest scare possible.'

'You mean he'll execute one of the false witnesses so that Volker Janssen will confess himself?'

Ann Kathrin nodded. 'He'd surely rather be punished for rape than lose his head.'

She wrote down the name Volker Janssen. Then she circled it with her pencil.

'What are his witnesses' names?'

'Werner and Michael Jansen.'

'Are they his brothers?'

'No. His name is written with a double s and the other two with only one. Or vice versa, I don't remember anymore. At any rate, they're brothers, but not related to Volker.'

*

It felt good to eavesdrop on Ann Kathrin Klaasen and Ubbo Heide in Café Philippe. Ubbo sympathised with him after all. It was music to his ears.

And the tip from Ann Kathrin wasn't so bad. Maybe, he thought, I could scare that scumbag so much that he'll run to the police and confess. That'd be a victory! He smirked. Maybe you have some more good tips in store for me, Ann Kathrin!

He laughed. In the end it'd be like with that secret tax CD. Although there are complaints that it's not right for the state to purchase data stolen from a Swiss bank, masses of goddamn tax dodgers hand themselves in, become remorseful and pay for fear of discovery. But they don't even know if their names are on the CD. If we put the fear of God into these people, then they'll all confess, take the lesser of two evils, and save their pitiful lives by begging for mercy.

I can already picture you on the front line with me. You, Ann Kathrin and me – what a team we'd be!

*

Rupert was standing in the queue at the supermarket when his phone rang. He had a case of beer and a bottle of whisky in his trolley – everything that a man like Rupert would need when giving up smoking.

Manni, his old buddy, who he loved to prop up the bar with in the Mittelhaus pub, kicked him when the phone rang.

Rupert briefly looked over at Manni, and then answered.

Agneta murmured in his ear with a husky voice. 'Hey, my stallion, how're you doing?'

Rupert was afraid that the other people in the queue would hear Agneta's voice and he coughed to cover the sound.

'Oh, I hope you haven't caught a cold. I thought I'd kept you warm enough.'

Rupert kept on coughing.

'I hope you'll come again tonight. I'm an expert in a couple of things you're not familiar with and I'd like to pamper you a little.'

Rupert tried to find a neutral tone. 'I'm working on a homicide right now. We're all under a lot of pressure. I can't make it tonight.'

'Didn't you like my shashlik?'

Rupert didn't know what'd been hotter, the shashlik or Agneta. But it'd be impossible to say that now.

'Didn't you like it?' she probed.

'Well, of course! But I—'

'I think I'm in danger! You told me that he could come and get me next! I thought you'd protect me?'

'I can try to get police protection for you, but I don't know if—'

'I don't want any of your deputies! I want you! Don't you care at all that you're putting me at the mercy of the killer? My husband's away on business, he'd protect me otherwise. But—'

'Well, as I said, I'm hot on the heels of the murderer here. We're really close to catching him and—'

By now, Rupert had the attention of everyone in the queue and the cashier had even stopped scanning goods and was staring at him.

Manni pointed to Rupert and chimed in. 'That's my friend, Rupert! Basically the boss of the police in East Frisia.'

Rupert turned around to him. 'Pipe down!'

'Are you ordering me to be quiet?' Agneta Meyerhoff asked.

'No, I didn't mean you. I'm not alone here.'

'Unlike me. I'm completely alone! Always! And I've had enough of it.'

If he wasn't mistaken, there were tears mixed with her fury. Her voice cracked, and she tried to soften her tone. 'I thought

I meant something to you, but apparently you don't care if I'm killed or not.'

'Of course I don't want the killer to get you, but there's a time and a place—'

'But you're not working night and day. Come to my place when you finish and I'll make you chicken soup. That's good for colds.'

'I don't have a cold. I-I can't come over tonight. I'm married, damn it, I sleep at home at night – normally.'

'OK, then, I'll just come to you. I don't want to be alone tonight.'

'To me?'

'Yeah, sure. I accept your protection!'

'I don't know if my wife will think that's such a good idea. She can really get jealous if—'

'That wasn't a serious suggestion, you idiot! I just wanted a response.'

Manni poked Rupert. 'Hey, if you guys have problems, I mean, if you need backup, protecting a hot chick or something – you can always count on me!'

'Yeah,' Rupert groaned, 'I know.'

'If I tell my husband you harassed me, he'll break your nose!'

'Harassed?' Rupert asked.

Rupert had already realised from her breathing that she wanted to hurt him. He was familiar with that reaction from women.

'I've never slept with a man who was so microscopic!' She yelled.

Rupert regretted it but couldn't help yelling back. 'It's not little!'

Several people at the till looked away, embarrassed. Others grinned widely at Rupert.

Manni patted Rupert on the shoulder and said, 'Don't put up with that, mate!'

*

Ann Kathrin Klaasen wanted to get her own impression of the situation in Achim and under no circumstances simply leave it to the local authorities. She didn't want to immediately blow her cover, so she chose to take her ageing, green rattletrap hatchback. But it didn't start right away when she wedged herself behind the wheel.

She coaxed her car, emphasising how important it was to her and that she'd never sell or junk it. But she needed to get to Achim, urgently, and it shouldn't be so stubborn.

Weller stood next to the car, his arms resting on the roof, and listened to Ann Kathrin.

'Some husbands would be pleased if their wives talked as tenderly to them as you do to your car,' he grinned and suggested taking the hatchback to a garage and hiring a car to go to Achim.

Ann Kathrin didn't react to Weller. Instead she told her car, 'He didn't mean it. He's just in a bad mood. Don't take it personally.'

'Ann, cars don't take anything personally. Please, we still have the C4. You can have it. I'll have Marion Wolters pick me up, and then—'

Ann Kathrin continued talking to her hatchback. 'Don't worry, my sweetheart,' she said and caressed the dashboard, 'You're not replaceable. Men think sometimes that if something isn't right or someone gets a bit old it's time to get a new—'

Weller slammed his fist on the roof of the car. 'No, damn it, I'm not like that!'

'I'm not talking to you,' Ann Kathrin told him.

'I know. You're talking to your car. Lord, if anyone hears us, Ann Kathrin, they'll think both of us are completely crazy!'

'You're the one who thinks I'm crazy, Frank. But the only people here are our neighbours. I live here. They know me.'

At that very moment the engine turned over.

'You see,' Ann Kathrin laughed, 'maybe the word "garage" helped. My sweetheart doesn't like that. You should understand. You don't like going to the doctor either.'

'What does that have to do with anything?'

'Could I remind you of the colon cancer test that's due?'

Weller straightened up, looked into the blue East Frisian sky and grunted like a hungry gorilla.

Ann Kathrin engaged the handbrake and climbed out to hug her Frank. She kissed the base of his neck and whispered. 'You don't have to worry, dear. Nothing will happen to me. I just want to get as close as possible.'

'Sure. What could happen to you? Your sweetheart will surely watch over you,' Weller said, sounding almost jealous. He had always had the old-fashioned idea that he had to protect his wife.

Then she left and watched him in the rear-view mirror as she turned the corner. He waved and looked concerned.

She turned on the radio and stopped at the North Sea Radio station because they were playing a song from the Fabulous 3, 'Over the Sea'. Music from Ubbo Heide's favourite bands could be heard more and more frequently on the radio.

Ann Kathrin hummed along.

'In the storm tighten your sails
The waves smash in the gales
Over the sea . . .'

Ann Kathrin gradually left the station's range. The radio started to crackle and pop. She switched to the next station. The news was still on there. A member of parliament who had downloaded child pornography from the Internet had been acquitted, but was to donate five thousand euros to a child protection association.

Ann Kathrin angrily hit the steering wheel, but then immediately apologised to her car for the attack. 'You can't do anything about it, sweetheart,' she said, 'but things like that make me furious. That man was lucky that he'd only downloaded child porn. It would have been really expensive if he'd illegally streamed a Hollywood blockbuster! What is wrong with the justice system in our country? A punishment becomes a donation. The child protection association should probably be grateful now. What's happening to the world? Has everyone gone crazy?'

Then the music programme started. Ann Kathrin changed the channel. She finally ended up with Radio Lower Saxony. Saskia Faust was apparently a guest in the studio.

Ann Kathrin turned up the volume.

'My father had recorded all these conversations and sent them to me.'

'Did your father suspect that he was going to be murdered? Is that why he sent you the tapes?'

'No, I think he did it because he wanted to show me that he wasn't necessarily loved for his work, he also had to overcome a lot of resistance. But he often sent me things like that when he was being attacked.'

'But why?'

'My father was a very sensitive person, even if many people thought otherwise. He was very affected by things like that and needed his daughter's support. Sometimes he lay in my arms, crying, and he often cried down the phone because he had to stay the night in another random hotel and—'

'Can we listen to the tape?'

'Of course.'

Ann Kathrin pulled over to the side of the road. She wanted to concentrate on what she was about to hear.

When she heard Rupert's voice she knew it was going to be bad.

'My wife always says that it only happens to me when the arsehole in front of me reminds me of the arsehole inside of me—'

'Don't be such a pussy! I'm apologising. Things like that don't happen to me. Only when there's an arrogant twit like you standing in front of me. Then I can slip out of my role and—'

'That's unbelievable,' the presenter said, sounding truly incensed. 'That's the way the East Frisian police treats a famous journalist?'

'Yes,' Saskia Faust said, 'and now my father's dead. They have him on their conscience.'

'Now we need to be clear, that's just conjecture, after all, but—'

Saskia Faust interrupted the presenter. 'I'm not saying that the East Frisian police killed him. I'm just saying that the wrong people are investigating this case. They're basically sympathising with the killer. He did the dirty work for them. My father collected material against that detective Ann Kathrin Klaasen. She's a kind of icon in East Frisia. I don't know what my father came across, but the public won't ever find out now—'

The presenter played some more music.

Ann Kathrin stretched out on her seat as if she were in bed and had just woken from a nightmare. While doing so, she touched the roof with her hands.

Her phone barked. It was like an alarm, a relief for her. She answered at once.

It was Holger Bloem.

'Ann! That Saskia Faust is live on the radio.'

'Yeah, I know,' Ann Kathrin groaned.

'It's directed against you. They really twisted it around. Rupert insults her father and it's your fault. I'm just calling to say that you can count on me. Regardless of what happens now. If you need someone to advise you on how to deal with the press, then—' He backtracked immediately. 'Not that you couldn't do it yourself, but—'

'What should I do, Holger? React or dodge?'

'Those are the two exact possibilities I see. If you react immediately you'll just escalate it. Sometimes it can be the right move to let a cold shower drip. I bet it won't take long for them to start chasing their next idiot. Excuse my language. Alternatively, you start a counter-attack. For example, with a big interview in which you share what all this does to you and what it means to you. You have a lot of friends in East Frisia. People know you and value your work. More people will stick by you than you think. To many people, that Faust was just a scumbag—'

'Thanks, Holger. I really appreciate it. I really don't feel like a press conference or anything. We've got bigger fish to fry. I think everything will calm down as soon as we've caught the killer. If the police can't produce a guilty party, then people like to blame us.'

'I could do a feature on you for the *East Frisia* magazine, Ann. This country has plenty to thank you for. There'd still be a lot of criminals running around if it wasn't for you.'

'No thanks, Holger. I don't think even more publicity would be good for me right now. I have to concentrate on this case first. But it's nice to know that people like you are on my side.'

'Always, you can count on that. Loyalty isn't a foreign concept for East Frisians.'

'Thanks, Holger. Bye,' Ann Kathrin said, and Holger Bloem added, 'Keep your chin up, Ann!'

Ann Kathrin walked twice round the car. It was good for her to feel the ground beneath her feet.

Then her seal barked again. On the screen she saw that her son Eike wanted to talk to her. She was immediately touched. He'd probably heard the interview and wanted to comfort his mother. Even if they didn't see each other very often, in the last few years she felt as if there was a kind of emotional connection between the two of them. For that reason alone it was good to receive the call.

She greeted Eike pleasantly while doing a couple of knee bends in front of her green hatchback. A trucker drove past and honked, enjoying the view. She paid no attention.

'Eike, nice of you to call. How are you?'

'Mum, I messed up.'

'She immediately forgot her anger and focused on her son. 'What's up?'

He sounded upset. His voice was shaky. At first Ann Kathrin thought he might be having trouble with his girlfriend, the resident physician Rebekka Simon. She would have greatly regretted that because she liked the young lady. But then Eike burst out, 'I'm such an idiot! I just didn't pay attention to my bank account and let everything slide and now they want to cut off my electricity, and the bank has cancelled my credit card. I'm standing at the ATM. I just wanted to take out fifty euros but—'

Ann Kathrin deduced. 'It's about money.'

'Yeah, Mum.'

'How much?'

'About two-and-a-half, at the most three thousand. Can you help me out? I'll pay you back.'

'Of course I can.'

It was easy for her to help her son; it even felt good. She had enough savings, and her money was safe at the Credit Union in Aurich-Norden.

'Should we go to the bank together and talk to them? I'll sort it out and—'

'Mum, can't you just send me the money?'

She smiled. 'You think it's embarrassing to talk to the people at the bank, right? If you'd done that sooner, maybe you wouldn't be in this position. I can't just transfer money, I'm out and about. I'm not at home.'

'Don't you do Internet banking?'

'No, I still go up to the teller and fill out the transfer forms. I like it better that way. I don't trust all that computer stuff.'

'Oh, Mum, that can't be true! What century are you living in?'

'At least I have my account under control. A transfer wouldn't even help you. The money just haemorrhages out of your account.'

'But I need a little cash now, Mum.'

She didn't want to hear the excuses. 'I could bring something over. I'm driving towards Bremen. I could—'

'Oh, Mum, that'd be fantastic. Could we meet in Oldenburg, and you'll bring me the money?'

'Where should we meet, Eike? In a car park near the autobahn?'

Eike laughed. 'Yeah, that's typical Mum. Money handover in a car park near the autobahn? You really are a detective!'

She was in a hurry, but she wanted to clear some space for her son. 'We could also grab something to eat and then—'

'How much money do you have on you, Mum?'

'Who knows? I have to look. I'd guess a hundred, maybe a hundred and twenty euros.'

'Mum, this is really embarrassing, but that's not enough. I need at least three hundred in cash. Three hundred and fifty would be ideal.'

'Then let's meet in front of a bank. I have to withdraw some money anyway. At the branch on Alexanderstrasse?'

'Fabulous, Mum! I'll be there in a half hour.'

'She looked at her watch. 'I might need a little longer.'

'No problem, Mum. I'll wait there. I love you; I'm sending you a kiss, you're the best!'

She wanted to thank him for the kiss, but Eike had already hung up.

*

Rupert drove his car into the garage, unloaded the case of beer and hid the bottle of whisky under his jacket as he walked towards the front door – he knew Beate was monitoring his alcohol consumption critically.

Inside it smelled of incense sticks, which immediately made Rupert's throat itch. He thought that stuff was worse than any cigarette smoke and he hoped that burning of incense sticks in shops and living rooms would be banned, like smoking in bars.

And then she was standing in front of him, in a flattering, strawberry-hued dress made of some kind of fabric that was, he assumed, woven by virgins next to a bonfire at full moon while they recited poems.

Beate had advanced to the level of reiki master, and was drenched in light. As a matter of principle, Rupert dealt with all of this by not letting it get to him. But something about her face was off. She wasn't as relaxed as usual. Her left cheek twitched and her lips were very thin. And then his well-mannered wife gave him a resounding slap.

Rupert stood very calmly. He felt his cheek. He couldn't believe it. Had she really just smacked him?

He pulled the bottle of whisky out of his jacket. He would have liked nothing more than to unscrew the lid and take a sip immediately.

'How dare you talk rubbish about me?'

'What? I didn't say anything about you! Why would I? You think I run around the police station letting everyone in on what you and your witchy girlfriends get up to?'

Shit, Rupert thought, Agneta Meyerhoff was here. The stupid bitch was taking revenge, telling Beate some rubbish.

He'd cheated on his wife frequently, and this wasn't the first time that she'd found out. But he'd never seen her so angry.

She pulled back to hit him again. He ducked.

'I heard it on the radio! How could you say something like that? I never said that it only happens when the arsehole in front of you reminds you of the arsehole inside you. What I told you was from a continuing education seminar for nursery school teachers that I completed in Delmenhorst a couple of years ago: '*When the child in front of you reminds you of the child in you.*' It was all about how teachers sometimes can't handle a situation with a child because it reminds them of traumas from their own childhood. How could you use it in this way?'

Rupert didn't understand. 'You heard what on the radio? I don't give radio interviews. I—'

Then he saw Saskia Faust in front of him in the police station, holding up the Dictaphone.

'Oh, fuck,' he said, 'has she really done it?' And he collapsed. He sat on the stairs, the bottle of whisky loosely between his knees, his head hung low, and his face was like that of a beaten child.

And Beate immediately touched him again. For some reason she loved Rupert. She didn't know why. She had explained to her girlfriends that it must be an old, karmic relationship. Perhaps the two of them knew each other in another life. Perhaps he'd helped her out of a fix and now she still felt indebted to him. Perhaps they had been comrades in arms. Yes, she could easily picture Rupert as a knight in shining armour.

She placed her left hand on his neck and stroked it. Then she ran her hand through his curls and said, 'You probably didn't mean it that way, right?'

'That twit made me furious,' Rupert said, looking more as if he was talking to his bottle of whisky rather than his wife. 'I would have loved to knock him out of his suit, as he stood there so smugly. For them we're all just East Frisian idiots. Sometimes I don't know what I should say, and then I remembered that saying of yours.'

She grabbed his hair tighter and pulled his head back so that he had to look at her.

'Those aren't preschool sayings, those are important, psychological insights into the human soul.'

'Yes, I mean, yes.'

Beate sat down next to him on the stairs and he felt enveloped in her energy like in a cocoon. He'd have bitten his tongue bloody before he'd admitted it, but he felt safe. He laid his head on his wife's shoulder and she whispered. 'It's not even really directed at you. I don't think she even mentioned you. They're really after Ann Kathrin.'

Rupert was offended. If the press would at least have a go at him, then that'd be something. The more danger, the more honour, he thought. But no, regardless of how much he worked himself to death, in the end they went to Ann Kathrin Klaasen, and she raked in the rewards when a case was solved.

Professionally he felt like he was on a downward slope, but at least his wife didn't know anything about Agneta Meyerhoff.

He unscrewed the lid on the bottle of whisky and went to take a sip. It always looked so good went movie stars did that. He could remember legendary scenes with Bruce Willis or Nicolas Cage. They wore vests when they drank whisky from the bottle and seemed unbelievably manly. But none of them had a perm and let their wife scratch their neck.

Beate put a hand on his arm when he lifted the bottle. 'That won't help,' she said. 'But I could treat you to reiki.'

'Can't I have both?' he asked, willing to compromise.

'I don't think that's good for you.'

'Oh, please, just a little sip.'

'You have to know for yourself what's good for you.'

As he drank from the bottle, she said, 'You look like a little boy sucking on a bottle of milk, but would prefer to have Mummy's breast.'

Rupert choked and spluttered a couple swigs of whisky through the bannisters. He asked himself if Bruce Willis, Nicolas Cage or his heroes Humphrey Bogart and James Bond, played by Sean Connery, ever had to hear such things. Surely not, he thought. What is the world coming to?

Beate hugged him and murmured. 'If you want to cry, you can let your tears flow. Crying is liberating.'

Oh man, Rupert thought. It was only a small step from action hero to crybaby. But by no stretch of the imagination did he want to leave.

*

David Weissberg sat by the fireplace in the romantic Menzhausen hotel with his wife Bianca, who was ten years younger than himself. He loved having breakfast in these comfortable armchairs rather than on hard ones. A spot just for two. The fire blazed.

It was just before twelve. A late riser's breakfast!

The coffee tasted good, the boiled eggs were just the way he liked them. Hard on the outside and with soft yolks.

He was already on his third egg. He had read that eating more eggs in the morning and less bread kept you fit and trim. Looking at his beautiful wife, he wanted to stay fit for a long time.

They'd married in this hotel. They'd met in Uslar, a little town in the Weser Uplands, and had fallen in love with the place, not just with each other. There were still cobblestones here. The streets gave you the feeling that the post would still be delivered by horse and carriage.

There were massages available in the hotel and everything was calm. Although several shops were empty on Langenstrasse, when the market stalls were opened up they filled the place with a peculiar charm.

David Weissberg and his wife Bianca were very fond of the good life. They only travelled first class and only stayed at good hotels. They didn't really have to watch their spending, but despite or maybe precisely because of that they were planning to eat soup at a café belonging to the local food bank. That's also what they'd done on their first date.

Naturally they wanted to give a good donation. Whoever ate there was supporting the food bank's work, and Bianca was emphatically of the opinion that people who were doing well had a responsibility for those who weren't having such a good time.

David Weissberg ordered another coffee. He intended to leave a generous fifty euros at the soup stand of the food bank because that was the way to his wife's heart. She couldn't stand stinginess or narrow-mindedness.

They'd had a wonderful night and there were still another two days awaiting them at the romantic spa hotel. They'd booked massages and wanted to go to the sauna that evening. The large bathtub in their bedroom was also beckoning. Bianca loved bubble baths.

David Weissberg stretched out his feet and felt like a million dollars. He didn't sense that his death had already been decided and that his killer had just parked behind the hotel.

*

He didn't need the parking sensors, but he didn't know how to turn off that annoying beeping sound that was telling him: 'Careful, there's a wall behind you.'

He had heard the same news that had made Ann Kathrin Klaasen furious, but he laughed bitterly.

A five thousand euro donation to the child protection association! Well, that's what I call a punishment! You certainly took drastic measures this time! How about giving him a bouquet and a box of chocolates? Perhaps you could fund a couple of hours of therapy? Just keep it up, the killer thought. I'll be working as executor for a will before you fools can catch me.

He suddenly had the feeling of having lots of time, and even if they did catch him one day, the people would elect him chancellor before they'd agree to convict him. Public opinion would shift soon enough and then they'd all be on his side.

You, David Weissberg, will be next.

He drummed out the rhythm from a crime show theme tune on his steering wheel.

No, he wouldn't take him to Emden and stick him in jail. The drive was too long. Too much could happen. The cops might set up roadblocks. He didn't want someone else to take the credit for his work.

*

Eike was continually astonished by his mother. He watched as she withdrew money for him from the bank's ATM. He'd almost forgotten, even though he'd grown up with it. She was talking to the ATM as if she were dealing with a nice, but slightly dull-witted human.

'Yes, my PIN. Wait. Zero seven zero seven – oh no, wrong, that's my birthday.' She laughed, as if she were joking with the machine. 'But that is the code for my phone. I have a different number for you. People shouldn't always use the same PIN code. I have Eike's birthday for you.' She turned around and smiled at him. 'At least that way I don't forget it.'

'You're afraid you'll forget my birthday?'

'No, Eike! My PIN. A mother would never forget her child's birthday.'

He hoped she wouldn't start retelling the whole story of his birth again. He knew it by heart. Back then on Juist, in winter, four weeks too early, and a helicopter had to come because there were complications.

Typical of my mother. She doesn't do normal, he thought. At least some stress and fuss had to be involved. Why just have a home birth when you could have a helicopter?

She typed in the number and withdrew five hundred euros. Eike hadn't asked her for so much cash, but she first thanked the ATM, then she gave Eike all of it. He was glad, but at the same time he emphasised that it wasn't necessary.

She suggested they go for a coffee together, but to him it sounded half-hearted, and he feared he would have to explain how and why he'd got into this stupid situation.

'You're probably in a hurry,' he guessed.

She shrugged her shoulders and nodded simultaneously. That meant: unfortunately yes. I'd prefer it wasn't so, but that's the way it is.

'Are you chasing another stupid killer?'

'Yes, but I'm afraid he's not stupid, as you put it. He's highly intelligent, but unfortunately mentally ill. And he's already selected a new victim.'

'Well then, I don't want to keep you waiting, Mum. I know what it's like. My mum is always busy saving the world.'

'Nice that you see it that way, Eike.' She held him by the shoulders, looked him in the eyes, and asked, 'Are you OK? Are you happy?'

He grinned inside. Yeah, that's exactly how she is: my mother. She doesn't just casually ask like other people. *'Hey, how's it goin'?'* No, she really wants to know. He laughed at her. 'Yes, Mum, I'm happy with Rebekka. She's a wonderful woman. Has a lot of you in her. She doesn't catch any killers, but as a doctor, she tracks down and fights illnesses, without mercy.'

Ann Kathrin regarded this as a huge compliment. She kissed her son.

They were still standing in front of the ATM when a large man wearing a peaked cap asked, 'Would you mind if I . . .'

The two of them made some space and apologised. Minutes later, Ann Kathrin left the car park in her rickety green hatchback. Eike watched her go. As if she couldn't afford a new car. He knew it was a question of loyalty for his mother. He recalled the last few minutes. My mother, he thought, had thanked the ATM more convincingly than I thanked her.

He was a little ashamed by the thought, but he knew that he was simply glad that she'd helped him. In a way, he'd even done her a slight favour with his request for financial support. Now she felt good. Needed as a mother.

*

Svenja Moers lay on the damp bed. Her clothes clung to her body and her breathing was flat and sounded as if air was being pushed through a narrow pipe. Her body was ravaged by a high fever.

Everything inside her resisted the thought of having to die there. She wanted to survive. But her strength was dwindling. She didn't know how long she'd been alone. When had she last seen him? Was it hours? Or days? What is time if you're living in a room without an outside world?

She wished so much that he'd turn on the radio again. They'll probably, yes certainly, be looking for me by now, she convinced herself. They've surely already reconstructed my last few days. It's certain that Agneta would have told them that I got a lift home with Yves Stern because my bike had been stolen. Or hadn't Agneta caught that? She's hot to trot for him . . . Surely they'll talk to everyone in the class. I was last seen in Emden on Wednesday. Is that a week ago? Or more? Has the class taken place without me? Have I been forgotten? Is he after his next victim? Maybe even Agneta?

She began to shake. Her legs jerked back and forth on the bed, as if someone were sending little electric shocks through them.

His name wasn't even Yves Stern, she thought. Of course not. He'd planned everything long in advance. He'd registered for the class using the fake name and it's certain that his address wasn't right either. Which is why no one has found me. I'm lost. Completely and utterly at his mercy.

At least she had water. The basin was still full.

Her dry, chapped lips hurt. They were covered in small bloody cuts. She would have liked nothing better than to plunge her head into the basin, but at the moment she didn't have enough energy to get out of bed.

The spasms in her legs subsided.

Dear God, let him make a mistake so they catch him! I don't want to die here! Not now. Not like this.

*

David Weissberg made him furious. All day long he'd been all over his Bianca. Couldn't they ever be apart? Such symbiotic relationships were simply not conducive to an execution.

He hadn't planned to kill Bianca too. Yes, it was about David, but how could he spare her if she was always stuck to him?

First the two of them participated in a historic city tour, holding hands, and then they took a stroll through the museum district. It occurred to him that they would probably go to the Potash Mining Museum and the butterfly park.

When they then went to the park, he was almost at the point where he'd happily kill her too. How idiotic love must make you, he thought, driven by hate, if it can bring you to walk barefoot over a forest floor, over colourful balls, squealing with glee when you feel the tilled soil under your feet. Being in love, he thought, is a form of insanity, and he was glad that he had been spared that fate.

Cheery Bianca didn't know that the man next to her had murdered his brother because he'd resisted the sale of the pharmacy and the two rental houses in Aurich and Esens.

At the time, Ubbo had even presented a signed confession from David Weissberg. But a clever lawyer and a psychological assessment had made an innocent person of David Weissberg, who in an emotionally stressful situation had supposedly been put under such great pressure by Ubbo Heide that he ultimately confessed to a murder he'd never committed. Everything was blamed on the big, anonymous burglar who, according to Ubbo Heide, had never even existed.

In his retelling in the book, Ubbo Heide had called David Weissberg 'Mr Silver Fox'. That was a sign from heaven. When he'd read that name, he knew that he had to do it for his mother. In her honour! She so enjoyed wearing that silver fox jacket. An heirloom. But by the mid-nineties she hadn't dared to wear it on the street, because of animal rights activists.

He reached inside his pocket and let his hand run over the bushy fur. He'd cut a piece out of the collar. He'd put it in David Weissberg's mouth. Once he was dead.

Ubbo Heide would get the message, and the source of the silver fox would be impossible to trace. His grandfather had purchased it in 1914 for sixty gold marks. At the time it was a fortune, as everyone in the family claimed, again and again. The piece had been hanging in his mother's wardrobe for twenty-five years.

The fur smelled a little musty, and would soon find a function as a bloody message to Ubbo Heide.

Now the couple were kissing. He could hardly stand it. They were acting like teenagers. Terrible! How could adults make such spectacles of themselves, he thought.

But as annoying as it was, the embarrassing smooching was saving Mr Silver Fox's life.

I'll get you. Just wait, I'll get you!

He stayed at least fifty metres behind the lovebirds, and when they bought ice creams, he looked at his phone to check on Svenja Moers. She lay lifeless on the bed staring at the ceiling.

'Perhaps,' he said, as if he were talking to her on the phone, 'perhaps I should have left some provisions in the cell. This is taking longer than I thought. Hold on, Svenja. Don't let go now. As soon as this Bianca leaves her David alone for a second, I'll carry out the sentence and come back to you. I could cook us spaghetti. A few carbs wouldn't be too bad right now, would they? But it's three or four hours from Uslar to Emden, baby. I don't think I'll get it done today. As long as they're kissing, you'll stay hungry.'

*

Ann Kathrin parked her hatchback right in front of the Bootshaus Hotel, between two black BMWs. Inside, she had a coffee and looked out at the Ueser Marina and the River Weser. She wanted to lose some weight so she ordered asparagus salad with crayfish tails and walnut oil.

Two men were engrossed in a conversation at the next table. They both wore light-blue summer suits. One of them sat with his back to Ann Kathrin, the other couldn't concentrate on the conversation, but constantly stared over at her instead. At first he only smiled in her direction, then he winked.

She thoroughly enjoyed his attention but when she stood up and walked past him to get a newspaper she pointed out her wedding ring. The papers on offer were *Die Welt*, *Achimer Kreisblatt* and the *Achimer Kurier*. Ann Kathrin trusted the local papers more than the national broadsheets. She looked in the *Achimer Kurier*. Before her asparagus with crayfish tails was brought from the kitchen, she had found a report that provoked her interest. Volker Janssen was mentioned.

He wrote poems. His first self-published collection had just appeared. The sixty-four-page collection was called *Goethe Is Dead, Schiller Is Dead, and I Already Feel Terrible.*

She looked at the picture. Was this the same man? He'd moved to Achim to start a new life. Janssen is a popular surname in Northern Germany. Did he really become a poet?

She googled him with her phone and although he didn't have a website, there was a review of his book. He hadn't done too badly. There was talk of a new, fresh tone in poetry.

Ann Kathrin enjoyed her meal, let the sun shine on her face and did some relaxation exercises after eating. She made her right arm heavy, and then her left.

The man on the next table got really nervous because he couldn't understand what she was up to.

She felt the rays of sunlight on her skin and imagined the sun's energy was wandering through her entire body and reanimating it.

When she got up, she stretched and yawned as if after a long, restful sleep.

Both men stared at her as she left.

She drove into the city centre and went to the Hoffmann bookstore. There she looked at the children's books, and when Veit Hoffmann spoke to her and asked if he could be of help, she immediately found him likable.

'I'm interested in a poet,' Ann Kathrin said. 'He's just published his first book with a funny title.' She acted as if she had to think.

'Volker Janssen. *Goethe Is Dead, Schiller Is dead, and I Already Feel Terrible*?'

'Yeah, exactly. Can I get a copy from you?'

'Sure. You can get everything from me except a map of Achim that isn't available anymore.'

He took the book from the shelf. 'Volker Janssen brought me a couple of copies. He doesn't have a publisher, does it all himself. His poetry is funny and completely original, but he himself is much more reserved. I wanted to organise a reading with him. He lives here in Achim, on Breslaustrasse. I think he inherited the little house from his grandma. Most of the houses there were built after the war for former refugees from the East.'

'Is there going to be a reading?'

Veit Hoffmann shrugged his shoulders.

'An author who avoids his audience?' Ann Kathrin asked.

'There are many of those. Salinger, Patrick Susskind—'

He wanted to list more, but Ann Kathrin said, 'That's too bad. I would've liked to have him sign my book. So that won't happen.'

'Unless you meet him here by chance.'

'Does he sometimes shop with you?'

'Sure, he doesn't just write poetry, he reads it too. And yesterday he bought tickets for the concert at Kasch.'

'What kind of concert?'

'Tonight. Iontach. A German-Irish group. My wife and I are going too.'

Ann Kathrin could hardy imagine a better way to get close to Volker Janssen.

'Are there tickets left?'

'Yeah, a couple.'

Ann Kathrin bought the book and a ticket, which he was also selling. Then she drove through the city. She looked at the big residential towers in the Magdeburg district before parking on Bergstrasse and exploring the neighbourhood on foot. The area between Gaudenzerstrasse, Allensteiner and Bergstrasse reminded her of the mining districts in Gelsenkirchen-Ückendorf.

*

Odysseus felt like an omniscient being again now that he had decided to kill Wilhelm Kaufmann. It was a wonderful feeling! It was itching under his skin.

Anyone who looked at him would think he was a normal person – he could be a teacher, a shop manager, or even a lifeguard. But he was something completely different, something that would terrify them — if they could see the entirety of his personality.

The final battle would take place on Langeoog. He knew this like he knew that autumn would come after summer. Where everything had begun.

Odysseus took the ferry from Bensersiel to Langeoog. He had the Langeoog Card, which also served as a ticket, in his jacket pocket next to the lethal capsule he'd bought in Thailand. It gave him the freedom to do everything he wanted.

A person who was prepared to leave this life at any time if something went wrong was truly free. He didn't cling to life; at least that was what he believed.

The warm wind was good. He consciously put himself in the airstream. He'd booked a place in a central location, in the spa district, close to the salt water pool and less than ten minutes' walk from the beach. He would rent a bicycle and would feel like the king of the island on his two-wheeled steed.

The closer he got to Langeoog, the more certain he became that the showdown was looming.

He climbed out of the island train. He walked the few minutes from the station in the town centre to the Island Roaster. Time seemed to have stopped in the little café, during a short, peaceful phase when the world was completely in order. If there had ever been such a moment, it was preserved here.

But there was nothing better than the smell here. He could sit and just breathe and take in the world.

He ordered a large coffee. Black.

Come on, he thought, and clicked his tongue. Come to Langeoog, Kaufmann. Come to die. I'll take care of you before you can behead me.

In fact, Wilhelm Kaufmann had been there for a while. He was walking barefoot by the sea, his shoes and socks in his left hand, his trouser legs rolled up to his knees. The tips of the waves licked his toes like cold tongues. The sand under his soles was still warm from the sun.

*

David Weissberg had enjoyed the day with Bianca in the spa in Uslar. He wanted to go in the sauna with her before dinner, but she wasn't quite ready. First she wanted to lie down for a while and talk to her mother.

David decided he didn't need to be there for that. Bianca only did one round in the sauna anyway, while he preferred two or three. He stuffed the fluffy hotel bathrobe into a sports bag and went ahead.

Lying on the bed, Bianca pushed a plump pillow under her back and dialled her mother's number. David blew her a kiss. Although he felt good, it was for the last time in his life. He'd only be alive for a few more minutes.

His annual physical check-up had brought good news. Although nearly sixty, from a medical perspective he was years younger, more like a forty-year-old. He was planning a huge party for his sixtieth birthday.

He wouldn't make it.

His murderer was already waiting in the sauna as he showered. He had overheard their short conversation in the café. 'I have to call my mother. You go ahead to the sauna.'

He had briefly considered entering the sauna fully clothed, stabbing David Weissberg, and then disappearing again. But then he changed his mind. He waited for David, naked and sweating, with the knife and the piece of silver fox fur lying next to him, wrapped in a white towel.

His body was already covered with sweat. He liked it. He enjoyed waiting here. It was like a ritual preperation for the execution.

Perhaps he should always do it that way, he thought. He needed rituals; otherwise everything would become so mundane. Of course he couldn't wait in a sauna for everyone chosen to die, but he could purify himself beforehand and proceed clean and clear to the deed. Perhaps David Weissberg wouldn't come alone; then he would use this round in the sauna as preparation and delay the execution until a later time.

*

There was even Irish beer at Kasch, and the guitarist, Jens Kommnick, tuned his guitar so gently that several thought the concert had already begun and gave him a spontaneous round of applause.

Ann Kathrin greeted Veit Hoffmann and his wife Iris. The two of them bought the musician a beer and pointed out Volker Janssen, who was looking a little lonely and lost in the crowd, holding his Guinness tightly.

Ann Kathrin walked over and spoke to him. She said she'd bought his volume of poetry and wanted an autograph.

He was standing very straight and still. A whiff of garlic surrounded him, and although he seemed shy, there was something in his gaze that she didn't like. She suddenly felt naked. Normally she would have asked him to dress her again after he'd undressed her without asking, but she didn't tonight. She thanked him for the autograph and asked if he was planning to keep on writing.

The hint of a smile flitted across his face. 'Will you,' he replied, 'keep on breathing tomorrow?'

'So writing is like breathing to you?'

He nodded. Then he brought his mouth very close to her right ear and whispered, 'I could paint your favourite poem very slowly on your naked body.'

He took a step back and stared at her, as if trying to inhale her reaction.

She tried to stay cool and tolerate his gaze.

'Believe me, it's a very special, highly erotic experience,' he promised.

'Are you usually successful with your offers to women or do most of them end up punching you?' she asked.

*

When David Weissberg entered the sauna he greeted the only other guest and sat on his towel opposite. He tried a little small talk but only received very curt responses.

When he saw the blade he flung both arms high in the air. But he in no way surrendered to his fate.

He tried to survive.

David Weissberg dodged the first thrust and could do nothing but grab for the blade. It went straight through his right palm. There was so much adrenaline coursing through his body that he didn't feel the pain.

He kicked his attacker in the shin and yelled. 'Are you crazy?'

The tall, thin man attacked David Weissberg's neck. He thrust firmly but Weissberg turned away and the blade hit his jawbone and slipped off.

Weissberg collapsed. His killer bent over him, thrust the knife into his heart and stuffed the silver fox fur between his lips.

Weissberg's blood had decorated the stomach and face of his murderer with tell tale red. He washed away the other man's blood in the shower, carefully cleaned the blade, got dressed, and left the sauna without being discovered.

*

A scent of jasmine and mango hinted at wellness and relaxation. When Bianca Weissberg joined her husband in the sauna after a rather unpleasant telephone conversation with her sick mother, she collapsed to the floor, screaming.

*

By then, the executioner was already on his way back. The radio was at full volume and he was singling along to 'Knocking on Heaven's Door.' The news came on after the Guns N' Roses cover of a Bob Dylan song.

The DJ with the gentle voice and the slight Franconian accent announced the horrors as if they were truisms: according to the *Washington Post*, the FBI and the Department of Justice had examined 268 trials in which FBI forensics had provided a DNA or hair analysis. In ninety-five percent of all cases they were wrong or at least very unreliable.

Thirty-two convicts had been sentenced to death on the basis of incorrect lab results, and fourteen had already been executed.

He slammed the steering wheel in fury. 'Sure,' he yelled, 'you think we don't know why you're announcing this shit? It's a huge propaganda show on the part of death penalty opponents! Now we're even supposed to feel sorry for those fuckers!'

Sandra Droege commented on these findings. She spoke of the greatest scandal ever for the US criminal justice system and accused the judges of being so uncritical of lab investigations having often watched the popular television series *CSI*. She claimed pencil pen-pushers and lab rats had been irresponsibly turned into movie heroes, and the nearly religious belief in those reports led to this devastating situation.

'And you don't say how many criminals have gone free due to incorrect analysis! Typical! You pack of liars!'

He screamed with such fury that foam from his mouth flew onto the windscreen. It slowly rolled down, leaving a trail of slime.

Sandra Droege now said that these findings would revive the debate about the death penalty. Innocent prisoners could now simply be released, false convictions reversed, but the dead couldn't be resurrected.

'Shut up!' he shouted, and turned off the radio.

Just after passing the city limit sign in Uslar he stopped and looked for Svenja Moers on his phone.

The way she looked scared him. He didn't want to be seen as someone who had let a prisoner starve.

How long could a person survive without food? At least he had provided her with water, but she looked sick. Did she need medication? Maybe he'd gone too far with the heat in her cell.

He didn't want to be unjust and cause a needless death. Life in prison was her sentence. But such a sentence only worked for people who had sufficient life expectancy ahead of them.

His GPS suggested a route via the A7, but he assumed there would be roadworks before Hanover and Bremen, which is why he intuitively chose a different way, via Osnabrück, Rheine and Lingen.

In contrast to his usual habits, he didn't pay attention to speed limits. He didn't usually like getting caught on camera and didn't like to attract attention by violating traffic laws. But at that moment he didn't care.

Hold on, Svenja, he thought. I'm coming! And he felt like a knight in shining armour.

*

Weller was looking forward to his evening at home. He'd purchased a herring sandwich at Weissig's shop, which was more than enough for his evening meal. He needed a couple of hours to himself. He knew himself very well. He became unbearable if he didn't get the chance to sink into a good crime novel from time to time.

Basically he needed three things in life: the feeling of being loved, a couple of chapters of exciting literature and at least once a week a herring or prawn sandwich – he called it 'East Frisian sushi' – then he was a happy and satisfied man.

Two crime novels were awaiting him, and a third, by Moa Graven, was lying in his letter box. The book had a dedication to him: *Have fun reading and thank you!*

Weller remembered. A couple of months ago a young author had called and asked questions as research for her new novel. She wanted an accurate picture of police work. That alone pleased him. He enjoyed answering her questions.

He opened a bottle of red wine and placed all three books on the arm of his reading chair: Moa Graven's *Pub Children*, *Shadow Oath* by Nané Lénard and *Murderous Monaco* by Jule Gölsdorf. Three crime novels by three women.

He was looking forward to a nice evening and grabbed two cushions. One for his back and one for his feet. Once he was comfortable, he considered reading the first sentence of each book and then deciding which one he would start. He loved first sentences! He even collected them. He had collected the best ones in a small black notebook.

He opened *Shadow Oath*, and just then his phone rang. He reached for it and immediately regretted the decision because Büscher was on the phone.

'He's struck again.'

'Well great,' Weller said, 'and I'd almost read the first sentence.'

'Huh? What?'

'Oh, nothing. Where did he strike?' Weller set the wine glass on the pile of books and lifted himself out of the chair.

'Somewhere in southern Germany. The name of the place is Uslar or something like that.'

'Uslar is in the Weser Uplands, not in southern Germany. It's in Lower Saxony!'

'Yeah, that's what I mean.'

Weller groaned. He had pictured a completely different evening. 'Who's the victim?'

'A certain David Weissberg. He was stabbed to death in the sauna.'

Weller focused his mind and hoped he would still have time for his red wine, his crime novels and his fish sandwich.

'That can't be our man. There's no David Weissberg in Ubbo's book.'

Büscher sounded strangely excited, almost asthmatic. 'I'll remind you of Faust. He wasn't a character in Ubbo's goddamn book!'

'Yes,' Weller said, 'but we all know him. I don't know any Weasel.'

'Weissberg!'

Weller sipped his red wine. It was a little heavy, but maybe just the thing to calm him down.

Weller tried to stop Büscher. 'I don't know a Weissberg either. I don't think it's anything to do with us.'

'But Ubbo Heide knew him. He almost went crazy when I mentioned Weissberg. Ubbo investigated him.'

'Crap!' Weller put his wine glass back down. 'That would mean that the culprit actually does come from our ranks because this case isn't described in Ubbo's book.'

Weller's own deduction hit him in the stomach.

'Or the murders have nothing to do with each other and it's all a coincidence,' Büscher said.

Weller could picture Ann Kathrin in front of him, how she would have reacted to that suggestion. He'd often heard the phrase *'I don't believe in coincidences and especially not of this sort,'* from her.

Weller quickly ended the conversation with Büscher and called Ann Kathrin.

*

Ann Kathrin Klaasen had put her phone on silent during the concert. She was listening to the music.

Volker Janssen sat two rows in front of her. Veit Hoffmann and his wife Iris were seated next to Ann and were sipping their drinks. Veit Hoffmann noticed that Ann Kathrin perceived her environment very precisely. She was interested in people who came close to Volker Janssen or even looked at him from a distance. This was more than mere interest in a poet. But for Veit,

Ann Kathrin didn't look as if she was in love. Her interest in Volker Janssen was different.

Perhaps, Veit thought, she was a private detective checking him out. There was supposedly – according to the rumours – trouble surrounding the inheritance.

Ann Kathrin had just come to get a good impression of Volker Janssen and his environment. But she liked the music from Iontach. She caught herself dreaming of Ireland.

She warned herself not to close her eyes now. From her perspective, Volker Janssen was the ideal next victim, and she played with the thought of how long it would take until the man who called himself the executioner would get Volker Janssen or one of the two witnesses.

Perhaps, Ann Kathrin thought, he's already here in this room. The killer had struck again with extraordinary speed. In her experience, serial killers often shortened the time between their crimes. Sometimes ten, fifteen years went by between the first and the second murders. Then the spaces became shorter and shorter.

Here she was dealing with a man who was under tremendous pressure and acted quickly. Bernhard Heymann. Yves Stern. Svenja Moers. Joachim Faust . . .

She pictured a restless person who believed he had to fulfill a task. Perhaps he heard voices, was motivated by inner pressure, or was afraid he'd soon be caught, and wanted to do as much as possible before then.

Some killers were glad when they were finally caught and everything came to an end. They left signs, whether consciously or unconsciously, for the investigators, so that they could better find them.

Had her killers also done something like that long ago? And had she overlooked something?'

He wants us to see connections. He wants us to know that it was him and not anyone else. That's why he had enrolled for the cooking class as Yves Stern. So we had to make the connection. To be completely certain, he sent us the pictures. He wants us to connect one crime to the next. He's proud of what he does.

She let herself be carried away by the music. It was as if the notes took her thoughts away.

She pictured Wilhelm Kaufmann disguised as an old woman.

Sometimes, she thought, he actually does have some feminine traits. He could be hard, but once in a while she had perceived a softer side.

Was he a master of disguise? If he was in the room, he would have noticed her long ago and retreated.

Her thoughts drifted. While her eyes searched the room, she began internally to consider whether she should delay the start of her new diet. She hadn't wanted to eat any more carbohydrates after six o'clock, but Veit Hoffmann had recommended an Italian restaurant. It was called Da Vito. She got hungry for spaghetti the way he had talked about it.

She thought of Weller when she had told him about her new diet and had wanted to motivate him to participate: he'd asked her with a grin, 'How do the carbs know how late it is?'

She liked his ironic way of handling things. Sometimes he acted much more stupid than he was, and the way he came to the point by asking questions – was that typically East Frisian?

During the interval she went to the ladies and checked her phone. Weller had tried to contact her with all available means of communication.

She had several text messages, simultaneous WhatsApp messages, emails, a Facebook message and two missed calls. Either he missed her greatly or something bad had happened. Probably both, she thought, and he was only using the case to get in touch. The thought flattered her a little.

But after she'd read the messages, she knew that she wouldn't spend the night in Achim and wouldn't visit Da Vito.

Good for my diet, she thought.

She paced back and forth in front of the door and called Weller. Should she come back to Norden or drive straight to Uslar?

Instead, she decided to talk to Ubbo Heide first. Somehow everything came back to him.

*

Odysseus wasn't at all the type who sat drinking at a bar for a long time. No, after just a little while he had already begun to feel uncomfortable, observed, even stalked. His therapist, who unfortunately had to die because he knew too much, had told him at the time that it had been his guilty conscience. The therapist claimed that others would sense his thoughts or even hear them, as if they were being broadcast across the room with a loudspeaker.

Psychobabble. He was simply someone who wandered about. He never stayed longer than one or two beers.

He liked to think of himself as a *flaneur*, not someone who was on the run in fear. Sometimes he actually forced himself to remain seated, play the role of the cool guy and have another drink. But then his bladder went crazy. He had to go to the gents.

He noticed that his gaze nervously swept around the room, studying everyone and wondering whether or not they knew.

He went into Dwarslooper intending to sprawl out on one of the cool pieces of furniture around the bar and have at least two draught beers. He wasn't hungry. When he was like he was now, he felt like a predator on the hunt, just about to pounce, ripping his prey to pieces.

The alcohol slightly damped his pugnacity – helped him to bridge the time until the prey appeared – and simultaneously made him courageous. But when he was sitting there and sipping his first beer, it was hard for him to look relaxed. He would have so liked to lounge around like the others.

Everyone seemed to have time on this island – as though time didn't really exist. Bad for someone who felt as driven as him. Nowhere else was this contradiction clearer to him than on the island. Stress was something for people from the mainland, for the big city. It belonged here as much as cholera or the plague.

Suddenly he began to doubt himself. He caught himself holding his hands in front of his face, as if he wanted to scratch his nose or wipe something out of his eyes. The fury directed inwards came with the shame and simultaneously the doubt.

Maybe I should just take the lethal pill here and end it all. Now is as good as any other time. I'm in control. Me!

He asked himself why he was so sure that he would meet Wilhelm Kaufmann here. His mind rebelled. It was always like this. His mind fought against his feelings, against his intuition. But in the end, something that was older than reason won out, even older than humanity. There was something reptilian inside him.

His skin felt dry, like a parched, callous material. He breathed with his mouth open, and would have preferred to walk on all fours. He felt lizard-like. Oh yes, he was familiar with those feelings.

In his mind's eye he saw himself as a moray eel. How did the animal, in its cave, know that prey would come by? How did it have the certainty?

Yes, that's the way he wanted to feel now, when he was sitting here: like an evil, poisonous predatory fish in the coral reef that is looking forward to food, and not like a sexual offender who fears being discovered and uses alcohol to fight the fear of the Devil. He felt comfortable as a moray eel.

He didn't speak with anyone. He didn't read a book. He just sat there and drank, his third beer already. He was able to sit tight as a moray. He was proud of himself.

No, he didn't want to go to the gents. He just ignored it. His bladder had to follow his orders, not the other way around. He wanted to sit here and play the role of relaxed holidaymaker, without ever in his life having experienced how that really felt: leaving his cares behind. He watched the cheerful Vietnamese waiter.

And then the door actually opened and he came in: Wilhelm Kaufmann.

Odysseus looked at his glass of beer. Was it a hallucination? Had he drunk his mind to smithereens? Or was that really Wilhelm Kaufmann, and once again there was evidence that his intuition was far, far wiser and more perceptive than his mind ever would be.

He looked at Wilhelm Kaufmann in astonishment and thought derisively: what have you contributed to humanity? This whole, goddamn, self-destructive civilisation is steered by reason. Reason is needed to solve a mathematical problem or do your tax return, but not to eat and not even to digest anything. And intuition helps with the hunt.

He wanted to become what he had once been: voracious and vicious. Shake off all the filth of civilisation, return to the source of his being.

As if he hadn't noticed Odysseus, Kaufmann walked to the bar, casually leaned on it and ordered a beer and a shot of sea buckthorn liqueur.

Odysseus heard his mind telling him, 'Men who drink liqueur can't be dangerous. You can take him easily.'

But his intuition told him something else. Be careful, he knows that you're watching him. He just wants you to think he's harmless. Normally he would have ordered a double shot of something at least forty percent proof, but he wants to keep his wits about him. He wants the duel to take place today.

Did I come here to look for him, Odysseus asked himself, or did he come to find me? He remembered a movie with the Three Musketeers. Someone hit d'Artagnan with a glove and demanded satisfaction for an insult. They arranged to meet in a park.

This was exactly the same.

Duels had already been banned back then, but he and Wilhelm Kaufmann would stick to this ban just as little as the Three Musketeers had. And resist the rest of the world if necessary.

We won't exchange any words here, Odysseus thought. When he leaves, I will follow. And today one of us will die.

*

Ann Kathrin talked with Ubbo on speakerphone while steering the car towards the autobahn.

'Can you explain it, Ubbo?'

She heard Carola's voice in the background. His wife was talking insistently to him. She was wanting to calm him, but sounded terribly nervous herself.

Ubbo's voice was so distressed, even shaky, that Ann Kathrin could hardly recognise her former boss. 'Ann, they found something in the mouth of the corpse. They said it was a piece of fur. They don't know any more. And I'm afraid that it is a fox fur.'

'Why do you think that, Ubbo?'

'My new book begins with the David Weissberg case. I call him Mr Silver Fox.'

Confused, Ann Kathrin asked, 'Yes, but your new book hasn't even been published. Were there any previews or anything like that?'

'No, Ann Kathrin, there's nothing like that. And I also stopped the publication. It won't ever appear.'

'But that would mean the killer knows your manuscript.'

'Wilhelm Kaufmann knows that I was working on that case. He was even at the trial back then.'

'What?'

'He was always there when things got tough. He was traumatised by this case. He was often in court when we had to testify and the accused's clever lawyer labelled us as idiots who hadn't done our work properly. When those big failures weighed down on us. At least for those people he liked. He sat in the back three times for me while I was being grilled.'

Ann Kathrin turned on her hazard lights, stopped in the middle of the street and got out of her car. She could think better when she walked. This was the case with telephone calls, not just interrogations.

The starry sky above her was clear. A cat yowled somewhere. It almost sounded like a baby's cry.

'Does Wilhelm Kaufmann know that you called Weissberg a fox in your book?'

'Silver fox.'

'Does he know that?'

'No, Ann, I don't think anyone knows.'

'Someone always knows something, Ubbo. I learned that from you. Nothing can ever truly remain secret. Who read your manuscript? Who typed it? You write longhand, right?'

'Yes, I always wrote in a notebook with a fountain pen.'

'And then?'

'Then Carola typed it up. Insa also did a couple of passages because Carola wasn't feeling well. We'd lent Insa money and she wanted to be nice to us. But the two of them are above reproach.'

Ann Kathrin said, 'Yeah, sure. As suspects. But not as informants. Where did your manuscript go then, Ubbo?'

'I printed it out for myself and sent a digital copy to my publisher.'

'And then?'

'Well, I have an editor there who was very excited. She wrote me an unbelievably nice email. She is smart and well read. She protected me from some mistakes or imprecise wording that could be misunderstood.'

'If you sent it digitally, then we have no clue how many copies there are. Maybe she sent it around to friends, acquaintances and fans of yours, to journalists – good Lord!'

'You have to follow up on this, Ann. I think the killer has made a mistake.'

'He doesn't make mistakes, Ubbo. He wants to surprise us. He wants to show us how powerful he is. That's exactly the way it was with the keys to your car. He wants to prove that he can get inside anywhere, has access to your private space. Now even your manuscript.'

'What are you planning, Ann?'

She took a deep breath of evening air. The air wasn't salty enough for her here. The wind blew over the smell of horse manure.

She had the urge to drive to the coast. But she said, 'I think it's time to officially issue a warrant for Wilhelm Kaufmann. We've lost him. And I'll also drive over to your publisher.'

'Should I come along?'

She wanted to make it easier for him and said, 'No, that's not necessary,' but he insisted.

'Ann, please, don't exclude me now. Let me come along. I know the people there. I know the game. And I know the rules.'

'No, Ubbo, I fear that this time neither of us knows the rules. At least not the ones the killer plays by.'

'We have to force him to play by our rules, Ann. Then we'll get him.'

'I'm getting back into the car now, Ubbo. I don't want to lose any time.'

'Wait, Ann!'

'Is there something on your mind?'

'Yeah. Is it really necessary to put out a warrant for Wilhelm Kaufmann? Can't we just try to find him and then . . . maybe he's just in Brake. We know where he lives. We know his friends. We know his relatives, his bank account and his habits. Good Lord, we did him a terrible injustice as a person. He was one of ours.

One of the really good ones. And we excluded him on the basis of flimsy arguments. I don't want us to treat him unfairly again.'

It hurt her to say it, but she did anyway. 'Ubbo, I can't make allowances for your feelings in this case, as honourable as they are. The murderer is killing at a great rate. I'm sure he's already on his way to his next victim. We can't afford to make any mistakes. If the worst comes to the worst, we'll apologise to Kaufmann later. I'd do that personally and would even take you along. But now we have to get him off the streets.

Ann Kathrin hung up, got back into the car, strapped in and then turned the key. But the hatchback didn't start.

She slammed her head back against the headrests twice. She gritted her teeth.

No, please not now!

She was furious. I should have sold this shitty car, she thought. Why don't I listen to Weller or Peter Grendel when it comes to things like this? I'm a sentimental cow. Now I'm sitting here in this heap of metal.

OK, she thought, no one's looking. She stroked the dashboard and said, 'I didn't mean it that way. We're all under unbelievable pressure. Please don't abandon me, sweetheart. Come on, start! I promise you that you'll get a great car wash with bubbles, undercarriage cleaning and a wax treatment if you like. I won't neglect you anymore, but please don't leave me now!'

She tried again and the car started.

Ann Kathrin bent over, touching the steering wheel with her chin. She looked up into the night sky. 'Thanks, Universe,' she said. 'Sometimes you just need a little luck.'

*

Odysseus' stomach tensed when Wilhelm Kaufmann went to the bar to pay. Had he made a mistake? Kaufmann could already have gone by the time he had got his own bill. Then the old detective would be waiting somewhere for him.

No, he couldn't let him out of his sight. He didn't want to walk back across the dark island without knowing where Kaufmann was.

He pulled a twenty-euro bill from his wallet, put it under his beer glass and called to the barman, 'Keep the change!'

Wilhelm Kaufmann stretched in front of the Dwarslooper bar, ran his fingers through his hair and didn't head back to his holiday accommodation. He had a bicycle with him, and Odysseus knew where he was going before him even got on it. To Flinthörn.

There were at least a dozen bicycles parked in front of the bar, and not even half of them were locked. Odysseus grabbed a Dutch roadster. He really had to pedal hard because Wilhelm Kaufmann had an e-bike and was easily doing thirty kilometres per hour in fifth gear.

The sky was midnight blue. It wasn't completely dark, as if twilight moved seamlessly into morning light here on the coast.

Wilhelm Kaufmann had parked his bike on the street next to the sign for tourists and had climbed up along the path over the dunes. Now he was up on top of them, with a clear view. The gentle breeze went through his clothing and felt good on his skin.

In his memory there was a rubbish bin attached to a metal pole at the bottom, straight ahead. But he couldn't see it. In this muted light, it looked more like a mediaeval cannon.

Wilhelm Kaufmann had been interested in the planets for a long time. The starry sky had always been very important to him. He could recognise the huge planet of Jupiter with his naked eye, revealing itself in the west as a bright point of light in the Gemini constellation. The other two bright stars were Castor and Pollux – if he wasn't mistaken. Together they formed an elongated triangle.

The bright sand was a huge natural source of light. Small dark shadows moved over the sand. Seagulls, crows. Maybe rabbits. Kaufmann wasn't exactly sure.

The longer Kaufmann looked, the more he came to the conclusion that there was a gathering of rabbits or hares there. He would have liked nothing more than to walk down and be close to them.

He took off his shoes and put his socks in his trouser pockets.

Now the gathering dispersed. The animals fluttered up, and as the first ones clearly rose against the sky, he recognised that they were seagulls.

He had concentrated too much on the animals and hadn't noticed that someone had crept up behind him. Only when Odysseus was two metres behind him did he hear human breathing, someone who sounded as though they had been walking too fast.

Kaufmann turned round and looked into the feverish eyes of a murderer.

'Hello, Mr Kaufmann. My name is Birger Holthusen. I saw you at Ubbo Heide's reading in Gelsenkirchen. And you were just in Dwarslooper.'

Kaufmann was dumbfounded at being addressed directly. Being addressed by name hit him like a blow to the head.

Odysseus reached into the pocket of his hoodie and wrapped his left hand around his dagger. The handle, which was made out of cherry wood, calmed him.

With a firm voice he said, 'You've come here to kill me.'

At the same time, he tried to climb a little higher up the dune to be on the same level as Kaufmann. He didn't like that he was being looked down upon.

'No, I came here on holiday,' Wilhelm Kaufmann corrected him.

The sand under Odysseus' feet was fine and slippery. He sank in slightly as he tried to find a firm footing. He would need a better position in which to thrust with a dagger.

'Holiday,' he scoffed. 'Holidays aren't for madmen like us.'

Odysseus watched Kaufmann's hands carefully. He was afraid that he would reach into his jacket and produce a gun from where his right pocket bulged. He wasn't wearing a shoulder holster. It had been quite warm in Dwarslooper, and he'd briefly taken off his jacket, but he'd held it loosely from his index finger instead of hanging it on the coat rack. It hadn't got any cooler but he'd already put his jacket back on.

Odysseus knew that Kaufmann was in a gun club in Brake and that he had two handguns registered under his name. A Walther PPK and a Sig Sauer. He was surely carrying the light, short Walther in his jacket pocket. He could hardly carry the Sig Sauer on his body, dressed as he was.

Now, the fact that he was standing barefoot in front of Odysseus eliminated the question of whether he was wearing a weapon on his leg; unlike Odysseus, who didn't leave the house without his boot knife.

'If you have something to say, then spit it out,' Wilhelm Kaufmann demanded.

'On the one hand, you feel drawn to me; on the other, you're scared of me because I'm like you. But unlike you, I follow through with my urges, while you try to stumble through a seemingly ordinary life. You killed Stern and Heymann to get rid of the sadistic child murderer inside yourself. Or do you still call yourself a paedophile? I gave it up. It sounds so friendly. In reality we're beasts, right? We don't love children, we destroy them.'

Kaufmann turned so that the moon was behind him, and tried to move so that his right hand was hidden from Odysseus' field of vision. Odysseus knew exactly what Kaufmann had planned and stepped to one side. There he sank ankle-deep into the sand.

'You killed the children, right?' Kaufmann asked. 'Stern and Heymann were actually innocent.'

'Yes, I did, damn it! Steffi Heymann and Nicola Billing. And two others.'

'Which others? And where's Steffi's body?'

Odysseus laughed. 'Now you're playing the role of cop again, right?'

Kaufmann had wondered why they were acting so formally with one another. Was this the last vestige of civilised behaviour that they wanted to preserve before the struggle began?

'I'm not on the police force anymore.'

'I know. They kicked you off. People like us always get kicked out at some point. When the carefully constructed façade gets cracked. When they sense that we are different from them and that something's not right with us. Sometimes they fire us without knowing exactly why. They just want to get rid of us because they feel uncomfortable in our presence. You know what I mean?'

Although Odysseus was being very familiar with him now, Kaufmann decided to keep things objective and to maintain some distance. 'I'm not at all like you. I have a temper. I've fought with many a man. But I've never harmed a child in my entire life.'

Odysseus held the dagger tightly in his left hand, still hidden in the pocket of his hoodie, but waved his right hand in the air and scoffed. 'Oh, come on! You can't fool me! And why? I've been watching you closely. Those were wonderful days on Langeoog. The ladies were wearing short skirts, as if their legs were only there for men's amusement, but you didn't look at them. You think I'm an idiot? Ten guys are sitting there and staring until their eyes fall out because a cutie just rode by, but it just didn't interest you or me in the least. We couldn't take our eyes off the little girl whose scoop of ice cream had fallen from her cone, making her cry.'

Kaufmann even remembered the scene. At the time he'd had the impulse to buy the kid a new ice cream. Then her mother had come running over. She'd been engrossed in a conversation with a friend somewhere and lost sight of her kid. Now she felt guilty and was grabbing the child, wiping away her tears and queuing up with the her for a new scoop of ice cream.

Odysseus had drawn his conclusions from those tiny sequences. How much the glasses you look through colour everything you see, Kaufmann thought.

'Where's the body of Steffi Heymann?'

Odysseus' face twisted into an ugly grin and he nodded knowingly, as if he understood everything now. 'So you're one of those. I knew it! That's why you followed me. That's why you didn't betray me. That's why you always come back here; you are turned on by dead children! How often have you broken into morgues? Come on, tell me, then I'll show you where she lies. And the names of the two others, if you're so interested.'

'I've never broken into a morgue.'

'Liar! You started just like me. How can you get close to a dead child's body if you don't have the courage to kill them yourself? And you couldn't do that; I can see that in you. You're a cleaner.' Odysseus pointed to the water. 'I buried her there. At low tide. There won't be much left of her. But I still like coming here. It's as if her little soul were still here, in this place. As if she couldn't leave it. I feel her presence here. Do you feel it too?'

'Nonsense! Don't tell me sick stories like that. If her body can't be found or rotted long ago, why do you come back here?'

The wind blew away his words. Kaufmann had difficulty understanding him. Was it a trick? Did he want to be closer?'

'All my life I have looked for someone like me. Someone I can swap ideas with. Someone who sticks with me, knows my worries.' He waved him away, but Kaufmann hadn't even said anything. 'Don't get me started on these so called paedophile clubs. I don't want anything to do with them. It all disgusts me. Besides, at some point the cover is always blown because the police have sneaked in and exposed them.

No, I was looking for a friend. A kindred spirit. A creature like myself. Perhaps you could have been that. I really could have pictured that, back then, when we met for the first time on this island. But we're too different. You're trying too hard to be like them and play on their team. That always goes wrong, as you must have noticed by now.

And now you're planning to kill me. Just like you killed Heymann and Stern. But you won't get anywhere because my senses are sharper than yours. I think more clearly. And I trust my intuition.'

Odysseus slowly pulled his left hand with the dagger out of the pocket of his hoodie. The blade alone frightened Kaufmann. He took a step back and reached into his jacket pocket.

Odysseus fell forward, knocking Kaufmann off balance, almost pulling him over, and thrust. He caught Kaufmann's upper right arm with the sharp dagger.

Kaufmann fell.

Odysseus was already sitting on Kaufmann's chest and pressing the tip of the dagger below his larynx. He could feel the gun, but couldn't reach it. He knew he was in extreme danger. If he paid the gun attention for only a second too long Kaufmann would use the chance to shake him off.

Then he had the Walther PPK between his thumb and index finger and lifted it up.

'Well, what do we have here?' he asked. 'The good old Walther. Wasn't that James Bond's service revolver? Do you have a phone? Give me your phone. I want your phone, damn it!'

Birger Holthusen briefly pointed the pistol in Kaufmann's face without taking the tip of his knife from his neck. It looked as if he were thinking about the best way to kill him. He put the Walther in his trouser pocket and grabbed the dagger with both hands.

Wilhelm Kaufmann carefully moved his head from left to right because he was afraid the blade could sink into his throat. He felt warm blood running down the left side of his neck.

'I don't have a phone with me,' he said quietly. 'I don't want to be constantly tracked.'

'Oh really, you're one of those. Old school, huh? I'll bury you where Steffi Heymann also lies. Hmm, no. By the time I'd have dug the hole, what's the point? I'll just cut your throat and disappear. That's what you did with Heymann and Stern. Isn't it ironic that now you'll die the same way they did? Next to the sea, head cut off? I can't promise you that I'll get your head completely off. I don't have a saw. Or an axe. Just this Swiss dagger. An old back up weapon for Swiss soldiers, created to silence opponents quickly. But hardly ideal for cutting through bones. I think you need a different weapon for that. Well, at least I'll cut your throat, you can be sure of that. Everyone will see the connection between you and the two others.

He lifted the dagger high above his head and held it with both hands.

He wanted to put all of his strength behind it, slamming it down, directly into Kaufmann's neck. But like this, for a tiny moment, his upper body became an unprotected surface.

Kaufmann took his chance and punched Odysseus in the ribs, immediately taking his breath away. Then when the knife came down, Odysseus was only holding it with his left hand, not with both.

Kaufmann grabbed it. The two of them struggled for the dagger, and now Kaufmann had a better chance because Odysseus couldn't get any air and pain paralysed his right side.

The dagger fell into the sand. Kaufmann tossed Odysseus off like a horse tired of its knight. Then he punched him twice in the face.

Odysseus' upper and lower lips burst simultaneously. He yelled something that Kaufmann didn't understand. His bloody mouth had something vampire-like about it, as if Count Dracula had been disturbed while sucking blood.

Odysseus jumped up and ran down the dune towards the North Sea.

Kaufmann searched the sand. He found the dagger because the stars reflected like diamonds on the sharpened blade. He didn't find the Walther. Perhaps Odysseus had it and was waiting for the night sky to offer him a good shot at Kaufmann.

Odysseus had arrived at the rubbish bin. It seemed like a warning on this long sandy beach not to drop litter in such a beautiful place.

'You're already where you belong!' Kaufmann called. 'In the rubbish!'

Kaufmann stumbled down the dunes, his legs wide apart, looking sort of ridiculous to Odysseus. He pointed the Walther at Kaufmann and fired the first shot.

Odysseus had never fired a gun like that before and the pistol's kick felt special. It propelled his insides forward. The bang hurt his ears. He felt numb. He didn't want to pull the trigger again. It wasn't like in the movies. No one would watch films with constant shooting if they were as loud as in real life, he thought.

Kaufmann stopped and raised his hands, the dagger in his right one. Odysseus held the Walther with both hands. In the moonlight the trickle of blood on his neck looked as though a spider was crawling out of Kaufmann's Adam's apple, heading for his open shirt.

'I'm aiming right at your head. Come down now! And drop the knife – right here!'

Odysseus asked himself why he hadn't just blown a hole in Kaufmann's head. It wouldn't have been difficult. He was only a couple of metres in front of him. He practically couldn't miss.

Maybe it was the noise the gun had made. At any rate, he didn't shoot again.

I'm a very old being, he thought. I'm from a time when people didn't use guns. Swords and knives are the weapons of choice for me. Or . . .'

Then he had an idea that pleased him greatly. 'You have the choice,' he said. 'Either I take you out with a bullet or you swallow this pill here. I bought it in Thailand. I've been carrying it around for ages so they can't take me alive. People like us should try not to be held captive, don't you think? What do you think they'd do with you if they found out that you beheaded two people so they couldn't be like you? It wouldn't be nice, believe me.'

Now he indicated Kaufmann's right hand with the dagger again. 'I said you should throw the knife over here!'

Kaufmann did so.

'OK, and now it's your decision. Poison or bullet?'

Wilhelm Kaufmann immediately chose the poison. He hoped he would be able to gain some time. Maybe someone had heard the shot. Maybe there were already people on the way. Possibly an animal activist who was on the beach because they were afraid that someone was hunting seals. But more than likely everyone would think the noise was someone setting off fireworks for a wedding party or something. Who on Langeoog would think of a shot from a Walther pistol? Here on Flinthörn, the most beautiful place on earth that Kaufmann knew.

Odysseus held out a hand containing the capsule, shaking with excitement. He moved around, agitated, and Kaufmann worried that he'd accidentally let off a second shot.

'If you're trying to trick me, I'll shoot you in the balls – and then in the head!' Odysseus yelled.

Kaufmann stuck the capsule in his mouth in such a way that Odysseus could see exactly what was happening. He even held it between his teeth for a moment. Then he let it disappear into his mouth.

He acted as if he were choking down a horse pill, but in reality he had stuck the capsule behind his teeth.

'OK, and now the two of us wait until you fall,' Odysseus said. 'Don't try to trick me. This stuff works. Can you feel anything yet?'

Kaufmann shook his head.

'Did you swallow the capsule?'

Kaufmann nodded.

Odysseus put the pistol in his trouser pocket and picked up the dagger. Using the dagger wouldn't cause any commotion.

The two of them stood opposite each other and stared. Seen from a distance, they could have been mistaken for a couple in love; perhaps sorting out some disagreement. In reality each of them was trying to see through the other's plans.

Kaufman was afraid that the saliva in his mouth would dissolve the capsule and that the poison would ultimately have its lethal effect, regardless of whether he swallowed the pill or not.

A bitter taste was spreading in his mouth already, and he felt the urge to vomit.

Odysseus feared that Kaufmann had found some trick to make the capsule disappear without swallowing it. If he doesn't collapse in the next two minutes, he thought, then I'll cut his throat and be done with it.

'Kneel down,' he demanded.

Kaufmann did so.

'Keep your upper body straight!'

Kaufmann followed this order too.

Odysseus now stood behind him, grabbed Kaufmann's hair with his right hand and pulled his head way back. He held the blade to Kaufmann's throat with his left hand.

At that very moment, Kaufmann's body went limp and collapsed.

The poison had worked after all.

Kaufmann began to twitch. He now lay on the ground, a pitiful picture, seizures overtaking his whole bode.

Odysseus watched him, but there was no feeling of triumph. Instead, he was sad that he wouldn't have this intended death for himself so as to avoid the justice system.

He decided to put an end to Kaufmann's terrible suffering. It was as though he were releasing himself as he raised the blade for the second time to thrust it into Kaufmann's throat.

However, as Odysseus raised his arms, Kaufmann took the opportunity to propel his legs forward, hitting Odysseus in the chin and then the stomach.

Once again the two of them struggled for the dagger. This time Kaufmann was on top. He spat terrible-smelling saliva into

Odysseus' face and then drove the double-edged blade into his chest. It missed his heart, but went deep.

Odysseus stared at his opponent with wide open eyes. 'So the pill didn't work?', he asked in a small voice.

'No, you scumbag! You've been tricked.' Kauffman said, and then ran to the sea to wash his moth out with salty water. He gargled and spat. He'd had no idea how delicious seawater could taste. As he vomited the water back into the Northsea, he was thankful for every drop that left his body. Who knows, he thought, what was in that pill.

Odysseus was bleeding to death on the beach. The pistol was still in his trouser pocket, but he wasn't able to reach it, otherwise he might have put an end to his suffering himself.

He lay on his back and looked up into the starry sky. He felt strangely peaceful, at ease with what was happening to him. He hoped that if his soul was reincarnated, he would get a good new start. Maybe be like everyone else. Get married, start a family, concentrate on work and hobbies. Not be constantly tormented by his inner demons as he had been in this life.

*

The police choir was interrupted in the middle of the song 'Super-duper Rupert.' They had wanted to combine a barbeque with a rehearsal that evening on police psychologist Elke Sommer's veranda, but Büscher explained that he needed all hands on deck, immediately.

Elke Sommer replied that people who have to forgo their free time for too long got worse instead of better at their jobs, but Büscher wasn't interested. He didn't even accept the arguments from Marion Wolters and Sylvia Hoppe, who claimed they were too drunk to drive and consequently unavailable.

It was shortly after midnight when the emergency meeting began in Aurich police station.

Marion Wolters smelled of red wine and charcoal, Sylvia Hoppe had difficulties accepting the seriousness of the situation because she couldn't get the lyrics from the 'Super-duper Rupert' song out of her head. She hummed to herself.

'A specialist at livin' large
If you ask him, he's in charge.
What'd they do without that cat?
They'd have nothing to laugh at.'

She asked with a grin, 'What does Rupert have to say about it all?'

Marion Wolters poked her, telling her to shut up, but that only made Sylvia giggle even more.

Elke Sommer attempted a particularly objective tone when she said, 'Please, despite the seriousness of this situation, there's still life outside our police duties. We had just put a couple of burgers on the grill. Can't all of this wait until tomorrow morning?'

As Sylvia Hoppe started giggling again, Marion Wolters apologised for her, saying, 'Sorry, she simply can't handle her alcohol.'

Büscher groaned, 'We're dealing with a very serious situation here.'

At that moment Rieke Gersema arrived, breathless from running.

'I'm afraid our culprit,' Büscher said, 'has struck again, and the victim is another suspect Ubbo Heide had investigated. This time it's a certain David Weissberg.'

'Yes, we already know that. But what are we supposed to do tonight?' Marion Wolters wanted to know.

'I need,' Büscher said thumping on the table, 'for you to all think, damn it! I'm new here and can't know every single detail as well as you do. The killer comes from among you – that's completely obvious!'

'Hear, hear!' Elke Sommer called, incensed. 'One of you!'

'Us,' Büscher corrected and continued, 'At the moment many of our lines of investigation are leading us in the direction of Wilhelm Kaufmann. So I need to know everything! When did you see him last? Who was in contact with him privately? I want to know everything about that man, even his relationships in our police station. Is that clear? Someone is giving him tips, clues, warning him. He's disappeared off the face of the earth. We've issued a warrant for him.'

Rupert raised his hand, which made Sylvia Hoppe start giggling again. 'Can't we just track his phone?' he suggested.

Marion Wolters said in Rupert's direction, 'He's not that stupid; he doesn't use a mobile phone.'

'What? You're stupid if you have a mobile phone?' Rupert asked in astonishment.

'We could,' Sylvia Hoppe suggested, 'suggest that from now on, everyone has to carry a phone. That way we could at least track them anytime.'

A part of her was still drunk, but not enough that she wasn't immediately embarrassed by what she'd said. She tried to force herself to shut up, but alcohol made her so chatty. Her first marriage had failed due to a combination of this and husband's lack of sense of humour.

Büscher returned to the fundamentals. 'So what do you know about him? Where could he be? Friends. Favourite places.' He let his gaze wander. He wanted to look each and every one of his colleagues in the eye once.

'Damn it,' he cursed desperately, 'you must know more than I do!'

*

A couple of minutes after Ann Kathrin had arrived in Aurich, Weller opened the door to Wilhelm Kaufmann's place in Brake. The local police had already searched the apartment and had found no indication of where he could be.

Weller put on some rubber gloves. He hated the things, but didn't want to contaminate the place with his DNA unnecessarily. He was alone in the well-decorated apartment. There was a view of the river through the window, as well as of the hotel and restaurant that Wilhelm Kaufmann had been running since his humiliating dismissal from the police force.

What would Ann Kathrin do now? Weller thought. Probably go to the bookcase first.

He immediately liked Wilhelm Kaufmann. He had a large collection of crime novels, and that pleased Weller.

And there were quite a lot of books on astronomy. A rather large telescope for observing the planets was standing next to the window.

Interesting hobby, Weller thought. But you need time for hobbies. Much more than I have. And it's a hobby you can only do at night. So Kaufmann was possibly a night owl. Maybe he had trouble sleeping and had chosen this hobby for that reason.

Weller looked in the fridge. None of it looked like it had been abandoned in haste. Weller could recognise at a glance homes that were abandoned because someone was afraid they would be arrested. This wasn't the case here. The apartment was tidy. The departure had been carefully planned.

There was nothing in the fridge that would spoil in the near future. Weller checked the expiry date on the yoghurts. Half a salami, a chunk of cheese wrapped in clingfilm, butter only in individual portion packages, but six of them.

Undoubtedly the home of a single man.

Weller liked the coffee machine. Wilhelm Kaufmann clearly didn't struggle for money, despite being dismissed from the police force, or maybe that was precisely why. He probably earned significantly more than he ever would have if he had stayed with the police.

There were many notes posted on the corkboard in the kitchen. The rubbish collection schedule, a tide chart, when the ferries to Langeoog ran, a postcard, the telephone number for a heating repairman, and then another small note with the words 'holiday apartment' and a telephone number below with the area code 04972.

Weller called Büscher and was transferred directly to the meeting room.

'Put it on speakerphone, Martin. Can everyone hear me?'

'Yeah. What's the news?'

'I'm here in Brake and I'd bet anything that Kaufmann is on Langeoog. He has a holiday flat there, which we can reach on the following telephone number.'

'How do you know that?' Büscher asked again.

'There's a note on his corkboard. The local authorities must have overlooked it.'

Rieke Gersema groaned and grabbed her head, but Büscher didn't let any accusations against his colleagues in Brake stand. 'Hey, hey, hey, that doesn't mean anything. I have countless telephone numbers posted on my pinboard, but that doesn't mean I go to these places.'

Büscher wrote down the number all the same, thanked Weller, hung up the phone, and then snarled at the others. 'Why don't any of you know stuff like this about Kauffman?'

Rupert had had enough. He burst out, 'How are we supposed to know where he goes on holiday? We don't even know him, damn it! That was all ages ago! Most of us only started here after Kaufmann was long gone. This is an old story between Ubbo and Kaufmann. We don't have anything to do with it. Even someone from Bremerhaven should be able to understand that, right?'

That was it. Büscher straightened himself up, then let fly. 'When I was in Bremerhaven,' he said, 'none of the suspects we weren't able to convict were killed! We did solid work and then put people behind bars if that's where they belonged. None of them became vigilantes!'

'You wouldn't have dared say something like that if Ann Kathrin Klaasen was sitting here at the table,' Elke Sommer said.

'My God, what's become of us?' Rieke Gersema asked. 'The atmosphere here is poisonous. We're tearing each other to pieces. That didn't used to happen.'

'Sure,' Rupert said, 'and this time it's nothing to do with me. ' He looked at Büscher, who feared he was being held responsible for the situation.

*

Wilhelm Kaufmann began to shiver. He was wet through and his clothes were sticking to his body. He was still coughing and spitting up seawater.

He saw Birger Holthusen, dead with the dagger in his chest. He knew that his own fingerprints would be on the weapon.

He considered what he should do. His right bicep was bleeding, but he wasn't worried. It wasn't deep, a flesh wound. He could still move his arm. But should he go to a doctor anyway? Had any of the poison made it into his bloodstream?

Or should he call the police? Tell them the whole story?

Something terrible had happened. He had a credible confession from Birger Holthusen, admitting he was responsible for the murders of Steffi Heymann and Nicola Billing as well as two other children. But now Birger Holthusen was dead. He'd killed him.

Doubt rose within him. The conversation he had had in Gelsenkirchen with Ubbo Heide had been really strange. Ubbo suspected him of killing Heymann and Stern, just as Birger Holthusen had done. There was some logic to it, but it still seemed unbelievable to him.

He felt the urge to wipe his fingerprints from the knife, retrieve the pistol that was hanging out of Holthusen's pocket, go back to his holiday flat, have a shower, and then drink himself senseless. He thought of the hours of interrogation if he went to the police. No, he wasn't up to it. Not today. He was exhausted. That fight had really taken it out of him.

I'm not as young as I was, he thought, and grabbed his heart. If this horrible poison doesn't work, hopefully my heart won't give up on me. A tight feeling spread across his chest. He knelt next to the dead man in the sand and wiped the knife clean, grabbed the pistol, and stomped back up the beach.

The sand will erase any tracks within hours, he thought. And I can still call the police tomorrow if I want to. For now I need peace and quiet. I need to get my thoughts in order, so I don't get tangled up and confused.

Kauffman was so worked up when he climbed onto his bicycle that he accidentally turned off the electric motor. He pedalled until his legs were burning. Only then did he realise his mistake and shifted down to third gear shortly before getting home; everything was really easy after that.

Never in his whole life had he showered as long as that night.

*

Svenja Moers felt like she was wrapped in spiderwebs or sticky cotton balls, as if she were pupating.

She heard a voice, swirling, with elongated vowels. She couldn't understand the meaning of the words; they were only sounds to her. A foreign, distorted language.

She tried to open her eyes, but she could hardly see anything through yellowish-white streaks. It was if she were looking out from inside a milky cocoon into an unknown, hostile world.

Someone was hitting her in the face. She didn't feel the pain, only heard the slapping and registered that her head shot quickly from right to left and back. It made her dizzy.

'Drink this! You are supposed to drink, damn it!'

She coughed. Something sloshed out of her mouth and ran down her neck. Her head was pulled upwards, hurting her neck.

Someone was pressing her lips against a glass. She would really have liked to drink, but her throat felt too narrow, as if it was swollen shut, every passageway clogged. It was hard for her to breathe and she gasped.

He wiped her face with a moist rag. Then he held something under her nose that smelled disgusting and she was racked by a coughing fit.

Eventually, she was able to sit upright. There were still stars dancing in front of her eyes, but the white streaks had become transparent.

She recognised Yves Stern with her in the cell.

He looked worried, almost friendly, like a doctor in a hospital.

'You can't die now. You're a part of something greater. That's not the way it's been planned. I brought you some fruit. You need a few vitamins. I'll bake us another cake. You must hold on! This is all far from over. You can be my witness, see my work come to light.'

He held a plate of peeled apple slices out to her. 'Eat.'

Am I awake? She asked herself. Is this a hallucination? Am I dreaming? Maybe I'm dead?

How many times had she wished he would come into her cell? Longing for the opportunity to attack him. But at this moment she wasn't in any position to do so. She'd have no chance of beating him. She wasn't even able to lift a piece of apple and bite into it. She had to gather her strength first.

He pushed a piece of apple between her lips. Then he showed her some photos. They were of figures made of wood.

'Look, this is the sculpture garden in Hude. I want to complete my work there, under the giant sculpture. The last body will lie underneath it. When the grass grows it looks as if the sculpture is floating. Then everyone will understand that I have not only brought justice, but I've also created a work of art – a sculpture as a comment on society. The society in which we live is something like a piece of wood. It has to be formed, hewn. What doesn't belong has to be removed so that in the end we have something that is beautiful. When I was walking among the sculptures I realised what I had to do. I'd gone on a cycling tour to Hude and had visited the monastery and the mill. The sculptures are on the banks of the River Hude, not far from the Peter Ustinov School. The artist is called Wolf E. Schultz.'

He's crazy, she thought, completely crazy. But for some reason he wants me to survive. That's good. Maybe he just needs a witness. Did he lose a friend? Does he feel lonely? He wants me to join him in what he's doing. He's putting me in a position of power – more than just a piece of meat that he can simply dispose of.

She chewed the apple wedge and was gradually able to speak.

'Give me some water.'

He held the glass for her and she drank greedily. She felt the vital energy flow back into her body.

'I know the art trail in Dangast,' she said, establishing a connection. 'I went there with my first husband.'

Immediately, she was scared. Had she said the wrong thing? His posture had changed. Was he now viewing her more as a murderer that he had before, rather than the sick person he needed to save from dying?

'Please let me go,' she said. 'I won't give anything away. I just want out. I'm dying in here. I can't take it. I can't breathe. It's too hot. I'm a girl from the coast. I need fresh air, space to move around. Surely you understand. Don't you?'

He silently pushed another apple wedge into her mouth. She didn't know exactly why he did it – to pacify her or re-energise her. 'I can't let you go. You're serving your sentence here. Just accept that.'

'But in every jail the prisoners are let out for fresh air! Don't you have a garden or courtyard? I could go outside and then come back.'

He laughed. 'You're promising to come back if I let you out of here? Why would you? Because you accept that this is where you belong?'

'Where would I go?' she asked. 'I confessed to the murders. It's all been with the police for a while now. I'd only go from one prison to another.'

'That is true. This prison doesn't have to stay as uncomfortable as it is at the moment though. We could agree on good food, regular meals, a pleasant temperature. What do you think?'

She chewed and nodded. He held out aother piece of apple. This time he didn't put it in her mouth but held it ten centimetres away from her face instead.

She opened her lips and reached for it. That's what he wants, she thought. For me to eat from the palm of his hand. And if that's what he wants, then that's what I'll do. The main thing for me is surviving. Regardless of how.

'I could cook for us,' she said. 'I could make your favourite dish. What your mother used to cook. My husbands always praised me for being a good cook,' she lied.

'I understand,' he said, 'you want to give me something for the mercy I've granted you. You realise that you haven't earned any of this? I could put you out in the sculpture garden too, under the giant. But that wouldn't work. After all, you're not the culmination of everything. It'd be like building a house without finishing the roof.'

He took a step back and looked at her. Although he was searching her body with his eyes, there was nothing sexual about it. Instead, she felt more like a slave at a market, being assessed for how he could best make use of her.

Now she was sitting up in the bed. She still felt dizzy, and her extremities were stiff. She had difficulty moving her fingers and her legs, which were under the blanket, felt as if they no longer belonged to her.

'There's a lot of work to be done here in the house. I have to do everything myself at the moment. And that's all your fault. I can't let a cleaning lady or any tradesmen in here. All because of you!'

He was speaking in an unstable tone, talking himself into a rage. His facial features became harder and he grew taller as he spoke. He must have grown used to walking hunched up so as not to be noticed, but when he stood up straight he was thin but huge.

'I could take care of much of the work. I could cook for us, clean, tidy up the place. We could live together like a married couple.'

'Yeah,' he grinned. 'You'd like that, wouldn't you? And then you'd kill me, like you always kill your husbands.' He grabbed her by the neck with his right hand and began to choke her. 'It won't work this time. I have you under control. I'm not going to fall for those pretty eyes!

'You could start with cleaning up your own cell and keeping it in shape.' He made a sweeping gesture. 'Just open your eyes to how it looks in here! Did you always do such a poor job at keeping house? I'm surprised your husbands didn't kill you.'

She tried to get up but when her right foot touched the floor it felt like she was stepping onto cotton balls. Her leg tingled, but she couldn't really feel the floor. Then she fell forward.

She had the presence of mind to extend her hands forward so that her face wouldn't slam against the floor. She tried to get back up, but she couldn't do it unaided.

He yelled at her, 'It's all your fault! You did all of this to yourself! If you'd have been more cooperative, I would have turned down the heat sooner, brought you food and water, but no, the lady always has to exert her will. You don't just need nourishment, you need exercise! You have to keep fit! Just look at yourself. You are doing a terrible job of looking after the body God gave you. You're a thankless bitch.'

He grabbed her by the arm and pulled her up. He pressed her against the bars and used both hands to hold her still, so she wouldn't collapse again as her knees went slack.

'You're all skin and bone! And that skin is loose.' He grabbed her bicep with his fingertips and tugged at her skin, as if it were a piece of fabric.

'Get on the scales over there! From now on we're going to keep you fit. I want to know how much you weigh.'

She tried to walk the two steps to the scales. She wobbled back and forth, but got there. Then she stepped onto the scale.

They read 72.9 kilos.

'How much did you weigh at home, before you came in here?' he asked. His voice was aggressive.

Because she didn't answer, he hissed. 'Don't tell me you don't know! Women weigh themselves all the time. You don't have any topics for discussion except your weight and stupid diets.'

'I'm always yo-yoing between seventy-four and seventy-six kilos.'

'Well, there you go,' he laughed, 'then you've lost weight in here. That must please you. But did you weigh yourself fully clothed at home? Be truthful!'

'No,' she said meekly, 'of course not.'

He reached into his side pocket and pulled out a notebook. He laid it in front of her, along with a pen.

'OK, starting now you'll write down your weight every day. Is that clear? You'll weigh yourself once in the morning and once at night. I want you to gain some weight. I want this to do you some good, and this notebook will prove it. You'll write down your precise weight and then,' he reached for a bag that he'd placed on the floor and she hadn't even noticed and took something out of it, 'you'll blow in here. This will measure your lung capacity. The instructions are in there. Blow in, nice and smooth. And then you write down your lung capacity every day. Besides that, your body temperature will be measured and everything you eat will be recorded. Once you've reached eighty kilos and have shown me that you can behave yourself, then you can watch television with me in the evening and move around the house. Maybe we'll even get some fresh air together.' He clapped his hands. 'Well, it's good to have a goal, right? From now on you can eat as much as you want. Pasta. Pizza. Cake. You no longer have to worry about keeping a slim figure. Now you're finally free behind these bars. The first goal is eighty kilos.'

He looked at her and her face twitched. She didn't know what to say or think and felt even more afraid.

'OK, now go and get undressed and weigh yourself so we can get some reasonable results. And remember, from now on you're going to do it twice a day. Morning and night.'

'I don't even know when it's morning or night,' she said, and was glad she was able to offer a little resistance. 'After all, I don't have a watch.'

'OK,' he said, and even seemed a little guilty. 'OK, I'll give you a watch so that we can run our experiment properly.'

He took his own watch from his wrist and tossed it on the bed. 'Eighty kilos,' he said, tapping the notebook, 'Write everything down nicely in here. It's the proof that I treat you decently, that everything here is orderly.'

Then he left her cell, locking it behind him and, without turning round once, disappeared between the steel doors and into the hall behind them.

On the one hand she was relieved. He hadn't demanded that she get undressed because he wanted to watch her. No, it was something different.

Although, maybe he's watching me now, she thought, through the cameras he's installed. I'm sure he's doing exactly that.

But she still got the feeling that her situation had just taken a turn for the better. No, she wouldn't give up yet. He wanted something from her and he needed the proof that he treated her decently. He wouldn't rape her or torture her. He was trying to do everything right. He believed he was good and wanted to collect evidence of that.

She quickly undressed and weighed herself again.

69.7.

My God, she thought, I've actually lost at least four kilos.

But what would have previously been a cause for joy now just worried her.

She quickly got dressed again, and then neatly recorded the number in the notebook.

When I'm fit and strong enough, then maybe I can ram the pen into his eye, she thought. At least he had been stupid enough to bring the keys with him into her cell. Maybe he'll do it again.

I'll regain my strength, she thought. I'll promise it to myself. I'll eat, I'll exercise, I'll get strong again, and then I'll kill you, my dear, just like I did my first two husbands. Only this time I don't have to make sure it looks like an accident. Oh no. I can do what I want with you. Any court in the world would say it was self-defence.

*

Ann Kathrin asked herself if it had been a good idea to drink black tea with peppermint leaves at this hour, but Ubbo Heide was holding on to his cup as if it were his lifesaver. .

The scent of tea filled the whole room and the hint of peppermint reminded Ann Kathrin more of a Bedouin tent in the desert than a home in East Frisia.

Carola Heide was very sensitive to light. She couldn't stand neon light at all, which is why there was only indirect lighting throughout the house and a couple of candles. For Ann Kathrin it felt almost like a sacred space.

There was a seal made of marzipan perched on Ubbo's knee. He petted the seal as soon as he put down his cup. Every once in a while he nibbled off some of it and pushed the little bits he'd rolled together between his fingers into his mouth.

Ann Kathrin thought he looked liked he'd aged by several years. His lips seemed oddly twisted and slanted, as if he had had a stroke. But she didn't dare express her suspicions.

'I need your advice, Ann. I'm at my wit's end.'

There he sat, the great figure of the Kripo in East Frisia, fatherly friend and role model for an entire generation of police officers – beaten by life, shaken, in need of help.

It was a given that she would stand by him. She didn't need to say anything, but looked at him quizzically.

He played with the seal while speaking quietly. 'I'm racking my brains. I have to do something. But before I act, I want to ask you what you think. It's important to me. In the end, I'll have to do what I think is right, but—'

'What are you thinking about, Ubbo?'

'Should I publicly appeal to the killer? Is that what he wants? Should I publicly ask him to stop? Tell him what a terrible mess he's making?'

'He wants to have a conversation with you. Everything points in your direction, that's obvious, Ubbo. But maybe you'd just incite him to do more.'

'That's exactly my fear, Ann. But I feel responsible for everything that's happened. I have to ask him to stop.'

'But what do you want to offer him, Ubbo? What's the deal? What does he get if he stops?'

Ubbo's fingers moved as if they were autonomous, not under his control. They ripped off the seal's head, then he dropped it and it rolled onto the floor between his legs. There the marzipan seal seemed to stare at him with its one remaining eye.

Now Ubbo's fingers tore the body to pieces, shaking with nerves.

'I have to meet him, offer him a conversation.'

'You want to show him that you understand him?'

'Ann, this is all much more complicated than it seems. He's turning my rage into reality. I got all it off my chest by writing it down, and sometimes I ask myself: isn't he just doing what I was too cowardly to do because I didn't want to put my family and career on the line?'

*

He listened to Ubbo's words with triumph. He clenched his fists and raised them towards the ceiling, yelling with joy. 'Yeah! Yeah! Yeah! You finally get it!'

He tried to turn up the transmitter. The reception was bad. It crackled, and the words became quieter, then louder. But the sentences still unleashed an unbelievable feeling of joy.

'So you want to set a trap for him, Ubbo? With yourself as the bait? We couldn't risk that. You're handicapped. You're stuck in a wheelchair. You're not the same old Ubbo. No,' Ann Kathrin said decisively, 'I don't want you to do that!'

'You're misunderstanding me, Ann. We'd order a SWAT team if we were setting a trap. I want to meet him – for real.'

'And then?' she asked, flabbergasted.

'Then I want to talk to him.'

'What's become of you, Ubbo? You can't seriously think that you can negotiate with someone like that! How would that work? You think that he'll stop and everything will be OK again? We'll retract the warrant? Are you dreaming? He couldn't let you go after that conversation, Ubbo. You'd know him then and—'

'I have to put an end to this, Ann. We can agree on that, right? It feels like I threw a snowball and triggered an avalanche that's now threatening to bury an entire village!'

*

If we meet, Ubbo, you'll understand that your avalanche is destroying Sodom and Gomorrah, and you'll be proud of having wiped out all that filth. I want to see whether I can make your wish come true.

Ann Kathrin received a call. He couldn't hear what she said. Either she was whispering or was too far from the recording device. He could only hear her words once she was speaking to Ubbo again.

'Kaufmann rented a holiday flat on Langeoog. I assume he won't be there yet, but we'll be waiting for him when he arrives. I think you'll be able to have a conversation with him soon.'

'Yes, Willy loves Langeoog,' Ubbo said, sounding resigned.

'We can't wait until the first ferry runs.'

'Ann – I want to come along!'

'But Ubbo; Willy Kaufmann—'

Ubbo didn't let her contradict him. 'I can talk to him, Ann. Then maybe I can convince him to give up, if it comes to that. Or do you want it to end in a wild shoot-out on a holiday island? Willy's a damn good shot; at least he was always much better than me.

*

The police on Langeoog were informed that very night, but were asked not to do anything because they were dealing with an extremely dangerous man who was surely armed and capable of anything.

Two helicopters landed on the island's airfield in the early morning hours. Martin Büscher, two snipers, and four young men from the SWAT team, exceptionally well trained, hooded, and wearing military clothing, climbed out of one. Ann Kathrin Klaasen, Frank Weller, the police psychologist Elke Sommer, Rupert and Ubbo Heide arrived on the island in the other.

Now, as a retired head detective, Ubbo Heide glanced at the people from the SWAT team and grumbled. 'They look like we're about to film an episode of *Star Wars*.'

There was a couple sitting on the dunes, newly in love. They'd just had the best sex of their lives, under the open sky, and were enjoying a joint. Their bodies were still perspiring. The sea air caressed them. Then they saw the advancing figures. Ubbo Heide's wheelchair appeared like a throne upon which the king was being carried across the island, surrounded by his brave knights.

'Man, this stuff is good,' the woman said to her partner. 'Did you grow it yourself?'

He shook his head. 'Nah, I bought it, but it blows your mind, doesn't it?'

*

The steel door opened. Svenja Moers could see far into the hallway, but no one was there. She could smell something, though, which transported her out of her cell and into an Italian restaurant. She heard some clattering, and then Yves Stern appeared, like a pizza delivery boy on his first shift.

He was awkwardly handling a huge pizza in a box, with two plastic plates, knives and forks and a litre of Coca-Cola balanced on top.

The plastic cutlery fell onto the floor, and when he bent down to retrieve it an aluminum container fell off the pile and spaghetti carbonara hit the floor.

He glanced at Svenja Moers, begging for forgiveness with a smile, and was with her, next to the bars, within a few steps.

'*The Grande Bouffe* can begin,' he said happily. 'With lasagne al forno, then an extra large pizza with the works – ham, cheese, tuna, everything they have.'

His manner was simultaneously amusing and terrifying.

Then I'll live, she thought.

She tried to read the writing on the pizza box. The cardboard was white and the red-and-green logo seemed familiar, but she couldn't recognise the name of a pizzeria.

He handed her the bottle of Coke, then the spaghetti and the lasagna through the bars. He didn't use the designated service hatch. He turned the pizza on its side and pushed it through.

The food was still hot. She didn't know where to start, and she realised that it would be impossible to eat everything.

Cold pizza still tastes good, she thought, and attacked the lasagne first.

After the second bite she knew that the food was far too heavy after the long period of fasting. She would have problems digesting it. Still, the main thing was that her body would receive sustenance and, in turn, energy.

She examined the pizza box up close, but couldn't find indication of a delivery service. There was a saying printed on it: *People need two things to live: food and drink.*

While she ate, he disappeared briefly, but was back a few minutes later, placing a folding chair in front of the bars. He took a seat, folding his left leg over his right, and watched with amusement while she ate.

'What's going on?' she asked. 'We're not at the zoo.'

She immediately regretted her comment, scared that she'd make him angry. But, at the same time, with the intake of food, her will to fight was returning.

*

The house lay invitingly before them, hidden in the darkness between the dunes. Only the windows on the upper storey were illuminated.

The men from the SWAT team prepared themselves. Two snipers took up positions in the dunes.

Ann Kathrin Klaasen stood next to Ubbo Heide. Behind them, Rupert was joking with the men from the SWAT team.

Thoughts shot through Ann Kathrin's head like overexposed photographs. One after another, fast as lightning, only interrupted by shots and screams.

A SWAT man kicked in the door.

Wood splintered.

People yelled.

Orders were mixed with screams of fear.

Wilhelm Kaufmann was hit by several bullets. Arms spread, he danced through the large room with big black spots on his shirt.

Then he was on the ground.

The rotating flashing blue lights illuminated the scene.

A police officer in the doorway fought for his life. Blood spurted from his neck.

These were only pictures in her head, but for Ann Kathrin they were so real. She screamed out loud for them to stop.

Everyone looked at her.

Rupert wisecracked in the direction of the elite unit, 'Girls! That's just the way they are. The lower they go, the higher-strung they get!'

Weller was furious with Rupert and went to punch him, but Elke Sommer calmed him, claiming it was gallows humour, and just the way that some people deal with severe high stress.

'No,' Weller stated, 'he's simply an idiot.'

Ubbo Heide trusted Ann Kathrin's instincts and took it very seriously when she called for them to stop.

'We should give him the chance to surrender. He knows our capabilities and that he won't get out of the place alive. The island is a trap anyway. We shouldn't just storm in and should instead make an attempt to reason with him.' Ann Kathrin pleaded.

'Yes,' Ubbo Heide said, 'I agree.'

But the power to give these orders did not rest in the hands of the retired chief of police.

'I have a very bad feeling about this,' Ann Kathrin continued, but didn't have the power to stop it either.

Rupert mimicked Ann Kathrin to the SWAT team. 'She has a very bad feeling. Uh-oh! We'd better call for reinforcements.

The last time she had a bad feeling the Sunday roast didn't turn out right.'

No one laughed at his joke.

*

Johannes Dunkel's friends always called him 'Johnny Dark'. He knew there was no courage without fear, and he was damn scared. He was afraid he'd be shot and spend the rest of his life like Ubbo Heide, in a wheelchair. Strangely enough, he didn't think about the fact that the bullet could kill him. He was still at an age when young men seem to think they're invincible.

But there was something else. For a couple of weeks now he had been in love like never before in his life. He wanted to get married, have kids, and never again sleep with another woman.

But his Vivien didn't like guns. She didn't see him as a hero who freed hostages or stopped dangerous criminals. She was a pacifist and believed peace was always the way. He was afraid she would leave him if an unarmed, perhaps even innocent person died because of him.

As he jumped from the roof and through the window of an unfamiliar house, while his comrades broke down the door below and stormed the rooms, he thought about Vivien.

He'd practised this operation with his team countless times and only once – truly only one single time – had he shot a target of an unarmed women with a baby in her arms that had popped up behind him. Before that he had correctly targeted the four pictures of a bearded man with a gun at the ready.

He didn't want to make this mistake again. Not for real. Especially since he knew that there was a former cop in the flat.

But this was a former cop who would know exactly how a raid played out. He wouldn't have the chance to get out. If he wanted to avoid getting arrested, he would have to shoot at the person coming through the window, use his rope to climb onto the roof, and disappear from there.

The former cop must be around sixty, maybe even older. But that by no means meant that he wasn't flexible enough to pull off that feat. It certainly meant that he had enough life experience to know that there wasn't any other option.

So Johannes Dunkel was prepared to shoot. Fortunately the room was illuminated. Dunkel rolled from the window into the middle of the room. He pulled up into a crouch in front of a table on which there was a half-bottle of Hennessy and a brandy glass.

Holding the gun in both hands, Dunkel pointed at the man standing in the doorway. He was naked and rubbing himself dry with a towel, which he now held up in front of his body for protection.

'Hands up! Show me your hands!' Dunkel yelled.

Wilhelm Kaufmann put his hands in the air, but he was still holding the towel in his right hand. There could well have been a gun concealed beneath it.

Dunkel was able to see into the bathroom and the kitchen and spotted a shirt hanging over a chair. It was covered in blood.

'Drop the towel!' Johannes Dunkel yelled.

Kaufmann did that too. He wasn't dry and drops of water ran down his body. His damp hair stood on end. His knees were shaking, and his member had shrunk, as if it wanted to pull back into his body.

'I'm unarmed,' Kaufmann said. 'Can I get dressed?'

Johannes Dunkel heard his colleagues storming up the stairs and said, 'No, you stay right there. And turn around slowly. Hands against the wall!'

Wilhelm Kaufmann was smart enough to do what he was told. He felt the young officer's nervousness. He didn't want to give him the slightest reason to pull the trigger.

He positioned himself exactly as he would have demanded of a criminal: legs wide, leaning forwards his hands pressed against the wall, and then he said, 'My name is Wilhelm Kaufmann. I'm a former police officer.'

'Shut up!' someone yelled.

Ubbo Heide was waiting downstairs in his wheelchair. Ann Kathrin, Weller, Rupert and Büscher ran up the stairs. When they entered the room, Kaufmann was lying naked on the floor, his hands behind his back and bound with the modern plastic cuffs that Weller always thought looked like cable ties.

Johannes Dunkel patted down Kaufmann's clothing which was hanging over a chair. He raised the gun he'd fished out of the trousers and sniffed it.

'He had a Walther in his pocket. It's recently been fired. He was probably having a shower to get rid of the powder residue and blood.'

Kaufmann griped at Büscher and Ann Kathrin. 'What's this about? Can't you people do a proper arrest anymore? Does it automatically have to be this Hollywood blockbuster shit? I would have rung you tomorrow morning anyway,'

*

Svenja Moers couldn't get through half of the lasagne, hadn't even tried the spaghetti or the pizza, but she already felt sick.

'What?' he asked. 'Keep eating.'

She burped. 'I can't.'

'You can't what?'

'I'm full.'

'I don't give a shit. You're supposed to eat!'

'But I'm not hungry anymore. I'll be sick if I eat more.'

He jumped up from the chair and completely lost it. Although he was, in her estimation, almost two metres tall, he still seemed to her like a furious, nasty little rat. He kicked out with his right foot, clenched his fists and sprayed spittle while screaming.

'You goddamn ungrateful bitch! I serve you with my best and what do you do? You insult me! Do you want to starve in here?'

Now she was glad that the bars were between him and her. She considered the steel bars as protection against his rage.

'No,' she said, trying not to let him sense her fear. 'I'm not ungrateful. But I'm being held against my will. This isn't a real prison. This here,' she pointed to her cell, 'is neither approved nor allowed by the state. The jurisdiction of the world is different. When it becomes clear what you're doing with me here, you'll be punished for torture, not just for kidnapping and false imprisonment. Is that what you want?'

'Torture?' He screeched. Did you say torture? You have no clue what you're talking about! Should I show you what torture looks like?'

Tears came to her eyes. She felt her cheeks suddenly become damp, and salty drops covered her lips.

She regretted every word she'd said. She'd got herself into a terrible situation. She didn't want to give him a reason to torture her.

'Please, she said,' I'm sorry. 'I'm already eating again.'

Then she took the lasagne, dug into it with the white plastic fork and shovelled up as much as she could. She didn't swallow, only stuffing more and more lukewarm, greasy pasta into her mouth.

*

The first interrogation took place on Langeoog. Ubbo insisted on being present, and no one had any objections when it became clear that Kaufmann would open up to him before anyone else.

Instead of taking Kaufmann to the police station, they took him one storey down into the other, empty holiday rental. They were in the living room, sitting around the table while the men from the SWAT team drank filter coffee in the kitchen, ate rolls, and Johannes Dunkel sent his beloved Vivien a WhatsApp message:

I'm so in love with you that I can barely stand not being with you right now.

Her answer was immediate:

I know that you're not allowed to talk to me about operations. But I prayed for you.

I believe, he wrote as an unbeliever, *it helped me.*

Wilhelm Kaufmann felt completely different now he was wearing fresh clothing. As if the old rules of the game were back in place.

'I didn't expect you so quickly. Have you already found the body?'

'Of course we have,' Weller said. 'What did you expect?'

Ubbo Heide motioned for Weller to take it down a notch and check his emotions.

Büscher agreed completely. He was leaning against the wall and watching everything calmly. This is the heart of the gang I have to lead, he thought. Take a good look at them. This is how they are. Maybe you'll be one of them someday. But that will be a damn long road.

Wilhelm Kaufmann addressed Ubbo Heide, as if he didn't take anyone else seriously. 'I would have called you early tomorrow morning. My report would have been on your desks at the start of work.'

'So you were planning on making a confession?' Ubbo Heide asked.

'Well, I wouldn't call it a confession. I wanted to make a statement. I did stab him.'

'We've already seen that,' Rupert muttered. Somehow he didn't like this conversation between Ubbo Heide and Kaufmann. He was tired and irritated. He turned round and looked at Büscher questioningly. But Büscher just kept on listening.

Ann Kathrin Klaasen considered this conversation between Ubbo Heide and Wilhelm Kaufmann to be exactly the right way to find out the truth quickly.

'What kind of statement,' Ubbo Heide asked, 'can be made at this point except for a confession?'

'It was self-defence. He attacked me.'

'Sure,' Rupert laughed and shamelessly scratched his balls, 'You're in the sauna when you get attacked, but luckily you have a knife with you and boom, you finish him off.'

Kaufmann considered Rupert's approach stupid and disrespectful and therefore didn't react at first. Instead, he said to Ubbo Heide, 'He thought I had murdered Heymann and Stern and believed I'd kill him next.'

Rupert smirked. 'Well, he sure was a smart one! Probably graduated from school.' He clapped his hands. 'Do you know what, Kaufmann, that's what we all think!'

Ubbo Heide looked at Ann Kathrin, who turned to Weller. 'I think it's better if you and Rupert step outside for a little while.'

Weller grabbed Rupert by the shoulder and pulled him up from his chair.

'What?' Rupert asked, 'What? Did I say something wrong again? Am I causing trouble at this little party?'

Weller didn't even allow himself to get drawn into a debate. Rupert looked at Büscher, hoping for support, but he was in agreement and didn't react as Weller pulled Rupert to the door and pushed him out of the room.

Ubbo Heide nodded to Ann Kathrin in thanks. Then he asked Kaufmann, 'Why David Weissberg?'

Wilhelm Kaufmann made a confused face and leaned back in his chair. 'David Weissberg? Do you mean *the* David Weissberg?'

'Yes, exactly. How did you know that I called him the Silver Fox in my new book?'

Astonished, Wilhelm opened his hands. 'I had no clue, Ubbo. I don't know your new book.'

'No one knows it. It won't be published.'

'I don't understand.'

Now Ann Kathrin chimed in. 'Mr Kaufmann, you stabbed David Weissberg in the sauna in Uslar and stuffed a piece of fur in his mouth.'

'From a fox,' Ubbo Heide added.

Kaufmann shook his head. 'Oh no,' he said, 'I've never been to Uslar in my whole life. I came to Langeoog for a holiday. I come here every year for two weeks. And I always rent the flat above this one. But this time Birger Holthusen was on the island. He attacked me on Flinthörn. He wanted to kill me. He confessed to having killed Steffi Heymann and Nicola Billing and two other children.'

Ubbo Heide collapsed as if he'd taken a punch to the stomach. For a moment Ann Kathrin feared he could be suffering a heart attack as Ubbo grabbed his chest in a way she'd never seen him do. Then his hands slid up higher to his neck.

'Does that mean Heymann and Stern were innocent?'

'Yes, Ubbo, that's what it means. You and I – we were both barking up the wrong tree.'

Ubbo Heide said nothing more. He looked to Ann Kathrin, begging her for help.

'Where,' she asked, 'is Birger Holthusen?'

'At Flinthörn. He couldn't get away. His own knife is in his chest. A dagger.' Kaufmann motioned with his fingers, 'This long. Almost a sabre.'

'My God,' Ubbo Heide said, 'we destroyed the lives of Heymann and Stern by false suspicion. And then in the end they were killed.'

'The courts,' Ann Kathrin said, 'had acquitted them.'

'Yes,' Ubbo groaned, 'the courts.'

Büscher pushed away from the wall. It was as if he'd only now entered the room. He straightened up in front of the others and said, 'Did I understand that right? There's another body? This Birger Holthusen?'

'Yes,' Wilhelm Kaufmann said. 'I caught Steffi Heymann and Nicola Billing's killer after all.'

'Can I have a glass of water?' Ubbo Heide asked. He looked pale as a ghost.

*

He had brought her a bucket so that she could relieve herself. What he viewed as a generous privilege he had given her, to her felt like a further means to humiliate and control her. She imagined how he would obtain urine and faeces samples in an improvised laboratory to analyse her condition precisely.

Was she part of an experiment? Was he one of those mad scientists that she remembered from the B-movies of her youth, when a trip to the Apollo Theatre represented the high point of a Sunday afternoon?

She felt heavy, as if she'd swallowed stones. She was suffering from constipation and stomach cramps. She kept on burping loudly, as if she were drunk. She felt embarassed, even here, alone in her cell, but she couldn't hold it in. The air came up out of the depths of her body like a scream and pushed its way out.

He brought her scrambled eggs with prawns, bacon and ham, accompanied by a thermos flask of filter coffee. He'd even provided milk and sugar, as if they were sitting out on the harbour in Greetsiel enjoying the view of the historic ships while eating.

He looked like he was in a good mood, but she knew how quickly this could change.

He demanded her notebook. She passed it through the bars and was surprised her hands wasn't shaking.

'It's impossible,' she said, 'for anyone to gain weight that fast. A body isn't a vessel you can just pour food into for it to become heavier.'

He smiled and spoke to her as though she were a child. 'But, my dear, that's exactly how it is.' He pointed to his open mouth. 'Things go in here and come out down there. If you put more in than comes out, then you gain weight.'

She didn't touch the food, but hoped that the coffee would help her digestion, although she would have prefered some herbal drops and a peppermint tea to help her with the stomach cramps.

'What you put into your body,' he said, 'also has to stay in there. You understand? There are two ways that happens. Either it can turn into fat or muscle tissue. The way you're hanging around here – just look at yourself – it'll turn into fat, if anything. But we'll change that. Look what I've brought you.'

He held up a rope.

Her first thought was that he was planning to hang her. But this wasn't the case.

'This is how every boxer prepares for a big fight. You coordinate balance, speed, body control, muscles from your calves up to your back. You must have liked doing it as a child.'

He began to skip in front of the bars.

My God, she thought, a child's game had never seemed so terrible.

He passed the rope through the bars. 'Now it's your turn. Get started! Go! The calories I bring you have to be transformed into muscle.'

'I can't, I have a stomach ache. Constipation. I—'

'Yeah, I'm sure. That's what comes from lazy living. But that's over now. In a few weeks you'll be fit as a fiddle. You'll see just how much you can improve your performance.'

She took the rope and let it slip between her fingers. It was made out of hemp and had bright handles.

With this, she thought, I could do more than just skip. I could tie you up or strangle you.

'Start,' he demanded. Otherwise your food will get cold. First you jump a little, then there's breakfast. And you'll be astonished what I've got for you then. We'll make your jail into a real little gym. Don't look so glum!' he screamed at her. 'This is the way it is. And remember to smile for the camera! After all, you know the show must go on. When I send the next pictures of you, you don't want to look like a cheap bitch, do you? Your pictures will be sent to the press throughout the whole country. What am I saying, you'll be an international star! Don't you want to look your best?'

She began to rotate the rope and hop as she had as a child. She had already stumbled by the second turn and almost fell.

'You're out of practice,' he grinned, 'but you'll get there. Look at it like this: you have the opportunity to atone for your sins here and become a better person. I'm a kind of personal trainer for you. Out there in real prisons they have people like that too. But at least I don't chatter on about social programmes or re training .Those things don't matter because you're never getting out of here anyway.'

*

Weller was really looking forward to the appointment. He, who'd spent some of the most pleasant and relaxing hours of his life with a thick crime novel in hand, was visiting a publishing house for the first time. He pictured it as a magical place where the rooms were drenched with artistic creativity the way other places smell of cleaning materials and photocopiers.

Ubbo Heide had become subdued and seemed broken to Weller, not at all as if he could at any moment get up out of his wheelchair and say: '*I've had enough, I'm back to being the old Ubbo.*' No, today he even let Weller push him. He was silent in a dogged way and seemed introverted and self-tormenting.

Weller was almost embarrassed because he was so excited. He knew several books by the crime novelists who were published here.

When the door opened Weller took a deep breath and briefly closed his eyes, like he used to do upon entering a bakery, in joyful anticipation of the delicious treat. The publishing director and an editor were able to spare some time to see them. For Weller they exuded intelligence in a sympathetic way. He was impressed.

They could be involved with fictitious crimes, with the possibilities, with language, but yesterday they surely hadn't stood in front of a paedophile who had bled out on the beach, Weller thought. He felt the desire to immediately swap places with these people, become part of this company. Learning from the bottom up.

Yes, why not stand at the photocopier or brew coffee for everyone? Here no one was in danger of landing in a wheelchair because of a knife, as had happened with Ubbo Heide. Weller tried to shake off these thoughts.

The publishing director looked like an ageing hippy. He wore a light blazer with the elbows worn thin; his formal shirt was open to the second button and he had curly grey chest hair. Everything here seemed easy and light, even superficial .

Although Weller had requested this conversation as a homicide detective, the talk now seemed to focus more on Ubbo Heide and his new book.

Weller drank his coffee black, and it tasted unusually good for filter coffee. The publishing director mentioned that he could also have a 'real' coffee from the espresso machine.

Ubbo Heide waved him away, and his editor said in a warm, empathetic voice, 'Naturally we completely understand the fact that you want to hold back your second book for the time being.'

'Although we regret it greatly in the light of the outstanding pre-orders and the importance of the topic,' the publishing director chimed in, and then handed back to his editor with a gesture.

The editor smiled and continued, 'Of course we hope we can publish the second volume as soon as the culprit has been caught. Which is why you can expect any and all support from us.'

'Of course not just because of that,' the publishing director corrected. 'We love crime in a literary way – we don't need it in the real world.'

Ubbo Heide remained silent, only looking at Weller, giving him the floor.

'I want to tell you how much I value what you do. I'm familiar with several books from your publishing house,' Weller said. 'I'm a real fan of crime fiction. But we have a problem. It's extremely important for us that we find out everything about the people who know the contents of Ubbo Heide's second book or somehow have obtained knowledge of it.'

The publishing director spread his arms and crossed them behind his head before stretching out in his chair. 'Our authors' manuscripts aren't exactly state secrets, but we do treat them with a high degree of confidentiality. We only ever have a few months' head start over our competition. Then everyone else can imitate us. Series, even entire programmes are copied. if you publish a successful book with the title *Monster Ships*, you can be sure that soon similar titles with similar contents will appear that could be called *Ships Monster, Monsters over Ships, Monsters in Ships*, and so on. So there's only a very small circle of people who know exactly what we're doing. I'd never tell you what book your favourite author is writing right next, for example.'

Weller levelled with him: 'Someone has read Ubbo Heide's manuscript and committed a murder for which knowledge of the contents is necessary. It even seems as if he committed the murder to demonstrate that he already knows the new book, although it hasn't even been published.'

The publishing director slapped the arms of his chair and exhaled. 'Wow. That's a bit much!'

'You can say that again,' Weller confirmed. 'I need a list of all the people who—'

The editor addressed Ubbo Heide. 'There aren't many people. I didn't send the manuscript round, or share it with any critics, or offer any galleys or anything like that.'

The publishing director coughed. 'Sometimes,' he said, 'we hire freelance editors.'

It sounded like an apology. But the editor shook her head, 'Oh no, not in this case.'

The two employees of the publishing house looked at each other, and the boss asked, 'Then you're the only one who is familiar with the manuscript?'

At first she nodded, but she seemed uncertain to Weller. 'This is enormously importantly to us.'

'Well, of course I wrote a short summary for the press, advertising and marketing.'

'I want to see that!' Weller demanded.

The publishing director raised his right hand conciliatorily. Under no circumstances did he want the tone to get combative. 'We'll cooperate fully and completely. One moment, please.'

He typed away at his computer and activated the printer behind Weller that he'd not even noticed. The editor handed Weller a piece of paper.

Weller registered that Ubbo Heide was called a 'bestselling author' and in the picture he looked ten years younger than in real life, but Weller couldn't find anything in the piece to give away the crime. Words like 'fox pelt' or 'silver fox' didn't appear.

He passed the paper to Ubbo, who held it with both hands, as if it were very heavy.

Weller decided to reveal more than he'd intended. Sometimes, if you were sitting around with good people it made sense to put all the cards on the table, show your hand to motivate them to play along.

'A man was stabbed in Uslar. He appears in Ubbo Heide's book as "Silver fox" and the killer left a piece of fox fur in his mouth as a message for us.'

The publishing director sank deeper into his chair. The editor held her hand in front of her mouth and exhaled. 'Oh my God! That sounds like the plot of a horror novel.'

'But it's the damn truth,' Weller said, 'and the killer has another victim in his clutches. He knows the manuscript. He can't have got the information,' Weller pointed to the paper that Ubbo Heide held in his hands like a heavy brick, 'from this text here.'

No one said anything for a while. Weller considered it a kind of pause for thought. Sometimes things had to sink in before they could continue.

'Where do you keep your manuscripts?' Weller asked.

The editor answered. 'On my computer. There's no print out of Ubbo's second bookd.'

'Well great,' Weller grumbled. He only now realised how ironic it was to be referring to a manuscript, literally hand written, while everything was digital these days.

'Who has access to your computer?'

'Well, me and—'

'Basically everyone in our publishing house,' the publishing director said and sat down again. 'Everything is password protected, but good Lord – anyone who works here can quickly get each others' passwords. It's all so . . . I mean, who expects something like this to happen?' He suddenly slammed his fist on the table, as if trying to kill an insect. 'Damn it, we had that hacker attack!'

Weller was on alert. 'What happened?'

'Well, we didn't know exactly what was going on, but our systems were knocked out. We couldn't get on the Internet. An issue with the router or something. I studied humanities; don't ask me things like that.'

'And what did you do?'

'Well, we hired a company that dealt with the whole thing—'

'Which company?'

The publishing director didn't know. He looked at his editor, who shrugged her shoulders.

'Well, I had a nice young man come to me. He didn't need very long, and then everything was back up and running.'

'Well,' Weller said, 'there must be an order, an invoice, or—'

'Yes, there must be,' the publishing director agreed, and punched a button on his telephone. An intern came through the door with excessive enthusiasm, as if she'd only been waiting for this all day. ACB was printed on her T-shirt.

Weller immediately liked her. He wished he had an intern like her too.

'You helped us when all the computers went on strike.'

'Yeah,' she beamed, 'my boyfriend works for a computer repair shop and—'

'Can I have the address?' Weller asked.

'Well, that's the funny thing,' she said.

Ubbo Heide looked like he was about to jump out of his wheelchair. It was exactly words like that made the alarms go off in his head. If something was odd or different from normal, then something monstrous could be hidden behind the apparent coincidences.

That's exactly what Weller was thinking as well. Now they were getting very close. Weller's skin was practically crawling, as if the culprit was within reach.

'My boyfriend came here to do the job himself – to surprise me.'

'And?' Weller asked. This conversation couldn't move fast enough for him.

'Well, everything was fine by the time he got here. Someone else from the company had been here first. But he couldn't say who it had been. There's only four people who work there. But sometimes, when they're really busy – which is all the time – they use freelancers. Schoolkids who are good at that sort of thing or—'

Weller couldn't stay in his seat anymore. He stood up. 'Wait a second. That means some random person was messing with the IT system here and you don't know who it was?'

'He was tall and skinny,' the editor remembered. It sounded like an apology.

'Did you have him show his ID?' Weller asked.

'No. I was happy that someone had come. He was competent, had everything fixed right away and—'

'And stole your data,' Weller declared. 'Good God, it's that simple, he makes your system crash, in other words, creating the problem. Then he offers himself as the solution. You probably even gave him a coffee while he stole everything he needed.'

She nodded. 'Yes. With milk and sugar.'

'Data theft,' the publishing director groaned. 'That's one of those awful things. Nothing's missing, and still something was stolen.'

'Yep,' Weller said. 'Welcome to the new millennium. Are there any surveillance systems here? Are there videos saved of people who park outside or come into the building, or—'

The publishing director showed his open palms like a sign of his innocence. 'Good Lord, we're not dealing with people like that! We're a publishing house. We publish crime novels. We normally don't deal with criminals, just with—' he waved them away and stopped talking.

'Yes,' Weller declared, 'maybe not normally. But you made it damn easy for them.'

'Now that sounds like an accusation,' the publishing director groaned, taken aback.

Well it is, damn it, Weller wanted to say, but Ubbo Heide stopped him with a glance.

'You're good people,' Ubbo said. 'No one's making accusations. But we're dealing with a cunning, evil person. He's exploiting our weaknesses. Not only yours, mine as well. And he knows us damn well.'

*

The formal way Ann Kathrin Klaasen addressed Wilhelm Kaufman was markedly different from the way she treated other suspects. He imagined there was a little more deference, even respect, in her voice, although he realised that he was sitting there as a suspect.

'I'll answer all of your questions, Ms. Klaasen. I know whom I'm dealing with. You're considered the interrogation expert for the East Frisian police. What am I saying? For the whole state of Lower Saxony, if not the entire country. It's said about you that—'

'Yes, it's said that I'm even able to get a chair or a case of beer to talk. I know. Now don't try to flatter me. You're above cheap tricks like that, Mr Kaufmann. For me there are only two possibilities: either you're an extremely cunning psychopath, who is trying to dispense his own kind of justice, or you're our best option for catching the killer. In either case, we have plenty of work ahead of us.'

'You're right about that, Ms. Klaasen,' he said. 'Let's get started.'

She paced three steps, turned, three steps. Glanced at him every time she took the last step.

He registered exactly what she was doing. Lies seemed almost absurd in the context. She would know straightaway if he wasn't telling the truth. She wants me to realise the hopelessness of his situation, he thought. Everything she does is planned. She has positioned me here so that I'm sitting with my back to the door. I'm supposed to believe that there is no way out and that this conversation is my last chance. She's presenting herself as the only person who can understand me. With her body language, her looks and gestures. She believes she can get everything out of me, and she wants me to believe that too.

'Then let's start with the lies first,' she said.

'Which lies?'

'You were in Uslar. We have video footage.'

He laughed. 'Pictures from surveillance cameras? From the sauna?'

'No, cameras aren't permitted in places like that, as you know. But there are plenty in the city. We spotted you three times. But if we looked long enough there would surely be more sightings. And believe me, we'll check every surveillance camera in Uslar for the time in question, second by second.'

He applauded her. 'Bravo,' he said, 'bravo. As a former detective, I can only say great job. But if I had been in Uslar, I would admit to it now. I've never been there in my whole life. I even doubt that I would have made it from there in time to meet Birger Holthusen in Langeoog.'

'Oh, I don't think that's a big deal,' she said.

'High tide and low tide cannot be shifted.'

'Thanks for the information,' she said sarcastically. 'Have to remember that one.'

Suddenly she stared at him as though trying to look deep in his soul.

'What do you want? To read my thoughts?'

'Good plan.'

'Ms. Klaasen, I went to Langeoog. I'd been planning to for ages. I always reserve the holiday flat a year in advance. It'd be easy to check.'

'And when did Birger Holthusen find out that you were there?'

He lifted both hands and then let them slap back to the table.

Ann Kathrin thought it sounded like butcher tossing chops onto the scales, but she didn't say so.

'It certainly wouldn't be hard for him to work it out. If someone has gone on holiday to the same small island at exactly the same time for ten years, then . . . But I have to be honest with you, Ms. Klaasen. I don't think he found out in any kind of intelligent way.'

'What do you mean by that? That he was stupid?'

'No, he certainly wasn't stupid. I want to say that he—' He gulped and didn't continue. His gaze seemed to pass through the wall and end up somewhere completely different.

'Yes?' Shouted Ann Kathrin.

'He just seemed to know. You should understand that. The instincts that you have, Ms. Klaasen.'

'Instincts? I do my homework, and then—' she began to scold. 'Don't you dare tell me it was a coincidence. I don't believe in them.'

'No, it wasn't a coincidence. He was waiting for me.'

She looked at him, disbelieving.

He tried to explain it with an example. 'Ms. Klaasen, if you go to a party, you know exactly who – besides yourself – is with the police, right?'

She nodded. 'Sure. But I couldn't tell you beforehand who would be at the party.'

He argued. 'I don't believe that. If you know that there's going to be free beer and scantily clad girls dancing on a pole, then you could tell me exactly which of your colleagues would likely show up.'

'Rupert,' she laughed. 'But this thing with you and Holthusen doesn't seem that simple.'

Kaufmann took a deep breath. 'He thought I was like him . . . Which is ridiculous, of course. Although I've not always dealt very well with adults, I truly am not attracted to little children.' He looked at her apologetically. 'Yes, many of my relationships have failed. I either avoided women or tried to dominate them, for fear of being inferior or becoming submissive.

'Please!' He pointed to the recorder. 'Can we turn that off? Is Ubbo Heide behind the window? Is my old friend listening to everything I'm telling you here?'

She didn't answer his question, but in her face he thought he sensed that Ubbo wasn't there.

She bent forward and pressed the stop button. 'If you're not the killer, then help me catch him.'

'Good God, of course I'm not. I've got a temper! I never wanted to be like this but I didn't get to decide! Sometimes things happen, and then I lose it. I react in a way that I shouldn't. I've got into fights and punched people before – more than once – and Ubbo and my other colleagues didn't want to cover up what I'd done anymore. You can understand that.'

'You're not a bad person,' Ann Kathrin said. 'All your life you've struggled to be one of the good guys. Right?'

He gulped and nodded. He wiped away a tear. 'Yes, damn it, I have. But to truly be one of the good guys you have to be able to control your feelings and I couldn't do that.'

'But a person with just a bad temper,' Ann Kathrin said, 'doesn't calmly plan a murder, get the tools, and—'

Kaufmann raised his hands. 'No! For heaven's sake, of course not! I lose it sometimes, but I'm not a calculating killer!'

*

He felt omnipotent. He had got back into the zone.

Oh yes, he was pulling the strings in this puppet show.

You know that I know your most secret desires and burn with truth. Yes, I realise what you want but don't dare to say out loud.

It gets to you too! You're not stupid! You read the papers and see the reports as I do, right?

Gravito is due to be released in Columbia, if he's not already been out for a while. He abused and killed one hundred and sixty children! But his confession led to his prison sentence being cut in half – to just twenty-four years – one month and seven days per victim. That is assuming we know about all of the victims.

In Columbia, people are often released after three-fifths of their sentence has been served. Which would mean only fourteen years for Gravito. If I have calculated correctly, that means the punishment per child was reduced to less than a month. And then he's free to do it all again.

Do you remember Degowski? He'll be getting out soon. No one could forget the pictures of him holding the gun to Silke Bischoff's head. In the end, three people were dead after that bank robbery went wrong. One of those was Silke Bischoff. And a five-year-old Italian boy.

Degowski will presumably be freed under a new name. That is usual; after all, you can't let famous criminals loose in public with their own names. Who would want to live near to them? So of course, he gets a new name and identity.

Degowski was prepared for his release gradually. He was allowed to go out for the day by himself. And we're all supposed to be happy for him!

Something is wrong in our society, friends. Cancerous tissue has to be cut out before it metastasises and kills the body that fed it. If you looked deep into your souls, you'd agree with me. You just don't yet dare say it out loud.

You're still thinking about the way in which I got my hands on Ubbo Heide's manuscript. If I grab one of those Jansen brothers now, then you'll know that I have an insight into your thoughts.

I'm a part of you. If you could finally think clearly and leave behind your blinkers, then I would no longer need to be the executioner. You could create order and free this country from all of the filth.

This feeling was better than any drug. Being completely in the zone. There was a chance for him to play his game and everything work out to his advantage.

Michael Jansen worked for the big CEWE Colour company in Oldenburg. He enjoyed jogging in the castle gardens after work. He openly shared information about his running schedule on his Facebook page. He had illustrated his routes with wonderful photos.

He appeared to have some knowledge of trees and wood because he included explanations under the photos: redwood, black walnut, red oak. Jansen was probably looking for fellow joggers to connect with. The whole Facebook page seemed like it was aimed this way. He had also posted numerous pictures of himself, of his firm calves, his fine-tuned body. His six-pack was especially prominent. You are probably accompanied by love-struck ladies with bouncing bosoms on your jogging route, he thought.

It should be easy to catch you in the gardens. I'll park my car next to yours, and when you return all sweaty at the end of your own macho Olympics, there are just two possibilities: if you've landed a chick and are accompanied to the car, then you're in luck and I'll let you go. If the ladies have lost interest in you, and you slowly climb into your flashy car all alone, then your time has come, Jansen.

He considered the disadvantages of putting Michael Jansen in the second cell. Strictly speaking, he hadn't actually committed a crime. He only needed him to retract his false statement, take back the alibi he'd provided, and then he could be released. There was nothing more at stake.

But anyone who'd seen that space couldn't be returned to freedom, regardless of whether he had accepted his punishment or not. The danger of blowing his cover was simply too great.

It'd be more effective, he thought, if they receive the confession and see that he is in a cell like Svenja Moers. Or would it frighten them even more to find a lying witness with his throat slit? And to top it off – as they suggested themselves – with a playing card in his mouth.

Everything pointed towards him killing Michael Jansen. The effect would be great, especially on his brother Werner. He would know exactly why his brother had died, and it would be clear that he was going after him next. Then Werner Jansen would confess, and not at the threat of prison. Instead, he would run to the police, or make a statement directly to the prosecutor's office. He'd say how sorry he was about everything and that he had acted under pressure. That he'd thought his friend was innocent and had only made the statement to help him. That would make the whole house of cards collapse and Volker Janssen would end up in prison. Probably even voluntarily, for fear of being beheaded.

He smiled. He was satisfied with himself. It was as if the blood was being pumped more swiftly through his veins, giving him a jittery, hot feeling.

He looked at the screen. Svenja Moers was staring at the bars lethargically and stubbornly – like a grounded pubescent teenager.

He needed to take her some more exercise equipment. He wanted to get her fit. He wished he could chase her around the house again and again, but that, unfortunately, wasn't possible.

I simply have too much to do for a single person, he thought. If I focus on training Svenja now, then I'll lose too much time. I have to take care of Michael Jansen first. The faster I wave the truth in front of your noses, the sooner you'll come to my side and play by my rules. It has been your game for too long. Your brains are clogged by notions of legality.

*

He pulled on his tracksuit, blue with three white stripes. He felt like he looked boring, adhering to society's dress codes. And that's exactly the way he wanted to look. He would blend in and not look suspicious to another jogger.

When he left his home in Emden, the worry of being watched crept up on him. Had snipers already taken up position on the surrounding houses? Where they more intelligent than he thought? Had they found out Yves Stern's real name?

He wanted to drive to Oldenburg via the A31 and A28 autobahns, but decided to take a detour to see if he was being followed. He drove towards Aurich via Ihlow. The silver-grey VW Golf looked suspicious to him. Its number plate showed NOR, so a driver from Norden and not Aurich. There was a young, long-haired woman with a hooked nose sitting behind the wheel. She was talking non-stop and gesticulating wildly.

Was she having an argument with a partner? Was she gossiping with a friend? Or did she have a direct line to Ann Kathrin Klaasen, Büscher and Ubbo Heide? Was she part of their team?

Her face didn't look familiar. He decided to test her.

He pulled over in a spot between the trees and acted as if he urgently had to pee.

The VW whizzed past him.

If they're really following me, he thought, she'll turn around and come back. Then it's your turn, girl. Before I deal with Michael Jansen.

But there was no sign of the VW. Maybe she had changed cars, or passed the baton to her colleagues.

He drove from Aurich to Wiesmoor. From there he drove towards Sande, then to Varel, and finally towards Westerstede and Bad Zwischenahn.

It had started to rain.

Shit, he thought, could it be that he was a wimp and wouldn't go jogging in the rain? Was this whole trip going to be in vain?

*

Michael Jansen was doing overtime in the office. A little shower became steady rain.

He sat in the car and smoked. He didn't take his eyes off the CEWE Colour entrance.

He had wound down the side windows slightly and turned up the fan, but the windows still steamed up.

If I'm in the zone, he thought, everything comes round in my favour. I have to have faith.

And that's exactly what happened. Michael Jansen didn't let the rain hold him back after such a long day at work. He was already wearing a tracksuit when he left the office. It was one of those ridiculous suits with water repellent microfibres and bright colours on the turned-down collar, colour coordinated with his salmon-pink running shoes.

Michael Jansen climbed into a light-blue BMW, equipped with huge loudspeakers.

Did you get the beautiful car in return for your false testimony? Or were you dumb enough to do it for free? As a favour? You never know when you'll need him again.

The rain eased during the drive to the castle gardens, but luckily there weren't any annoying female joggers around. Perhaps he hadn't presented himself well enough on his Facebook page.

They were alone in the park, running next to each other for a while, as if they had known each other for years. They didn't say a word, but each was listening to the other's breath, and their feet were in sync as their shoes hit the rain-soaked ground.

Now he ran a little slower, remaining two strides behind Michael Jansen. It would have been easy to ram the dagger into his back. But he didn't think much of cowardly methods such as that.

He called his name. 'Michael Jansen?'

Jansen turned around in astonishment. The two looked each other in the eyes. Michael Jansen saw the blade, but couldn't believe what was in front of him.

His first attempt to push the knife into Jansen's neck failed as Jansen bent back, stumbled, and fell into a puddle. He threw his arms up, flailing like a bug that had fallen on its back and couldn't get backup.

'You can have my money! I have a bank card. I can take money out. I—'

'It's not about the money, you idiot! You protected a killer and rapist with your false statement!'

He severed the aorta with one clean cut and the rainwater in the puddle mixed with blood. Michael Jansen struggled hard, trying to get up despite the four-or five-centimetre cut in his neck. A stab to the heart ended it and Michael Jansen died with his mouth wide open.

Wiping the blade on the leg of Jansen's tracksuit leg, he cleaned his hands in the puddle and pulled out a playing card. He hoped that it would cause the desired panic throughout the entire police force. He shoved the card into Jansen's mouth, but it fell back out.

I can't have that, damn it! He pushed the card deep inside Jansen's mouth, and then pressed against his head and chin, as if he were a nut cracker.

He looked left and right to check they were still alone in the park. Then he took two pictures on his phone and walked away back the way they'd come, passing the cedar that Michael Jansen had praised on his Facebook page.

*

Ann Kathrin stood by the flipchart and wrote down what was known about the killer.

Weller, Rupert, Sylvia Hoppe, Rieke Gersema and Büscher pitched in energetically, not unlike a group of nerdy schoolkids, observed Ann Kathrin.

'Now we're going to pull together everything the killer knows about us, because this will ultimately lead us to him. Very few people have this information.'

'He knows Ubbo and his daughter, Ubbo's current book and details in the next,' Büscher began.

Ann Kathrin wrote 'Insa and Ubbo' and drew a red circle around the names.

'He knows his way around computers, otherwise he wouldn't have been able to do the thing at the publishing house,' Weller said.

Ann Kathrin wrote 'computer specialist' on the wall and drew a circle around that too.

'Maybe I should take a crack at Wilhelm Kaufmann,' Rupert suggested. 'You always put on the kid gloves.'

'He belongs in our group of suspects,' Ann Kathrin said, 'but we can't let that restrict our vision.'

Marion Wolters opened the door without knocking and spoke into the room. What she had to say couldn't wait. 'The Oldenburg police found a jogger in the castle gardens with his throat cut. It's Michael Jansen.'

Ann Kathrin had been just about to write something down. As the marker fell from her hand it made a squeaking noise and left a long line down the paper.

'Presumed or clearly identified?' asked Weller, who didn't want it to be true.

'His car was parked only a couple of hundred metres away. He had his ID with him. There's no doubt. And he has a playing card in his mouth.'

Weller felt sick. He jumped up, hitting his knee hard against the edge of the table. There was a clattering that sounded like a gun shot.

'That wasn't funny!' Weller yelled.

Marion agreed with him. 'It really wasn't!'

Ann Kathrin was breathing heavily. She was thin-lipped and pale. 'I only talked about Jansen here in this room. How we would find a witness with his throat cut.'

'And I,' Weller groaned, 'said I bet he would have a playing card in his mouth.'

'Yes,' Büscher nodded, 'I was there, damn it.' Then he continued, 'Either it was one of us, or someone's listening in on us.'

Weller had difficulty staying conscious. Vertigo made him sit down again and he wondered how Ann Kathrin could stand up giving clear orders. 'I want specialists in here immediately to check the room for bugs.'

'And the whole building while they're at it,' Büscher added. 'Then we need to look after the brother, Werner Jansen, immediately. He needs police protection, and we need to pick up Volker Janssen.'

'We'd all do better to keep our mouths shut,' Weller yelled at Büscher's, 'before he uses our next bright idea against us!'

Ann Kathrin nodded, but said, 'He won't go after either of those two now. I think he's banking on one of them giving in and confessing.'

'I think Charlie Thiekötter has one of those devices you can use to find and neutralise bugs,' Sylvia Hoppe said.

Rieke Gersema held her glasses tightly with both hands. 'We're finished if it gets out that the killer has been getting his information directly from the police station in Aurich.'

'He is too, if we could only get our hands on him,' Rupert said and slammed his right fist into his left palm.

*

Ubbo Heide had asked Ann Kathrin to bring some files to him at home. This was breaking all the rules, but they were beyond that. All they wanted was to catch the killer. And under no circumstances did she want to dispense with Ubbo's expertise.

Büscher had come along, uninvited.

Ubbo's wheelchair stood in the hallway. They were sitting in the living room – Ubbo like a wise old man in his wing chair. Oddly attractive. There was a look in his eye, such a wise gaze that it touched Ann Kathrin deeply.

It looked as if they were working here to be more comfortable, but in reality they needed to get out of the police station as they were now working under the assumption that they were being listened in on.

They didn't know who was doing it and how. But it seemed perfectly obvious.

Martin Büscher heard a commotion in the kitchen and went over to Carola Heide to make himself useful. His wife had always said that he hadn't been very helpful with the housework – but only after the divorce – and he'd learned his lesson.

He didn't like this whole thing at all. They were working in someone's home and not the police headquarters. But he'd still come because as long as the bugs hadn't been found in the police station, continuing to discuss the case there was just too risky and gave him stomach pain.

Büscher had a thought that was constantly turning over in his mind, something he hardly dared to voice. Could the executioner be Rupert, that macho idiot? He had been there in every one of those meetings. He had a rudimentary and archaic idea of the rule of law, and wasn't one who liked long debates. Instead, he preferred to take drastic measures and then apologise later if he was wrong.

There were two files lying open on Ubbo Heide's lap. He appreciated digital files and the images that could give a 360-degree view of a crime scene while sitting at a desk, but there was nothing better than a paper reference file. He was just old school like that.

He patted the paper. 'Ann, so it's like this: whenever we really close a case – sometimes only years later – in the end we often find that the solution was in the file all the time. We just didn't see it.'

'Because we interpreted things incorrectly?' she suggested, but he shook his head. 'No, because we didn't look closely enough. Because we overlooked things. Because our vision was obstructed by the chaos of everyday life.'

'Sometimes,' she said, 'we're simply overwhelmed by the sheer amount of information. How can I filter out exactly what's important to us from among those seven thousand pages?'

He smiled gently. 'Only your intuition can help there, my dear, not a computer. Instead of constantly producing new files, we should read what we already have carefully, so we can ask the right questions. But one thing is clear: we know the killer. Later we'll say: of course it was him! Who else could it have been? How could we missed that?'

Ann Kathrin needed to tell Ubbo Heide something. It was difficult, but this was exactly the right time. 'Ubbo, when you received the package on Wangerooge the sender was listed as—'

Ubbo finished her sentence: 'H. TAO. From Hude.' H. TAO.

'If you read it backwards, it spells OATH. That made me take another look at your book, Ubbo, and you—'

Ubbo's lower lip quivered as he formed the words. 'I wrote: "*I swore an oath not to let the two of them get away, but I wasn't able to definitively prove they were guilty of killing Steffi Heymann. The trial became a catastrophic defeat for our entire team of detectives. I even blamed myself. Sometimes I lie awake at night and think that it shouldn't have happened to me.*"'

He quoted almost perfectly from the book. It was easy for him to remember because he'd frequently read aloud from this chapter at events. But he'd never made the connection with the name 'H. Tao' before.

He leaned over to Ann Kathrin. 'As I've been saying!' he said.

She just looked at him.

'Well!'

'What should I say?'

'He's fulfilling my oath!'

Carola Heide came in from the kitchen with a tray. She was enveloped by a cloud of scent: East Frisian tea, peppermint and apple cake.

Büscher returned to the living room with Carola. He carried the teapot and the tea warmer. Carola enjoyed having this gentleman around, but Ubbo seemed a little annoyed at his presence. He would have preferred to talk to Ann Kathrin alone, but couldn't really send away her boss.

Büscher tried to understand the relationship between Ann Kathrin and Ubbo Heide. Sometimes he almost got the impression that there was something intimate going on between the two of them, but at others it was more like a father–daughter relationship. Either way, it was not like that of any normal former boss and employee.

'OK,' Carola said, 'enjoy and take your time.'

She deposited the tray.

'Perhaps,' Ubbo Heide said, 'we should drink the tea with cream and sugar this time.'

Carola stared at him and asked herself if he was serious. 'Not with peppermint leaves?'

'Dribble the cream anticlockwise,' he said, 'to turn back the clock. We may find some answers to our questions in the past, not the future.'

Carola shrugged her shoulders. She knew that her husband liked to wax philosophical if he wasn't making progress in a case.

The sugar was crackling in the cup when Carola said in passing, 'A journalist from Gelsenkirchen has already called twice today. She wants an interview with you, Ubbo. I tried to shake her off, but she—'

'Silke Sobotta from the *Stadtspiegel*?'

'Exactly,' Carola answered, 'that was her. She was ill when you were in Gelsenkirchen and—'

Ubbo waved her away, as if he didn't want to hear about it. 'I already gave her colleague an interview. That lanky young man.' Ubbo thought for a second but couldn't think of his name.

Ann Kathrin helped him out. 'Kowalski.'

Ubbo nodded in thanks.

'Perhaps you should call her back,' Carola suggested.

Ubbo Heide shook his head. 'No, everyone wants to know why my new book won't be published, and what that has to do with the case. We really have more important things to do.' He leafed ostentiatiously through the file, as if searching for an important passage.

Carola lowered the teapot and apologised with emphatic gestures. 'But I told her that she could call again. She had such a nice voice. I simply couldn't get rid of her. I always have your back otherwise, but I'm not a secretary, damn it, and recently it's been—'

The phone rang.

'That'll be her. I did agree.'

'Go on, answer it,' Ann Kathrin said to Ubbo reassuringly. 'You don't have to speak for long.'

Disgruntled, Ubbo accepted the telephone and answered sullenly. 'Hey. Heide here. With whom do I have the pleasure of speaking?'

Ann Kathrin tried the tea while Ubbo attempted to fend off Silke Sobotta.

'I really don't have any time, Ms. Sobotta. As much as I'd like to talk to you, I don't feel well and am in the middle of an important conversation. And I already did an interview with your colleague, Mr Kowalski. Didn't that get published?'

The answer hit Ubbo like a sucker punch.

'I don't have a colleague named Kowalski and we haven't published an interview with you. This man has to have been from another paper, but he's certainly not from Gelsenkirchen because I know the reporters here.'

Ubbo and Ann Kathrin looked at each other questioningly and she immediately used her iPhone to Google Kowalski, but couldn't find a journalist by that name.

Ubbo pictured the scene. The tall, gaunt man hadn't even introduced himself as a reporter from the *Stadtspiegel.*

Although his ability to remember names was diminishing, Ubbo could remember faces, conversations and situations even better than he used to. 'I practically put the words in his mouth, damn it. He'd only introduced himself as Kowalski and said "I'm here to interview you." Then I assumed he was from the *Stadtspiegel*. I even told him that Ms. Sobotta was ill. Weller didn't believe him at first, hadn't wanted to let him through. He was excellently informed, had read my book and—'

'Damn it, Ubbo,' Ann Kathrin said, 'you gave the killer an interview!'

Ubbo said, 'And Weller was right! The killer was in Gelsenkirchen.'

'That means,' Ann Kathrin deduced, 'that we have a picture of him. We can put a warrant out with a picture.'

Ubbo lifted the phone back to his ear. 'Ms. Sobotta? You have to keep our conversation completely confidential. You just gave us a critical lead. But please, we have to keep it to ourselves. You can have your interview, as long as you want. I'll pay for your trip to East Frisia, and we'll put you up at a first-class hotel. Just not now. And please don't say a word to anyone!'

She instantly recognised the explosive nature of the situation, promised to keep her lips sealed and he ended the conversation.

'I believe we can count on her,' Ubbo said Ann Kathrin.

She tried to summarise what they had. 'We all know what he looks like, how he moves, we certainly have pictures of him. We'll issue a warrant for him.'

But Ubbo raised his hands defensively. 'Not so fast, Ann, not so fast.'

He beckoned her closer, as if she were at the end of the street, and not in his living room, just three metres away. He wanted to whisper something into her ear, but before he did so, he gestured to his wife to turn on the radio.

Carola instantly understood and did as he desired.

The local station Radio Lower Saxony was playing old songs. Ubbo Heide gestured again, asking Carola to turn it up louder. Only then did he whisper in Ann Kathrin's ear. 'I know where he gets all his information. He gave me a tin of mints. From Bochum. I had them with me in my wheelchair. I bet there's a—'

'A bug.' The word slipped from Ann Kathrin's lips and she immediately held a hand in front of her mouth.

Büscher, who had been listening as well, stepped into the middle of the room and raised both hands. He motioned Ann Kathrin and Ubbo Heide to stop talking. He took the file from Ubbo's lap and wrote on the back of a piece of paper. *This is our chance. If he's really listening to what we say, then we can lay a trap for him.*

Ubbo and Ann Kathrin read it, looked at each other, and Ann Kathrin gave a thumbs up.

Ubbo did the same.

*

There hadn't been anything for quite some time, just static and a crackling noise. He worried the battery was dead or the bug had been discovered. He wanted to be there now, know what was going on.

Being among them, unseen, that got him into the zone, giving him this wonderful feeling of omnipotence and superiority.

He pictured their reaction to the playing card in Michael Jansen's mouth and to the piece of silver fox fur between David Weissberg's teeth. Would they finally understand that he was the one making their secret dreams a reality? Would they finally support him? Finally join in with him as the righteous executioner? Could the great clean-up now begin?

He was making good progress with Svenja Moers. She appeared to have understood that she was responsible for all of her own, reprehensible deeds. She ate and exercised with gusto.

He was playing with the idea of training her to become a fighting machine. He'd seen an American movie where a beautiful young woman who had committed a crime was turned into a killing machine. Perhaps it could still be possible with Svenja Moers. Then she could be let out of the cage from time to time so she could carry out a job for him. It was becoming more and more difficult to find new disguises. At some point they would see through all his masks and costumes, and unfortunately he couldn't change his size. If only he could become a small, fat man – just for the day.

Perhaps he'd direct the strikes from a chair at some point. Like a guru. A man on high ensuring the country became worth living in again. So that people no longer needed to be afraid to go out at night. With a dozen determined men and women – willing to do anything – he could create a country where only the criminals would be afraid because they would be pursued mercilessly like wild animals being hunted. No one would mourn this endangered species.

There was something intoxicating about these ideas and he saw himself as Ubbo Heide was: a recognised, beloved authority whose advice was valued, and who made that wheelchair he sat upon into a royal throne.

He drank cocoa, like his grandma had made him and watched Svenja Moers on the screen. She was using the exercise machine and pedalled away for a good twenty minutes. Sweat pearled on her forehead.

Did she know that he was watching her, could even read the level of difficulty? The machine was set at sixty and she rode at a speed of twenty-three kilometres per hour. That was already pretty good for her, he thought.

He turned on the loudspeakers and said, 'You're doing really well. Keep going. And don't forget those nutritional drinks: they were expensive!'

She looked up into the camera, nodded and smiled at him.

Yes, he thought, maybe you'll be my fighting machine. Maybe, just maybe, I'll give you the chance to atone for your sins by fighting on our side.

Then he heard something again. They were driving and the police radio was on.

There'd been an accident with several injuries on Issumer Strasse in Wittmund. A driver was out of control. Apparently it was a criminal who had been wanted for a long time.

But they were going to the police station in Norden, on the market square and not to Wittmund. He heard Ann Kathrin saying, 'The officers in Wittmund will have to deal with that by themselves. Everyone from K1 is gathering in Norden.'

A shiver ran down his spine. *Everyone from K1.* That meant the homicide squad was getting together, and he'd be there, live.

It must be about him. What else? An accident in Wittmund was meaningless by comparison, even if a criminal was involved.

He felt good and drank his cocoa, leaning back in his chair, stretching out his legs. Ubbo Heide is with them, he thought. My activities have brought him back into the line of duty and made him the head of the Kripo. In the end, that wimp Büscher will have to either get in line or go back to Bremerhaven.

Ubbo Heide is the key to everything. Whoever has Ubbo on their side has won. Ann Kathrin will be the first to toe the line, and in the end the whole gang will too.

He heard Weller crackling over the police radio. 'I'm almost at Werner Jansen's place in Oldenburg Ofenerdiek. Should I turn around and come to Norden or—'

Luckily Ann Kathrin spoke loudly and clearly, 'No, Frank, it's important that you talk to him.'

'But the police in Oldenburg could do that.'

'I would prefer for you to be there. He has to have police protection so just arrest him if he doesn't cooperate.'

'I can't just do that.'

'Work it out, Frank.'

He laughed loudly and called out, as if his voice could reach the car. 'How stupid are you? Do you really think Werner Jansen is next? I killed Michael Jansen so his brother would run to you. He will be terrified and will surely retract his statement. Then that damn Volker Janssen will no longer have an alibi and you can finally catch that animal.

*

Werner Jansen was listening to Sandra Droege on Radio Lower Saxony. She was covering the murders and had made a clear connection to Ubbo Heide's book. She reported that the body in Oldenburg's castle gardens had a playing card in his mouth. Although the police hadn't said which card it was, Sandra Droege assumed it was an ace because there was a lengthy chapter in the book where witnesses were described as 'poker brothers'. Droege claimed that their statement had undermined Ubbo Heide's detective work, reducing it to absurdity.

She read a passage aloud from the book, describing how the culprit still had two aces up his sleeve and had produced them during the trial. Two witness who in Ubbo Heide's opinion had lied and then stuck to their statements despite interrogation.

Werner Jansen immediately broke into a cold sweat and knew that the game was over. Even back then he'd had a bad feeling about it, but you couldn't abandon a friend in a situation like that, and his brother had been insistent. They were friends, after all, and you have to help each other out. It had only taken a court deposition to free their friend.

He had already received a call notifying him about his brother's death and he'd been invited to identify the body, but the police officer hadn't mentioned a playing card in his mouth. He had thought it had sounded like a mugging gone wrong. Of course his brother, a fighter by nature, wouldn't just hand over the money and avoid a struggle, that's not the way he was.

But it all looked very different now. The playing card was a clear sign.

There was something in the recent press speculation. It seemed as though someone was trying to solve Ubbo Heide's cold cases.

He didn't want to think about the future; he just wanted the whole thing to end before it was his turn. Should he go to a lawyer first or straight to the police?

Once he had worked out exactly what he needed to do and was ready to get the ball rolling, it felt as if he was nailed to the chair. His arms and legs were heavy and his body became inert and lame while thoughts raced through his head faster and faster.

Had he had a stroke?

His brain sent out orders, but they didn't arrive at his muscles and joints.

The sound of the doorbell ringing shocked him out of it and it was as if his body was acting independently.

He watched himself open the door. There was a man standing there in a light summer blazer. He wore jeans and an open-necked shirt. He held up his ID in his left hand. He was in his mid-forties and had a friendly manner, like someone who had popped over for a coffee.

'My name is Frank Weller. I'm from Aurich Homicide. Your brother is—'

'I know, I know. Did you really find a playing card in his mouth? I just heard it on the radio.'

Weller nodded.

'It's the man who's trying to solve Ubbo Heide's cases. Please help me, Detective Weller! I made a terrible mistake when I gave Volker an alibi. We weren't playing poker at the time of the crime. I don't know if he tried to rape that woman but I don't think he did. He's actually a nice guy. We only wanted to help out a friend, not cover for a criminal, but then that crazy guy came along and—'

'I'd like to record your statement. Then you can sign it. I don't think you need to fear any additional punishment if you help us voluntarily and freely. But I would suggest that we go to the police station now. You need to be safe. We can't guarantee that the killer won't—'

'Yeah, sure, arrest me, damn it! Please take me in! I don't want to end up like Mikey.'

He was crying like a child.

Weller thought about the executioner when he saw the picture of misery in front of him, asking him to arrest him and finally confessing. Whoever you are, he thought, your methods are damn successful.

*

Rupert walked up the narrow stairs in Norden's police station, following Marion Wolters. He thought that her behind had become wider and she had finally really earned the name fat arse. He grinned to himself. She could be called double fat arse. There wasn't a seat big enough for her bottom.

Rupert reached for his back – climbing stairs really made it ache. The pain raced up his spine, all the way to his head.

If I threw away my badge and had them guess my age, I bet I'd be able to retire, he thought.

Rupert was upset because he had to sit upstairs in the office with Marion, while all the others met down in the big conference room with Ubbo Heide. Downstairs there were smells of tea and baked goods, like when Ubbo Heide had run the place, always good to his loyal followers and careful to create a pleasant work environment.

Having arrived upstairs, Rupert found the room far too small for the two of them. He needed at least three metres distance from Marion.

Rupert had understood that he was supposed to start an 'innocuous conversation' with Marion Wolters, in the hopes that they would be listened in on. The conversation only served one function: to distract the killer from what was being planned downstairs.

Rupert didn't mind the task – meaningless conversation wasn't a problem for him – but he'd have preferred a different partner. Anyone but Marion Wolters.

Rupert looked at her very closely. She didn't like being here with him either. She had wrinkles on her neck and face and crow's feet around her eyes.

Rupert wondered whether he should tell her that it was possible to have liposuction on the buttocks and then use what was extracted to smooth out the wrinkles on your face and neck. Rupert had heard that it was far better than that poisonous Botox stuff.

Although he hadn't even said anything yet, she was ready for a confrontation.

Their conversation had yet to begin. The bug would be brought up to them so the killer wouldn't get suspicious. If Rupert had understood correctly, the thing was in Ubbo Heide's wheelchair, and he asked himself who would have to carry Ubbo and his wheelchair up the stairs.

Why don't we have our conversation down there and they have their meeting up here, Rupert thought? But then the world was simply mad, and not everyone in the police station was as clever as he was, not by a long way.

He had no desire to be constantly giving instruction and pointing out their mistakes. It was up to them to realise the mess they were making of everything.

*

One storey below, Ann Kathrin was pouring Ubbo Heide a cup of tea, and Büscher was happy to note that Ubbo had left him the executive chair and positioned himself in the wheelchair next to it.

Despite that, Ubbo opened the meeting. 'We have plenty to discuss. But,' he picked up the tin of mints from Bochum, shook it once, making them clatter, 'these are addictive, friends, and I've been putting on weight since I've been in this wheelchair. Could somebody get rid of this?'

'Those are Marion Wolters' favourite sweets, I'm sure!' said Sylvia Hoppe, following the plan. Ann Kathrin thought it all sounded a little too staged.

Ubbo Heide made a sweeping gesture, like a king in an operetta who was giving land to his nobility. 'Then give them to her.'

Sylvia Hoppe took the tin and left the room.

Büscher wanted to get started as soon as the footsteps on the stairs had faded away, but Ann Kathrin interrupted him with a gesture.

'I think we should continue our meeting after the lunch break. I suggest we all need to eat.'

Then she wrote on the flipchart with a red marker: 'The Galley or Ten Cate'?

Rieke Gersema pointed to 'The Galley' and silently communicated that she'd already rung them and everything was sorted.

They left and silently walked across the market square towards Osterstrasse. Ubbo Heide was embarrassed to see an entire display window in the Hasbargen bookstore of his books. There was also a large portrait of him on display. He pretended not to see it.

Ann Kathrin walked next to Ubbo's wheelchair. She knew that the decisive minutes were approaching. She wanted to be close to him, was moved by an odd urge to protect him.

It wasn't the first time that a K1 work meeting had taken place in The Galley. They wouldn't be disturbed around this time. Although there were still people down below in the restaurant, breakfast had long been finished and Ann Kathrin's friend Melanie Weiss enjoyed serving everyone coffee and tea. She was considered very discreet.

Büscher found all this strangely foreign. Maybe it was an East Frisia thing. Having a meeting in a hotel and a retired boss who led the investigations without question while drinking tea in his wheelchair.

Melanie Weiss hugged Ann Kathrin, and the two of them whispered something.

What a tight-knit community, Büscher thought. Love it or leave it.

He assumed that once you'd won them over, they'd let themselves be torn to shreds for you. At least that's how he gauged the relationship between his colleagues and Ubbo Heide, and with Ann Kathrin Klaasen.

Ann Kathrin said, 'Dear colleagues, we're working on the assumption that the killer has installed a bug in Ubbo Heide's tin of mints. Now he can use it to listen to Rupert and Marion. We probably won't be disturbed here. We've left the police station because we can't be certain that there aren't any bugs hidden in Aurich or in Norden.'

She nodded and gave the floor to Büscher. He cleared his throat. 'Yes, I'm honoured to open the gathering here. It's a little strange to me to be meeting in a breakfast room, but there you go. Needs must.'

The smell of lunch rose up from the restaurant. Rieke Gersema's mouth started to water, and she wished she could order a lamb burger, but repressed the impulse by putting her glasses very low on her nose and trying to focus.

Sylvia Hoppe asked, 'Has he been listening to us the whole time, damn it? That means it doesn't even have to have been one of our colleagues. He got his inside info by—'

She clenched her fist and then extended her middle finger, as if she wanted to show the killer what she thought of him.

'This whole thing is a big chance for us,' Ubbo Heide explained. 'Now we can pass false information to the killer and maybe trap him.'

The police psychologist Elke Sommer lifted her hands in defence. 'No we can't. That'd mean pointing him towards a new victim and then trying to catch him there. That's not ethical!'

Büscher looked to Ubbo Heide for help.

Ubbo Heide reassured her. 'It'd be unethical if we had a chance to get him and didn't use it. We have the advantage now, we know something that he doesn't. And we know that he has let his actions be directed by our conversations.'

Ann Kathrin took over. 'Weller has visited Werner Jansen and it is exactly as we predicted. Jansen has now admitted to lying and even asked to be arrested. This means Volker Janssen's alibi is gone. However, the question is whether he can be put on trial again. Once acquitted—'

Büscher asserted himself by speaking more loudly. 'I'm a little uncertain about this. For example, if the killer could hear us right now, he'd have to – to be consistent with his logic – try to get that young poet. We could catch him—'

'And what if he succeeded?' Elke Sommer asked, incensed.

Ann Kathrin didn't like what she was hearing. 'People, how's this supposed to work practically? Of course we can set a trap for him. But that would mean we were giving him a new victim. And then? Such surveillance of a potential victim is very personnel-intensive. We could maintain it for twenty-four hours, maybe two or three days. But what if he doesn't strike during that time?'

Büscher took over. 'Exactly. We don't have the staff numbers. What if he waits three weeks or a month, then the whole police service would be paralysed. Here at the Aurich-Wittmund police department we're responsible for a quarter of a million people. We can't drop everything to—'

'On the other hand,' Ann Kathrin said, 'he's always struck very quickly in the past.'

'The question is also whether we should inform the bait beforehand,' Büscher cautioned.

'*Bait*, my God,' Elke Sommer groaned and grimaced in disgust. 'We're talking about people's lives here and not about fishing!'

Ann Kathrin emphasised, 'Naturally whoever is playing the decoy has to agree and actively support us, otherwise the plan's off.'

Rieke Gersema couldn't stay seated any longer. 'Good heavens, I feel sick when I think about what could happen. We're laying a trap for him and the next person dies! Then it'll come out that he basically followed our lead. I can already see the headlines! This could cost us all our heads, people.'

'You're right,' Büscher said. He was calm and seemed like he had complete control of the situation. 'Unless the next victim is a former police officer.'

For a moment it seemed as if the air had been sucked out of the room. The buzzing of a fly became audible. A bird was twittering somewhere outside.

Ann Kathrin's mouth opened, but it still took a couple of seconds before she spoke. 'You think Willy Kaufmann would play along?'

Ubbo Heide pointed to Büscher. 'That's a brilliant idea.'

Thanks, Büscher thought. If my plan works, they'll finally accept me. If not, I'll be glad to return to Bremerhaven.

*

Marion Wolters was transformed since Sylvia Hoppe had deposited the tin of mints on the table. She no longer looked morosely at Rupert, and she also no longer drummed nervously on the table. Instead she acted as if she was head over heels in love with him and wanted to impress him.

It seemed to Rupert that she didn't have to search long for a topic. It was as if she knew exactly what she should talk to him about. She liked the fact that someone else was listening, regardless of whether it was the killer. This whole thing would probably be played in court, or heaven forbid, be broadcast on the radio, like the exchange of words Rupert had had with that journalist, Faust, on the beach in Norddeich.

Everything had been strange recently. The police department was under scrutiny. If Rupert wasn't mistaken, the increased media attention meant that his female colleagues had been arriving at work far better coiffed than they had in a long time.

'You know what, Rupi?' Marion Wolters said. 'The women's' police choir are working on a song about you.'

He leaned back, looking interested. 'Yes, I've caught wind of something like that going on. Recently everyone has been calling me Rupi and not Rupert.'

Then she began to sing. Rupert considered her singing voice far less annoying than her speaking voice.

She positioned herself as if the tin was a microphone and there was an attentive audience listening.

'Rupert is East Frisia's top
Super-duper cop
A specialist at livin' large
If you ask him, he's in charge
What'd they do without that cat
They'd have nothing to laugh at.'

The song pleased Rupert so much that he would have liked nothing more than to jump up and dance after hearing it, but his sacroiliac joint didn't permit any circular hip movements at that moment.

Is she after me? Rupert asked himself. Surely not. Now Marion Wolters raised her hands over her head, snapped her fingers, turned around, and stomped out a fiery rhythm on the floor with her orthopaedic shoes.

He could understand why a woman like Marion Wolters would secretly fancy him. Maybe that's why the others were constantly making fun of him. In reality these feminist sympathisers who talked their way into women's beds weren't real men.

Rupert crossed his arms behind his head and looked at Marion Wolters. Suddenly he no longer found her as ugly or too fat. Quite the reverse. She had a fabulous Rubenesque figure. That's what his Beate called overweight women, if he remembered correctly. Rubens – he must have been some painter who couldn't afford real models, Rupert assumed, and for that reason used overweight women from his town.

She messed up a verse or had forgotten the lyrics. At any rate, she now clapped her hands and invited him to join in with her swinging hips.

'Whether blond or brown
Super-duper Rupert!'

She almost got him to sing along.

'Super-duper Rupert!'

He pictured the entire women's choir of the East Frisian Kripo serenading him with the song.

How much they must like me, he thought, that they'd make the effort to sing a song to impress me.

But then there was something in Marion's eye. A twinkle.

Perhaps, Rupert thought, they're pulling my leg. Are they making fun of me? Or does Wolters actually want to jump into bed with me? That fat arse, of all people. Who'd have thought it?

*

'Stop that singing!' he yelled. That voice was taking him completely out of the zone. It was terrible. Instead of being there with the homicide team as they discussed his plans, he was listening to this caterwauling! What the hell?

He imitated Sylvia Hope's voice. 'Ubbo says you like them and too many mints make him fat.'

'Typical boss!' he complained. 'Passing something on to his minions as soon as he gets tired of it. You're no better than the others, Ubbo!'

This 'Super-duper Rupert' really drove him crazy. He felt anger rising inside himself and wanted to do something destructive and unfair without any plan or goal, only to vent his own rage. Completely different from the executioner who had acted with precision and approached life like a game of chess.

He hoped that someone would take the bugged tin back to the right meeting. How could fate be so cruel to him?

He turned down the receiver and turned on the radio instead. Local news.

'Jean-Claude Juncker, EU Commission head, expressly warned Hungary against reintroducing the death penalty. This is prohibited by EU agreements. Juncker claimed the country could no longer remain in the EU if Prime Minister Viktor Orbán continued to insist on his plan.'

He didn't know what to do with his rage. Wherever he turned, the wind was in his face. He had to think of the old East Frisian adage: *the wind always comes from in from the front.*

At least the topic was back on the table. People were even starting to rethink the death penalty in Old Europe. A tumour had to be excised, a bacterial infection was treated with antibiotics, and not by reasoning with the bacteria.

They needed an outfit like the Navy Seal Team 6. The elite unit was so secret that the Pentagon wouldn't confirm its name. It was responsible for the killing of Osama bin Laden. It was used to hunt down criminals all across the world. It operated in war zones, tracked down suspects and neutralised them.

The *New York Times* wrote that killing had become routine for them. Some nights they had liquidated twenty-five or more people. The press had repeatedly accused them of killing innocent people, even children. But no member of the team had ever been indicted. At most the elite fighters had been moved to different positions.

That's exactly what we need, he thought. A Team 6. First for East Frisia. Then for the state of Lower Saxony. And ultimately for the entire country. We could be used as an example of the first crime-free region. Here no criminal would escape their fate.

He turned on the radio again. For a moment the air was still. Even the wind in Emden wasn't blowing around the house. There appeared to be no traffic on the streets, as if the world paused briefly to give him the time to breathe deeply and reorient himsel.

Was all this with the tin a stupid coincidence or were they doing it on purpose? Had they cottoned on to what he was doing? Did they want to provoke him?

Everything went his way when he was in the zone. Then there were only fortunate coincidences and twists of fate. Everything in the right place at the right time.

Was fate no longer on his side? When he was in the zone, it seemed as if an entire army of guardian angels had been ordered to help him, support him, clear the way for him. Why hadn't any of these spiritual helpers made sure that the tin of mints was in the conference room? Were his guardian angels revolting against him now?

Suddenly he didn't know what to do with his feelings. A shaking that began in the middle of his body took hold of him and he was immediately soaked with sweat. He was familiar with the feeling from his childhood. So much fear, overshadowed by a monstrous, murderous rage.

Should he go downstairs, tie Svenja Moers to the bars and whip her? Would her screams get him back in the zone? Or should he drop her off at the police station with dynamite in her bag? She'd run inside looking for help and then he could blow the whole place to pieces.

Yeah, that's what he felt like doing. They didn't have any right to exclude him from their meeting. He didn't want to have songs like that sung to him.

The shakes receded. He became calmer, and his brain turned back on.

If you blow the police station to smithereens, you'll just harm your cause and do the criminals in East Frisia a big favour, he told himself. They'd be free to move around at will and no one would stand between them and their crimes.

Regardless of how inadequate, even pitiful the police were in their indecisiveness, there was only one way: he had to make them his allies. And he was really close to doing that.

Once I have the chief, then they'll all follow me.

One more time, he ran through how he could kidnap Ubbo Heide to show him how true justice worked and make him into a collaborator. Better still, as the special ops leader for Team 6.

Something had always held him back from doing that. Fear of not being able to match up to this man of being defeated by his charisma and his arguments.

He laughed at himself. What kind of a wimp am I? I'm afraid of a retired, wheelchair-bound police officer.

He turned the receiver back on in the hope of good news.

He heard Rupert. 'You know I'm not really fond of beanpoles. I mean, as a man you want to be able to get hold of something. I prefer love handles to bumping against hip bones.'

His laughter sounded like a rooster crowing.

*

Is he really hitting on me? Marion Wolters asked herself. Is he really so dense that he can't see how much we're making fun of him? Or is he so desperate for sex that he doesn't care?

She began to find the situation increasingly enjoyable. This is how actresses must feel, she thought. Playing a role, and playing it well. Her audience believed her. She hoped this was the case with those listening in as well, not just with Rupert. That they hadn't realised that the police were on to them.

As long as the killer's listening to me, then he's not doing anything else, and our people have time to think up a plan.

But maybe Rupert was also just playing a game. Did he want the killer to think that he was witness to a ham-fisted attempt at a pick-up? The start of an unsuccessful flirtation? Did Rupert think he could keep the stranger listening in that way? Or was he serious about all this?

It wasn't possible to confer with Rupert to find out. With anyone else it would have been easy to communicate with glances and gestures, but with Rupert you never knew where you stood.

Will this make me the laughing stock of the team later on, she asked herself. Are we both making fools of ourselves? Will the recordings be played in court? Would the press be there? Maybe it would be spread all over social media. You have to be prepared for anything these days.

'Are you actually hitting on me?' she asked in a strident voice that would have been a turnoff for anyone who wasn't a fan of BDSM.

'Sure, I can understand why you'd hope for that,' Rupert replied.

'You think I don't know that you call me fat arse?' she scolded, and was immediately upset with herself for spreading the nickname further.

'I feel bad about that,' Rupert said, 'but anyone can see it.'

'What?'

'Well, that you've never had good sex.'

She was so incensed that she couldn't breathe. She would have liked to punch him, but she kept herself under control, still searching for the right words, while Rupert continued, 'You can see it in your face, there, the corners of your mouth. Although, I, for one, prefer to look at people's behinds. They tell me the unvarnished truth. You know a face can be kept under control, people have their expressions in check. Then they smile at you nicely and think: burn in hell, you piece of shit. But a bottom, it tells you the whole truth.'

He drew circles in the air with his fingers.

'A really good arse tells you whether someone is happy or sexually frustrated.'

Marion Wolters turned around so she wouldn't have to look at Rupert any longer. But in doing so, she was putting her backside on display, which she didn't like either. She couldn't really hide behind the curtains, though. She had a job to do. She hoped she would be relieved soon because she didn't know how much longer she could stand to be in the same room as Rupert.

'A behind,' Rupert continued, waxing philosophical, 'reveals much about one's character. For example, the pear-shaped ones are usually fairly phony. This is true for men as well as women. Although it's much more accentuated with women. The very round, firm half-spheres,' he used his hands to form such a bottom in the air, 'belong to the honest. You can trust them. Those with the small, pert, boyish behinds are usually uncomplicated and cheerful. But,' Rupert raised a finger, 'beware of those who are well-exercised. There's been a lot of work put into them. They're egocentric, training the whole day, want to be the best at everything.' Rupert waved her away. 'I always say: keep your hands off, it won't be any fun with them. The ones with a really expansive derriere, one of those ample, soft cushions, are often sensual, drawn towards enjoyment and—'

She stood up in front of him, arms out. He still persisted. 'But be careful with those who are saggy here.' He pointed to her thighs. 'They can be damn moody.'

'Shut your trap, Rupert! I can't listen to any more of this!'

'You see, that's what I mean. First nice and friendly, sweet, making you feel desired, then if not everything goes exactly as they hope, they immediately get aggressive. That's typical for your butt shape. That's also why you can't land a man. You scare them away.'

She groaned. 'What kind of idiot are you?'

She couldn't explain even to herself what she did next. She took the tin of mints, opened it, grabbed a white sweet, and popped it into her mouth. She crunched loudly.

She couldn't handle being in the same room as Rupert anymore. Either I choke him, or I get out of here, she thought.

She stormed past him to the door, stopped in front of it, and took a deep breath.

Rupert called to her from inside the room. 'Well, what's the story? Can't you take the truth? A big behind like yours is something beautiful! You just have to own it!'

She opened the door, went outside and wrote with a red marker before sticking it on the outside of the door: *This room is bugged by the perpetrator. Please no conversations related to the case.*

Then she walked down the stairs. She wanted to go to Café Ten Cate. She was craving apple cake with whipped cream on top.

*

Weller had received the message from Ann Kathrin via WhatsApp: *Meeting in The Galley.*

Weller liked that. On the way from Oldenburg to Norden he was looking forward to beef roulade, or perhaps he should have the dyke lamb? Just before reaching Norden he decided to have the daily special.

He parked behind The Galley. Because he had turned from the narrow street into the courtyard too quickly a couple of pebbles flew into Peter Grendel's yellow van, which was also parked at the back. Peter was just getting out. He patted the top of Weller's roof with his large mason's hands and laughed, 'Well, the cops are in a hurry! Do we need to save the world?'

'Even worse,' Weller said, 'all of East Frisia.'

Peter Grendel watched Weller go, disappearing into The Galley with large strides. 'As long as the dyke holds!' Peter called, but Frank Weller didn't hear him.

He quickly placed an order for the daily special with Melanie Weiss: stuffed bell peppers. Then he raced up into the breakfast room.

He briefly nodded to his colleagues so as not to interrupt the flow of the meeting, pulled up a chair and sat down close to the old radio. His parents used to have one like that. It was one of his better childhood memories. He'd sat in front of the device and listened to his first radio show, watching the green and yellow lights.

'I'm up for it,' Ubbo Heide said, 'having Ann Kathrin talk with Willy Kaufmann and proposing our offer.'

'Wouldn't you prefer to do it?' Ann Kathrin asked. 'You're old comrades in arms.'

'That's precisely why I don't want to,' Ubbo Heide explained. 'He'd always feel obligated towards me. I think it's better if you talk to him, Ann. You interrogated him. It's your case. I, dear friends, am only your adviser.' He pointed to Büscher. 'That's your new boss, and I think that he's a good catch.'

Büscher appeared to grow as he stood leaning against the wall, rocking back and forth, the soles of his shoes squeaking.

'Now we're going to make a plan for how we can make sure that Kowalski is interested in only one possible victim. And then we'll construct a trap that will snap shut on him. We're being provided with a special command next week. After that we'll make it quick and push our man to strike quickly.'

Melanie Weiss brought Weller the fragrant stuffed bell peppers. He sat down at the breakfast table, but only then realised that no one else had ordered anything to eat.

'Your fellow officers,' Melanie Weiss said, 'didn't want anything. But I'm sure you'll enjoy it, Frank.'

'Oh yes,' he smiled, 'I love stuffed bell peppers. Give my best to the chef.'

Elke Sommer pursed her lips and said, 'Enjoy your meal.'

Büscher felt that it was no longer necessary to keep quiet. He spoke calmly. 'I think that we'll leave the tin upstairs and lock down the room. Then our culprit can listen in for a couple of hours. Later, we can hold a fake meeting upstairs so we can make Wilhelm Kaufmann our—' Büscher didn't continue because the word 'target' didn't seem appropriate. Instead, he gestured to Elke Sommer and interjected, 'Naturally only if Mr Kaufmann is in agreement.'

'Then we'll have to get Ubbo up the stairs. There's no lift,' Sylvia Hoppe added.

'Normally,' Ubbo Heide said, 'former police officers don't participate in meetings.'

Büscher looked at him gratefully; he really is handing over the reins, he thought.

Weller spoke with his mouth full. 'Why? We could just as well bring the tin downstairs and hold the meeting in the conference room. A little tin is lighter than Ubbo, after all.' He laughed at his own joke, but Ubbo waved him away. 'I'm too old for this nonsense, kids. We just need to put this behind us.'

'You're not leaving us in the lurch, Ubbo?' Rieke Gersema asked, but Ann Kathrin knew that he couldn't keep on going the way he was.

'I only have one wish: I want to sit on Wangerooge and look at the sea and know that everything's all right,' Ubbo said.

'You can do that again soon, Ubbo,' said Ann Kathrin. 'I believe we can now show our culprit a door that he'll gladly run through. And we'll be waiting on the other side.'

'With handcuffs,' Weller grinned, chewing.

*

Why can't I hear anything anymore, damn it? Just a second ago it was very clear, that stupid singsong. It's not because of the battery. They must be meeting in another room, damn it!

He would have liked to go to the Norden police station disguised as an old woman. He could go inside, reposition the tin and add another surveillance device. He still had half a dozen of them. They were dirt cheap on the Internet.

But that move was too dangerous. He didn't want to take any risks now.

He watched Svenja Moers on the screen. At least he still had her under control.

He hated losing control, not knowing what others were doing. It returned him to the impotence of his childhood, when he didn't know where his father was, when the old man would come home, or what would happen then.

Helpless, powerless, defenceless, he never wanted to be that again.

He went down to Svenja Moers. She sat on the bike and pedalled away. By now, she could tell from the small light signals on the side when the camera moved or when he zoomed in on her. But it was completely different when he entered the room. The adrenaline immediately shot through her veins, and she pedalled even faster.

She called out to him obediently. 'I'm making an effort!. I'm exercising all day long! I'm already in much better shape!'

'Give me your notebook,' he demanded.

She jumped off her bike. The pedals kept on spinning without her. She fetched her notebook and passed it to him through the bars. He leafed through it but didn't look closely at the numbers.

'I'm wondering,' he said, as if to himself, 'whether you can help me to take care of a small job. If you're worthy.'

She smelled a chance for herself and nodded. 'I'll take care of it. What is it?'

'Be proud that I've chosen you. If you show you're worthy, then you can be my helper.'

I won't be able to snatch Ubbo Heide myself, he thought. But what could convince him more than a confessed murderer who's changed sides and joined us?

*

The detention centre in Aurich was closed. It no longer met the security standards and there weren't enough funds to renovate it. Since its closure, the East Frisian officers had to drive to the jails in Lingen or Oldenburg after arresting suspects.

The increased distance made it a drain on resources.

It was Wilhelm Kaufmann's wish to be locked up in Lingen. He looked composed. His jacket hung over the back of the chair. He wore civilian clothes, but to Ann Kathrin they looked something like a uniform.

He knew that he was safe here in pre-trial detention. He placed his hands on the table, as if in prayer, and breathed through his nose. It sounded to Ann Kathrin like wheezing, as if he had trouble getting air or was getting a cold. However, he exuded a calm, relaxed air.

She hung her bag over the back of the chair. 'You seem,' she said, 'like a traveller who had a heavy burden and is now glad to have put it down somewhere.'

'Very well put, Ms. Klaasen. That is how I feel. As if my burdens have been lifted.'

'Because you stabbed Birger Holthusen? Or because you escaped with your life?'

He shook his head slowly. 'Here in detention I feel so oddly free, as if I've had a great victory.'

She sat down next to him and folded her hands. To an outsider it looked as if she were imitating his posture. She did things like this unconsciously, as if she could better put herself in the other person's shoes.

Kaufmann did, in fact, register it.

'Maybe it's all over for you, but not for us. We still have a murderer out there. But we know now what he looks like, and that he has a prisoner. Svenja Moers. You could help us save this woman and several other people from a terrible fate. If we don't stop him, he'll keep on killing.'

'Yes, I'm sure you're right, Ms. Klaasen. He'll keep on killing. It will be difficult for you when the Birger Holthusen story goes public. How will he feel then? As someone who beheaded two innocent people. My God, how could he possibly turn this thing around?' Kaufmann looked at his fingers and continued, 'No, he can't. At best he can try to make people forget.'

'Make people forget?' Ann Kathrin asked. 'By distracting with new murders?'

'Yes, and by denying what happened. The whole thing must make him furious. How will you even publicise it? Is the press informed?'

'They know about the dead man on Langeoog. But they don't know everything.'

'He'll go crazy if he reads it in the papers.'

'Yeah. I hope that we'll catch him before that.'

'Do you have a plan?'

She looked him in the eye now. He could handle her stare.

'You play an important role in our plan, Mr Kaufmann.'

He smiled and didn't lower his gaze.

Ann Kathrin reached behind herself and fingered her purse. Then she took one more deep breath and explained. 'Birger Holthusen thought you were the culprit. He was afraid that you would kill him too. And that's why he went for you. Right? He just wanted to get in first.'

'Yeah, that's exactly how it was.'

'And we also suspected you. In fact, there were many factors counting against you.'

He didn't stop smiling, as if he were proud of it. She asked herself if he knew where she was heading.

'You also saw the killer. He was at Ubbo's reading in Gelsenkirchen. He did an interview with Ubbo in the Intercity Hotel.'

'That tall, thin guy with the sweets? Looked like a marathon runner, but needed a cigarette every couple of minutes?'

'Exactly. Do you know what he's been doing?'

Kaufmann shrugged his shoulders. 'How should I? I don't know him. I only saw him that one day.' He thought about it but shook his head again. 'No, I haven't had anything else to do with that person.'

Now Ann Kathrin decided to tell him the whole truth. 'He's eavesdropping on us. We even know exactly how he does it. That means we could establish contact with him and—'

Kaufmann's smile became a wide grin. He slapped an open hand on the table, pointing at Ann Kathrin with his left index finger, and exclaimed, 'I'm supposed to be the decoy!'

'Yes, that's the plan. If we—'

Kaufmann gestured for her to be quiet. He wanted to prove that he still thought like a real detective who'd caught the scent and was just about to strike.

'You won't tell the press that Birger Holthusen killed Steffi Heymann and Nicola Billing. No one knows that except us. Instead, you'll present me to the press as their killer. Then that man, who already looks like the Grim Reaper from a distance, will not only know that he has beheaded the wrong people, he'll also know that the real culprit is still alive. Then he'll come to get me.'

Kaufmann giggled with glee and starting tapping his finger on the table. 'That's a crazy, but good idea. And it'll work. We'll have him when he comes to get me.'

Ann Kathrin asked herself where this joy came from. Was it just Kaufmann's gallows humour?

She hadn't imagined it could be so easy. She had been prepared to give him time to think it over, to convince him, but things couldn't move fast enough for Kaufman.

Her own experience told her that people who said yes quickly also backed out quickly. That's why she remained cautious. 'Of course we don't have to tell the press anything. We don't want to cause harm to you. Something always sticks. We could keep the press out of it completely. After all, he's listening to us.'

Kaufmann whistled through his teeth. 'That's good. That's very good! And how do we want to set the trap? He won't just walk in here to finish me off.'

'First I wanted to make our offer to you to find out if you were prepared to—'

'Offer? What kind of offer? Ms. Klaasen, I thought you were coming with a request.'

'Well, it is a request. No one would hold it against you if you don't play along. The whole thing is extremely risky.'

He pushed back his shoulders and puffed out his chest.

'It's a deep-seated desire of mine to do this, Ms. Klaasen. I can finally make a meaningful contribution. Now that I'm not a part of the force, I'll become your most important man. You have no idea how good that feels.'

Ann Kathrin promised, 'He won't know where you are. We'll put you up at a hotel.'

He made a sweeping gesture. 'I'm already in one of your hotels. I don't consider it charming, but the safety standards are impressive.'

'We don't have time for jokes, Mr Kaufmann. We can have three, maybe four police officers guard you. Our man will receive clear information from us regarding when and where he can get to you. And that's where we'll catch him.'

Kaufmann pushed back with his feet, making his chair balance on the two back legs. The back of the chair was now at such an angle that the hem of his jacket touched the floor and it looked as though he could fall at any moment.

'I once attended a workshop on a similar topic. It was years ago. A professional decoy from the USA was there and—'

Ann Kathrin raised her hands, showing her palms.

'I know, I know. The whole thing is highly dangerous, and I can't advice you to participate with a clear conscience. But I have to ask you these questions.'

He locked his hands behind his head and leaned back further. Did he want to show her that he was prepared to take risks? He reminded her of a schoolboy at the back of class trying to provoke his teacher by doing tricks with his chair.

'Stop it, Ms. Klaasen, stop it,' he requested. 'You're giving me a gift.'

'A gift?'

'My life is over anyway. For me, this is the chance to rehabilitate myself.'

'I can't promise you that you'll be able to rejoin the police force.'

'That's not what this is about. If we bring this to an end, no one will say: "*That's Willy over there. Didn't they let him go because he didn't have his emotions under control and beat the living daylights out of people every once in a while?*" No, they'll say: "*That's Willy, who helped us catch a dangerous serial killer. He risked his neck for us.*"'

Ann Kathrin nodded. 'Yes, Mr Kaufmann, you could become a hero.'

'Well then, I'll call it a gift. You tell me what's supposed to happen, when and where. And then you'll come back for me here.'

'Here?' She couldn't believe that he actually wanted to remain in detention. But he thought it was a safe place. For now.

'The only thing that I'm missing here is a good spaghetti carbonara delivery. I'd also like a beer and – it doesn't have to be oysters, but a plate of seafood and maybe a grilled wolf fish would be really nice.'

She stood up and took a step closer. 'That won't be any problem at all.' She wanted to put her hand on his shoulder. Sometimes a touch made a conversation more real. 'We'll take really good care of you here.'

He held her hand tight. She didn't like that and tried to pull it back, but his grip was hard. He looked her in the eyes. 'For me, good food is as important as a gun. I have to be able to defend myself in case—'

'That's impossible. It's against all of the rules.'

'It's not about the rules. It's about not having him grab me before your plan becomes reality. He doesn't care about rules. If we stick to the rules, then he's far ahead of us.'

'Yes,' Ann Kathrin said, 'he probably would have put it like that. I can take you to a hotel, have police in the rooms on either side. And of course you could have a gun there. But here—'

'You have your gun in your bag, right?' Now he released her hand.

'Yes, I have my service revolver with me,' she admitted.

He held out his hand.

'This will never happen again,' Anna Kathrin said, opening her purse and retrieving it.

He casually put the gun in his trouser pocket.

Terrible images raced through Ann Kathrin's head. A shoot-out in the hallway. An injured guard.

No, these weren't premonitions, they were terrifying fantasies. She'd always had a very vivid imagination, even as a child, and over the years she had learned to picture horrific scenes.

Where would this leave her? She'd given her service revolver to a man who had just admitted to having stabbed Birger Holthusen to death on Langeoog. She'd smuggled a weapon to a man whom they had just recently suspected of being the murderer of Heymann and Stern. What if everything turned once again and it suddenly emerged that he had? How many times had she seen how a tiny piece of information suddenly changed everything, cast everything in a different light?

She asked herself what Ubbo would think of her for having armed Wilhelm Kaufmann. And then she heard her father's voice in her head: *'Trust your instincts, Ann. They're always faster than reason and usually far more precise.'*

Kaufmann stood up, took his jacket from the back of the chair and held it so that the Heckler & Koch in his right trouser pocket was covered.

Clever, Ann Kathrin thought. Anyone else would have put the gun in their jacket, but not him.

Ann Kathrin knocked on the door and a prison guard came in.

Projecting his voice and using a completely different register from before, Kaufmann said, 'Thank you for your visit, Detective. You really don't need to worry. I'm being treated with respect and I want for nothing.'

She smiled at the guard. 'Mr Kaufmann would like a food delivery. Can we get that done?'

The guard grinned and led Willy Kaufmann back to his cell.

*

The sight of him made Svenja Moers realise something was different. He was acting like a neighbour who had come asking to borrow some salt, but in reality was hoping to find someone to unburden their heart to. His movements were somewhat feminine without seeming fey. His facial features were softer than usual, almost a little twitchy around the corners of his mouth. He spoke with a voice begging for recognition.

She remained cautious. She knew how quickly his mood could swing, and maybe this was just another one of his tricks, to scare her. He found pleasure in her fear. He liked her tears, and she wanted to give him as few of them as possible.

She had an English voice in her head. She couldn't say where it was from. It said: '*Don't feed him*.'

Was it a split part of her personality? Was her soul beginning to crack? Did part of her soul speak the English that she'd learned while on holiday with her parents in Torquay? She'd met her first boyfriend – a boy with beautiful hair and a great body, but who sadly didn't speak any German – and had spent two weeks falling in love with him and improving her English skills far more than years of memorising vocabulary in school had done.

Was it his voice that she heard – warning her not to trust him?

It was as if the memory hit her like a pain from deep inside her body. She'd taken sandwiches, sausage spread and grilled chops and had fed a dog who had followed them. She'd thought it was cute, and it looked half-starved, but it turned out to be a feral, mangy, aggressive animal.

'Don't feed him,' Oliver had called, but by then it was already too late. In the end, they were surrounded by four dogs and forced to flee the beautiful, deserted part of the beach.

Oliver had acted bravely and had fended off the dogs with a stick and by throwing stones. But they had still been followed, for what felt like at least three kilometres.

At the time she hadn't planned to kill one of her husbands, and perhaps, she thought, if I had married Oliver, then I would still be a happily married woman with three nearly grown children in Torquay.

She snapped out of the memory and realised he had brought coffee that he served in two delicate teacups. The smell revived her spirits and memories of much better times.

She didn't think about whether he might have drugged it, making her defenceless. He was already in complete control of what she ate anyway.

She tried the coffee and the feeling of it burning her lips and tongue was fantastic.

Take what you can get, she thought.

'I have a question,' he said.

She looked at him in disbelief. *He* had a question for *her*?

'I want to send a message to everyone about how you escaped your just punishment. And I was asking myself how I should do it. How would you do it?'

His voice was quiet, reserved and completely different from what she was used to from him. That's precisely what scared her. Would he suggest something terrible to scare her? Something like cutting off her fingers and sending them?

She thought he was capable of anything.

But he tilted his head, asked if she thought the coffee tasted good, or if it was maybe too strong, and if she preferred hers with milk or sugar.

'I prefer mine black,' she said. He silently raised his cup in her direction, took a sip himself, then sniffed at it and whispered, 'I could send them a letter. But letters are so old fashioned, don't you think? I mean, who writes letters these days? Besides, it would take too long. I want them to know right away. I want to put them under pressure. The less time they have to think, the more mistakes they will make. I have most of their email addresses. But email is so impersonal and with a little bad luck, they could be flagged as spam and land in the junk mail.'

She sipped the coffee loudly, buying some time. 'I don't know what to say.'

'Well, what would you do?'

'I'd call them. Voices on the telephone are very direct.'

He laughed. 'You're just trying to trick me, you fucking whore! You know a call can be traced. Besides, I don't want to call two dozen people. The police would storm this building before I had the third one on the line.'

'I-I really didn't want—but I'm not—'

She didn't dare say it. 'Not what? Not a criminal? You killed your two husbands. Already forgotten that? I thought we could talk on the same level!'

The cup began to clatter against the saucer as Svenja Moers' hands were shaking so much.

'I've never sent out a ransom note or message or anything,' she said.

He pointed at her with the index finger of his left hand. 'Message. That's the important word. It has to be a message and every one of them has to know the others have also received it. What do you think about a video? You could read the text aloud, and I'll film it and upload it to YouTube. You already have a channel, right?'

She had no idea what he was talking about. Then she remembered. Of course, she'd uploaded a little holiday clip once. How the hell did he know about that?

He was pleased, clenched his fist and threw a right hook, as if he were knocking out an invisible opponent. 'That's it! We'll make a video! You'll say who you are and a little bit about your situation, and then you'll reel off all the names and tell them I'm coming to get them. Really scare them!'

'And then?' she asked, no idea where he was headed.

'And then they'll run to the police and confess because the penalties that our courts have in place are far more lenient than what I'd do with them.'

Realising again that he was insane, she decided to do what he demanded. At some point, the police would see the clues. Maybe this video would be her chance.

*

Weller was in a better mood than the others. Perhaps that was because he had eaten a stuffed bell pepper, washed down with a non-alcoholic beer and rounded it off with an espresso, while the others had eaten nothing.

Weller knew that this behaviour would not go down well, but the harder they worked, the more intense the hunt for the culprit was, the more he needed to eat. He firmly believed that only a sated person would have enough energy to think through the complicated issues and be able to dense imaginative solutions.

'We should lure him onto an island,' Weller suggested.

Büscher agreed. 'An island is good. Then we can easily control the access. The smaller the island, the better. We let him onto the island, but not back off. He can't get away if we're prepared.'

Rupert had returned to the team in the meantime. The tin of mints was all alone in the police department in Norden.

'I think an island is a stupid idea,' Rupert blustered. 'Our people would be noticed immediately. The smaller the island, the faster.'

Elke Sommer smiled. 'A SWAT team can hide better in a tower block than on Baltrum. The island is so small that you can almost throw a ball over it.'

'Yeah, Baltrum is really too small,' Weller noted, 'but we should choose an island that is dependent on the tide.' He continued, 'In peak tourist season there's a ferry that goes to Norderney every half hour. That would be hard to keep under control. I would suggest Wangerooge, Spiekeroog or even Juist. But Borkum is too big.'

Büscher raised his index finger. 'Langeoog would make sense. After all, Kaufmann goes on holiday there every year. So it wouldn't be unreasonable for him to go back to his holiday flat. It's booked anyway.'

'We've already upset lots of people on Langeoog,' Sylvia chimed in. 'After all, Birger Holthusen was stabbed there. We grabbed Kaufmann there. Won't people think it's odd if he suddenly reappears?'

'But the killer might not realise that.'

Everyone looked at Ubbo Heide, as if they expected a decision from him.

'Although Langeoog doesn't depend on the tide, it's certainly the right choice,' Ubbo said thoughtfully. 'We will have to take over the whole house. There can't be any holidaymakers there under any circumstances. Willy Kaufmann musn't take a step without us and has to be wearing a wire. Team, we can't mess this up! You will all be looking for new jobs if Willy is found lying on the beach with his throat cut.'

'Is what we're planning here at all legal?' Elke Sommer asked.

Rieke Gersema groaned and looked as if she'd prefer not to know.

Büscher answered, 'If Kaufmann plays along, yes. And if not, we won't do it.'

Both Weller and Büscher's phones rang almost simultaneously. They both answered immediately. Ann Kathrin informed Weller that Kaufmann was up for it, and Büscher heard from Achim that Volker Janssen had turned himself in at the police station. He insisted on police protection, refused to leave the building and wanted to be put in a witness protection programme.

'Witness protection programme?' Büscher asked. 'That'd actually be a criminal protection programme, right?'

Büscher listened for a while, then he let rip. 'Yes, he's considered innocent, legally speaking. They delivered a verdict of not guilty. But—' He waved them away, as if it wasn't worth wasting his breath. 'Well, let's forget that nonsense. What do I care about his lawyer? You might as well put him in one of your drunk tanks and keep him there until he's had enough of it himself.'

Weller thanked Ann Kathrin for the information and was glad he could cut Büscher down to size. 'We can't assume that the culprit will do what we plan. Maybe he'll pull the wool over our eyes. He might know our plan, laugh to himself and then take someone else. Volker Janssen, for example!'

Büscher played it down. 'We can't possibly protect everyone while watching Kaufmann and setting the trap. We don't have the military at our disposal, just our own teams.'

Ubbo Heide chimed in. 'Weller's right. We should be happy that our fellow police officers in Achim are offering us some support. Janssen won't run away – on the contrary – and they'll keep him safe.'

'And if he wants us to do precisely that?' Elke Sommer asked. 'He's always been one step ahead so far. He knows that you don't have a couple of hundred people available. It's also completely clear that we can't protect everyone in Ubbo's book. After all, this means about twenty-two people who are still alive and at risk, and I'm not even talking about the second volume here. He wants you to lose sight of the whole picture and then show you how pitiful your means are in comparison to his.'

Weller didn't like that Elke Sommer said you and your, as if she was consciously excluding herself, as if she didn't belong. As if she was already trying to distance herself from an impending defeat or simply didn't want anything to do with it. But Weller thought it wasn't that simple.

Although many considered him far too nice, he strongly rebuked Elke Sommer. 'Aren't you one of us anymore, Elke?'

She looked at him as if she had no idea what he was talking about.

'Yes,' Ubbo Heide said, 'I noticed that too, Elke. Your words suggest you are distancing yourself from us. At a time when we need your analytical expertise. Give us your take on the situation.'

She swallowed and moved her shoulders jerkily. 'My take is that he's pulling the damn wool over our eyes. He's bringing out the worst in us. He wants us all to become murderous beasts. And we're on our way there.'

'At least you're saying *we* again now,' Ubbo Heide noted with relief.

*

He'd set the camera up in front of the bars. He was agitated, as if he were a real director now, making a film and afraid to fail his audience.

'No! Don't stand like that! I can only see the bed behind you. Actually, it'd be better if we could see instruments of torture behind you or something. That would scare people.

'Don't smile so much when you talk, understand? They have to be frightened! The whole thing becomes a joke if you smile at them. That doesn't work!

'You look far too healthy and happy. If we were making a real film now, then there'd also be someone doing make up, and she'd give you a black eye and a fat lip. We don't have anything like that. But it's more authentic if everything's real. What do you think?'

'I-I could put a bandage on my face.' Svenja suggested. But he shook his head. 'No, no, that won't do. They'd see through it right away. Seems you've never seen a face beaten to a pulp, right? It has to swell up and crack. We can't fake that. The best thing would be for me to punch you a couple of times.'

'No,' she said, 'please don't.'

She was afraid of what he'd do, but then had an idea. 'I think it should look like you're treating me well. Why am I keeping the log, gaining weight and keeping in shape? How would it look if my face has been beaten? The criminals might be afraid, but that's not the way to convince people like Ubbo Heide that you're doing the right thing.'

Her clear logical reasoning made him think. 'OK, let's try it. Do you know your lines?'

She was afraid she couldn't learn the speech by heart. There were so many names. 'I don't know. I'll certainly get tangled up. Can't I have a piece of paper to read from?'

'Yeah, but it looks much better if you do it without. It makes it seem more spontaneous. And don't try to play any tricks on me and smuggle any messages into the text. If you do that, then you can read everything aloud once again, but this time with a split lip and a black eye. OK?'

She nodded.

He took up his position behind the camera. 'OK, let's go. The show can begin. We're making history now, and it's like in Lotto, you're pulling names out of a hat and telling them who's won. But the prize isn't money. Instead, it's death or a trip to prison.'

She began. 'My name is Svenja Moers. I'm doing time in this prison for my crimes.' She pointed to the bars. 'The courts acquitted me even though I killed my two husbands. A fair penalty also awaits you. The executioner will get you. One after another. Unless you face up to your crimes and confess! If you fear the shame and want to avoid the courts, you could choose suicide and face divine justice instead. But hurry, otherwise the executioner will get you and take off your heads like he did Yves Stern and Bernhard Heymann. I'll read the names aloud now: Volker Janssen. Johannes Kleir. Professor Ludwig. Susanne Sarwutzki—'

'Sewutzki, not Sarwutzki!' he scolded. 'Now we have to do everything again!'

*

Weller saw the message on his screen while he was listening to Ubbo Heide.

Volker Janssen's lawyer smelled – Weller now remembered – like motorboat oil. It was said of the man that, 'If all the criminals he got off were jailed overnight, then in East Frisia they'd regret having closed the prison in Aurich. They'd need another wing added. Lawyers like him save the state lots of money because so many criminals are running around free. But it's not good for the victims – former or future.'

According to the message, the lawyer had advised Volker Janssen that because he was now without an alibi he should deny the killing in Syke, but instead cast the incident in Bensersiel in a different light. He claims now that yes, there was sexual intercourse with mutual consent, but the woman was clearly ashamed after the fact and didn't want her boyfriend to think she had cheated on him, which is why – inspired by press reports – she'd made up an attempted rape and while doing so, was very precise in matching her descriptions of what had happened to what she had read about the murder in Syke. Which made it his word against hers.

As soon as Weller read who had been hired as the defence and the statement the lawyer had produced, he knew that Volker Janssen would leave the courtroom a free man.

Weller caught himself hoping quietly that the executioner might snatch Janssen before he got his next victim. Weller bit his lips so he wouldn't say anything.

He could practically smell that lawyer and his terrible aftershave.

Ubbo Heide explained. 'We don't know exactly what that supposed journalist, Kowalski, has heard. Maybe there are bugs elsewhere, and one careless statement by any of us could lead to a sick mind like his to monstrous conclusions. Regardless of what he knows, we have to take all of that into account when luring him into our new plan.'

'He wants to be close to you, Ubbo,' Büscher said with almost envious respect. 'He's even searching for recognition from you. If he senses he can get that somehow, he'll do exactly what he needs to get it.'

Ubbo Heide nodded. 'I think so too.'

'Which is why,' Weller demanded, 'you, Ubbo, should be part of the conversation at any rate. We'll fetch the sweets, put the tin on the table and then—'

'He'll go berserk if he realises that we're tricking him. And then we'll all become his targets. We only have one shot, people. We have to take good aim.'

Rieke Gersema hadn't decided for herself whether this was legal or not. She'd have to sell it all to the press later as spokesperson. But she said nothing, only hoping that everything would work out.

*

They had given up trying to develop a screenplay, writing sentences that people would actually say. It all sounded fake, memorised. No, he'd catch on straightaway. It needed to flow through conversation. It was supposed to sound light, impromptu, spontaneous. No complex, polished sentences. No rustling of paper, no reading from the script.

Ubbo Heide was pale around his lips and highly focused.

Rieke Gersema had asked to come along. She didn't want to speak, just listen. Ann Kathrin had been against it, but Ubbo Heide had agreed. 'Perhaps she can learn something. At some point we'll no longer be here, and we are role models for many, despite our failures and our fears. You can only learn if you've seen others act.'

They were now down on the ground floor of the police station in Norden with a view of the market square. Rieke entered the room with the mint tin, shaking it well to wake the device if necessary, and to get the eavesdropper's attention. She opened with the words, 'I'm sorry, Ubbo. I was at Ten Cate. They didn't have any more marzipan seals. Sold out. But maybe you can make do with these mints from Bochum.'

Ubbo Heide groaned. 'What, they don't have any more marzipan seals? And no nougat balls either?'

'No,' Rieke said, 'Jörg Tapper came personally and said that he'd bring over the first batch when they're ready. The tourists have practically emptied the shop. It was a huge run—'

Ubbo Heide winked at her. She was doing well. It sounded believable and everyone who knew Ubbo knew that this sounded like him.

Ubbo reached for the tin, removed a mint, and cracked it loudly between his teeth. The culprit would have heard it if he was listening in on the conversation.

'If I have to make decisions like this or listen to such awful news, then I need marzipan for my stomach. Nothing else really helps, but thanks, Rieke. Could you please leave us alone now? I have to discuss something with Ann Kathrin – just the two of us.'

Rieke Gersema opened the door and then closed it loudly, but she stayed in the room and took a seat. She placed her index finger over her lips and made a gesture as if she were locking them closed.

'I'd quit now if I wasn't already retired, Ann. I've never felt so helpless and clueless.'

Ann Kathrin cleared her throat. She looked intensely at Ubbo while she spoke and tried to read his face, whether she was doing it right or if it was too artificial. Her own voice sounded strange, but Ubbo looked at her encouragingly. He even gave her a thumbs up.

'Birger Holthusen was our last chance to catch Willy Kaufmann. That's why he killed Holthusen on Langeoog. But we can't prove it. The judge will see it as self-defence, if anything.

A former cop attacked on the beach, who defended himself and—'

'That means the deaths of the two children, Steffi Heymann and Nicola Billing, won't be avenged!' Ubbo Heide spat out the words as if they were choking him.

'Yes, that's exactly what it means. There's no judge who would want to reopen the case. We already failed with our indictment back then, against Heymann and Stern. We don't have the slightest chance against Kaufmann. It's all so long ago. Witnesses no longer remember and Kaufmann neutralised the only witness for the prosecution.'

'That means he will get away unpunished?'

'Yes, that's what it means. And what's worse, the executioner has beheaded two people who were innocent. The real child murderer is still running around free.'

'Yes. We have to let Kaufman out of detention and back to his holiday flat in Langeoog. He's already asked me,' Ann Kathrin said, about the ferry times. That was his first concern.'

'And what do you think of it, Ann?'

'What?' she answered. 'I'm going to try to get the executioner and liberate Svenja Moers. The thing with Kaufmann is meaningless. We won't get anywhere with that.'

Ubbo Heide hit the arm of the wheelchair with his fist, making it squeak oddly. 'What upsets me the most,' he complained, 'is that Kaufmann is one of us. He worked closely with me. He took advantage of his investigative work to make Heymann and Stern take the blame for the whole thing. No wonder I ultimately failed in court with that case and stood there like a fool. How am I supposed prove a murder by two people if it wasn't them? My God, he must have had a laugh in court! He didn't care if the two were acquitted or convicted. The main thing is that he didn't get involved.'

Weller ripped open the door, contrary to the agreement, and stood in the hallway, gesturing to Ann Kathrin to get her to come out. She answered by shrugging her shoulders and making a face. Ubbo Heide clutched his head, as if asking himself how anyone could be so stupid as to barge in at this moment.

Weller pointed to the tin of mints and waved again. Whatever it was seemed so urgent that it couldn't be delayed any longer. Weller only very rarely behaved like this, and then never without reason. Ann Kathrin hardly recognised him.

She went out into the hallway. They stood outside, whispering with their heads together. 'He's released a video on YouTube announcing that he's going to kill them all. The entire list from Ubbo's books. Svenja Moers read the list aloud. Forty-one names in total. We thought we were hunting him, Ann. But he's hunting us.'

If it's on the Internet, then we should be able to find out the IP address, and then—' Ann Kathrin said excitedly.

'Yeah, of course,' Weller replied, 'we've already got that far. Charlie Thiekötter, our computer nerd, said there are two possibilities: either the computer's in the German chancellor's office, or the killer has tricked us again. Although I think our government is capable of many things, I think in this case the killer just wants to show us what he's capable of.'

*

It was as if his mother were in the room, laughing at him. He was familiar with the feeling from his worst nightmares. He felt very small, trying to defend himself, firing justifications like an anti-aircraft auxiliary fires a barrage against the approaching bomber squadron, knowing something would be destroyed.

Yes, that's how he felt every time his mother got at him, in her sneering way.

'That's not right, Mum,' he said to the wall. 'They're lying. They want to make a fool out of me, embarrass me and force me to give up. I didn't execute the wrong people! They're just saying that to—'

He felt terrible when he was like this and only wanted to get out of the situation. He'd never manned a flak gun, had never run to the bunker under a hail of bombs. He only knew about these things from his grandmother's stories. She'd helped out with the anti-aircraft service. But it was as if she'd passed her fitful dreams to him on her deathbed. Like this house which had first been left to his parents, and then to him.

The attack came in the dark. You just heard the terrible humming in the air. By then the bombs had already started falling.

He took the big bread knife out of the knife block and cut a deep flesh wound in his left bicep. It felt good to see the blood flowing. It brought him back to reality. He wasn't part of that war generation. Those were all old family experiences, not his own. He had to get rid of those thoughts. Exorcise them.

As a child he had cut himself when the dreams from his grandmother's stories had become overwhelming. It usually helped.

On the one hand, he wanted to bandage his arm so that he wouldn't lose too much blood and so the wound wouldn't become infected. He still had so much planned. He needed his strength. On the other, it was wonderful to watch the blood pulsing out. He still had so much life inside him.

He wrapped a bandage around his arm calmly. It was like a healing ritual. How good pain could feel! Now he was back to reality. No bombs in the night.

He wasn't defenceless, not helpless.

He could act. He set the pace.

He was in control of the situation.

Perhaps every new situation offered new possibilities. If he really had been mistaken and Heymann and Stern had been innocent, then it was also Willy Kaufmann's fault. He'd made him his instrument.

How freeing it must be for Ubbo Heide and his team when he took work off their hands, and was now going to bring everything to a great conclusion. It couldn't be that someone like Kaufmann could get off scot-free.

I'm catching the real culprits while you're guarding the killers and criminals who Ubbo Heide exposed in his book.

Why not Langeoog? He liked the island, although it was a long time since he had last visited it. His mother was still alive back then.

He would have liked to take the ferry dressed as an old woman, in her honour, but the danger that his disguise was too well known was too great. He smiled. You don't know all my tricks yet. I'll surprise you all once more. You'll be surprised if you're planning to trick me!

*

Büscher managed to mobilise 104 police officers in no time to protect all the people named in the video and to inform them about the danger they were in. A firestorm was unleashed on the Internet, leading the East Frisia Kripo servers to crash.

Ann Kathrin Klaasen decided the Rupert should work as a waiter on the ferry between Bensersiel and Langeoog.

'What?' Rupert asked, incensed. 'I'm supposed to—?'

Ann Kathrin calmly explained, 'The culprit was definitely in Gelsenkirchen. We don't know who from our team he knows, but he's familiar with all the officers who were involved in Gelsenkirchen. He'll try to come to Langeoog. At least one of us should be there in case he takes the ferry.'

'But don't immediately knock over every old lady who's trying to spend her holiday on the island,' Weller teased.

'We have six people from a SWAT team on board. They're already on their way to the ferry.'

'Oh, are they also turning into service personnel?'

'Sure,' Weller grinned, 'and you'll be the head waiter and boss them all.'

Ann Kathrin remained serious. 'No, they'll all be hidden in a room, in full gear. Probably in the engine room or the luggage room. And they'll only attempt a seizure on your command.'

Rupert liked that. His chest puffed up. 'So I'm playing the head waiter and the gang is at my command!'

'Why attempt?' Weller asked and looked at Ann Kathrin critically. She shrugged her shoulders. Had she given something away with her choice of words? Did she not think that the SWAT team could catch him on the ferry?

Weller rubbed his hands, like he sometimes did while cooking, looking forward to the food. 'The airfield is easier for us to watch. We'll catch him at the departures if he flies from Harlesiel.'

Ann Kathrin nodded. 'Of course, for us it'd be best if he doesn't even come to the island.'

'Surely there are more ways to reach the island. Maybe he'll approach in his own sailing boat or suddenly show up as a surfer or—' Weller speculated.

Ann Kathrin gestured to Weller not to open up more cans of worms.

'Yes, Frank,' she said, 'we'll roll the dice and hope to win the game. But we have to take into account that we're dealing with a very sophisticated killer.'

'People, I'm telling you,' Rupert called out, actually proud. 'He'll try using some kind of crap disguise to get on the island, via the ferry, in the crowds of tourists. That won't exactly make it easier for our SWAT team. Unlike him, we won't risk having bystanders become casualties, and he knows that perfectly well. But maybe I can—'

Rupert stood up and intimated how he would bring a tray to the table as a waiter. The pain caused by his sacroiliac joint made the whole show look somewhat stiffer than he'd hoped.

Before he could continue, Ann Kathrin said, 'No, please don't play the hero, Rupert!'

'What do you mean, play the hero? If he's sitting in front of me, orders a prawn sandwich and then a beer, then I can bring it to him, put the gun to his head and say, "*The three of us think you're disgusting, and are of the opinion that you should put your hands up now.*"'

'The three of us?' Ann Kathrin asked.

Rupert opened his blazer, flashed his holster with his service revolver and grinned, 'Heckler, Koch and me.'

Weller knew how stupid Ann Kathrin thought it was to show off with guns and was surprised how badly Rupert had judged the situation. Did he really think that he could score points with Ann Kathrin like this? Or was he making a show of himself because in his heart of hearts he was afraid of the situation and hoped that he'd be spared?

'Just a little more of that, Rupert, and you can be put on file-sorting duty. There's a huge pile of papers to work through on my desk, and it's growing all the time. For example, there are some statistics on field service that urgently need to be compiled—'

Rupert played the server, and nodded at her in a subservient gesture. 'No problem, boss. Got it!'

*

The door opened with a whirr. And that was when her next nightmare began. He was standing there, his left arm bandaged and a piece of the bandage dangling down. He reminded her of Michael Jackson doing the moonwalk, and he moved towards her in almost a dreamy way. He carried a large pink toiletry bag in his right hand. Large, horn-handled, with silver clasps.

He opened the cell door.

Her heart raced with excitement.

He swung the bag into the room, letting it fly through the air. He closed the door again, stopped in front of the bars, reached behind himself and took a page from a glossy magazine from his jeans pocket. He held it out to her. It showed a woman with her hair in a glamorous updo.

'Can you manage that?' he asked. 'I want you to look classy.'

What does he want, she thought. Am I supposed to make another video, or is he going to let me go?

At first she made an effort to improve his mood. 'Of course, I can manage that. But something like that takes time, of course. That hairdo is from the sixties, or seventies, or eighties. I haven't ever had anything like that myself, but my mother—'

'Mine did too,' he said, and for the first time there was something that connected the two of them. That made Svenja Moers hopeful.

'Are you ready to help me? Do your regret your crimes? Do you want to fight on the side of the good guys?'

She nodded enthusiastically.

'You need a different hair colour. Pick something out! There's everything in there, from bottle blond to bright red. The main thing is that you look different from how you do now. There are also glasses with plain glass in the bag.'

She opened the bag. The glasses made her think of ABBA concerts although she didn't know why exactly. They had big frames and dark glass.

'These would make you look like a fly,' she said, and he laughed. 'Whatever you say.'

'What do you have planned? Why am I putting these on?'

She was afraid she'd gone too far with the questions and would trigger a new fit of rage. But he remained calm.

'I need you to pass on a message. When you do it, I want you to be wearing this exact hairdo, a pair of glasses and these earrings here.' He held them up.

'I-I can't wear earrings because of an allergy,' she said, her voice showing her fear. 'I would like to wear earrings, but my ears swell up, I get a sore throat, it itches like mad, and then—'

He acted as if she hadn't understood him. 'I said I want you to wear these earrings.'

He held out the earrings with his right hand, through the bars. She took the earrings and looked at them. They were round, made of gold, and there was a small black jewel in the middle of each of them. There was nothing remarkable about them. She asked herself if these were the earrings his mother had worn.

'Show me if they look good on you, or I can bring you different ones.'

'I-I don't have holes in my ears anymore. They've closed up. I haven't worn earrings for over thirty years. Like I said, I have an allergy—'

'Then we'll just have to pierce your ears. It doesn't work without earrings.'

'Maybe I could wear clip-ons,' she suggested. 'If we put a different clasp in the back, then—'

He pulled a face. 'Clip-ons could fall off – you could simply pull them off,' he demonstrate, pulling imaginary clips from his ears, 'and throw them away.'

'I wouldn't do that!'

'I don't have a piercing gun, but I do have a leather punch. You know,' he pointed to his belt, 'I always have to tighten it. It's hard to get a belt in the right size.'

'No, please!' she said.

'Go ahead and start dyeing your hair. I'll get the leather punch. That'll give us nice, even holes.'

He disappeared through the door. It closed behind him with a hiss, reminding her of the mouth of a monster in a horror movie she'd watched with her first husband, who'd liked that kind of thing.

She collapsed, crouching on the floor in front of the bed, and squeezed her hands into the backs of her knees. That's the way she had sometimes sat as a girl, when fear of the big, incomprehensible world grabbed hold of her.

*

Ann Kathrin was astonished to see how Büscher and Ubbo Heide exploited their old contacts with the criminal justice system with perfect coordination, within minutes making possible complicated things that would normally have required many forms and official channels. It was almost a sublime feeling to watch them handle these things on the phone.

Minutes later, they had all the papers they needed to pick Wilhelm Kaufmann up from the detention centre.

Neither Büscher nor Ubbo had needed to raise their voice to get it done.

Ann Kathrin tried to learn from them how you held your nerve with all that red tape and got what was necessary.

'Ultimately,' Ubbo Heide said to her, 'all these rules and laws are made by people and interpreted by people. We always have to make sure that they fulfill their function. The laws are made for people, not the other way around.'

The tin of mints was now located in Ubbo Heide's former office, with North Sea Radio turned up loud.

Ann Kathrin picked up Willy Kaufmann personally in Lingen. He was lying on his bed, her gun under his pillow when she entered his cell.

First she drove to the police station on Wilhelm Berning Strasse. There were two specialists waiting there who would wire Wilhelm Kaufmann.

'Tomorrow,' Ann Kathrin said, 'we'll take the first ferry from Bensersiel to Langeoog.'

Wilhelm Kaufmann stood there, his upper body naked, and bandaged as if he had a broken rib. The first microphone was under the bandage. A second was in one of the buttons on his jacket, and there was a third in his shoe.

'You got the injury,' Ann Kathrin said, as if giving him a backstory, 'while struggling with Birger Holthusen. That's plausible.'

'Is the mic on his shoe picking up what I'm saying?'

'No idea. But if you have to warn us that you don't have your jacket anymore, and the one on your ribs isn't working for some reason, then you can just pull off your shoe and let us know where you—'

'It won't come to that,' Kaufmann assured her, and he sensed that there would be a fourth transmitter somewhere that she hadn't told him about so he couldn't trick her and get rid of all the bugs.

He drank water from a bottle. He was very thirsty. He kept on running his tongue over his teeth and puffed out his cheeks as if to gargle the water.

'Tomorrow morning. And where will I stay the night? In my home in Brake?'

'That's up to you, of course. But we suggest that you stay at the North Sea Hotel Benser Hof in Bensersiel, opposite the marina.'

Kaufmann whistled. 'That's a four-star hotel. Can I assume that the tax payers are footing the bill?'

Ann Kathrin smiled. 'Yes, and in this case they'll even pay for a suite.'

'Will you stay by my side?' he asked.

'No, but there will be four local police officers watching over you. They have rooms on the same floor and there'll be a squad car in front.'

'Great. And how's it labelled? "*Caution, we're protecting a child murderer*?"'

'No it's undercover.'

Wilhelm Kaufmann laughed. 'Sure. *Get Your Bricks on Route 66*. One of Peter Grendel's vans, then no one will realise that you're behind it.'

'Nope. *Theo Hinrichs, Buttforde*.'

Kaufmann nodded. 'Theo's travelling cake shop.'

'This is a tourist area. No one will be suspicious. The vehicle looks like it's waiting for its next tour.'

'The police officers will eat jam doughnuts and apple turnovers until they're silly if Theo leaves any in there,' Kaufmann joked. 'But why will we be taking the first ferry? Do you think he's already over there?'

'We can't rule that out. He could have taken an air taxi from Norddeich, from Harlesiel, or even from Bremen.'

'You need an ID to get onto a plane.'

'But I still think he'll take the ferry. The *Langeoog III* has space for eight hundred passengers. Someone like him will feel safer there than in a cramped plane, where he might not be able to escape.'

Wilhelm Kaufmann pointed to Ann Kathrin. 'You think exactly like them, Ms. Klaasen. As a detective, you're the worst thing the criminal world could imagine. The ferry goes almost every hour. Believe me, Ms. Klaasen, he won't take the first one, he'll go when there are a whole lot of tourists on board.'

*

He'd even given her two painkillers before he did it, but now it wasn't just her ears burning, the pain went all the way to the roots of her hair. The left earlobe just wouldn't stop bleeding.

He was clearly sorry. He stammered, 'Well, an ear sure isn't a leather belt. But there's no other way. Or do you think it'd be better to use a nail?'

The hairdo wasn't big enough for his taste. She asked herself what he meant exactly, and he explained to her. 'It's not firm enough! It has to look almost structured, glamorous, you understand? You're supposed to attract people's attention.'

These words – attract people's attention – made her forget the pain. He was actually planning to let her out into some kind of public place, however that might be defined. He wasn't doing this for himself and his own pleasure. It wasn't about a new clip that needed to be filmed. No indeed. She was going to be leaving this prison!

'I want them all to look at you, understood? You're supposed to move your hips like Marilyn Monroe. The wives should pull their husbands closer, afraid you'll seduce them. You should look like a man-eater! Do you have it in you? Find it!'

'But why?' she dared ask him.

'They expect to see either me or a feeble old lady with a walker. No one is imagining an eighties vamp in a mini skirt.'

But he'd found one.

*

Rupert wore the Heckler & Koch in his holster under the fake blue uniform jacket of a maritime waiter. He was below decks and, he thought, it was rather humid. He wished he could take off the jacket and leave the white shirt unbuttoned. He wasn't wearing the stupid, black bow tie Büscher had offered him.

'Waiters don't need stuff like that in East Frisia,' Rupert had claimed.

Rupert was enjoying his job as the ferry cast off because there were four very cheerful young women seated at a table inside. They weren't wearing any more clothing than absolutely necessary for this sunny day. It truly wouldn't have been an easy choice if Rupert were forced to pick between them.

They waved to him and he went over immediately.

'Hey. What can I do for you?' He asked.

The one with the spaghetti straps wanted a glass of bubbly – dry, nice and cool.

'I happen not to like the taste of warm Prosecco!' she laughed.

Her friend, who was wearing an orange T-shirt that was far too tight, wanted a rooibos tea and a piece of cake without whipped cream, and the cake only if it didn't contain any gelatin.

'Sure,' Rupert said, 'vegetarian apple cake, so to speak,' and beamed at her.

She felt understood.

The redhead with the hook nose and the sharp, promising gaze ordered a coffee with milk and emphasised, 'But from the espresso machine, please, not filter coffee. I can't stomach it!'

The one in the striped summer dress wanted a hot boiled sausage with double mustard. 'But you can keep the roll. And give me a slightly fizzy mineral water, without ice and no lemon.'

The one with the spaghetti straps called out. 'Oh, you with your low carbs, Miriam! In that case, I'll have the roll!'

Rupert walked over to the bar and wondered to himself which one of them would scream the loudest in bed.

He was genuinely unsure if he'd be able to deal with those young things when the chips were down. When was the last time he'd had a thirty-year-old in bed? But never mind, they were feisty, looked great and he had fun letting his fantasies run wild.

Many of the guests were standing at the bar, trying to order beers and brats.

Rupert couldn't really recall the girls' order. His new colleague behind the counter pointed to the pad. 'You wrote everything down, right?'

Rupert didn't react. His colleague took the notepad and looked at it. It read: *The one with the striped dress is named Miriam.*

'Well great,' the waiter said.

Rupert turned round and let his eyes scan the room. He didn't mind that the other waiter wasn't happy with his work. He had another job to do. And with a little luck, he would become a hero in front of those four ladies and arrest a serial killer.

What kind of woman wouldn't be impressed? Regardless of whether they were twenty years younger than he was.

'So what do you want? Four coffees or what? Just tell me. Can't you see I'm busy here?'

'I don't have to write it down. I keep such details in my head. So I need a tea—'

'What kind of tea? East Frisian?'

'Nah, one of those that women always drink.'

'Harmony herbal tea?'

'That stuff that's not even real tea.'

'Rooibos?'

'Exactly!'

'Vanilla?'

'Are there other kinds?'

'You don't have a clue, man!'

'And then a boiled sausage with double mustard, a piece of apple cake with whipped cream.'

'We don't have any more apple cake, but I do have East Frisian torte.'

'Fine.'

Rupert only knew the man they were looking for from the descriptions and pictures Weller had taken in Gelsenkirchen. He was tall and thin. Because he'd apparently disguised himself as a woman once, Rupert assumed he could use any hairdo as a disguise.

The guy over there with the dreadlocks almost down to his bottom looked very suspicious. Surely that hair wasn't real. And the beard as well.

Rupert couldn't remember ever having seen someone with both dreadlocks and a beard. He thought people only wore their hair like that because they couldn't grow a real beard.

He was at least six foot five, maybe six foot six tall. Shoes at least size twelve. His right shoe was loose. The ends of the shoelaces clacked against the ground with every step. His shoes were more suitable for mountain climbing than an island holiday.

He was carrying a bag on his back, with plenty of room for a weapon.

The waterproof fishing vest he wore with all the pockets could also be a bulletproof vest in disguise.

'Bingo,' Rupert said. 'I think we've got him.'

The answer from the button in Rupert's ear was unpleasantly loud. 'Do not arrest! I repeat: do not arrest! Stay as close to him as possible. We'll get him, if he goes to the bathroom or disembarks. Not now. There are too many people—'

But Rupert saw his chance that very minute. No more than two metres away, the beanpole was bending over to tie his shoelaces with a nice double bow. It didn't get better than this!

Rupert was there in two steps and kicked him in the back. The man slammed to the ground and Rupert had already overwhelmed him.

The dreadlocked guy screamed. 'Help! I'm being attacked! What do you want?' But before Rupert could slap the cuffs on him, he was attacked himself, by Miriam and the girl with the spaghetti straps.

'Leave Lars alone! Let him be, he didn't do anything to you!'

Miriam grabbed Rupert's nose and twisted it. He'd been through plenty in his lifetime, but he'd never seen that kind of self-defence.

It hurt like crazy, and Rupert didn't dare hit away her hand because he was afraid his nose could suffer serious damage as a result.

He whined, although he couldn't recognise his own voice through the nasal tone. 'Ouch! Ouch! I'm . . . in —olice.'

He wanted to pull out his badge, but Miriam slammed her elbow against his lower ribs. Rupert had the breath knocked out of him. He knelt on the floor. Lars, the man with the dreadlocks, stood up and went to the women's table, protected by the four of them, who were grouped around him like professional bodyguards.

Rupert's colleague laughed behind the bar. 'It really isn't your day, is it? Are those your daughters? Was that guy hitting on them? He looks like a pothead. I wouldn't like it either if my daughter came home with someone like that. My God, I don't even want to think about it!'

Rupert touched his nose and tried to get his breathing back under control.

Should he call up the SWAT team now and initiate the arrest, or should the whole thing be filed under 'mistakes can happen if you're nervous'?

*

He made her prance up and down repeatedly, insisting she sway her hips and smile. He didn't think she had enough makeup on, but he liked the hairdo now.

She was already outside of the cell. What a feeling! Although there was still a locked steel door and she had no idea how it was opened, she could already feel freedom was in touching distance.

'I'm going to do everything you ask,' she said, 'and I'll follow your directions exactly. You can rely on me.'

'Yes,' he laughed, 'it's nice to be on the right side of things, isn't it? It's a good feeling, like being praised by your parents because you've completed a difficult task.'

She made an effort to smile. 'Yes, that's exactly how it feels.'

'There are transmitters,' he said, 'in your earrings. I'm listening to every word you say. And I'll know soon enough if you take them off. It makes a rustling sound that I—'

'No, I won't do that! I won't disappoint you!'

He wants to send me somewhere with these stupid earrings. I don't care what he hears, though, she thought. I'll run to the police and ask them for help. And then this madman will finally be arrested.

'And I also have a wonderful belt for you,' he said. 'Look.'

She shook her head. 'No.'

'Women wear things like that these days. Instead of a handbag. You tie it around your stomach and you keep your money and phone inside it, so they can't be stolen.'

He sounded so friendly and had such a wide smile that she knew there was something else going on.

'You've already guessed, right?'

'No.'

'Come, tell me: what's inside?'

'A phone?'

'Oh, come on! Don't pull my leg. What do you think it could be? Don't act so stupid! It's an explosives belt. It just looks better than those things the terrorists always wear.'

He raised a little transmitter. It resembled her old Nokia phone that had died years before.

He was giddy, like a kid with a birthday present. 'I can use this to trigger the explosion. It works remotely, like a phone call. So if I hear,' he said, stroking the left side of his face, 'anything I don't like, then . . . baaaaang! If you try to take it off or throw it away – baaaaang! There's only one way to get rid of it, sweetie: you come back to me, and then I'll free you of it. And then we'll celebrate together. Don't try to cross me!'

*

In keeping with his request, Wilhelm Kaufmann had received a Walther pistol. Since he'd been carrying it in his right blazer pocket, he almost felt as if he'd been reinstated to the police force, a volunteer member of the team.

'Shouldn't we be on a first-name basis,' he asked Ann Kathrin Klaasen. 'We're practically colleagues again.'

She only nodded gently, but then he called out enthusiastically, 'Give me five!' and she did as he asked. What they needed now was a little hope and a lot of luck.

Ann Kathrin dialled Büscher's number, in Kaufmann's presence. He answered immediately.

'It's not a good idea to take the first ferry, Martin.'

'Why not?'

'We're pretending that Willy Kaufmann is a tourist, off to the island for fun, for a break at his holiday flat. He's stayed in the Benser Hof Hotel in Bensersiel before. Wouldn't it be better to let him sleep in, eat breakfast and then catch the ferry? If he's already being watched, then it will be much more credible.'

Büscher immediately agreed with her. 'Of course. You must do what's best. Should I inform the SWAT team that you—'

'No,' she answered, 'that's exactly what I don't want.'

And Büscher understood that she didn't trust anyone. From the very beginning, she hadn't planned on having Wilhelm Kaufmann take the first ferry at 6.45. She'd only said that to prevent any possible disruptions, to mislead eavesdroppers. She'd have him go at 9.30, maybe even at 11.30. Maybe Kowalski would already be over there and waiting for his new victim.

*

Weller had taken a plane to the island. They still had their suitcases in the Strandeck Hotel. Weller had been lucky. There was still a room available.

The killer, Weller thought, would hardly be surprised to see detectives on the island. After all, Holthusen had been murdered there. He might even think that we are still trying to arrest Wilhelm Kaufmann. Besides, Weller was planning to explore the island with a pirate's bandana underneath his helmet, to disguise his face.

You will have used a bike too, Weller thought. There's no better, faster transport here. The island isn't that big. If we meet, I'll recognise you and then—

In his dreams he was duelling with the culprit. But in reality he wasn't really looking forward to that. Instead, he hoped the boys from the SWAT team would be able to put an end to it on the ferry without spilling too much blood. Then he would carry out the official arrest here on the island and accompany the killer back to the mainland.

*

Twelve cameras recorded everyone who parked their cars in the car park in Bensersiel, purchased a Langeoog Card in the ticket hall or waited for the ferry. No one could board the ferry without being recorded from at least two different angles. There were also several surveillance cameras on the ferry itself.

The staff at Café Waterkant were helpful and provided a room for Ann Kathrin Klaasen and Martin Büscher, who now sat there in front of the monitors. They were accompanied by Sylvia Hoppe, who was able to move the individual pictures onto another screen. Then they could immediately send any pictures they wanted to all of the police officers on duty.

'When we identify him here, he will be done for,' Büscher said. He was delighted that the fact they had been present at Ubbo Heide's reading in Gelsenkirchen had given them a definite advantage: they knew what Kowalski looked like.

Büscher was so nervous that he couldn't drink coffee or tea. His hands were sweaty. He kept wiping them on his trouser legs. Everything he'd heard about Ann Kathrin Klaasen appeared to be true. She was completely calm in situations of total crisis. She only got worked up in her everyday life when the washing machine didn't work or the car wouldn't start. The words 'cold-blooded' came to mind.

She checked every person with a quick glance.

'Please zoom in on the Japanese woman in camera one!'

'The man in the wheelchair! I want to see his face. He's under the camera frame!'

'Can I please have the blonde a little bigger? Watch out, she's about to walk in front of the second camera and I need her from the front.'

She gave clear instructions and was highly focused. In between times, she called Rupert and reprimanded him. 'No more going it alone, you understand?'

'What do you mean, going it alone?' Rupert defended himself. 'I just didn't want the chance to slip away.'

'The chance to die for justice?' she asked harshly. 'Or to become a superhero?'

'OK,' Rupert grumbled. 'I'll admit I think I'm capable of more that the kids from the SWAT team. They all have to show their ID in the cinema if the film is an 18.'

'Rupert!' She reproached him. The way she said his name was sufficient to convey her feelings.

'The main thing is for this to end soon. I'll go crazy if I have to play the waiter any longer. It's just not a job for me. It looks so easy if you're sitting at a bar, but in reality—'

'Do you want us to bring you out? Are you not up to the job?'

'No, I am. I'm still serving boiled sausages. But if another one of those tourists messes me around, I'll pour pea soup on their head!'

Büscher grinned. He liked the way Ann Kathrin dealt with Rupert. He decided to learn from her.

Weller checked in. 'I'm trying the apple cake here in the café. I'm about to ride my bike around and then return to the ferry terminal. I'll recognise him if he's already on the island.'

'Thanks, Frank. I'd like an update every fifteen minutes.'

'Sure, sweetie.'

'Don't call me sweetie on an official operation. This is all being recorded, and maybe later on—'

'Sorry, sweetie.'

Ann Kathrin hung up.

'What kind of trip is he on?' Büscher asked.

'He's jealous of you,' she said, and Büscher looked astonished.

'Of me?'

'Yeah.'

Büscher liked that. Somehow it made him feel better. He wanted to say something, make a gesture, but Ann Kathrin motioned to the screen. 'This is where the action is.'

*

Carola Heide had brewed tea and set the table for two. The teapot was on a warmer and there were peppermint leaves on the table, filling the room with their scent.

Ubbo was exhausted. Carola was worried about him. When he thought no one was looking, he threw his head back and exhaled in a way that she didn't like at all. It was as if he was fighting for air.

He liked to downplay his physical weaknesses. He'd learned that an enfeebled boss had much less authority that one who was fighting fit. Everyone at the police station could be ill, but he couldn't. He'd lived according to this principle for too long.

'Good that you're at home,' Carola said to him. 'I was afraid for you.'

He waved her away but even that gesture was difficult for him.

'Oh, you,' he tried to smile. 'My job is done. I can't make an arrest as a volunteer. It's the young officers' turn now. I'm keeping out of operations. This was my final show.'

She looked at him with relief. 'A couple of weeks on Wangerooge will do you good,' she said.

'Do us good,' he added and saw in her gaze how much this woman loved him, after all these years. It made him feel better, and in that moment he knew that he was prepared to do anything for her. For her and for their relationship. Life would have very different priorities from now on. He just wanted to spend a couple of good years with his wife and take better care of their daughter. He ignored the knocking on the door. But then someone rang the bell.

'Send them away,' Ubbo said, 'whoever it is.'

'You can count on that,' Carola promised. She cleared her throat, put on a stern look, and went to the door. She feared there might be a police officer standing there with some important message, wanting to take Ubbo immediately to the headquarters on Fischteigweg. Well, they'd get an earful!

The man was carrying a duffle bag. He looked like a marathon runner. Tall and gaunt. He gave the impression of being both energetic and burned-out at the same time.

She was familiar with these contradictions in high-performance athletes, who played close attention to a healthy lifestyle, but then forced themselves to overcome their limits without paying attention to the body's signals to stop. Ubbo was a little bit like that.

'I have to speak to your husband,' he said, immediately trying to squeeze through the crack of the door.

She held the door with her foot. 'I daresay. Lots of people want to see him. But my husband's not available at the moment.'

'You're mistaken. He'll be very glad to see me.'

'I think I know you,' Carola Heide said.

'Yes. I once gave your daughter private lessons. She's stupid, far less intelligent than her father.'

With a gentle power he pushed the door further open and forced her into the hallway.

'You can't just—'

'Oh yes. I can.'

From the living-room window Ubbo Heide couldn't see who was at the door. It didn't interest him because it had never occurred to him that Kowalski would arrive on his doorstep.

*

The ferry docked at 11.20.

Wilhelm Kaufmann listened to the roar of the diesel engine. He liked the noise when the ship's propellers swirled the salty water. He knew something about ships and ferries. The *Langeoog III* was 45 metres long and 10 metres wide. It had a draught of 1.32 metres.

Kaufmann stood in line and ticked off these facts mentally. It made him feel secure.

He proudly stepped on board. He in no way felt prepared to die. Instead, he felt a crazy will to survive. All his colleagues were there. Those who had just been investigating him were now on his side. The tide had turned.

He felt an enormous strength since he'd won the fight against Birger Holthusen.

Everything's going to be OK, he thought. Everything's going to be OK.

He stepped onto the ferry as if heading to a new life.

Svenja Moers appeared three times on Ann Kathrin's screens. She was visible for several seconds, both from the front and from the back.

The resolution quality was exceptional.

But Ann Kathrin wasn't interested in a woman who was decked out like a diva from the eighties.

Büscher pegged her as freshly divorced, looking for a new husband, or at least a lover. A holiday on the coast was an ideal opportunity. He never would have thought that the kidnapped Svenja Moers could be moving around unaccompanied. Even if he had noticed the similarity, it wouldn't have made any sense. A prisoner who had been released usually went straight to the police or their relatives; they didn't take the next ferry to Langeoog looking like that.

Aside from her provocative stride, she didn't act in any way strangely. She even stood very close to Willy Kaufmann in the queue, which was when she showed up again in the pictures.

'She won't get very far on deck with that hairdo,' Ann Kathrin joked, trying to lighten the mood. 'The East Frisian wind laughs at things like that.'

'She's not from here,' Martin Büscher said.

*

Kowalski placed the duffle bag on the floor, adjusted Ubbo Heide's wheelchair and patted him down. 'You're exactly the type who would carry a gun at home,' he said.

Scared stiff, Carola Heide was leaning against the wall and watching.

'What do you want from us?'

'Why,' Kowalski asked aggressively, 'do I have to listen to North Sea Radio all day long?'

Ubbo Heide patted his stomach and said, 'I left the tin of mints in the police station.'

Kowalski sniffed. There was a smell of black tea and fresh peppermint. He pranced around excitedly, like the favourite stallion in a race. 'You were trying to trick me. Right? You think you're cleverer than I am.' He laughed as if he'd made a joke. 'You're not. I revere you, Mr Heide. You're a great old man. You have vision, and you know what's going on. But you're not rigorous enough. I'm bringing your work to its conclusion. Together we could change East Frisia and the whole world along with it. It could start here, in your backyard, with your cases. You have always suffered from the inconsistency of the penal process, the soft approach of the justice system. If you join me, Mr Heide, then Ann Kathrin will join too. Weller, Rupert – your whole team. An East Frisia free of criminals – isn't that the goal?'

He clenched his fists and raised them like a burning torch.

'The good guys are differentiated from the bad by their actions,' Ubbo Heide said, but Kowalski wouldn't stand for this.

'But also by omission,' he scolded. 'And the way the justice system acts in our country, they're stabbing you and your people in the back. That's failure to lend assistance, if not worse. Why did you write the book? Do you not believe in your own arguments?'

'Leave my husband in peace!' Carola Heide demanded, moving towards Kowalski as if she intended to fight him.

He pointed to the sofa. 'Please sit down and shut your trap. Don't make me have to tie you up and gag you.'

She did ask he requested. She placed her hands on her knees and tried to keep the shaking under control.

I have to be strong, she thought. I have to be very strong now, and I have to stand by my man, regardless of what happens.

'We could become the Navy Seal Team 6 for East Frisia . People will love us.'

Ubbo Heide looked at Kowalski as if he was an idiot. Kowalski was aware that Ubbo was so used to dealing with psychopaths that he always assumed he was dealing with one. He realised his first task was to show Ubbo that he was a highly intelligent man who was following a well thought out plan.

'Mr Heide – think about it for a second! There's work being done on intelligent weapons! Rockets that independently look for their targets—'

'I'd prefer intelligent politicians,' Ubbo Heide said, in all seriousness. 'People who don't think of carpet bombing the first time a problem comes up, but instead are wise enough to find peaceful solutions and demonstrate negotiating skills.'

Carola Heide nodded to her husband.

Kowalski tried to dismiss his arguments with a hand motion. 'Yeah, that might be the way to deal with whole countries. But we're not talking about countries, we're talking about people, individual criminals—'

Ubbo Heide interrupted him. 'No. It's always about people and ultimately human lives – usually innocent ones.' Ubbo Heide pointed to him. 'You, for example, killed two innocent people, namely—'

'Heymann and Stern. I know. Good Lord, there's always collateral damage! We have to live with that.'

Ubbo Heide's face gained more colour. His eyes had a feverish sheen. Something of his old charisma emerged, the way he could persuade anyone with a couple of sentences and bring them into line. 'That's exactly what I don't want.'

Kowalski didn't accept these words. He pulled a monitor and a transmitter out of his bag and set everything up on the living-room table, as if he were a television technician who wanted to demonstrate a new piece of equipment.

'Wilhelm Kaufmann, that true child killer – he won't escape us. He's on board the *Langeoog III* right now. Svenja Moers is with him. The woman who killed her two husbands, and the man who killed at least two children are on the same boat! Isn't that ironic?'

On the screen Ubbo Heide only saw the swinging hips, then a bald man from above.

'We can't expect especially great pictures. After all, our camera person doesn't know that she's filming for us. There's a camera installed in her hairpin. She's also wearing two mics in her earrings. We have her completely under control. We can hear what she says and see what she does. She's on our side.'

Ubbo Heide didn't believe that. 'Don't talk such nonsense.'

'Well, not completely voluntarily,' Kowalski admitted. 'She's wearing an explosive belt that we can trigger with this,' he pointed to his old phone. It's enough for her and Kaufmann. The number is on speed dial. Press one button and the world has two fewer murderers. The justice department doesn't need to worry about them anymore. If we don't do it, they'll both get away scot-free, Mr Heide. You know it's true. I've heard you talking about Kaufmann, and Svenja Moers has already been acquitted of her crimes.

'Do you want to spend the rest of your life in that wheelchair waiting for the news that somewhere a child has disappeared, has been fished out of the water, dead? Could you live with that guilt, Mr Heide? And Svenja Moers will certainly marry again and propel her next husband into the great beyond if there's not enough money involved. And she'll do it more cleverly than before. She's learned from the first two times. That's the problem. She's getting better and better. You do an excellent job of describing that in your book, by the way.'

Then Kowalski moved his face very close to Ubbo Heide's. Their noses were almost touching and Ubbo could smell Kowalski's nicotine breath.

'One word from you, Mr Heide, and I'll press the button, and both of them will be blown up. She'll stay very close to him, as I've ordered her to. She'll sit down next to him as soon as the ferry casts off. We can direct her from here. Say yes, and I'll do it in your name! Or do you want to press the button yourself?

He held out the phone for Ubbo Heide.

'Never,' Ubbo said.

Kowalski almost dropped his phone and shouted, 'For a better, crime-free world! You've fought for that all your life.'

'You can't protect freedom and justice by eliminating it,' Ubbo Heide said. 'And I don't want to live in your brave new clean world.'

Carola nodded to her husband. 'Me neither!'

Kowalski wanted to light a cigarette, but Ubbo Heide stopped him. 'This is a smoke-free home.'

Kowalski hadn't expected that. 'And you think I'm going to step outside to light one up?'

'No, I expect you to respect the rules. There's no smoking in my home. I don't care what you do in your house.'

'Don't push your luck, Mr Heide. I'm armed and you're in a wheelchair.'

Kowalski looked at his revolver, as if he had to reassure himself it was still there.

Ubbo Heide smiled at him. 'But that's no reason to abandon all your manners. Are we going to start eating with our fingers next?' He pointed to the floor. 'Will we shit on the carpet? Or will we continue to behave like civilised people? I don't want smoke in my home and you have to respect that.'

'I need to smoke,' Kowalski said, 'when I get nervous. And I'm damn nervous.'

'I would be too, if I were in your shoes,' Ubbo Heide said. 'But I also wouldn't take any prisoners, and I'd step outside to smoke. Back when I was still smoking and Carola wasn't, I always—'

Carola Heide interrupted her husband. 'Shouldn't we make an exception?'

Ubbo shook his head. 'No. Why? It won't harm him if he doesn't smoke but it is harmful to us if we smoke passively. This is our home and we didn't invite him in.'

Kowalski groaned.

Carola was afraid her heart would stop, but then she was astonished to see Kowalski push the cigarette back into the packet.

*

A light drizzle drove many of the tourists off the deck. They fled to an inside room and ordered hot cups of tea and coffee.

In Rupert's estimation, Svenja Moers was the hottest woman on board by far. He'd almost jumped up to push a chair under her, like a gentleman, because she was looking around so indecisively for a place to sit. He hoped she'd sit next to the aisle, and not next to the window, so he could better admire her legs.

He thought she was exactly his cup of tea. She was looking for attention and he'd give it to her.

He pictured what kind of acrobatics she'd be able to do in bed. He wasn't at all bothered by her ridiculous hairdo. After the problems with Agneta Meyerhoff he'd actually been planning to stay true to his Beate for a while, but he didn't have the capacity to say no to such a tantalising offer.

He would have liked to go over to her and brag that he was an undercover detective, not just a waiter. That would probably make him more interesting to her.

Women were really strange creatures, Rupert thought. On the one hand, he didn't know one who liked war movies or violence. But they all loved muscular gunslingers. They married gentle teachers or social workers, but dreamed of Bruce Willis, Arnold Schwarzenegger, or Sylvester Stallone.

He'd seldom been as annoyed by Ann Kathrin's voice as he was now. It was as if she were sitting directly in his ear.

'Kaufmann isn't positioned correctly. We don't have a clear view of him. He needs to move a little to the right.'

Rupert wished he could shout at her to tell him herself. But he didn't do that. It was still better to be following Ann Kathrin's orders than serving that squawking horde of children with the three single mothers that was rolling towards the bar.

Now that fantastic woman was sitting next to Willy Kaufmann. It didn't get better than that! Hurray! Bingo! Rupert thought. If there's a God, he's on my side.

She leaned back in her seat, stretched out her legs, and leaned over to Kaufmann.

Lucky you, Rupert thought, she's whispering something in your ear. Why's that woman hitting on Kaufmann? Why isn't she reacting to my glances and winks? What does Kaufman have that I don't?

He wanted to go over to adjust Kaufmann's chair, to improve Ann Kathrin's view.

Svenja Moers draped an arm around Kaufmann and whispered into his ear. 'My name is Svenja Moers. I'm a tool for the executioner. He can hear and see us. I'm supposed to give you this.'

She handed Kaufmann a little box, which he took, dumbfounded.

'Tool for the executioner. Are those your own words?'

She didn't respond. Instead, she said, 'Keep the device with you. I'll be blown up if I move more than two metres away from you. And you'll go with me. From now on, we should keep very close. We're supposed to hold hands like lovers. Our fates are now entwined.'

Rupert stood next to their table. 'May I move your chair slightly? You're sitting in the aisle. If I need to get past when I'm serving someone—'

Kaufmann snapped at Rupert, 'No, you may not!'

To Rupert's astonishment, Kaufmann held out his open hand and the woman with the never-ending legs placed her hand in his. From a distance, the two of them now looked like a couple, but Rupert registered how the woman's hands shook and the corners of her mouth twitched.

He didn't understand what was going on, but something was wrong. Was that woman a colleague from the federal police force, doing personal protection independently? Or had they just neglected to inform him?

A forty-five-year-old woman called over to Rupert. 'Hey, you! Are you still working here or is your position available? I know a couple of people who'd apply immediately! Who doesn't want to work where other people take holidays?'

Her husband acted impressed and her children even more so.

Rupert shot back. 'Now listen to me, bitch! You'll land in the North Sea if you don't shut up!'

'Mum, what'd that man say?'

'And keep your spawn close to you,' Rupert scolded.

*

'Damn, damn, damn!' Büscher cursed. 'That bastard has tricked us! What now?'

He stared at Ann Kathrin with big eyes. She'd never seen him so helpless.

It's always that way, she thought. You have a plan, but the only thing that works is improvising when things get going.

Ann Kathrin tried to summarise the situation objectively. 'He's not on board as we expected him to be. We have all our forces tied up on Langeoog, and our SWAT team is on the ferry. We're protecting forty-one additional individuals. We're working ourselves into the ground and he's somewhere completely different.'

'Where, damn it, could he be?' Büscher asked, and there was a hint of panic in his voice. He spoke frantically. 'He's going to blow the two of them to bits. Right now there are two hundred and twelve tourists plus the crew and then our people on the ferry. It'll be a bloodbath!'

'That's not his goal,' Ann Kathrin said, 'that'd only pit us against him and make Ubbo Heide furious. He wants something else. He wants . . .' her voice went quiet. The end of her sentence was barely audible, 'to win Ubbo over.'

Ann Kathrin ran her hands over her face as if to brush away cobwebs.

Büscher activated the connection to Kaufmann and gave his orders. 'We have to prevent lives from being endangered. Find a place on board where there are as few people as possible. Best of all outside, up on deck. Maybe you could climb into a life boat or—'

Ann Kathrin pushed him aside and contradicted his orders. 'No. Don't do that. Do the opposite! You have to stay with the crowd. He won't risk having innocent people die. He wants to punish criminals.'

Kaufmann replied sarcastically. 'It's nice that everyone's in agreement!'

*

Kowalski, who clearly still hoped he could get Ubbo Heide to join his side, spoke flatteringly. 'Now we'll show the world our power. We're a hard-hitting, effective team.'

'No,' Ubbo Heide said, 'we're not a team. You're a sick man, Mr Kowalski. Is that even your real name?'

As if Ubbo Heide hadn't even spoken, Kowalski was now making contact with Svenja Moers and giving her orders. 'You two will now identify yourselves loudly and clearly. With your full names. Then you will confess in front of everyone. I demand a public confession. This is Judgement Day.'

He giggled.

Svenja Moers asked. 'Are we really supposed to—'

'Oh, yes! You should. And you'll start, Svenja. Then Wilhelm Kaufmann. Loud and clear, so everyone can hear you. We're watching you. One little mistake and you'll be blown sky-high.'

*

Svenja Moers stood up and called out in a voice that cut through the noise. 'My name is Svenja Moers! I'm wearing an explosive belt. I'm a prisoner of the executioner! I killed my two husbands – the courts acquitted me! That's why I'm here now!'

Her final words were drowned out by the screams. People moved, trying to get as far away from her as possible. Fathers stood in front of their families, mothers hugged their children tight and turned their backs on Svenja Moers, pushing towards the exit. The aisles were clogged immediately.

Only Rupert remained with them.

Wilhelm Kaufmann was sitting very calmly, as if used to such situations.

The redhead with the hook nose oscillated between the impulse to run and the exciting feeling of being a part of something truly big and important for the first time in her life. Finally having something you could tell people about. Exclusive material for her Facebook page.

She held up her phone and filmed the situation while her friend in the striped summer dress next to her fainted.

*

Sylvia Hoppe's voice quaked. She sounded like an old, fragile woman staring down death. 'This was a mistake. We shouldn't have done it. It will be a catastrophe.'

Büscher called for the bomb squad.

Ann Kathrin seemed as if she were physically present, but in a completely different place internally. It was as if she were talking to the killer. Very quietly and with utmost concentration. 'Where are you? What do you have planned, damn it?'

If I were him, she thought, where would I be directing this from? He is looking to attract as much attention as possible, and could be on the ferry. At the same time, the whole thing will be broadcast via phone, the pictures and clips, faster than any television company could be there with a camera crew. It'll be unfiltered, and can't be controlled. But he's not sitting on the mainland somewhere and drinking a cup of tea. He's—

It was as if every pore of her body were giving her information. A chill ran through her body. She raised the phone to her ear while watching Svenja Moers and Wilhelm Kaufmann on the screen, and she dialled Ubbo Heide's number.

*

'Can I answer the telephone?' Ubbo Heide asked.

Kowalski nodded and played with his gun, like other people play with pens. He was pleased with the situation on the screen. Everything was working exactly as he'd pictured it.

Now it was Kaufmann's turn. He also stood up. Then he said, 'My name is Wilhelm Kaufmann! I'm a former police officer and the man who calls himself the executioner now wants me to say that I murdered children and killed Steffi Heymann and Nicola Billing! But that's not right! I'm here because we wanted to trap him! And that seems to have worked! But now I'm in the trap, too!'

He appealed directly to Kowalski. 'If you blow us up, then it won't just be this young woman next to me who dies. I will too, and you can believe me when I say I'm innocent! I had nothing to do with the whole thing!'

'What a piece of shit,' Kowalski cursed. 'Such a goddamn piece of shit!'

Ubbo Heide's wife Carola stood up. It was hard for her to stay on her feet. She reached the phone by the second ring, handing it to her husband by the third. She recognised the name on the screen. *Ann*. Even reading the letters did her good. It was a connection to the outside world. And she sensed it would save them.

Ubbo answered in a completely normal voice. 'This is Ubbo Heide.'

'Ubbo! We're watching what's happening on board. Things are getting out of hand! He's fitted Svenja Moers with an explosive belt.'

'I know.'

'Who is it, damn it?' Kowalski asked.

'Ann Kathrin Klaasen.'

Kowalski grinned, as if he'd thought as much. 'What does she want?'

'I assume,' Ubbo Heide said, 'she wants to ask her former boss for advice in a difficult situation. Unlike you, Ann Kathrin isn't resistant to advice.'

'Pass her to me,' Kowalski demanded.

Ubbo Heide did what Kowalski asked of him.

'What can I do for you, Ms. Klaasen?' Kowalski asked. 'I'm here with Ubbo Heide. We're watching what's happening. We're not at all pleased with what Wilhelm Kaufmann is saying. Did you tell him to do that? He's spoiling everything. I wanted a public confession. For all of us. To show our weak justice system how you can make progress by really cracking down. But this is muddying the waters. Either way, the two of them must die. Tell him to shut up!'

'Kaufmann is clever,' Ann Kathrin answered. 'He's making you look like a fool, Kowalski. He's showing the man who calls himself the executioner that he's actually a pitiful amateur. You don't actually care if you execute the right people or the wrong ones. In the end, there's just a bloodbath if we make justice arbitrary. Only a proper court can convict Kaufmann.'

Kowalski didn't want to get into this kind of discussion. He was afraid he'd leave the zone. This wonderful, well-planned attack was to be a glorious triumph, not a sloppy compromise.

'If you want to bring about a world free of criminals, Mr Kowalski, then it'd only be consistent for you to slit your own wrists now. You'd be setting a good example. Maybe there would be imitators. These days any idiot can find imitators.'

Ubbo Heide motioned to Carola and she immediately understood what he wanted. Kowalski was so distracted by the action on the ship, which he was following on the monitor, and by the conversation with Ann Kathrin Klaasen, that he lost sight of his duffle bag.

Carola picked up the bag and carried it to the kitchen. It was heavy and there was the sound of metal clinking together. She undid the zip and saw a Samurai sword and an automatic gun.

Carola carefully placed the bag on the kitchen floor and, trying to make as little noise as possible, pushed it under the table so he wouldn't see it immediately.

She took the big bread knife from the knife block.

Yes, she was prepared to fight.

Ubbo Heide hoped the tea was still hot enough. He poured it as if at a tea party. Then he motioned to the fresh peppermint leaves in the middle of the table for a little assistance. Kowalski, despite the tense situation, did as his mother had taught him and politely helped the old man. While talking with Ann Kathrin Klaasen, he leaned over and pushed the peppermint leaves in Ubbo Heide's direction. He barked into the telephone, 'Ms. Klaasen, don't think that you can—'

He didn't get any further, because the hot East Frisian tea landed in his face.

He dropped the telephone and screamed. He flailed his arms furiously, but there was no one there to hit.

'You goddamn idiot!' he yelled. Then he launched himself at Ubbo Heide, grabbed him by the throat and choked him. 'You stupid old man!'

*

'He's with Ubbo! All available units immediately to Ubbo Heide's house! Ann Kathrin screamed.

*

Kowalski grabbed Ubbo Heide's collar with both hands and lifted him out of his wheelchair until they were eye to eye.

'We could have been such a good team. But you don't want that! Don't think you can hold me back. I want to blow up those two criminals now, finishing what you started, old man.'

The way Kowalski said those words it sounded like he was giving Ubbo Heide a generous present.

He let go of Ubbo, who tried to hold on, but fell next to the wheelchair. His bottom hit the floor hard and his head hit against a rubber wheel.

That very moment, Carola Heide drove the bread knife into Kowalski's back with all her strength. Then she let it go with a scream.

Kowalski turned around to her very slowly, as if he couldn't understand what had just happened. He reached for his back, trying to pull out the knife, but wasn't able to reach it. Then he fell forward, toppling over Ubbo Heide.

Ubbo hit him with a punch to his left temple as he went.

Carola, still screaming, stamped her foot on the carpet. 'I stabbed him in the back with a knife! I stabbed him in the back with a knife!'

Ubbo said, 'Carola, go into the kitchen and get the packing tape! We need to tie him up. This is an arrest!'

His words immediately calmed her and she went to the kitchen, as if in a trance. She didn't have to look long in her well-organised household. She immediately found the packing tape and a pair of scissors. The knife moved back and forth as Ubbo tied Kowalski's hands behind his back.

'Did I kill him?'

'No,' Ubbo answered calmly, 'I wouldn't be tying him up if you had. It's a flesh wound at the most. He's bleeding a lot, but—'

'I feel sick,' Carola said.

'You're allowed to,' Ubbo smiled. He shoved Kowalski off him, who was now was lying on his stomach on the floor and cursing. 'What kind of goddamn idiot are you! You've ruined everything!'

Ubbo pulled himself up on the table so he was sitting upright on the floor. He pressed the button on the screen and made contact with Svenja Moers. 'This is Ubbo Heide speaking. You don't have to be afraid. I have the perpetrator in custody. He was arrested just now. He is no longer able to trigger the explosives. Please calm down and take a seat. A specialist will come and free you from your explosive belt.'

*

It was more a falling than a sitting down. Svenja Moers suddenly felt that all the blood was rushing from her brain and upper body into her legs as she flopped onto the chair.

*

'It's over,' Ann Kathrin celebrated. 'Over! The rest is a job for the specialists!'

'Where's our bomb squad?' Büscher asked into his phone.

'On their way to Langeoog by helicopter.'

'That means the ferry has to dock first, and then—'

'It won't work any other way.'

Ann Kathrin called Ubbo first. 'How are you doing?'

'Fabulous. I could use a tea, and a little marzipan wouldn't go amiss. This was all a little too much for my stomach.'

He was already back to his old jokes.

Ann Kathrin checked in with Weller. 'The ferry is about to dock. First of all we have to let all the tourists disembark. Only our people, Svenja Moers and Wilhelm Kaufmann will remain. Then our explosives specialists can go on board and free them. It's over.'

'Is the scumbag still alive?' Weller asked.

'Yes,' Ann Kathrin said, 'and now he'll have to answer to the justice system. We'll see if he still thinks it's too soft.'

Ann Kathrin turned to Rupert. 'Stay very close to those two and keep them calm. They should move as little as possible and not touch the explosive belt. Our people will be handling everything. No going it alone—'

'The two of them are in the best of hands with me,' Rupert promised, bowing and asking the half-conscious Svenja Moers, 'How are you doing?'

Svenja Moers coughed.

'Could be worse,' Rupert said. 'Our people will come and take off the belt any second now, and then it's all over for you. By contrast, if I even think about what kind of paperwork we'll have to deal with for this operation!' He waved it away. 'I can't even imagine all the files that will be coming our way now!'

Kaufmann leaned over to Rupert, pointed to the package in his hands and said 'Just shut your trap, Rupert, and go and get us a drink!'

'I'm not actually the waiter here, but of course I'll make an exception.' Rupert reflected. After all, he knew how many people were listening in. 'A beer? What would you like?'

'I think Mrs Moers needs some water, and I could use a shot.'

'Me too,' Rupert admitted.

Above them, they heard the sound of a helicopter's rotor blades bringing the explosives specialist to Langeoog.